MW00883870

An Invincible Summer

A novel

by

Betta Ferrendelli

Author's Note

The story in this novel takes place during the mid 1990s when "mental retardation" and like phrases and terms were commonly used. Thank you for reading.

Dedication

In Memory

Jenny Tapp

1977-2000

One

Jaime Monroe pummeled the heavy bag in an Ali-like flutter of powerful punches.

The first time she put on a pair of boxing gloves, she felt like a cartoon character.

Until she hit the bag.

Then her adrenaline began to surge, sweat ran and she felt powerful.

An avid athlete, she excelled in all sports, but boxing was her outlet. It toughened her for long hours as a deputy district attorney in the Domestic Violence Unit of the Denver County District Attorney's Office. At twenty-eight, Jaime was in her third year of the demanding, high-stress job, which she worked with an ardent passion. Boxing sharpened and focused her attention, cleared her mind. It was a stress-management tool she used to turn negative emotion into positive energy.

Tonight, well into an intense workout, sweat darkened her gray T-shirt and clung to her slender back.

An image of Kelly Jo Cox's broken and battered body flashed before her and Jaime stepped back from the heavy bag, tasting bile in her throat. She looked toward the window, her reflection staring back at her. She was 5-feet 8-inches tall, agile and lean with brown hair that reached to her shoulders. Her broad, smooth face gave an impression of calm. She had strong cheekbones, a long, slender nose and a generous mouth with a wide, ready smile. She took a deep breath and attacked the heavy bag again with an onslaught of punches, as hard and forceful as a man. The center of the heavy bag was dented inward by the solid impact of her punches, fueled by a fervor that lived within her.

Kelly Jo had been raped and murdered and Jaime was prosecuting her attacker. Closing arguments would begin in a few days. It was Jaime's first major trial and she was ready. For months she had worked to build an airtight case.

With Kelly Jo's case, Jaime needed the energy she got from boxing. She would begin every routine with a half-mile run. Push-ups, sit-ups and dips were done at intervals. She finished in the club's training room with a combination of free and circuit weights, a rowing machine, stationary cycle, trampoline and jump rope.

Men would often ask what she was training for.

"Nothing," she would reply, wondering why they paid so much attention to her. "I'm just working out."

They would laugh. Shake their heads. She heard their whispers behind her back.

"Why would a doll like that want to work the heavy bag?"

But she ignored them.

There was no reason to smile tonight. Kelly Jo's case made her question her profession. Though it made her consider another line of work, she would never give up. She could not. There were other reasons why. Deep-rooted motives that kept her going. Deep-seated demons of guilt she needed to exorcise. This was the only way.

With a final quick flurry of punches, Jaime stepped away from the heavy bag. She wiped her forehead with the back of her glove. She removed the gloves and grabbed her water bottle. She took a long drink and stared out the window, letting her body cool.

Downtown Denver was fascinating at night. Her club was located on the fifth floor of a tall building off 17th Avenue. She could hear sirens as they passed by on the streets below, devoid of the crowds who walked along them during the day. Lights from tall buildings stared back. She could not see anyone in the building across the street and thought of the many evenings she had worked well into the night, only realizing it was late and time to go when the cleaning crews came, or the night security guard would startle her by saying, "Ms. Monroe, you still here?"

She took another long swallow of water and picked up a jump rope. It tapped the floor in an even rhythm, keeping pace with the thoughts about the case as they turned in her mind.

Kelly Jo was fifteen when she died, but had the mentality of an eight-year-old. Kelly Jo's younger sister, Beverly, was a cute, freckled-faced little girl, with honey-blonde hair. She was nine, precocious and old enough to know that something bad had happened to her sister. But when it came to testifying, Beverly froze with terror. She could hardly speak.

Why shouldn't she be afraid? Jaime thought.

It was nearly impossible for her to build a rapport with Beverly because their mother was loyal to her boyfriend, the man who killed Kelly Jo. Jaime finally broke through the little girl's fortress to earn her trust. The process moved at a glacier's pace, but Jaime did not give up.

Jaime had learned quickly how to get reluctant and frightened children to speak with her. She did not "interview" them. To gain their trust she would often color with them, other times they went for walks, or ate hamburgers together. Many of their confessions came riding while they were in the car, as did Beverly's. Jaime guessed it was because the car was closed and intimate and the child was free to look out the window. Beverly was no exception. Just getting Beverly to the courthouse was an ordeal that tried Jaime's patience. Beverly had first refused to go, but with gentle reassurance and coaxing, Jaime finally managed. Only she could testify against the man who had raped and beaten Kelly Jo, killing her. The two of them had a practice session earlier.

They stood outside an empty courtroom at the City and County building on 14th Avenue and Bannock Street, in downtown Denver. Jaime was able to gain permission to take Beverly inside so she could see what the room was like before she had to testify.

"Jaime, I don't wanna go in there. Please don't make me." She was frozen with fear.

"Beverly," Jaime said softly. "I won't make you do anything you don't want to."

She lowered herself to eye level with Beverly. She smiled, put her hands on Beverly's shoulders, and rubbed. "Remember when we talked about how you wanted to help your sister?"

She nodded, her blue eyes glassy with tears.

"And I said you would have to go into a courtroom, just like the ones you see on TV and sit in that chair and tell everybody what happened. Remember?"

Again Beverly nodded. Her tears, with nowhere else to go, spilled over tiny lids, already red and swollen. Her bottom lip quivered as she tried to stop crying.

"What's beyond this door right now, Beverly, is an empty courtroom, but the one you will enter soon will be filled with lots of people and they'll want to hear what you have to say. And you'll tell them, just like you've told me. But we can't do it out here. We have to go inside."

She waited, allowing Beverly time to consider her choices.

Jaime was learning that she had to be more than just an attorney. She had to be a social worker, mom, sibling and best friend.

"Will you go with me if I go inside?" Beverly asked.

When Jaime nodded, Beverly took a small step forward. Jaime pushed the door open and took her hand. Slowly, they walked inside, cool air hitting their faces. The empty room seemed large to Beverly, and her grasp on Jaime's hand grew tighter. She pulled Jaime's hand closer to her chest as they neared the witness stand. Beverly hesitated, but she didn't stop. They walked in silence until they reached the wooden railing, the threshold that separated the public from the lawyers and the judge.

Jaime stopped and looked at Beverly. "We'll be on this side when it's time for you to testify. When your turn comes, Beverly, you will walk past the railing, like you and I are going to do right now."

Jaime took a step forward, hesitating a moment before Beverly decided to follow. She had been squeezing Jaime's hand so hard, both their hands were clammy.

"I'll be here at this table. Your mother's boyfriend will be sitting there," Jaime said, pointing respectively to the two long wooden tables.

Beverly pulled her hand free and began to tug at the tips of her fingers. She looked at the two tables, then wide-eyed, scanned the perimeter of the courtroom, taking in the judge's bench, the witness stand, the jury box and finally the seats that would fill with spectators.

"It looks just like on TV," she said finally.

Jaime smiled. "Yes, it does."

First they sat together on the witness stand, Beverly on Jaime's lap. Then Jaime left her and walked to the prosecutor's table and then to the defense table. She folded her arms lightly against her chest, leaned onto the table, and studied the little girl.

"Do you think when the time comes, Beverly, you'll be strong enough to tell us what happened?"

Beverly's hands were folded and resting in her lap. She wore a pale blue print dress with white lace around the collar. Shiny black patent leather shoes covered little feet wearing white socks trimmed with small pink roses and fine lace. Jaime had purchased the outfit for Beverly so she would have something decent to wear when it came time to testify. Beverly's foster mother told Jaime that Beverly kept the dress and shoes at the foot of her bed where she could see them.

Beverly looked down and studied the print of her dress a long time before she spoke. There were tears in her eyes when she looked up at Jaime. "I can," she said in a fragile voice. "For Kelly Jo."

On the way out of the courtroom, they held hands as they walked down the hallway.

"Jaime?"

Jaime looked down at Beverly, with eyes that were large and brown.

"Now that Kelly Jo's gone, me and my brother are gonna need a new mom."

Jaime stopped. They stepped closer to the wall to avoid traffic in the hallway. Jaime lowered herself and looked into Beverly's eyes.

"Yes, I know you will, honey."

"So, uh, could you be our new mom? You're taller and more fun and smarter than our mom. Our new foster mom is OK, but I know we can't stay there. And you're prettier, too, 'cause my mom never combed her hair."

Jaime kissed her lightly on the forehead.

"Jaime, why was Kelly Jo always the one that got hurt and not me and my brother?"

Beverly had asked Jaime that question constantly. Law school had failed to prepare her to answer it. Jaime knew Kelly Jo was the "target" child in an abusive family, but how could she explain that to a nine-year-old?

"People are different, sweetheart," Jaime began by saying. "I know it may be hard for you to understand, especially now, but your mother does love you and your brother. And she loved Kelly Jo, too. But sometimes people can't cope with what happens to them so they do things to hurt themselves and those they love. Do you understand why you and your brother had to be taken away from your mother?"

Beverly nodded. "'Cause Kelly Jo got hurt and died?"

"That's right."

"Kelly Jo didn't have no friends, 'cept me," Beverly said proudly, standing a little taller.

Jaime cupped her hands around Beverly's soft, round face.

"You were an angel to your sister."

Beverly regarded Jaime levelly.

"So does that mean you can be our mom now?"

Jaime took Beverly's small hands. She swallowed slowly. "Sweetheart, I can't be your mom. But I can be someone who can be there for you. We can find a better home for you and your brother. Would you like me to help you?"

Beverly nodded and wrapped her arms tightly around Jaime's neck. Jaime felt her heart pound against her rib cage so hard it almost stopped her from breathing.

Jaime could feel the same pressure against her ribs tonight. And it wasn't coming from jumping rope or hitting the heavy bag.

She finished her workout and left the gym anxiously, looking forward to a steam and cool shower. She hustled past the basketball court. If Mitchell was playing, she did not want to see him. The last thing she wanted to do was talk to him.

The moon lit up the January sky, shining like a new dime. It cast a chilly eye at Jaime as she left the club. She was glad she lived within walking distance. Darts of frosted air spurted from her mouth as she hurried across the street to her apartment, a smooth glass and tan-brick building. She reached the entrance to the lobby and glanced quickly at the address, Eighteen Hundred, written in script. She had shared the apartment with Mitchell until two months ago when he left, or, better, when she had kicked him out. He was living somewhere in Capital Hill now. Just as well. It was better he was gone.

Over dinner, Jaime reviewed Kelly Jo's case. Later she cleaned up and read the Denver News-Dispatch. Jaime liked reading reporter Leigh Roberts' accounts of the Cox trial. Her stories were precise and detailed, her quotes accurate. And Jaime liked the way Leigh was able to capture the mood of the courtroom each day.

Her body cried for sleep, but she was doing everything she could to avoid going to bed. Sleeping brought nightmares. Ever since she had started work on Kelly Jo's case, they had grown steadily worse. Exhausted, she fell into bed and turned on the TV. It was 11:45 p.m.

She woke suddenly, blinking several times as though she were looking into the sun. The TV was still flickering and the room felt as thick as the ocean floor. She turned toward the clock, squinting at the numbers, surprised she had managed to fall asleep. The red digits showed 3:40 a.m. Jaime's pillow and nightshirt were drenched in sweat. Her hair was matted on the nape of her neck.

Why did she feel so scared? She closed her eyes. She had been dreaming, but all she could recall was the tree.

The cottonwood tree with a trunk as thick and wide as a mountainside stood at the hairpin corner. Jaime had not driven that route in Boulder where she lived as a child in years, but she knew the tree still owned the corner. Jaime's sister had crashed her car into it — the car folding as easily around the trunk as if it were aluminum. The accident had ended her sister's life. But she had stopped living long, long before.

To them, it had been a beautiful tree with branches stretching toward the sky and leaves that turned into distinct, crisp autumn hues. It was naked in the winter, bloomed in green glory in the spring, shielded and cooled them with shade from the summer sun. It was their landmark, a signal that home was only two left turns and a mile away. When they trained, they ran from home to the tree and back.

But not anymore.

"*Sarah.*" Jaime called out her sister's name, the darkness carrying the sound of her voice.

At 5:30 a.m. the alarm sounded. Jaime didn't need it. She had been staring into the blackness, staring at that old cottonwood tree.

Two

Jaime rose from the prosecution table, straightened her black wool skirt and looked at the judge.

"Your honor, we call our final witness, Beverly Cox."

Jaime watched Beverly wearing her print dress, take small, deliberate steps toward the witness stand. She waited for Beverly to get settled and take the oath, feeling relieved they had rehearsed this part.

She walked to the witness stand and smiled at Beverly. "Sweetheart, what's your name?"

"Beverly Cox."

"And how did you know Kelly Jo?"

"She was my sister."

"What do you remember about Kelly Jo?"

"She cried all the time because Will was mean to her."

"You mean William Blair, that man over there?" Jaime pointed to the defense table.

"Yes, that's my mommy's boyfriend."

"How was he mean to your sister?"

Beverly looked down at her hands. "He hurt her with his hands and other things."

"What other things, Beverly?"

"He stuck pens inside of her."

"In her mouth, Beverly?" Jaime asked.

Beverly shook her head. "Down there, you know, where you go to the bathroom."

Several of the jurors fidgeted in their chairs. Beverly glanced at them and then to Jaime. Jaime nodded slightly with a small smile that reassured the little girl.

Beverly nodded and then went on. "He'd hold her down on the bed so she couldn't move. Kelly Jo wasn't very strong and … and then he would stick stuff inside her."

"How often did this happen?" Jaime asked.

"All the time," Beverly said.

"How do you know this?"

"We shared a room. We had twin beds. And every night after my mommy would put us to bed, Will came in the room and he always went to Kelly Jo's bed."

"What do you remember about the last week of Kelly Jo's life, Beverly?"

"One day we went to the playground."

"Did Kelly Jo break her leg coming down the slide, as your mother told the social worker?"

"No. Nothing happened like that. We just played and then went home."

"How did Kelly Jo break her leg shortly before she died?"

"In our bedroom."

"Did she fall off the bed?"

"No."

"What happened then?" Jaime asked.

"Will came in the room, really mad and slapped my sister so hard she just went flying off the bed."

"Your sister was a small child, wasn't she?"

"Uh huh, a really little girl," Beverly replied. "When my sister fell, she screamed really loud and I heard a really weird sound coming from her leg … it kinda went pop."

"A week after that incident, after your mother put you to bed that night, did Will come into the room as he usually did?" Jaime asked.

"Yeah," Beverly said.

"And then he pulled down his pants," Jaime said.

"Objection! Your honor, please, Ms. Monroe is leading the witness," attorney Burt Palicano said from his place at the defense table.

Jaime rephrased her question. "How could you see what happened, Beverly? Wasn't the room dark?"

"Yeah, but the light from the hallway made the room bright so I could see better. Will took his pants down."

"So Mr. Blair pulled down his pants…"

Beverly nodded. "And then he climbed on top of Kelly Jo and she started to cry right away and she just kept crying even though Will told her to be quiet."

"Did he tell her in a mean way?"

"Yeah, he said in a really nasty voice, 'Shut up, retard.'"

"And then what happened, Beverly? What did Mr. Blair do to make Kelly Jo stop crying?"

"He took off one of his socks and stuffed it in her mouth."

Jaime drew a deep breath. She wanted to close her eyes, but she forced herself to keep her attention on Beverly. "And then what happened, sweetheart?"

"He held a hand over her mouth and then the bed kept moving back and forth and then he made a really loud grunting noise and then the bed stopped rocking."

"What happened after that?"

"He left the room."

"Was Kelly Jo still crying?"

Beverly shook her head. "She didn't make any more sounds after that."

Jaime stared at Beverly and when Jaime turned to leave the witness stand, she didn't realized how hard she had been gripping the railing until she saw the imprint of her hand on it. Jaime walked slowly back to the prosecution table. She stood in front of her chair, looking darkly at the judge.

"Your honor, I have no further questions for Beverly Cox."

The judge, an elderly man with bushy eyebrows and a fleshy face, looked at his gavel and then at defense attorney Burt Palicano.

"Your witness, counselor," he said.

Palicano struggled to heave his bulk from the narrow confines of his chair. He waddled toward the witness stand, his pants rubbing together as he walked. He stood looking at Beverly, his hands squarely on his hips, his suit jacket open and his large belly falling over his belt. Jaime noticed Beverly's eyes were wide and she had seemed to shrink in her chair.

"You're very good in school, aren't you Beverly," he said, staring intently at her, his expression ominous.

Beverly couldn't help smiling and she sat a little taller in her chair. "I guess. My teachers tell me that all the time."

"What's your favorite subject?"

"English," Beverly answered without hesitation. "I like writing stories."

"Yes, your teachers are full of praise for you, aren't they? Telling you what a good little storyteller you are."

Jaime sprang to her feet. "Objection, your honor!"

"Overruled," the judge said.

Palicano continued, glaring at her. "This is just another story you made up, isn't it, Beverly? It didn't really happen like that, did it? Of course not. It's just your imagination."

"It did! Everything happened just like I said it did!" Beverly's voice broke and she fell back against her chair.

Palicano shifted to one side, giving Beverly the opportunity to look directly at Jaime, her eyes pleading for help. Jaime clasped her hands in Beverly's direction. She hoped it would convey that she was doing the right thing. They had rehearsed this.

Palicano went on, "A man's life is a stake here, Beverly, do you realize that? This isn't a game. Tell us what really happened."

"Objection!" Jaime said, rising to her feet again.

"Overruled," the judge said.

"Kelly Jo broke her leg coming down the slide, just as your mother told the social worker, didn't she?"

"No, it didn't happen at the playground!" Beverly protested. "It happened in our bedroom. Will hit Kelly Jo and knocked her off the bed and her leg broke."

"Isn't that what you told the social worker?" Palicano asked.

"No! I told her the truth!" Beverly said, who was sobbing now. "I never said anything bad about my sister! I only wanted to help her!"

Palicano spoke in a huff. "Well, you're not doing much to help her now…"

"Objection!" Jaime was still on her feet. "Your honor, the defense attorney is badgering the witness!"

"Mr. Palicano," the judge said, pointing his gavel at the lawyer, "please make your point and let's move on."

Palicano stood directly in front of the witness stand, watching Beverly weep as she took in deep gulps of air. "I have nothing further for this witness, your honor." He turned and waddled back to the defense table.

"Beverly, you may step down," the judge said to her.

The little girl bolted from the witness stand and fell heavily into Jaime's arms.

THREE

"If the world were a perfect place we might not be here today," Jaime said in a smooth, even voice as she began her closing remarks the next morning. She walked to the jury box and looked at each juror as she let them digest her words. She was dressed in a gray diagonal tweed jacket with a high-button, double-breasted front that complemented her skirt.

She was about to end her first solo trial. She was nervous, but determined the jurors wouldn't see it. She rested a hand on the railing to steady herself. After months of building a case and more than a week of hearing testimony and presenting evidence, Jaime wanted nothing more than to make Kelly Jo's rapist and murderer a lifetime resident of the state penitentiary.

"What now falls into your hands, ladies and gentlemen, is to decide the case of 15-year-old Kelly Jo Cox and the fate of the man who raped her and left her for dead. You've heard testimony that proves this man is guilty of raping and murdering an innocent child."

Some of the jurors looked beyond Jaime to the defense table. Jaime turned slowly from the jury and stared across the courtroom at the man accused of killing Kelly Jo. But he did not meet her stare. He rubbed a finger over a mustache hardly more than peach fuzz, and kept his gaze fixed on the table.

Jaime pointed to him. "That man, William Blair, sits in this courtroom today."

Jaime paused long enough to allow the jury to have another good, long look at him. He was twenty-five. A wide tan tie and brown polyester suit covered his tall, lanky frame. His dishwater-blond hair was thick and kinky and old acne scars pockmarked his long, thin face.

"Kelly Jo only lived fifteen years and we know those weren't happy years," she went on. "Not once in her short, tragic life did she know what it was like to be a child. For Kelly Jo, Christmas never came. The tooth fairy never left money under her pillow and the Easter Bunny never hid colored eggs. Instead, Kelly Jo could celebrate only when her mother and Mr. Blair left her alone because the monster under her bed was very real and it came for her every night."

Jaime returned to the prosecution table, picked up a yellow legal pad and studied it for a moment. She took a pen from the table and, returning to the jury box, ran her hand along the smooth surface. She looked at each juror thoughtfully.

"But the world is far from perfect and Kelly Jo, a 15-year-old mentally disabled little girl, was raped and murdered. Our lives will continue, ladies and gentlemen, but Kelly Jo's life is over. There was something, however, that Kelly Jo took with her, something that Mr. Blair failed to think about when he raped her. It spoke the volumes that she could not..."

Jaime's voice trailed off and she deliberately waited a minute before speaking. "He left his calling card with Kelly Jo. She went to her death carrying the semen of Mr. Blair."

William Blair was looking at Jaime when she turned toward the defense table. She stared straight into green eyes. Throughout the trial as she watched him, she noticed that a certain way he held his head made his facial features look young, the way she imagined he looked in boyhood. She would catch his eyes shifting nervously back and forth and allow herself a small smile. She knew she had him.

"Abuse—domestic, physical, sexual and emotional—has run rampant in this family since Kelly Jo was born. And nothing, nothing gives a man..." Jaime pounded the railing with her fist, "The excuse to beat and rape a child. No child should have to endure the suffering Kelly Jo did at the unmerciful hands of Mr. Blair."

Jaime clutched her pen as she slowly walked the length of the jury box. "You might ask yourself, ladies and gentlemen, as I often did when I was assigned this case, how could a woman who has felt the first signs of life began to move within her, or who has nuzzled her baby's sweet, damp head against her breast, or watched her baby sleep innocently before her, allow such a heinous crime to continue?"

"Objection! Your honor, is the district attorney auditioning for a Broadway play?" Burt Palicano struggled to squeeze out of his chair. "Would you please remind Ms. Monroe," he wheezed, "That these are closing arguments and not some political soapbox."

The judge cast a weary eye at Jaime. "Sustained, counselor. He's right," the judge said. "This is a courtroom, not a forum, Ms. Monroe. Confine your statements to the testimony we've heard in court."

Jaime nodded, feeling her face flush. "Yes, your honor."

The judge looked at the jurors. "The jury will disregard the prosecutor's last statement."

Jaime waited as the fleshy Palicano attempted to stuff himself back into his chair.

She went on. "Kelly Jo's leg had been broken only weeks before she was raped a final time. You were told this was a case of accidental injury. That social workers accepted the mother's claim that Kelly Jo and Beverly were on a swing set when she broke her leg coming down the slide.

"But each of you heard for yourself the real truth when Beverly took the stand and testified that her sister wasn't anywhere near a playground the day she broke her leg. Each of you heard Beverly tell us in her own words how she and Kelly Jo were playing in her bedroom when Mr. Blair barged in and slapped Kelly Jo—a small, fragile child—so hard she fell off the bed.

"You heard Beverly tell us in her own words how Kelly Jo fell, and her leg went pop. And you heard how Kelly Jo screamed in pain."

Jaime paced the length of the jury box. "This was no *accidental* injury, ladies and gentlemen. It was an *excuse* that came from a mother who has been a drug addict since she was a teenager, a mother who has her own log book with the Denver Police Department on 911 calls for assault, domestic violence and on and on and on."

Jaime turned from the jury and looked again at William Blair sitting hunched over the defense table, hands folded tightly. She wanted him to be an old, old man, if he ever was released from prison.

"So, ladies and gentlemen, who are you going to believe? Are you going to believe the druggie mom?"

"Objection! The child's mother is not on trial here, your honor!" Palicano said as he pulled his legs under his chair ready to stand.

"Overruled," the judge said.

Jaime continued. "And, since we didn't have the opportunity to hear from Mr. Blair…"

"Objection!"

"Sustained."

Jaime went on. "I know it wasn't easy for any of you to listen to Beverly's testimony about the day Mr. Blair raped Sarah…"

Jaime stopped abruptly and stared at the floor, instantly realizing her blunder.

Am I losing it? Can't I get through a day anymore without thinking about her?

"Counselor?"

Jaime looked up at the sound of the judge's throaty voice.

"Counselor? Are you all right?"

"I'm sorry. What?" She looked at him as though she were hearing him for the first time.

"Is everything all right?" the judge asked with a hint of impatience in his voice.

Jaime felt the weight of every eye in the courtroom on her. She nodded at the judge. "Yes, your honor. I'm sorry," Jaime said and flashed a small, apologetic smile. "It was difficult, as I said, to hear Beverly's account of the day Kelly Jo was raped. Beverly cried. Even some of you cried."

Jaime walked to the prosecutor's table and rested the tips of her fingers lightly on her chair. "When you leave here and go into the jury room, ask yourself, ladies and gentlemen, who are you going to believe? Think about how you felt when you heard how Kelly Jo had been found, his semen inside her. Remember that Beverly's testimony only confirmed existing forensic evidence. Ladies and gentlemen, this man is guilty of rape and murder. Thank you."

When the judge sent the jury out to deliberate, the courtroom emptied quickly. Jaime was alone. She sat down, kicked off her heels and slumped back against her chair. Her sigh echoed off the surrounding walls. She felt satisfied, the nervous pit in her stomach gone. Her closing went well, *except for the slip with Sarah.*

Damn.

It was over and she was glad. Kelly Jo's case had drained her and brought back every unpleasant memory of Sarah. Kelly Jo's trial would end just after the anniversary of the night her own sister had been raped.

Ten years have come and gone since that New Year's Eve party.

She looked around the empty courtroom. Jaime could still hear Beverly on the witness stand remembering Kelly Jo pleading and crying.

She called out for mommy, but mommy did not come.

"No. No. No."

Had Sarah said the same? Did she feel the same pain? Experience the same horror? Jaime would never know. Her sister had vowed to keep that she had been raped a secret. She had wanted to protect her older sister. Jaime had meant the world to her.

Within two hours the jury returned.

"Madam Foreman, has the jury reached a verdict?" the judge asked.

"Yes, your honor, we have."

"How does the jury find?"

"We find the defendant, Mr. William Blair, guilty."

Jaime closed her eyes. It was finally over. She left the courtroom and was hardly down the hall when a booming voice came from behind her.

"Excellent, counselor!"

Dan Walker, an energetic, middle-aged man with thick, curly black hair, caught up with her. He had been her mentor when she first came to the DA's office. Jaime had been second chair on several of his trials. He had since left the DA's office to form his own firm, but both were avid runners and still ran together. She smiled broadly when he reached her and they embraced.

"I just heard! I knew you had that poor dumb bastard from day one."

"The guy should have pled," Jaime said.

"With that kind of evidence, you're damn right he should have! But he didn't and they did right by giving you that case."

Jaime shrugged her shoulders. "I don't know. I was nervous as hell."

"It didn't show."

"Thanks, Dan. Is that a compliment?"

"Of course it is. Haven't I always said that mind of yours is always clicking, always working in fast forward?" Dan said and flashed his familiar wide grin. "Haven't I always said that you could spar with the best of 'em? And that sixth sense you're building against defense attorneys really helped you stay ahead of old Burt didn't it?"

"Dan, *that* wasn't too hard," Jaime said, thinking of the flabby Palicano trying to hoist himself from the chair.

"Jaime," Dan said smiling again. "You know what I mean. Congratulations, you did well! We should celebrate, and if I didn't have this damn hearing, I'd take you to lunch."

"Another time," she said and smiled.

But she didn't feel like celebrating, really. After watching Beverly on the witness stand, Jaime couldn't help wondering if she had done the right thing. It was an open and shut case. *Did I really have to put that child through that?*

As Jaime watched Dan Walker turn the corner, she thought about how he had helped her learn their profession. She recalled the times he would tell her how she was quickly gaining a courtroom savvy. She smiled. Maybe Dan Walker was right. She did love the challenge of putting the pieces together and making it work. It was only her third year and she was fast making a name for herself.

Jaime agreed with Dan when he said she was hardest on herself. She remembered telling him she couldn't help it, that she was obsessively dedicated to her profession. She was aggressive, articulate and focused. She was a woman with a knack for paying attention to detail. That's why he liked her. She felt honored when Dan had asked her to join his firm when he left the DA's office, but she had declined. She said she wanted to stay on the side of the angels.

Jaime left the city and county building, thinking of the day Sarah was forced to tell her and their parents she had been raped. The sideways glance Sarah had given Jaime told her everything.

She had been trying to keep it a secret.

She thought of Beverly on the witness stand, of Kelly Jo, and of Sarah's funeral that she could not attend.

Dan always told her what a great prosecutor she was becoming.

She laughed sadly, having a difficult time believing in herself the confident way Dan Walker did.

For if it were true, why did she felt so rotten?

Four

The temperature was near freezing when Jaime stepped from the Denver City and County Building. She wrapped her long dark coat against the cold and pulled on a pair of gloves.

Snow remained on the ground, as a dirty and frozen reminder that winter still had claim to the calendar. Patchy gray clouds covered the sky, but Jaime caught a fleeting glimpse of the sun as she walked down the stone steps. Her mood improved with the appearance of the sun and she turned her face toward the sky.

Her breath rose in wisps as she walked the few blocks to catch the 16th Street Mall shuttle to Market Street Station. From there it would be a short walk to Lower Downtown. She had promised herself if she won for Kelly Jo, she would eat at Café Gardenia, a new Italian restaurant housed in a red-brick building between 18th and 19th avenues on Blake Street.

Jaime entered the restaurant. Despite the rush of waiters and people, the atmosphere was cozy. A rich smell of tomato sauce filled the air, raising her spirits. The place was small and the tables were close together and Jaime had to squeeze by a line of people at the deli. Her hopes of dining faded quickly, all the tables were full. She was about to leave when she spotted a woman sitting alone at a table. The woman looked familiar and Jaime took a second, longer look.

It was Leigh Roberts, the *Dispatch* reporter and syndicated columnist, whose column, BETWEEN THE LINES, appeared in the paper every Tuesday and Sunday. Leigh wrote about contemporary issues and life. Her writing gave Jaime the impression she was open and approachable.

After Kelly Jo's verdict was announced, Jaime had given Leigh and a group of other journalists a statement when they had approached the prosecution table. As Jaime spoke, she watched Leigh write furiously in her reporter's notebook, occasionally meeting Jaime's eyes when she looked up.

Any other day Jaime would have left the cafe, but the guilty verdict had boosted her confidence. Leigh was sitting near the back of the cafe. Jaime made her way to the table.

"Excuse me," Jaime said.

Leigh stopped squeezing fresh lemon into hot tea and looked up.

"Hi," Jaime said and waved.

They studied each other. Jaime knew from her column that she was in her mid-forties, but she had a natural beauty about her that made her look a decade younger.

Jaime cleared her throat. "I thought your coverage of the Cox trial was excellent. Your stories were always accurate and to the point and, being the prosecutor on the case, I appreciated that. And I love your column."

Leigh looked at Jaime and said nothing. Her thin, oval face was smooth, with the smallest hint of laugh lines appearing around eyes that were round and blue. She looked around the busy cafe and then to Jaime. "Would you like to share the table?" she asked.

Jaime nodded. "Do you mind? I've wanted to try this place since it opened."

"I've been here several times already. The food is wonderful," Leigh said.

She rose and removed her briefcase and laptop from the chair so

Jaime could sit down. Jaime noticed Leigh was slender and about two inches shorter than she.

"So you're Jaime Monroe," Leigh said.

Jamie tilted her head, then added, "Actually the last name is Monroe-Price. But I'm dropping Price when my divorce is final. You're brave to eat spaghetti sauce with your top. It's beautiful," Jaime said remarking on Leigh's white cashmere sweater.

"Thanks," Leigh said and tugged slightly at the collar, pulling it toward her chin. "I wanted something warm today. They said it was going to be cold and I hate being cold."

When Jaime had settled at the table, Leigh said, "I have to say I enjoyed watching you during the trial. That chubby defense attorney never had a chance."

"None whatsoever," Jaime said. "Aren't you writing a story about what happened today?"

"I'm in no hurry. The verdict came back so quickly, so I've got plenty of time to file before deadline," Leigh said. "So you've read a few of my columns?"

"Quite a few," Jaime said. "I agree with what you write. Most of it, anyway. Even if I don't, you'll say something that gets me thinking."

"That's good to hear. I guess that means I'm doing my job."

A waiter came to the table and they both ordered linguine in a tomato and basil sauce.

"I'm here to celebrate," Jaime said when the waiter left. "Kelly Jo's case was my first major trial on my own."

"I'm sure you're glad it's over, especially now that we won't be in your face anymore."

"Yeah, I am."

"I've been wanting to do a column on that case from the day I did my first story on Kelly Jo," Leigh said. "It would make a wonderful piece. I'd *love* to get inside that guy's head."

"Believe me, you wouldn't," Jaime said.

They were silent as the waiter set two steamy bowls of minestrone soup and a basket of fresh bread in front of them.

"What happened to that child was awful," Leigh said.

The din of the restaurant seemed to grow and Jaime and Leigh moved closer to the table.

Jaime nodded as she buttered a slice of bread. “When I thought it couldn’t get any worse, it did. The first time I saw X-rays from some of her injuries, it amazed me that people are capable of inflicting such pain and violence on other human beings. It wasn’t like this little girl could defend herself.”

“How many times did he rape her?” Leigh asked.

“Who knows? He used anything he could get his hands on—a toothbrush, his finger, a ball point pen. I guess since she was mentally challenged he thought she couldn’t stop him or tell anyone what had happened to her.”

Leigh took a slice of bread and bit into it without buttering it. She chewed slowly. “He might have gotten away with it if it hadn’t been for Beverly. Kelly Jo fell into a low level of cognitive development. She could’ve never testified to what had happened to her.”

“How does it compare with the other levels?” Jaime asked.

“There are four degrees of severity with mental retardation, mild, moderate, severe and profound.” Leigh finished the last of her soup and set her spoon down. She looked at Jaime. “Kelly Jo was considered severe.”

“Can people like Kelly Jo really learn?” Jaime asked.

“Of course they can and do, but it’s limited, very limited,” Leigh went on, gesturing with her hand. “They benefit only a small extent from instruction such as familiarity with the alphabet and some simple counting. They can master some survival words, mommy, daddy, I’m hungry, I want to eat and I have to go to the bathroom.”

Jaime cocked her head. “Your knowledge of the subject seems extensive. You were the only reporter who came every day. You were interested in the proceedings and your writing showed that you know a lot about such disabilities,” Jaime said, as if she wanted to know why.

Leigh shrugged and her smile hardly registered on her face. She leaned against the tall back of the chair.

“Oh, it’s just a mild interest, really,” Leigh spoke in a tone that evoked no further response.

They ate a moment in silence.

“What else did the jerk do to her?” Leigh asked, shifting the focus of the conversation back to Kelly Jo Cox.

"Besides the broken leg?" Jaime said. "There were burn marks all over her torso and she had welts on her back as thick as my finger where he hit her with an electrical cord. Little bastard, I hope he rots in prison."

Jaime's face was animated and lively and her eyebrows rose slightly every time she spoke. She gestured repeatedly and there was a sense of quickness, of urgency, and of passion in her voice as she talked about the trial.

"There must be a reason for your intensity," Leigh said.

Jaime looked at Leigh wide-eyed and swallowed over the sudden lump in her throat. Yes, there was, a deep-seated reason few people knew. Jaime avoided eye contact and turned to watch people order at the deli. When she spoke again, her passion gave way to a professional calm.

"I just wanted to see that the bastard got what he deserved."

Leigh picked up her tea and raised the cup to eye level. "A toast," she said. "A toast to victory."

Jaime raised her water glass. They ate for several minutes in silence.

"We really should change the subject, anyway," Leigh said, and grinned.

"How long have you been with the *Dispatch*?" Jaime asked.

"Almost fourteen years. I got my start at a small daily in upstate New York."

"Are you from New York?"

Leigh nodded. "That job was the best thing to ever happen to me," she said. "It made me appreciate what reporters and attorneys, some of them at least, have to go through."

"Meaning?" Jaime leaned forward.

"My first big story was a young mother brutally murdered by a drifter who robbed the gas station where she worked. I remember the editor … a scruffy guy with a big belly," Leigh said using her hands animatedly. "He came into the newsroom and I could tell he was looking for someone with more experience to send to the scene, but the newsroom was empty. He saw me, but he kept looking around the newsroom, like he was hoping another reporter would walk in."

The smile on Leigh's face was wide and Jaime smiled with her.

"He finally pointed to me and said 'you, Lisa, come here.'" I replied from across the newsroom, "It's Leigh." He said, "'Well, whatever, come here.'" He told me to get to the gas station. I couldn't help it, but I pointed to myself and said "Me?" He nodded and said, "You see anyone else in here? Get your ass out there!"

Leigh was silent as she thought a moment. "It was covering that story that I knew I wanted to be a journalist."

"Seems like you've done very well for yourself," Jaime said.

Leigh leaned away from the table and looked carefully at Jaime. "I've had some successes in my career and personally for that matter. And failures, too, of course," she said with feeling. "When I get down, I think back to my successes, like probably most people do. In the end though, they don't make me feel as good about myself as I would like to feel, especially at this point in my life. But for the most part, I can't complain about what I've done so far."

They finished their lunch in silence. It was after 2 p.m. when they stepped from the cafe. The sun had slipped behind heavy dark gray clouds. The wind had picked up. Both women buttoned their long coats and threw scarves over their shoulders to shield themselves from the piercing winter air.

Leigh looked to the sky. "It'll probably snow tonight," she said.

"I'll walk with you to the shuttle," Jaime said and they moved along Blake Street toward the 16th Street Mall.

Leigh would return to the *Dispatch* building on Welton Street and Jaime to the DA's office on Colfax Avenue. When they reached Market Street Station, Leigh spoke.

"I'm going to walk. I've got to make a stop before I go back to work. You go ahead, Jaime. Lunch and the conversation were nice."

"Same here and thanks for letting me join you," Jaime said. "I didn't want to celebrate alone."

"Maybe we can do it again," Leigh said.

"I'd like that."

Jaime waved and moved in the direction of the waiting shuttle. Before she boarded, she turned to see which direction Leigh had gone. But she had disappeared into a sea of people. And only stranger's faces stared back.

FIVE

"Good morning, counselor," the honorable Pearl Priestly said. The woman's scratchy voice emanated from Jaime's voice mail. "Jaime, dear, can we meet for lunch tomorrow? I'd like to pick your brain about an interesting case."

Jaime had been in court all morning and was back at the office listening to messages. Jaime first met Pearl after the judge lectured during one of her pre-law courses and again when the judge gave another lecture during Jaime's second year in law school. They became and stayed friends.

Pearl Priestly had helped Jaime land her first job. She came highly recommended by Pearl, who had taken an immediate liking to the young, ambitious law student.

Pearl remembered Jaime vividly from the first lecture and was instantly impressed by her acuity. She posed several hypothetical situations that could have resulted in serious ramifications had they not been litigated properly. When Jaime introduced herself after her second lecture, Pearl recalled Jaime seemed surprised she remembered her.

"You remembered my name and everything," Jaime would tell her later.

When Jaime returned from Boston University to earn her law degree in Denver, Pearl became her mentor, taking her to parties and introducing her to attorneys and judges. Like Pearl, Jaime's interests were mainly in cases of abused and neglected children. It was a common bond that linked them. As a former prosecutor, Pearl had tried and won many child abuse cases.

Pearl and Jaime met often for lunch. They would discuss impending cases, murders of the day and trials in progress. Often they talked of their personal lives. Pearl was a widow and had been for years. She had a son and daughter who were both involved in missionary work in third-world countries. When she heard about Sarah, their parents and what had happened to the family, a mother's love rose within her. It surfaced one night when Pearl and Jaime went to a dinner party. Jaime drank too much and stayed the night at Pearl's place. Jaime didn't remember the conversation they had the following morning. But Pearl did. Jaime had told her about her family. Pearl also accepted Jaime's distance and her reluctance to be close.

Jaime dialed the number from memory and left word she would be happy to meet the judge the next day at Washington Park. Lunch, whenever the winter weather permitted, was always hotdogs from a vendor and a walk in the park. Pearl loved hotdogs.

A pale yellow sun was shining in a clear blue sky when Jaime reached Wash Park. It was crowded with people enjoying a warm winter day. Runners and bikers exercised along the asphalt road and anglers rested in folding chairs by the lakes waiting for fish to bite. When Jaime stepped from her car, she left her long coat behind. Her winter-white wool slacks and tailored blazer would be plenty to keep the chill from her body.

She arrived at the north entrance at noon. Pearl was there waiting. It wasn't hard to spot her from a distance. Pearl stood as though the wind was pushing her forward. She was a small, painfully thin woman. Almost brittle. She wore a long, thick tweed coat with a belt tied tightly around her waist. A pair of black gloves protruded limply from a side pocket. The temperature didn't matter, with little body fat, she was always cold.

Her body was a thin disguise of the woman's character. Short, fine silver hair framed her face. She was a frail, but forceful woman, spry and energetic and she tackled her work with a strong, efficient conviction. She was a powerful judge, mighty in her courtroom, well known for the stiff, uncompromising sentences she handed down.

They greeted each other with a hug. When Jaime pulled away, Pearl kept her bony hands tightly on Jaime's shoulders, studying her. Whenever Pearl saw Jaime, her love grew. Always in those early moments of meeting, Pearl would fast forward through Jaime's life. A painful process.

She smoothed Jaime's hair from her eyes. The emerald green blouse Jaime wore beneath her blazer deepened her brown eyes. Her smile was warm. "You look so good, Jaime, dear."

Jaime nodded and returned the smile. Pearl slipped her arm under Jaime's elbow and they entered the park and walked to the flowerbeds. The beds were empty now, but come spring, the large patches of dirt would be filled with brilliant, vivid flowers. Jaime bought three hotdogs, two of them for Pearl, drinks and chips.

"What's this big case you're so interested in?" Jaime asked, as she gave Pearl her hotdogs.

"I know this young woman with mental retardation who lives in a group home near Congress Park. But she'll be moving into a host-home soon. An apartment, I think, the ones off Speer Boulevard. You know, those near the college?"

Pearl looked at Jaime and she nodded.

"She works in a sheltered workshop now, stuffing sports bags with newspaper," Pearl went on, "But she's going to start work with a cleaning crew at the food court in the Tabor Center in about a month."

"What's her name?" Jaime asked.

"Ashleigh Roberts."

Jaime looked at Pearl waiting for her to say more, but she didn't. Jaime shook her head slightly, confused.

"Ashleigh's mother wants to have her sterilized."

Jaime raised her eyebrows slightly. "Sterilized?"

"Ashleigh's mother is afraid people will take advantage of Ashleigh in many ways, sexually for one and Ashleigh won't know how or be able to take care of herself. Her biggest fear, I've been told, is that she's afraid Ashleigh could be raped because she won't be careful enough. So the mother wants to eliminate the risk of pregnancy by having her sterilized."

"That's pretty drastic," Jaime said.

"Of course, that's not going to eliminate the risk of getting raped, but who knows what the mother's thinking."

"What are the state laws on sterilization?" Jaime asked.

"I'll give you a thimble-size overview," she said, patting Jaime lightly on her arm. "Sterilization of people with developmental disabilities is intentionally strict in Colorado."

"To prevent involuntary sterilization?" Jaime asked, meeting Pearl's blue eyes. She never remembered Pearl to look any different, even from the first time she saw her in college. Her ripened face showed every bit of its near-seven decades of life. Every wrinkle was deeply etched in her face and skin folded around her eyes and throat.

Pearl nodded. "Courts have a statutory provision when the primary purpose is to prevent pregnancy. Since the guardian can't substitute their consent for sterilization for that of an incapacitated person, my guess is the mother in this case went to her doctor to ask about doing the procedure without getting the courts involved, but..."

"That's what happened," Jaime interrupted and nodded at Pearl. "The doctor told her no and that's why you're telling me."

"That's why we're here," Pearl confirmed. She took a bite from her hotdog and chewed slowly, then patted the corners of her mouth with a crumpled napkin. "Here's the short answer, dear," she continued. "The law provides for a hearing that judicially determines the person's capacity to consent, if consent was not obtained. It's a hot-button topic in the fields of medical and social ethics. For historical reasons, you know, eugenics fans and the like."

"Eugenics." Jaime said. "The science of improving the human race by careful selection of parents. Keep the able by encouraging reproduction with parents who have good, strong genes. Sterilize the bad who have the defective, faulty traits."

"Hard to imagine isn't it?" Pearl said, frowning.

"Just to keep it confusing," Pearl went on, "Some who promote the rights of mentally disabled people to be sterilized argue the reverse that, in fact, sterilization may present a desirable birth control method for some. It's a matter of personal privacy that the Constitution protects from interference when the decision is an informed and intelligent choice of the disabled individual."

"Sounds complicated."

Pearl laughed. "It's not supposed to be easy, dear."

They finished lunch and began to stroll toward Grassmere Lake near the south end of Wash Park. They walked in silence for several moments.

"How did you hear about Ashleigh's case?" Jaime asked.

"Erin Greene, Ashleigh's group home supervisor at Morningside Heights, called me. We've known each other for years. She voiced her concerns and I met with them last week. A nice young woman. Erin said she was worried that Ashleigh's mother was extremely fearful about an unwanted pregnancy, almost to the point of obsession."

"Does she have a reason to be, I mean, besides Ashleigh being mentally disabled?"

"Ashleigh also has health problems."

"What kind of problems?"

"She has diabetes, a mild form. It's controlled through diet and exercise, for the most part. Her mother fears getting pregnant would, of course, be detrimental to her health. Erin said Ashleigh's mother had every intention of going through with the operation to quote, get her daughter fixed so that wouldn't happen."

"What about Ashleigh's father?" Jaime asked.

"They're divorced. He apparently hasn't been in Ashleigh's life for years, but he does send her money on a regular basis."

"Who's the judge on the case?" Jaime asked, feeling a growing dislike of Ashleigh's mother.

"You know him," Pearl said. "Jessie Gutierrez."

Jaime nodded with familiarity. Jessie Gutierrez had a voice that hummed like a bass note and a soft, round body that reminded her of the Michelin Tire Man.

"From what I understand Ashleigh's mother thinks going to court is just going to be a formality. She'll tell the judge what she wants and the health risk it poses for Ashleigh and that's it," Pearl said flatly.

Jaime had been watching a small group of runners, but turned her attention to Pearl. She shook her head in disbelief.

"The first time she went to court it may have been that simple way," Pearl said.

"When was that?"

"When Ashleigh turned eighteen, her mother went to court to have her declared incompetent. She became the child's legal guardian. That may have been a formality, but not this."

"If that were my case," Jaime returned without hesitation. "I wouldn't stand by while Ashleigh's mother got approval to do a snip here and there." She paused a moment and thought. "I can't believe Ashleigh's mother actually believes that's all there is to it. Who is this woman, anyway?"

"Her name's Leigh Roberts…"

"Leigh Roberts? *Her*? You mean the columnist and reporter for the *Dispatch*?"

Their eyes met. Pearl nodded.

"I would've thought she'd be more progressive than that."

"You know her?" Pearl asked.

After a weighty pause Jaime answered hesitantly. "Yes. Well, I mean, sort of. I read her columns. She's good."

"Didn't she attend Kelly Jo's trial every day?" Pearl asked.

Jaime nodded. "We ended up at the same place for lunch after the verdict, so we shared a table."

They walked beyond the empty flower garden and reached the lake and Jaime told Pearl what Leigh had said about people with mental retardation.

"A mild interest," Pearl said and laughed. "I'd hardly call it mild, my dear."

"We had a nice lunch," Jaime said. "But she never said anything about having a daughter with developmental problems. She didn't mention having a child at all."

"Well, she does," Pearl said with conviction.

Pearl flashed Jaime a look of caution. "But don't put Leigh into that mean-rotten-horrible-mother category all by herself, dear. She's not the only parent with a disabled child wanting the procedure done. It used to happen all the time. For most of the 20th century parents had little problem getting their mentally challenged children sterilized. They'd walk into doctor's offices and get it done for all kinds of reasons. But now, doctors and lawyers are saying 'hold it.' The parents no longer have that right. Now you need court approval."

Pearl stopped talking and they walked in silence for a time as Jaime weighed what she heard. They reached the lake. The sun's image shimmered and glistened on the water. Jaime closed her eyes against the glare and the sun's reflection off the water warmed her. She felt Pearl's serious stare. She opened her eyes and they exchanged a heavy glance.

"It's a thorny issue," Pearl went on. "Cases like these can be very time consuming and complex. Most parents are split on the issue and not many are riding the fence. Some parents say they should be the ones to make the decision and others say the *courts* should weigh the matter."

Pearl stopped to collect her thoughts. "Doesn't matter how you look at it. The courts have stepped onto an emotional mine field. Reproductive rights for the disabled are, to put it mildly, riddled with social and ethical questions, controversial as they are complex."

"How old is Ashleigh?" Jaime asked.

"Twenty-four. I thought of you, dear, the moment I met her. She'd like you."

Jaime watched the water as it rippled toward her. It made a soft, lapping sound.

"Leigh is Ashleigh's legal guardian," Pearl said. "She has the authority to make decisions for Ashleigh because she lacks the mental capacity to make some on her own. But what fails about that all-or-nothing phenomenon is that while some individuals can't make certain kinds of decisions for themselves, they can make up their own minds on other matters."

They walked from the lake to a bench. Nearby, a group of South High School literature students were having their Shakespeare lesson under a cottonwood tree.

"Has Ashleigh given consent?" Jaime asked as they sat down.

"No. Erin Greene says she was part of a heated conversation between

Ashleigh and Leigh recently and Ashleigh distinctly told her mother no, she would not do it. This is heading for court. I can see it coming. Any exercise of state power to order nonconsensual sterilization must be scrutinized carefully."

"Does Leigh have a lawyer?"

"Yes. Winston Ross, one of the best. Have you heard of him?"

Jaime nodded and then glanced from the students to Pearl, studying her. Her cold blue eyes had the look of fire in them.

"It has to be scrutinized carefully because of the individual's rights and interests," Pearl added.

"So, it will be up to Ashleigh's attorney to prove she's competent," Jaime said.

Pearl nodded and went on. "Many people who have mild mental retardation understand the implications of such an operation and what it means. They are capable and competent enough to make their own decision. They understand the responsibilities of parenthood."

"Does Ashleigh have an attorney?" Jaime asked.

"Not yet," Pearl said. "I'm trying to find someone, too. If you can think of anyone who might be interested let me know."

Jaime raised her eyebrows. "I will." She paused a moment then added, "Tell me more about Ashleigh's disability."

"Ashleigh's classification makes up the largest percentage of people who have a mental disability. About 85 percent of people who have some retardation, have it mildly." Pearl went on. "Ashleigh does much on her own. And she's competent enough to understand what being sterilized would mean."

"I guess that's for the courts to decide," Jaime said.

"She is competent enough," Pearl said, emphasizing the word is.

Pearl grew quiet and they both turned their attention to the literature class. As the students started to recite a Shakespeare sonnet and what remained of the dead leaves on the cottonwood tree, began to rustle, Jaime felt her heart skip a beat. Her breath rose and caught in her throat as a girl read the opening lines.

"When in disgrace with Fortune and men's eyes,
I all alone beweep my outcast state,
And trouble deaf heaven with my bootless cries..."

A cold sweat absorbed her and she trembled involuntarily. Their shoulders were touching and Pearl turned to Jaime the moment she felt her shiver. She saw the ashen color in Jaime's face.

"Jaime, dear. What's the matter?"

She was too shaken to respond.

"Dear?" Pearl rested her hand lightly on Jaime's lap.

Jaime lifted her hand off her lap and pointed to the students. Pearl looked to the students and then Jaime, confusion showed in her wrinkled face.

"It's the 29th sonnet. What does it mean to you?" Pearl had lowered her voice. It was sympathetic, soft and even.

"I ... I first read it in a literature class when I was a freshman in high school," Jaime whispered. "One night Sarah and I were studying in my bedroom. And I read it to her for the first time. It was our favorite. I read it to her all the time. I still know it by heart, but I don't read it much anymore…"

They did not speak again until the students had collected their notebooks and returned to the school building.

"Pearl, I just can't shake Kelly Jo's case," Jaime said with feeling. "It has pushed everything with Sarah to the surface again. A day hardly goes by that I don't think of her anyway, but ever since this case, she's on my mind constantly. Sarah died the night she graduated from high school crashing into a tree just like that." Jaime pointed toward the cottonwood. "No matter what I do, I ... I can't stop thinking about her. It's making me crazy."

Pearl patted her lightly on the back and left her hand there. She nodded. "Yes, I know, dear."

"Sarah was a great tennis player, you know," Jaime said looking at Pearl. "The summer after she was raped, she went from playing and practicing tennis six days a week to hardly playing at all."

Jaime was twenty-two and graduating from college when her sister died. After Sarah's death, Jaime was determined to get on with her life and leave the dark shadows behind.

For a time it worked.

She moved back to Denver, started law school that fall and buried herself in her studies. Jaime graduated in the top ten of her class. She met Mitchell Price. She knew she should not have married him, but she did something she didn't often do, she ignored her inner voice and married him anyway. In the beginning, married life was exciting and work consumed the majority of her time. She thought little of Sarah and had not spoken to her parents since her sister's death. But with Kelly Jo's trial everything bubbled back to the surface. And coupled with the separation from Mitchell, it was becoming more than Jaime could handle.

Pearl glanced at her watch. It was 2:25 p.m.

"Dear, I've got a three o'clock appointment," she said, disappointment clear in her voice. "But I can skip it if you want to talk."

Jaime shook her head.

"You won Kelly Jo's case," Pearl said quietly. "That's some justice. It's time to put that case behind you, pick yourself up and go on."

Moving on for Jaime was always an effort. She had told Pearl she couldn't decide whether it was strength or weakness. Whether she was a fighter or a fool.

Jaime looked at Pearl and smiled weakly. "I've got to be at the police station, anyway," she said. "I'll give you a ride."

Six

A misty rain greeted Jaime the following morning as she set out to run.

The warmth of yesterday was gone, fading into her skin like a memory. She wore a hooded Boston University sweat top pulled loosely around her neck. Dressed in long stretch pants, molded around the toned muscles that shaped her legs, she felt warm.

Ashleigh Roberts was the first thing on her mind when she woke and Ashleigh stayed in her thoughts throughout the entire run and her working day.

Before she left work that evening, Jaime called Pearl.

"You asked me yesterday if I knew someone who would be interested in representing Ashleigh."

"You've found someone?" Pearl asked and Jaime could hear the lift in her voice.

"I have," Jaime said.

"Who?" Pearl asked unable to keep the excitement from her voice.

There was a pause.

"Me."

Another pause.

"You?"

"Yes, me."

Pearl laughed. "I was hoping you'd say that."

"Ashleigh has been on my mind since yesterday. You know that still, small voice inside me that I've always told you about?"

"Yes, the one you said you didn't listen to when it came to marrying Mitchell?"

"That one. Well, Pearl, it started talking to me when you did yesterday and it's been talking very loudly since."

"That means you'd have to quit the DA's office, dear. You know that."

"Yes, Pearl, I know."

"Are you prepared to do that?" she asked.

"I am," Jaime returned.

"Do you know you'd be turning your back on a career that's just beginning to take off for you, my dear?"

"Yes, I know, I've taken all that into consideration." Jaime thought about Beverly Cox crying on the witness stand. She won Kelly Jo's case, but at what cost? "I want to help Ashleigh."

"That's wonderful to hear. But I'd wish you'd take some time to think this through, Jaime. We can find someone to represent Ashleigh."

"I have," Jaime said softly. "It's something I have to do. Maybe I can do some good."

There was a pause.

"I can't wait for you to meet Ashleigh."

"Neither can I."

"You'll like her, she's a sweet young thing."

That night Jaime had a light sparring session with her partner, Frank Powers. He wanted to go for Chinese food, but Jaime declined. She said she was tired. She went home, but before she started dinner, she made a phone call, dialing the number from memory.

"Dan Walker," the cheery voice said.

Jaime closed her eyes and smiled. He was at the office, as she knew he would be. Dan worked long, hard hours.

"Dan, it's me."

"Jaime! What's up?"

She spent the next few minutes telling him what had transpired in the last few days.

"You're sure you want to quit?"

"Pearl asked me the same thing and yes. I've thought it through and I'm doing the right thing."

There was a pause and Jaime sliced tomatoes as she waited for him to speak.

"How 'bout partner?" Dan said. "Walker, Monroe & Associates?"

Jaime laughed into the phone.

"No, Jaime, I'm serious. We'd make great partners."

She was silent as she thought a moment. "I'll come on one condition."

"Name it," Dan said.

"My assistant comes with me."

"Deal. I'd love to have Tia Ranch on board," Dan said without hesitation. "When can you both start?"

"A month or so. I've got some stuff to wrap up."

"Lunch tomorrow and we'll talk more."

Jaime agreed and hung up the phone and finished making pasta. Sarah was in her thoughts throughout the workout and as she fixed dinner. Pasta was her sister's favorite, too. They used to prepare it together. Jaime remembered the two of them laughing in the kitchen and cooking dinner while music from the stereo in the living room blared loud enough to make every wall in the house vibrate. The television was on, but the talking heads were mute.

Her apartment was silent now. The living room was dark and dormant. There was no music coming from the stereo. No talk on the TV. The only noise came from the rustling of the pots and pans, water running and the thoughts that worked against her mind. A memory welled within her. She smiled, though it made her sad.

Sarah's first tennis tournament.

She was just a child. Eleven years old. She won her first tournament. Sarah was the only one to enter in her age category, so she had to play in the next age bracket if she wanted to compete. She wanted to. Sarah made it to the finals without dropping a set. She beat a 14-year-old girl in the finals in straight sets, 6-4, 6-0, in less than an hour.

If only I hadn't had the party, Jaime thought.

After dinner, Jaime was exhausted. She leaned back against the bed. She wanted to read, but nothing interested her. She flipped through the channels but, as usual, there was nothing on. She got off the bed, went to the window and stared out. The world was as silent as the snowflakes that fell and landed on the windowpane. Beyond, a city that never slept, met her gaze.

Jaime didn't want to sleep. Sleep meant dreams and dreams meant Sarah. Dreams meant cottonwood trees. She felt a tension headache begin to work its way from the back of her skull forward. She tried stretching her shoulders to loosen the knots. She looked to where sleep beckoned her.

The warm tumble of the bed was inviting.

She gave in and crawled beneath the blankets and pulled them under her chin. As sleep began to fade her thoughts to hazy, distant images, the words of Shakespeare's sonnet remained clear...

"For thy sweet love rememb'red such wealth brings,
that then I scorn to change my state with kings."

SEVEN

Jaime had worked out over the noon hour and was returning to the DA's office, but not before she stopped at Café Gardenia to get lunch to go. She looked inside to see how long the line at the deli was. However, it wasn't the line that captured her attention. She moved closer to the window and cupped her hand against the glass. Leigh Roberts was sitting alone at a table.

The thought of Ashleigh filled her and Jaime wondered if Leigh knew she was going to be her daughter's attorney.

Leigh glanced up when the cafe door opened and looked directly at Jaime. She smiled widely and motioned her to the table. Jaime made her way toward the table thinking, *she doesn't know yet.*

"Jaime, good to see you." Leigh's voice was bright and upbeat.

Leigh took her laptop off the chair. "Can you join me for lunch? I'd love to share a table."

Jaime grinned as she pulled the chair out to sit down.

"I've already ordered. I'll get the waiter," Leigh said.

"Thanks, but no. I'm going to order at the deli. I worked out at lunch and I have to get back to the office."

They were silent as the waiter set tomatoes topped with mozzarella and fresh basil in front of Leigh. Jaime felt a surge of nervousness. She wondered if there was an easy way to say she would be representing Ashleigh. The noise of the busy restaurant gave Jaime time to consider how to begin the conversation.

"I didn't know you had a daughter," Jaime said finally.

Leigh stopped eating and looked carefully at Jaime. She nodded slightly.

"Her name is Ashleigh," Jaime continued.

"Yes," Leigh said, sounding surprised. "Do you know her?"

"I will," Jaime said and squinted at her. "I learned about Ashleigh through a friend. She was looking for someone to represent her."

Leigh set her fork down, folded her hands over her plate, and regarded Jaime. She nodded slightly, as if she knew what was coming next.

"I've decided that person should be me." Jaime spoke matter-of-factly.

"You're willing to quit the DA's office?" Leigh asked.

Jaime nodded. "I'll be Ashleigh's attorney when her case goes before the court."

Leigh looked from Jaime to the tabletop and smoothed out an imaginary wrinkle.

"When did you hear about Ashleigh's case?" Leigh asked.

"A few days ago," Jaime said.

Leigh blinked several times, as though she were trying make sense of the information. She shrugged her shoulders and looked at Jaime. "Obviously you and I feel differently about what's best for Ashleigh," she said.

Jaime's eyes were impenetrable. "Yes, it appears we do."

"Have you met my daughter?"

"She's coming to the office in a few days."

They were silent again while the waiter removed the salad and set a plate of pasta in front of Leigh. She stared at it blankly.

"I've never read anything about Ashleigh in your columns," Jaime said.

"I've never written about her."

"Why not?"

"I just haven't," Leigh said, trying to keep the irritation from her voice. "Some things aren't meant for the printed page. Nothing about her life is the business of anyone but me."

"You can imagine my surprise when I learned Ashleigh was your daughter. Why didn't you say anything about her the other day?"

"Why should..." Leigh's voice began to rise in anger, in defense, so she stopped and looked away from Jaime. She watched the bustle of activity at the deli counter for a moment. When she spoke again, her voice was calm, but firm. "I haven't written about Ashleigh because there's never been a reason to."

Leigh pushed the plate away from her and looked at Jaime, wounded. Jaime remembered the day they met and their discussion on mental disabilities.

"This is a mild interest, Leigh?"

Leigh looked at Jaime and said nothing. She glanced at her watch.

"I've got an interview and I need to get going," she said and rose from the table. She threw her napkin down and left without saying good-bye.

Jaime remained seated. She watched over her shoulder as Leigh paid her bill and left the restaurant.

EIGHT

"I thought you said you were tired."

Jaime looked up to find herself staring into the eyes of Barry Winters, an employee at the athletic club. He had worked at the club for nearly ten years managing the front desk.

He was leaning his tall frame against the weight machine Jaime was using. Barry stood 6-foot-3-inches. His body looked fit and trim despite being ten pounds overweight. He had a full head of curly sandy hair attractively threaded with gray. At forty-five, his long face had few lines, and there was a kindness to his facial features.

Jaime finished her reps and pushed the hair from her eyes. "I was," she said. "'Til I got here. Now I feel great."

Jaime was in a light and airy mood when she came to the club this early February evening. She seemed to sparkle. He hadn't talked to her since the Cox trial.

"Things went well during the trial?" Barry asked. His manner was easy going and his voice soft spoken.

"Things went wonderful," Jaime replied, grinning as she began another set on the weight machine.

Barry waited for her to finish.

"I take it you're glad it's over," he said.

Jaime nodded.

Barry handed her a towel. "I saw your trainer just before I left the desk to come find you. You have a workout planned tonight." His jaw was firm and a mustache framed white teeth and a smile that was friendly and warm. His pool-blue eyes were calm, but tempered with a sense of sadness, much like his disposition.

"I was just loosening up a little."

Barry watched Jaime grab the bag with her equipment and walk toward the stairs. He continued to stare in her direction long after she was gone.

Jaime greeted Scott McIntyre, her personal trainer, with a quick hug on the steps to the third floor. He took her bag and carried it the rest of the way into the boxing gym. Jaime guessed Scott to be in his late thirties. He could have been an attractive man, but his blunted nose had been broken more times than he could remember, giving his face an uneven, peculiar appearance. He was a small, but powerfully built man who wore his dark brown hair pulled back in a thin braid. Scott was easily three inches shorter than Jaime. But he had not earned the title "Zen Boxer" because he was a pushover.

A friendship formed instantly with Scott. She had visited several clubs before selecting the Athletic Club at Denver Downtown. She found what she was looking for—a speedbag, heavy bag and double-end bag. When she stepped foot in the gym in Denver, the overpowering smell of leather and sweat took her back to Boston, where boxing had become her outlet.

When she wasn't studying or in class, she spent her free time working out. She motivated herself to exercise. And since she had already stopped playing tennis, there was no need to find a partner. She did not even bring her racquets to Boston. It was often hard for her to imagine that a game she once so deeply loved had become a sport she could hardly bring herself to watch, much less play. Whenever she walked by tennis courts now and heard the familiar sound of a ball leaving a racquet, she quickened her steps to leave the area.

Scott had helped Jaime develop an inner discipline and with that came empowerment. The workout tonight was what she needed. Three ten-minute segments of jump rope made her lungs feel as though they were about to combust. It felt as though she was doing abs and sit-ups for the first time, grimacing and feeling her muscles burn each time she sat up. Stretching was the only thing that had not left her in pain.

Jaime was unaware she was being watched as she warmed up, hitting the heavy bag. Scott and Frank winced each time she hit the bag hard and fast.

Scott shook his head. "I'd hate that to be me," he said, keeping his eyes fixed on her.

Frank had his arms crossed over his chest. "She's too damn skinny to hit the bag that hard."

Frank Powers made a good sparring and training partner for her. He was almost as good as Scott. What Scott lacked in height and weight, Frank, at 6-feet-3-inches and two hundred and sixty pounds, more than made up for. Everything about Frank, his arms, chest, neck and legs, was thick and solid. Whenever Jaime saw Frank's body, trees in the Redwood Forest came to mind.

In the beginning, Frank was hesitant to spar and train with Jaime. His reluctance came because he refused to hit women. He saw it too many times growing up from the men living with his mother. He had promised himself on the many nights he sat waiting in emergency rooms, while doctors tended to his mother's latest injuries, he would not hit a woman. Scott wanted Jaime to spar with Frank, a well-seasoned boxer, who knew how to avoid throwing overly zealous punches. Frank was a moving target for Jaime. They finally began to spar regularly together and both improved. While Frank did more covering up than throwing uppercuts, his facial expression during their sessions proved Jaime's punches were no wisps of air. "Feel that, Frank?" Scott would yell when Jaime connected against his body.

When Jaime finished hitting the bag, she walked toward Scott and Frank, pulling off her gloves.

"Hey, big guy, how's it going?" Jaime asked.

"It's going," Frank replied, and tousled her hair.

"That was a good round," Scott said, handing her a water bottle.

"Thanks. I'm dying of thirst," Jaime said and took a long swallow. She looked at Frank. "Are you ready?"

He nodded. They waved to Scott and walked toward the sparring area. As Frank put on his gloves, she noticed he seemed distracted and preoccupied.

"Is everything okay?" There was softness in her voice, a hint of concern.

His eyes held hers for only an instant before he looked away. But it was long enough for Jaime to see a distant, worried look within them. His disposition was stormy, but he managed a weak attempt at a smile. "Don't know. Can't seem to get a handle on it, Jaime." He was silent for a moment. "But I don't want to talk about it now. Maybe later. Maybe over coffee."

They began their workout in silence. Frank blocked a few of Jaime's punches, but he was listless. After a few minutes Jaime stopped abruptly and began to remove her gloves.

Frank looked at her, puzzled. "What?" he asked.

"I'm taking off my gloves."

"What for? We're not finished yet. Your work has been pretty sloppy tonight."

Jaime looked at Frank, the scowl on her face showing her current distaste for him. "*Your* work has been sloppy, too. And, besides, I've already finished my workout."

Frank lowered his arms and studied the palms of his gloves. He looked at her sheepishly. For a moment it seemed as though his bulky body had lost its stature.

She moved closer to Frank and rested her hand on his shoulder. "What's wrong?"

Frank looked at Jaime. "Let's go."

Within a half-hour they had showered and dressed. They waved to Barry and walked in silence out of the club and into the winter night. The sky was milky white and the air was thick with the threat of snow. The wind kicked up around their heels and they walked briskly for a block before getting in Jaime's car. They drove in silence to the Brown Palace Hotel on the corner of Broadway and Tremont Place. With their coats turned against the icy night air, they walked quickly toward the hotel.

They passed through the elegant lobby and headed for the Churchill Bar, an equally elegant setting filled with the rich smells of tobacco and fine wine.

Quiet and dark, the Churchill Bar was a favorite place for them. They had spent many hours there in the past three years immersed in quiet conversations. For a long time they sat in silence in the comfortable burgundy leather chairs. The small lamp that topped the glass table allowed Jaime to study Frank. He avoided her gaze, and looked instead in the direction of the humidor where red wine and cigars were perfectly chilled. They often came because of his penchant for cigars. She wasn't a fan of cigar smoke, but she didn't mind coming here with Frank.

Jaime glanced out the long window to Broadway, but the street was quiet now, the snow absorbing every sound. She grew tired of watching the snow fall, turned her attention to Frank and watched as he ran a stocky index finger around the ridge of his coffee cup. She waited patiently for him to speak, her arms hunched over the table.

Frank was hurting and in trouble and it upset her. They were good friends, but their relationship went deeper, more like blood, more like brother and sister. She had talked with him often, especially when she and Mitchell were fighting. He knew what to say to make her feel better. When she could, she wanted to return the favor.

"What is it, Frank? The gambling's gotten out of control." It wasn't a question.

He looked up long enough to signal for more coffee.

"What was it? A basketball game?"

Frank laughed. "Well, let's just say I got lucky on the horses and let the bet ride and before I realized it, I was down five grand."

Jaime wanted to remind him of their conversation where he had promised her he was going to quit. She knew she didn't have to remind him.

"Is it money? Do you need money?" she asked.

He did not answer as he removed a pack of cigarettes from his coat pocket. He tapped the cigarette against the tabletop before lighting it. He watched as the smoke rose quietly and funneled up around him.

Jaime looked at him, the disdain in her face showing. "I thought you said you were going to give that up just like you said you were about gambling? As health conscious as you say you are, you still smoke."

"I just light up when I'm tense. It's not like before."

Frank looked at Jaime through the hazy smoke from the cigarette. She held worry and care in her eyes for him. She had always been there for him. He had her friendship, her love. He took another quick drag and crushed the butt out in the ashtray.

As he leaned back in his chair and folded his big hands over the top of his head, Jaime took a moment to study him. His auburn hair, thinning on top and graying at the temples, was cut close to the sides of his head. His eyes were more gray than blue, like the color of steel. His nose was straight and narrow against a face of keenly carved features. He managed a smile, but it was empty of any mirth.

"The kind of money I need, Jaime, you don't have."

"How much, Frank?"

"It doesn't matter. Besides, for a change, it has nothing to do with how much cash I need. Can you believe it?"

"What's happened?"

Frank took a deep breath before he could find courage to tell her. When he began to speak his voice was low and Jaime moved closer to hear him.

"Carol is gone," he said. "She took Rachael and they left and went back to her mother's in Pennsylvania."

"When?"

"Last week, sometime, Tuesday, I think. I'm not sure anymore. I've lost track of time."

Frank lit another cigarette. The tension in his eyes told her the inevitable, even before he said a word. She knew the day would come when his wife and 12-year-old daughter would leave, unable to handle the gambling habit that had long ago driven a wedge between them.

"What was the final straw?" she asked.

Frank took the cigarette from the ashtray and tapped the ash. He took another long drag and left it there, dangling from the corner of his mouth. "Our problem. Carol used to call my gambling our problem because she really thought she could help me. You know, change me and make me a new and better man. But last weekend, our problem became my problem..."

His voice trailed off and Jaime looked on, waiting for him to continue.

"We had gone to her sister's home in Colorado Springs for a weekend visit. Carol's sister called a week later and told her that $15,000 in checks were missing. Carol confronted me and what could I say? I took the checks."

Jaime said nothing.

"I'm not any different than the others," Frank went on, "I thought the next bet would change everything."

Heavily in debt and running short of marks, Frank took the checks and cashed them. When Carol found out, she took Rachael and left.

"They left with the clothes on their backs, Jaime. I came home from work and they were gone. I knew something was up. Carol had been acting strangely. I came home and the house was empty. It had that uninhabited, vacant feel. You know, how a house feels sorta stale when no one has been in it for a while? Do you know what I mean?"

Frank looked at Jaime earnestly, as though he needed her assurance she understood. She nodded and responded quietly. "I know."

"She couldn't have been gone more than a few hours. But it was like she'd never been there at all."

"Why didn't you say something earlier?" Jaime said. "You know you can come to me. I've always thought we had that understanding."

Frank shrugged. "I guess I kept hoping she'd come back so I wouldn't have to."

Jaime put her head down on the table, resting it on her forearms. She stayed still and quiet for a long time. She lifted her head and stared at him, her lucid, brown eyes penetrating.

"Would you stop looking at me like that," he said and took another deep drag on his cigarette. When he blew the smoke from his nose, Jaime mumbled something Frank could not understand and then, sounding very much like his sister, said, "Would you stop that! It looks like your brain is on fire!"

Jaime laughed and for the first time that evening Frank smiled, too, but only a moment before his facial features clouded. She eyed him suspiciously, as though a thought had just come to her. "You're not messing around with your job are you?"

Frank's bulky frame did not allow him to have a svelte businessman look, but he was very much the businessman—one of Denver's best investment brokers. A reputation he had worked hard to earn. He said nothing and met Jaime's stare.

She spoke slowly and cautiously. "Until now, your job has been sacred, or has that changed too? You know they'll come after you."

"I could get your husband to defend me," Frank said, adding a small laugh.

Jaime's eyes narrowed as she shot Frank a disgusted look. "I fail to see the humor in that statement." She grew quiet, wounded by his comment. "This is going to catch up with you."

"Hasn't happened yet."

"Why press your luck? Can't you try to get some help? Do you know what a prison cell looks like?"

He looked at her, unsure of where she was headed.

"That's where you're going if you don't get help. These lies, deceit and stealing from your friends, acquaintances and now your family will catch up with you," Jaime said. "What's next, Frank?"

The cigarette in his mouth had burned its way to the filter, and he put the butt in the ashtray. He studied it and then looked at Jaime. She knew the look. He was ending the conversation.

"Thanks for talking tonight," he said.

He looked at his watch, 10:15 p.m. "Gotta go. I have to be in the office by seven. Got a big meeting in the morning." Frank caught the bartender's attention. A thin, young man came with a pot of coffee, but he waved him off. "No thanks. No more, we're leaving."

Nine

The photograph of Sarah and Jaime was blurred.

But the images were clear in Jaime's mind. They were pressed shoulder to shoulder, grinning at each other behind a thicket of trees green with summer. Sunglasses covered their eyes. When Jaime looked at the photograph, she remembered how happy they both were at tennis camp that summer. It showed in their beaming smiles. Jaime did not remember that someone had snapped the picture until the photos came back.

She kept it on the wall in her living room, along with another of her favorites. The second was a picture of their shadows Jaime had taken that same summer. Their faces could not be seen, but their images had been captured, silhouettes on the blacktop trail they had been following. In the photo, Sarah had turned toward Jaime, her hand on her shoulder. Jaime was fifteen, Sarah eleven. When Jaime looked at the photographs there were times she was filled with a deep, abiding, protective-kind-of-love for her sister. Other times the still life filled her with an ache that lingered like a phantom pain.

But her favorite picture was another of Sarah playing tennis. She was hitting a forehand, with perfect form. Her auburn hair was pulled back tight in a ponytail, away from her smooth, round face. She wore a white cotton top with capped sleeves that showed the strength in her arms. A red-pleated tennis skirt covered only a small portion of Sarah's long, tanned and muscular legs. She was fourteen, tall and slender and already had the body of a grown woman.

In the photo, her tongue protruded slightly between a pair of firmly pressed lips. Her determined, emerald green eyes, deep in concentration, were fixed on the tennis ball now on its way over the net toward her opponent. It reminded Jaime of happier, simpler times in their young lives.

Jaime's attention shifted among the photos and rested on the one with their shadows until the images seemed to move.

Thirteen years ago we were at camp. Has it been that long? You were alive then, little sister.

Jaime moved away from the photos, feeling exhausted. She had felt tired and drained all day. Of course, she knew why. It was this way every February, as it had been for the past ten years. She opened a can of soup and ate in front of the television. She knew she had watched some kind of drama and that every so often there were commercials, but nothing registered. She stretched out on the couch. Her head was hardly on the pillow before she fell into a deep, troubled sleep.

And the dream came …

Sarah woke with every muscle and joint aching. She had felt this way for more than a week. She recalled her tennis workouts, weight and conditioning training over the last several days. She had not done anything different with her regimen to cause such discomfort.

She hadn't said anything to anyone, not even Jaime.

Although, on the tennis court earlier this week, Jaime had commented that her strokes did not have their usual power. Sarah shrugged off her sister's notion saying her timing was off. That seemed to satisfy Jaime and she did not question her about it again.

That was Tuesday. It was now Thursday and she only felt worse.

She woke to severe cramping in her lower abdomen. The pain was so bad, she doubled over in bed. Almost as quickly as the pain came, it subsided. She had managed to drift off to sleep. She woke again several hours later with a dull pain in the middle of her back. The pain seemed to spread up her spine like a slow moving fire before it settled in her shoulders. She managed to get ready for school.

The pain stayed with her the entire morning at school. She wasn't sure, because she never had the sensation before, but several times, she felt as if she would faint. By noon she felt so dizzy, she was afraid to walk to her classes. Sarah hoped eating lunch would help, but it didn't. All she could think about was the couch in the living room. Her middle school was within walking distance from home. The nurse called Sarah's mother, Nora Monroe. Sarah assured her mother that although she did not feel well, she was well enough to walk home.

"I'll be fine, mom. I'm just tired that's all. Maybe I'm getting a cold or the flu. I'll be fine 'til you get there. Besides Jaime doesn't have to work after school today. She'll be home by three o'clock."

Sarah made it home, but the normal ten-minute walk took a half hour. She had to stop every few minutes to hold on to something to steady herself and quiet the vertigo. By the time she reached the front porch steps, her heart was pounding and her forehead was beaded in sweat. She felt as if she had just completed a grueling game of singles.

"What's the matter with me?" Sarah asked herself as she put the key in the lock.

The moment she stepped inside, an excruciating, stabbing pain pierced through her lower abdomen. Her backpack fell to the floor. She cried out and dropped to one knee. She wrapped her arms tightly around her stomach and pressed firmly. It was the same pain that had awakened her earlier that morning, only stronger and sharper. After a few minutes the pain had eased and she struggled to her feet. She headed for the couch. Something was wrong. This was not a cold or the flu. It was something she had never felt before. She decided to tell Jaime when she got home. Sarah rounded the corner to the living room, bright with sunlight.

Relief settled over her, but her sense of comfort was short lived. The pain returned acute and sharp enough to make Sarah shiver. She cried out, doubled over and fell to the floor. She felt herself slipping into unconsciousness, as though a pair of hands had reached up from within and pulled her downward. Everything in the room seemed as though it was spinning and moving away from her. The traffic on the street sounded muffled and distant. Sarah succumbed to the darkness, as if someone had dropped a heavy veil over her eyes.

"Sarah?" Jaime called as she opened the front door. She listened but the house was quiet and still. "Sarah?" Jaime called again and frowned. "Sarah, are you here?"

Jaime saw Sarah's backpack on the floor. "Sarah, mom's gonna yell at you if she comes home and sees your bag still here in the hall," Jaime said, sensing trouble. Sarah usually never left anything out. Jaime called louder. "Sarah? Mom called at school and said you were coming home early."

She put her backpack next to Sarah's and started down the hallway toward the living room. "Mom said you were sick. Don't you want to play tennis this afternoon?" Jaime asked playfully. "What's the matter? Afraid I'll win?"

The smile on Jaime's face was wide when she entered the living room. When she saw Sarah lying on the floor near the sofa, the smile fell from her face, and her breathing stopped. A knot formed in her stomach.

Jaime raced across the room to her sister. "Oh, my God, Sarah!"

She called for help. Within minutes, the Monroe home was ablaze with emergency lights. Jaime rode in the ambulance with Sarah. John and Nora Monroe were already at the hospital when they arrived. They thought Sarah had appendicitis and kept that thought when she was taken for emergency surgery.

Jaime and her parents went to the waiting room. The time it took for Sarah to emerge from surgery could have been measured by the calendar. Jaime sat by herself in a chair by a window. She watched as cars traveled in and out of the hospital parking lot. Every so often she looked at her parents. They sat together on a couch.

John and Nora, both forty three, were real estate agents and made a comfortable living selling commercial properties. They were a close-knit couple and devoted to their daughters. Holidays, birthdays and anniversaries were always big celebrations. Much of their home life centered on Sarah and her tennis. When she started to play tournaments, John and Nora only missed her matches if they absolutely had to. Expense was not an issue when it came to Sarah's equipment and coaching. She had whatever she wanted.

Jaime watched as her parents made poor attempts to concentrate on the magazines that lay open over their laps. Nora, the tall, thin, willowy dark-haired ex-model, was striking. Sensitive brown eyes, above strong cheekbones, matched a warm, wide smile. John was a tall, slender man with an engaging manner. His eyes, the same emerald green as Sarah's, were deep-set and intense. He wore a full, neatly trimmed beard.

Jaime's nerves had settled slightly by the time the doctor, a stocky middle-aged man, with pearl-gray hair, found them in the waiting room. She joined her parents on the sofa.

The doctor smiled grimly. He pulled up a chair and sat facing them. He studied his folded hands, considering what he would say.

Nora spoke first. "Doctor, what is it? What's the matter with Sarah? Is it cancer?"

The doctor's smile was moderate. "It's not cancer."

He saw the worry in their eyes. "Nora," the doctor started slowly by saying. "Has Sarah complained lately about having pain in her lower abdomen or shoulders, or just not feeling well?"

It was Jaime who spoke and they focused their attention on her.

"Tuesday when we practiced, I noticed Sarah winded easily and it was an effort to run after the ball. She seemed like she was in pain. She didn't chase anything down I'd hit to her. I ... I asked if she was okay. She just said her timing was off."

"And was she unconscious when you found her this afternoon?" the doctor asked.

Jaime nodded. "But she didn't say anything to me about not feeling well."

"And I haven't noticed anything different about her," Nora added. "Sarah would tell us, certainly Jaime, if she didn't feel well."

The doctor looked from John to Nora. "Does your daughter have a boyfriend?" he asked matter-of-factly.

"No, why?" Nora said without hesitation. A sense of suspicion grew in her voice.

"Well, if Jaime had not come home when she did, it's likely, Mrs. Monroe, Sarah would no longer be with us."

Nora's bottom lip began to quiver and her hand trembled noticeably as she covered her mouth. "What on earth do you mean?"

John tried to calm her by resting his hand on her lap.

"Your daughter had an ectopic pregnancy," the doctor said.

Nora raised her eyebrows. "A what?" Her voice sounded peculiar and forced, as if she needed to say something to break the silence.

"She was pregnant, Mrs. Monroe. Sarah was pregnant. But it was ectopic."

"What does that mean?" John asked and frowned.

"An ectopic pregnancy forms in one of the fallopian tubes," the doctor said. "It eventually breaks through the wall of the tube and causes serious internal bleeding." He stopped a moment to make certain Sarah's family could handle what he was telling them. Nora was on the verge of tears. John was stoic. Jaime's expression was numb.

"Sarah could have bled to death had Jaime not come home when she did," the doctor said and paused briefly to collect his thoughts. "Sometimes ectopic pregnancies are reabsorbed by the body, with no harm done. Other times, such as, and unfortunately in Sarah's case, they rupture and cause hemorrhage. It can be life threatening, particularly when the patient faints and cannot call for help."

"She's only fourteen, how could this have happened?" John spoke, directing his comment to no one in particular.

The doctor went on. "There are no procedures that will rule out ectopic pregnancies in advance and they are often not easy to diagnose, Mrs. Monroe, but I can safely assume Sarah was pregnant and it was ectopic."

The doctor rose from his chair and returned it to its original place.

"When can she go home?" John asked.

"She's a strong girl. She should be out in a few days," he said.

"Can we see her?" John asked, his voice stifled, but firm.

"Not now. She's in recovery. I'll have a nurse come to get you."

A few days later Sarah went home. The ride from the hospital was uncomfortably quiet. Jaime and Sarah sat in the backseat, staring out the car windows. John and Nora rode in silence. They had decided to wait until Sarah went home before talking to her. Nora watched the passing landscape, but saw nothing. She had been unable to keep her mind on anything since the visit with the doctor in the hospital waiting room.

She kept repeating his words over and over ... *Does your daughter have a boyfriend? ... If Jaime hadn't come home when she did, it's likely, Mrs. Monroe, Sarah would no longer be with us ... Does your daughter have a boyfriend? ... Your daughter had an ectopic pregnancy, Mrs. Monroe ... An ectopic pregnancy, Mrs. Monroe ... Does your daughter have a boyfriend?*

When John stopped the car in the driveway, he was the first to speak. "Sarah, when you've had the chance to rest, your mother and I want to talk to you."

John did not look at Sarah in the rearview mirror as he spoke, but he could feel both his daughter's eyes on him. Sarah did not know what had happened, but she had an inkling. She was certain she must have been pregnant and something had gone wrong.

Dreadfully wrong.

She had said nothing about that New Year's Eve night in the horrible dark of her bedroom. Not even to Jaime. Least of all Jaime.

When Sarah and Jaime reached the living room a few hours later, there was no sun to warm it. Snow began to fall in large flakes not long after they had arrived home. Their parents were seated near the fireplace reading when they entered the room. When John saw them, he let his newspaper fall against the side of the chair. Nora marked her place in her novel and studied her husband.

Sarah, still recovering and in pain, walked slowly toward the couch. Jaime matched her slow steps. Sarah, at 5-foot-10-inches, was already two inches taller than Jaime. If one didn't know them, it would be easy to mistake Sarah as the oldest. They settled on the couch. The last of the dying fire popped and crackled quietly, but no one spoke. Sarah, her eyes down, studied the palms of her hand. Jaime kept her eyes on an intricate pattern on the couch.

"Sarah." John's voice caused both of his girls to look at him. His voice was firm, but gentle. "Sarah, we nearly lost you and we're glad that didn't happen. As long as the both of you are safe, we can weather anything." He paused briefly. "The doctor said you were pregnant. It had started to form in the wrong place and ruptured and that's what caused all of your pain. You could have bled to death had you not gone to the hospital when you did."

Sarah sighed and looked from her parents to Jaime. "I know," she said simply.

John studied her a moment, unable to hide his surprise. "What do you mean you know?"

Sarah spoke calmly. "I just know that's all."

Nora finally spoke. "How did you know, Sarah? Did the doctor tell you?"

Sarah shook her head and answered quietly. "Well, no."

"Sarah, I understand you must've felt afraid to come to your father and me about this. But we're here to help both of you," Nora said, looking from Sarah to Jaime.

"I know, mom," Sarah said, her voice a sad whisper.

Nora spoke calmly. "Would you like to tell us what happened?"

Sarah closed her eyes tightly and rubbed her hand firmly across her forehead. She hoped the tears that were on the edge of coming would not. She had mentally replayed the scenes of him on top her so often she wondered why her brain had not exploded from the torment. Nora sensed her daughter's discomfort. She began to rise from her chair to comfort her. Sarah waved her back.

"No, mom, please ... give me a minute. And please stay there until I finish speaking. Please. Can you do that for me?"

Nora nodded. The room fell silent and they waited for Sarah to speak. She could not look at any of them, so she fixed her attention on the large bay window across the room. Outside it was cold and dreary. Lifeless. The way Sarah had felt since the night of Jaime's party. The party Jaime had the holiday weekend her parents were out of town. The party they had refused to let her have because they would be away. The party Jaime had anyway. The one that Jaime's boyfriend came to. The wild party where everyone had too much to drink and everyone had ended up passed out, even Jaime.

Everyone except Ryan McKenna.

It took all the fortitude, Sarah had within her to begin to speak. Then, the words, the ones she could not utter that night, finally came.

"He ... he raped me."

John shifted uncomfortably in his chair and his foot caused the newspaper to rustle slightly.

"Who, Sarah? Who raped you?" her father asked.

Sarah finally looked from the window to Jaime, then to her parents. "Ryan McKenna."

Jaime gasped. Now she knew why Ryan had made himself so scarce.

"Ryan raped me."

"When?" her father's voice was shaky.

"New Year's Eve."

John leaned forward in his chair. His eyes narrowed as he quizzed Sarah. "When?"

"The weekend you and mom were out of town."

"What were you doing out of the house?" he asked.

"I wasn't," Sarah said without hesitation. "It happened here. In my bedroom."

John looked from Sarah to Jaime. Jaime knew his anger was mounting. Sarah's eyes were fixed on Jaime, too. They knew Sarah had no choice but to continue.

"Jaime had a party and a lot of her friends were here ... Everyone got drunk and after a while it got really quiet and I just figured Jaime had sent everyone home. I opened my bedroom door ... and ... and he was standing there like he was just about to open it himself ... There was this look in his eye ... He put his finger to his mouth like telling me to be quiet and he pushed me, kinda soft at first, back into my room ... He said it was only me and him that were still awake ... Now we're going to have a little fun he told me ... He said he always thought I looked 'hot.'"

Sarah was cut off by Nora's crying. The sound sent a chill through Sarah and fear wedged like a pillow in the small of her back. She buried her hands in her face and began to sob softly at first. Before long, the sobs came in uncontrollable bursts of despair.

"Why didn't you tell us, Sarah?" John's voice was heavy with emotion.

Sarah cradled herself with her arms and began to rock back and forth. "He ... He threatened me. He said he'd deny everything, he even threatened to kill me ... and, and I was really afraid he would hurt me again ... and I didn't want him to ... to hurt me."

Nora, sobbing, got up from the chair and wrapped her arms around

Sarah. John glared at Jaime. She looked like a little girl lost.

Jaime woke with her heart racing and the sound of her blood roaring in her ears like an inferno. She sat up quickly and swung her feet to the floor. As sleep slowly left her, she realized she had only been dreaming.

She noticed the lamp on the end table had cast a ghostly light on the three photographs on the wall, leaving them in shadows. They were taken long ago in happier times when Sarah was alive. Many years had passed since those summer days. Jaime longed to go back to the simpler and happier time in her life when those photographs were taken.

Ten

Manila folders covered Jaime's desk, containing child abuse reports so despicable that even the most inspired Hollywood screenwriter would have difficulty putting them on paper.

"Where would you like to start?" Tia Ranch asked Jaime.

They were in Jaime's office. Tia picked up a file so heavy she had to use both hands to avoid spilling the contents all over the desk.

"We've got the case of the three-year-old girl who was raped repeatedly in her own home," Tia said. "Her injuries were so bad she had to have surgery." She set the file back on the desk and grabbed another one. "Or we have the case of the 58-year-old school bus driver who's pleaded innocent to fondling four girls on his bus route, all younger than eleven years old."

Tia took another minute to examine the folders. "It's an amazing situation," she said, placing her hands on her hips. "We sit here every morning and try to decide which case needs the most attention. The baby who's been beaten. The two-year-old with the broken leg, or the drug-addicted infant who's been in the hospital going through withdrawal." She rolled her eyes toward the ceiling.

Tia and Jaime began their case ritual the same way each morning. Tia gave Jaime a summary on each case, which they discussed at length. Tia had been Jaime's assistant for just over a year. It was a partnership that ran like proverbial clockwork.

Tia Ranch was a big, magnificent-looking, balloon-breasted woman, tall and stunning with a broad forehead and cheekbones like an Egyptian queen set against ebony skin. She was a single mother, raising two boys with help from her mother.

"Let's start with the bus driver," Jaime said, grabbing a pen and legal pad.

After they finished the rundown on their cases, Tia leaned back in her chair and exhaled deeply. "We have more cases here than we'll ever know what to do with," she said. "Of course it doesn't help matters much every time Oprah runs a show on sexual abuse against children and *more* cases get reported."

Jaime did not respond. She did not have her usual vigor this morning when they discussed their caseload. She seemed distant.

Their usual morning briefings often lasted more than an hour. This morning, they had finished in half that time. Jaime hardly participated. She would only nod and ask an occasional question about the cases, but nothing more. Since the Kelly Jo Cox case, Jaime had a difficult time thinking about anything else. She couldn't help replaying the defense attorney questioning Beverly so harshly.

"Jaime, what it is?" Tia asked gently.

Jaime looked up from a file she was studying and into Tia's dark, absorbing eyes. Tia's expression was cautious and alert.

"Nothing," Jaime said and turned her attention back to her file.

"Girl, who do you think you're talkin' to? You expect me to believe that? Come on," she said. "It's me you're talking to, not your mama."

Jaime leaned back and tucked her arm over the back of her swivel chair. "I talked with Pearl last week."

"And?"

"And she told me about a young woman whose mother wants her sterilized."

"How old is she?"

"Twenty-four."

Tia frowned and used the end of her pencil to scratch her scalp. She thought for several moments then cleared her throat and spoke. "What's the reason she needs her mother's approval?"

"She's mentally disabled."

"Like Kelly Jo?" Tia asked.

"Not as bad," Jaime said. "She's higher functioning and does more on her own."

Tia absentmindedly began to stack the case folders together as though she was about to leave, but then stopped. "I've read stories in the newspaper about parents who want to have their daughters sterilized," she said. "How could they do such a thing?"

Jaime shrugged. "When people think their principles for doing something are right, then to them, it is right. It's that simple, but from what Pearl tells me, this young woman is competent to make that kind of decision herself."

"And the mother wants to take the decision away from her by going to court to force the sterilization?"

"That's right."

The two women searched each other's faces in silence.

"Pearl tells me the reason the mother wants to go that route is because her daughter lives in a group home, at least for now…" Jaime's voice trailed off while she studied her desk calendar. "Let's see, it's almost the end of February. So she should be moving from the group home into a host home by the end of August, September at the latest."

"So, she'll go from a protected environment to one where she's more on her own," Tia confirmed.

"Exactly, but there's more. She now works in a sheltered workshop."

"That's changing, too?" Tia asked.

Jaime nodded. "Pearl said she's going to start work in a few days at the food court on the 16th Street Mall."

"She'll go from a protected working environment to an unprotected one," Tia said.

Jaime pressed her lips together and nodded. "Pearl said the mother is afraid there's a greater chance her daughter will be taken advantage of when she gets into those kinds of public settings. Apparently she's all for her daughter gaining more independence, but she'd be happier knowing she couldn't get pregnant. And it also doesn't help that her daughter has diabetes."

"But she wants to take some of that independence away by making her daughter have the operation," Tia said.

Jaime nodded. "I get the impression the mother thinks going to court will be a formality. I guess she thinks her daughter's attorney is supposed to just stand there. You know, nod and make all the appropriate noises, then case closed and thank you for coming."

Tia's eyes grew round and wide. Her eyebrows drifted upward. "Well, she's in for a big surprise, but what does that have to do with us?" Tia studied Jaime intently for a moment. "Girl, I know what you're thinking, you want the case, don't you?"

Jaime nodded and then told Tia about her conversation with Dan Walker. She ended by saying, "I told him I'd come only if you could come, too."

Tia looked dismayed. "I'm surprised you're even considering it." Her voice turned playful and she looked at Jaime with a wide grin. "I know why you said yes, girl. Why you're considering leaving the DA's office. You didn't want to hurt Pearl's feelings. I know how she feels about you. You could be her daughter. She loves you that much."

"No, that's not it."

"What then?"

Jaime looked at Tia. She opened her mouth to speak, but nothing came.

"You don't know why, do you?" Tia said, surprised at Jaime's indecision.

"Of course I do."

"Then what is it?"

Jaime tossed her pen on the desk, left her chair and went to the large window. She stared out unseeing. It was a long time before the skyscrapers and weather came into view. Overcast. She kept her attention focused on the sea of office buildings, some clouded in a light, foggy mist.

"I know why," Jaime said, quietly. "When Pearl and I met last week and she started telling me about Ashleigh…"

Tia interrupted her, speaking in a hushed tone. "She reminded you of Sarah."

Tia watched as Jaime's shoulders stiffened. She was right. They had not been working together three months before they started to finish each other's sentences. Jaime and Tia were as different as January and June. Jaime, the athlete, was meticulous about what she ate and how much. Jaime had always been lithe and trim. Tia tried to diet, but for her, weight had always been a problem. She was a big-boned woman who carried extra pounds easily on her large frame. What Jaime didn't eat in junk food, Tia more than made up for. She loved pastry. Her passion was Twinkies and diet Pepsi, or corn chips and a V-8. Tia would inconspicuously raise her can of V-8 to show Jaime she was consuming something healthy whenever she walked by the desk and eyed what she was eating.

When it came to family, there were no children in Jaime's future, especially now with Mitchell gone. Tia was divorced. Derrick was eight and Darryl, ten. She was a devoted mother who put her sons before everything. Her sons were the essence of her. The very substance of her being. They gave her a sense of balance. Their laughter gave Tia hope. Above all, they gave her love. And she loved back.

"A case like this could take a long time," Tia said. "Are you sure you know what you're doing?"

Jaime nodded.

"I know. I know you do," Tia said softly. "But I'm playing devil's advocate here. I just want to do what's right for us."

Jaime turned from the window and smiled at Tia, a warm, gracious smile. "I appreciate your help in thinking this through with me. I couldn't do it without you, Tia."

Tia grinned broadly. A long silence filled the room.

"Well would you be willing?" Jaime asked finally.

She looked at Tia and the smile spread quickly over her face. The look in Tia's eyes said it all.

"The change might do us both good," Tia said.

It was exhausting to work in a profession that revealed the dark side of humanity. Burnout was commonplace in a line of work that forced one to think ugly, horrific thoughts. It did not help matters when offenders threatened their victims with death or worse, leaving already intimidated children unwilling to speak out to help themselves.

Jaime nodded and returned to her desk. "Incidentally, Ashleigh's mother is Leigh Roberts."

"The woman who works for the Dispatch?"

"That's her."

"The same one you had lunch with? The one you liked so much?"

"The same one."

"Does Leigh know you're considering representing her daughter?"

"She does. We met again after Pearl and I spoke."

"You didn't tell me about that encounter."

"It wasn't as pleasant as the first time we met."

Tia scanned the piles of paper and folders that covered Jaime's desk. "Lordy, Lordy help the next attorney who will take over all these cases," she said and looked at Jaime.

Jaime's intensity, her eagerness and her determination had already taken over. They would not let up until Ashleigh Roberts had her day in court.

"When's Ashleigh coming?" Tia asked finally.

"Tomorrow."

ELEVEN

From Morningside Heights, near Congress Park, where Ashleigh Roberts had lived comfortably and safely in a sheltered group home for the past twelve years, she took the bus to downtown Denver.

The bus stopped on Colfax Avenue across the street from the District Attorney's office. Ashleigh got off the bus, squinting as she looked into the morning's strong winter sun. The air was brisk as she walked to the traffic light and waited for the signal to change before crossing. She remembered to look both ways.

Ashleigh knew she had reached the building Erin Greene described. It was sitting on the corner of Colfax Avenue and Court Street, just as it was the Saturday before when they did a practice run to the office where Jaime Monroe worked. Erin wanted to come with Ashleigh the day of her appointment, but Ashleigh insisted on going alone.

Ashleigh walked immediately to the elevator and pushed the up arrow. She did not bother to stop to scan the office directory. Most of what was printed on the directory Ashleigh could not read, and it meant nothing to her.

Ashleigh's appointment with Jaime was at 10 o'clock. Though on her left wrist she wore a watch, Ashleigh had difficulty telling time. Erin had also drawn a clock face on the index card to show Ashleigh what the hands looked like when the big hand was on the twelve and the small hand was on the ten. Ashleigh loved the way a watch felt against her wrist. She had tried wearing a digital watch, as both Erin and Ashleigh's mother thought it might be easier for her to tell time that way. Ashleigh, however, often transposed the numbers. Though it was still difficult, she did better wearing an analog watch.

When the elevator door slid open Ashleigh stepped inside. In her hand, she carried a white, three-by-five card, which she used to help find her way. She carried another card in her right shoe, just in case she lost the first one. She found the number to Jaime's floor and pushed the button. She waited, along with the rest of the passengers who filed in, for the door to close. Ashleigh caught sight of herself in a mirror against the back of the elevator. She had a good, straight nose and a heart-shaped face with a delicate chin. She wore no makeup and her skin was clear and smooth. Hazel eyes, soft brown flecked with green, were framed with long lashes. A small beauty mark on her cheek, beneath her right eye highlighted the hint of brown in her eyes.

When the elevator reached her floor, she was alone. The lighted number for her floor would darkened and the elevator door opened, just as Erin said it would.

When she stepped off the car, she studied the white card. To her left, she saw the reception area and a woman there waiting. She smiled at Ashleigh and Ashleigh smiled back.

"This must be her," Tia Ranch said looking from the receptionist to the young woman approaching her.

Tia greeted Ashleigh before she reached the receptionist's desk.

"Hi, you must be Ashleigh Roberts," Tia said.

Ashleigh looked at Tia and nodded. She sounded nice and friendly. "Uh-huh. That's me."

"I'm Tia Ranch. I work with Jaime."

"Jaime Monroe?" Ashleigh asked and pointed to her card. "It says I have to see a Jaime Monroe."

"Come on," she said and smiled reassuringly and then motioned for Ashleigh to follow. "There's only one Jaime here. I'll take you to her office."

Obediently, Ashleigh began to walk behind Tia, following her as she headed down the hallway.

"So, I hear you're starting a new job at the food court on the mall."

"Yep. I'm gonna be cleaning tables and stuff. I'm excited and I start next week."

"And you're going to get a new place to live, too. That's great."

Ashleigh nodded. "I'm going to be living somewhere off a busy street. I can see a river that runs outside the window."

"That's Cherry Creek, Ashleigh. That's pretty cool, you'll be living in a nice place," Tia said, knowing that Ashleigh's new home would be the Riverway Center Apartments that paralleled Speer Boulevard.

"And I'll have my own room and everything, but not 'til August. That's a long time from now," Ashleigh said.

"I bet you can't wait," Tia said.

They walked a moment in silence. "I've never been inside a really big building like this before," Ashleigh announced as they turned one corner and then another. "But I said the number of the floor over and over a whole bunch of times on the way here, so I wouldn't forget and get lost."

They reached Jaime's office door. It was open, but Tia knocked lightly before she entered.

"Jaime?"

Jaime looked up from the legal pad she had been writing on.

"Ashleigh's here."

"Come in," Jaime said, and rose from her chair.

Ashleigh walked in behind Tia. Jaime came from around the desk. Their eyes met as she met Ashleigh at the door, her hand extended.

"Hi, Ashleigh, I'm Jaime Monroe. I'm going to represent you."

"Erin said that you're the one who's gonna help me."

"Erin's right, Ashleigh. I'm going to do my best to try and help you." Jaime looked from Ashleigh to Tia, who had watched the encounter between them with all-absorbing eyes. "Tia and I are going to do everything we can to help you."

Ashleigh glanced from Tia to Jaime and Jaime took in every feature of her face. Then Ashleigh smiled. It was full of innocence. Easy and effortless. The way ice becomes water.

Jaime's immense brown eyes grew wider. She raised her eyebrows and swallowed over the sudden constriction in her throat. "Let Tia take your jacket, Ashleigh. You sit here and we'll get started."

Ashleigh removed her jacket. Beneath the pale-blue down-filled parka, her attire was plain and simple. She wore a neatly pressed long-sleeved cotton shirt, buttoned at the cuffs. It was white with vertical beige stripes. She wore tan chinos and tennis shoes that looked as though she had just taken them from the box. Ashleigh was slender and Jaime guessed she was about 5-foot-6-inches tall. Her chestnut-colored hair reached to center of her back.

As Ashleigh made her way to the chair in front of the desk, Jaime noticed her coltish, loopy grace, and she felt a sudden and fierce dislike toward Leigh Roberts. *How could she want to do such a thing to such a beautiful human being?* She pushed the angry thoughts from her mind.

"I hope you didn't have any trouble finding us," Tia said, once they had settled.

Ashleigh shook her head. "I have my card, so it was easy." Ashleigh told them about the directions written on her card and where she kept the spare copy.

An awkward silence filled the room as Jaime considered how to start.

"Tell us about your diabetes, Ashleigh," Jaime said.

"I've had it since I was twenty. But it's not too bad," Ashleigh replied.

"And you're twenty four now, is that right?"

"Uh-huh," Ashleigh said.

"Can you tell us what you have to do on a daily basis to take care of yourself and your diabetes?" Jaime asked.

Ashleigh's eyes drifted toward the ceiling as she considered her answer. She replied in a slow, halting voice. She wanted to be certain not to miss something that was part of her daily routine. "Well, uh, I have to eat three meals a day and three snacks at the same times every day. And, uh, I can't skip any meals, even if I'm not very hungry, 'cause sometimes I'm not, 'cause if I miss my meals and snacks, Erin gets really mad at me."

"Why is that?" Tia asked.

"Erin says that my blood sugar will get all messed up if I don't eat like I'm supposed to. And, let's see, ah, oh, I have to poke my finger to check the blood." Ashleigh thought a moment, then added quickly. "Well, I don't poke my finger 'cause it hurts when I do it. Erin does it for me. When she does, it doesn't hurt so much."

Jaime and Tia looked at each other and smiled.

"Erin told me you're not insulin dependent that your diabetes can be controlled through the foods you eat and exercise, is that right, Ashleigh?" Jaime asked.

"Uh-huh. Sometimes I miss having a candy bar, or ice cream. I like chocolate, but I don't eat any 'cause I don't like what happens to me when I do. My body gets really out of whack. And I feel really funny all over."

"Do you remember how you knew you had diabetes, Ashleigh?" Tia asked.

"When it happened I kinda felt there was something wrong with me. I would get dizzy and then hot and then cold…" She stopped and thought a moment. "I just didn't feel good and one night I woke up 'cause I couldn't feel my arms and legs. They felt kinda tingly, like getting poked with a pin, you know? I got scared and went to get out of bed to call Erin. But I fell. Erin said the noise scared her right out of bed and she came running into my room to see what had happened to me."

"And then what happened, Ashleigh?" Jaime asked.

"I went to the doctor and that's when we knew. But my mom and Erin helped me get a routine going and so it's really easy now."

"And you know if you became pregnant, Ashleigh, it could be detrimental, or harmful, to your health and that your baby could also suffer from the effects of your diabetes, if you didn't continue to take care of yourself," Tia said.

Ashleigh looked from Jaime to Tia and nodded. "Uh-huh. That's what Erin and mom tell me."

"Do you have a boyfriend now, Ashleigh, maybe someone you like?" Jaime asked.

Ashleigh shook her head. "I've never had one. Is that bad?"

"Of course not, sweetheart," Tia said.

"Erin tells me your group home is just for women," Jaime said.

"Uh-huh."

"But what about the workshop where you work now," Jaime went on. "Are you interested in any of the young men you work with there?"

Ashleigh shook her head. "They're all kinda dorky."

Jaime looked from Ashleigh to Tia and smiled slightly.

"Do you think you'd like to have a boyfriend someday, Ashleigh?" Jaime asked.

Ashleigh's eyes drifted toward the ceiling. "Maybe someday."

During the next hour, Ashleigh listened as Jaime and Tia explained to her how they would prepare for her hearing. Jaime told Ashleigh they would meet often during the next four months.

When they finished, Jaime looked at the calendar. She flipped ahead to July and scanned the month a moment in silence. "Let's see. We go to court July tenth. That's a Thursday. The hearing itself, Ashleigh, should last a day. The judge will take a few weeks to decide and we should know…" Jaime hesitated as she pointed to the calendar with her index finger. "We should know by ... mid to late July."

Jaime glanced quickly at Tia before she turned her attention to Ashleigh.

"How does that sound?"

Ashleigh nodded. "Good."

She began to fidget with the white card she held. She kept her attention fixed on the floor beneath her. She looked at Jaime with uncertainty.

"I, uh, have a question," she said quietly.

"Sure. Go ahead, Ashleigh, what is it?" Tia's voice was smooth and yielding.

"Will my mom be mad at me if we win?"

Jaime and Tia exchanged a long, quiet stare. It was Tia who answered.

"Honey, she might. But we have to do what's right for you, Ashleigh. And if she does get angry, maybe we can work together and help her overcome that anger. Would that work for you?"

Ashleigh nodded. "I don't want her to be mad at me."

Tia smiled and patted Ashleigh gently on her arm. "Of course not, and we wouldn't want that either. We'll make certain that doesn't happen. Sound like a deal?"

"It's a deal," Ashleigh said.

Jaime looked relieved. She didn't know how to answer Ashleigh's question and was glad Tia took over. It needed a mother's touch.

"All right, it's settled then," Jaime said. "Ashleigh, we'll keep in close touch with you and Erin and go from there."

They rose and walked to the door. Tia handed Ashleigh her parka and Ashleigh followed Jaime from her office putting on her jacket.

"Don't forget, Ashleigh," Jaime said as they neared the elevator, "When we meet again Tia and I are going to be working in a new building, one not too far from here. Erin will remind you before we meet again."

Ashleigh looked at Jaime and nodded.

"I guess you won't have any trouble finding your way home," Jaime said as they waited for the elevator to arrive.

Ashleigh showed Jaime her card detailed with the instructions for coming to the office and returning to Morningside Heights.

"I have this remember?"

"Oh, yeah and another one in your shoe. Good thinking," Jaime said and she smiled.

The elevator arrived. The door opened. Ashleigh stepped inside.

"Be careful, Ashleigh," Jaime said. "I'm glad you came. I'll be in touch soon."

Twelve

The last image of Ashleigh that Jaime saw was a small, sure smile and piercing hazel eyes.

Jaime became consumed with Ashleigh as she returned to her office. She was iridescent, illuminating, warm and bright. She had life and luminescence about her like sunlight shining through stained glass windows. She was not refined, or cultured, or well spoken. But she was polite and well mannered. Gracious. There was gentleness and naiveté about Ashleigh that seemed far removed from the effects most people assume from living in an often harsh and callous world. She may have been simple and marred in mind, but Jaime knew when Ashleigh walked through the door she was capable of shedding love like a shaft of sunlight.

Jaime entered her office and went to the window. Below, the city streets were filled with people and cars. She looked at everyone and hoped to see Ashleigh in their midst, but no one with a light blue parka stood out. Tia walked up softly behind Jaime. For a moment they watched the streets below in silence.

"You all right?" Tia asked finally.

Jaime shrugged. When she spoke her voice was level and quiet. "I woke this morning a long time before the alarm went off, so I stayed in bed and thought about Sarah. I felt different when I woke, but I'm not sure why."

"How did you feel?" Tia said.

Jaime shrugged. "I don't know. I felt the way I used to when Sarah would be coming home from tennis camp."

Jaime looked at Tia with little animation on her face. Her complexion was pallid. Her spirit was heavy and drained, her words weighted. "Lots of times she'd leave early on a Friday afternoon and come home late Sunday. I'd wake up Sunday morning excited she was coming home. I'd be so anxious to see her."

"Is that how it was today?" Tia asked.

Jaime blinked at Tia, then nodded. "It occurred to me this morning that's how I felt all week when I thought about Ashleigh coming. Isn't that silly? I was so excited to meet her and anxious for the time as it got closer." Jaime clenched her hand into a hard, tight fist. "I didn't realize, until now, how much I really missed seeing and being with Sarah until it felt like I was going to see her again. It was good to feel that way. Even though it wasn't really my sister."

Jaime felt emotions begin to stir within her. To keep from crying, she imagined herself throwing a few shadow punches, then she turned her attention from the crowded streets and looked above the tall buildings. The pale, yellow February sun was weak and low in a hazy sky. Moments later, it disappeared behind a thick, dark cloud, leaving the day draped in a heavy shadow.

"I still miss her," Jaime said.

"I know you do."

Jaime worked to collect herself and get her emotions under control. "It was such a good feeling this morning, Tia. For the first time I felt alive again."

Jaime's words sent them into a long silence.

"You got here early this morning," Tia said softly and rested her hand lightly on her shoulder and squeezed. She left it there to let Jaime know of the love and concern she had for her. "You look beat. Go home and pamper yourself tonight. You need it."

Jaime turned from the window and glanced at where Ashleigh had been sitting. She left the window and headed for the door.

"In a little while," Jaime said, as she returned to her desk.

It was eight o'clock when Jaime finally became aware of the time. The office had been empty and quiet for nearly two hours. She had done little since Tia had left the office after six. Except think.

She turned her attention to her legal pad and began to make notes from the meeting with Ashleigh. But they were not notes she could use in a courtroom, or anywhere else. When she finished, she tore the paper from the notepad. She had always considered herself a closet poet. She had been writing poems for years, but never showed them to anyone, not even Sarah. She kept them in a frayed school notebook, hidden in a dresser drawer.

But this one she would not keep. She tore the page in half and continued to tear until only tattered pieces remained. She let the slips of paper fall like snow into the wastebasket beneath her desk.

THIRTEEN

Tia's long, manicured nails, a fire-engine red, moved swiftly and proficiently over the computer keyboard. She wore no rings or bracelets, just an old wristwatch that had once been her grandmother's. Her smooth, dark hands were graceful and slender. Beautiful, as though they could be used in a dish soap commercial.

Jaime broke her concentration, calling from her office door. "Tia, where's that file on the bus driver? And bring me Ashleigh's, too, please."

Tia stopped typing and crumpled an empty bag of Nacho-Cheese Doritos into a tight ball and tossed it in the trash. She cleaned the tips of her fingers on a napkin, grabbed the files and headed to Jaime's office.

"Here you go," Tia said.

"Thanks. You're the greatest."

Tia smiled at the compliment. "Hump day," she said, studying the calendar on Jaime's desk. "Girl, it's gonna be different come Friday when I leave here knowing that on Monday I won't be back."

Jaime looked up from the file she was reading and put her pen down on the desk. "Are you nervous about leaving, Tia?" she asked, studying her friend and co-worker.

"Me? Heavens no! Don't get me wrong, I've loved working here. I couldn't have asked for anything better…" Tia stopped as if to catch herself. She chuckled. "Whenever I say that, mama scolds me. She tells me things can be better and things sure can be worse. She's right. New things are always a little scary, but that's not gonna stop me."

"I'm glad you built in a couple of weeks off before we start at Dan's," Jaime said.

"I've got vacation time coming, might as well use it," Tia said.

Jaime glanced at the calendar and tapped her last day as a deputy district attorney. "I'll be right behind you, just ten days for me."

Tia's glanced at her watch. "It's almost seven o'clock. The boys are gonna think their mama has skipped town. Gotta run. See you in the morning."

"Night, Tia," Jaime said and resumed reading the file.

Tia left the office, but stopped at the door and turned to face Jaime. "Hey, we're planning a trip to the zoo Saturday. The boys and I, and mama's coming, too. A picnic sort of thing, to celebrate our new jobs, provided the weather cooperates and it's supposed to. You interested? The boys asked if you were coming."

Jaime closed the file and looked thoughtfully at Tia. "Sure. Sounds great. Frank and I are running in the morning, but the rest of the day is wide open. I'd love to come."

With a quick wave of her hand, Tia was gone.

The night air was cool. Tia Ranch turned her coat collar to a light breeze that greeted her as she stepped from the DA's building. In those first few moments after leaving work, Tia's thoughts often returned to New York City. It was there she met her husband, Douglas. If only that hadn't happened. She returned to Denver and home, two years ago, leaving New York and Douglas behind. She had stayed with her mother until she finished paralegal school and landed a job with the DA's office. Then she found a place for herself and the boys.

She caught the local bus, which would take her to home off Alameda Avenue and Colorado Boulevard. Tia liked to ride the bus. It gave her time to unwind before she made it home to her sons, who would demand all of her time and attention. Douglas also found his way into her thoughts as the bus lumbered from the stop. Enough time had passed. Now she hurt less whenever she thought of what he had done to her.

She had been driving home from a church outing and the boys were asleep in the back seat. Something told her to stop at his office. The shingle read Dr. Douglas Ranch, DDS and the office doors were open. Tia took it as an invitation to enter. She walked inside. The smell of antiseptic filled her nostrils. She thought she was prepared for what awaited her, but she wasn't really. She had a feeling things between the two of them weren't right. She wanted to ignore it, but what she saw confirmed it.

She found Douglas embracing one of his dental assistants. They were kissing. The sight filled her with fury. Douglas looked up. Their eyes met. Tia glared at him, her nostrils flared. She stormed out of the office.

He raced after her. "Tia! Wait! It's not like it seems! Listen to me!"

Tia slammed the car door and locked it. She drove away with him pounding on the glass. She did not go home that night, but to a motel. Douglas had followed her and stayed outside the door half the night begging her to let him in the room. Tia refused. She woke the next morning and looked out the window. Douglas was gone. He came home that night and found his clothes on the front steps of their apartment building, piled in a heap, covered by a light dusting of snow.

Douglas begged Tia relentlessly for another chance. She said no. Douglas finally gave up when Tia served him with divorce papers. Then he turned ugly, became verbally abusive. He told Tia she would not amount to anything. She would never make it on her own with the boys. Douglas told Tia that with her lack of education she would get nowhere. She would end up on welfare and would crawl back to him. But she did not come crawling back. She was determined. Tia could type. At ninety words a minute, her skill was a priceless commodity.

She wanted to be a paralegal so she went to the Denver Paralegal Institute when she returned to Denver. She looked for a job immediately, but there were few offers. Tia interviewed for several positions, but was always the runner-up. For six months, she spent five days a week going from law firm to law firm. She spent Sundays combing the want ads, a depressing and dismal task.

Hopes of finding a job had dwindled the day Tia finally entered the DA's office. The day had been unmercifully cold and the weather had drained what little of her energy remained. The frigid wind whipped relentlessly, sending a chill through her body, assaulting her every time she came around the office buildings on every street corner.

She was exhausted when she entered the DA's building. She had deliberately not applied with the DA. It was a last resort. She felt depleted, but knew she had to apply, to say she had tried every avenue. Just one more resume, her last for the day. Her feet ached and she longed to feel the cushion of carpet beneath them.

She didn't plan to see anyone. She did not know if she had the strength should, by chance, someone be there to talk to her. Tia just wanted to leave a resume and go home.

She was only applying to make her mother happy. That morning before another day of job hunting, her mother had asked if she had applied with the DA's office.

"No, not yet, mama."

"Well, Tia, honey, why on earth not?"

"I don't know, mama. I told you they're not going to hire someone like me."

"Why, Tia, I don't know why you go and talk that fool kind of talk about yourself. Shame on you. If they only knew how good you were, they'd hire you in a minute."

Tia frowned and flashed her mother a skeptical look. It was just mother talk. The same kind of boasting she had done many times for her own sons.

Tia's mother smiled. "Don't be so down on yourself. I know the Good Lord has something special planned for you. Why, He wouldn't take you all this way just to go and leave you now. Don't you remember what Pastor Bill said Sunday?"

Tia looked at her mother, but did not respond.

"He was talking about prayer, remember? For what man among you would ask for a loaf of bread and receive a stone? Do you think the Lord would leave you standing at a locked door, if you've been out there knocking the whole time?"

Tia swirled her spoon around the remains of her oatmeal. "No, mama."

She continued to fidget with her spoon while her mother spoke. Then she looked at her mother sitting across the kitchen table and smiled. She rose from the chair and grabbed her briefcase filled with resumes. On the way out the door, she kissed her mother lightly on the forehead.

The conversation with her mother filled Tia's mind as she stood at the entrance to the DA's office. It was 6:25 p.m. when she pushed the door open and walked to the elevator. Tia took a long, deep breath as the elevator door closed and she pushed the button. She watched the numbers light up until the elevator reached her floor. The elevator bell chimed slightly as the door slid open.

Tia stepped out of the elevator and clutched the handle of her briefcase firmly as she walked toward the reception area. She ran her tongue along her lips to moisten them, her red lipstick just remnants now.

The area was empty. As Tia moved closer to the reception desk she stopped near a large potted plant to open her briefcase. She rested the briefcase against her leg as she pulled out a resume. The moment she did, a woman, her attention fixed on a document, came around the plant and bumped into Tia. Her briefcase and everything inside went crashing to the floor.

"Oh! Pardon me! I'm so sorry for not paying more attention! It's just that I didn't expect to see anyone here this time of night."

Tia studied her quickly and evenly. She was as tall as Tia, dressed in a dark wool blazer and skirt and very attractive. The first thing Tia noticed was the woman's eyes. They were immense and sensitive, taking everything in. They were a chocolate brown that lent a warmth and richness to her face.

"Let me help you pick those up," the woman said.

The woman bent down with Tia and helped her collect the resumes that had scattered all over the office floor. The woman scanned one of Tia's resumes quickly before handing it back to her.

"Looking for a job?" she asked.

Tia felt her face flush as the heat began to rise.

"Jaime Monroe," the woman said and extended her hand. "Nice to meet you."

Tia hoped hers wasn't too clammy. "Tia Ranch."

"Mind if I take a look?" Jaime asked, pointing to the resume.

Tia nodded and then looked at Jaime as she scanned her resume. Every few moments Jaime would arch her right eyebrow, which Tia hoped was because she read something she liked about her qualifications.

"What kind of work are you looking for?" Jaime asked.

"Paralegal. I graduated from DPI six months ago."

"You've been looking ever since?" Jaime asked, looking from the resume to Tia.

Tia nodded.

"You look beat."

Tia sighed heavily as she spoke. "I am. It's been a long day. I was ready to call it quits, but I was in the area. I didn't expect to see anyone. And I'm sorry to bother you and take up your time. Are you an attorney?"

Jaime nodded. "It's no bother. If you want to leave this with me I'll make sure it gets to HR first thing Monday."

"Thanks," Tia said. "That would be wonderful. I'd appreciate it."

"It's the least I can do for almost knocking you over."

The telephone rang Sunday morning just as Tia finished getting her boys ready for church. Her mother answered. Tia frowned when her mother called her name. She was not expecting any phone calls. Her hello was reserved.

"Tia? It's Jaime Monroe. We met Friday at the DA's office."

"Yes, Jaime, how're you?"

"Fine, thanks. Do you think it's possible to come to the DA's for an interview tomorrow morning at ten o'clock?"

Tia almost dropped the telephone. She cleared her throat and tried to sound relaxed. "Of course I can."

"I've been looking over your resume and I can't pass it up."

"That's great. I'll be there. Thanks, Jaime."

"Wonderful, see you tomorrow morning."

When Tia put the phone back into the receiver and turned around, her mother's dark eyes were probing. "Who was that, Tia?"

"Jaime Monroe. She's the one I told you about. I have an interview at the District Attorney's Office, in the morning at ten."

The bus had reached her stop, interrupting Tia's memories. She got off and began to walk toward home and the wind did not feel as cold.

Jaime left the DA's office shortly after Tia. She had gone to the club anticipating boxing with Frank, but he did not show for their workout. Jaime checked with Barry at the front desk to see if Frank had called to cancel. He had not. She called his apartment, but hung up when the answering machine clicked on. Instead, Jaime ran three miles on the treadmill. She stopped at Café Gardenia and was home by 9:30 p.m. Exhausted, she went to bed at eleven o'clock and within minutes fell into a troubled sleep, her subconscious lost in the depths of tangled dreams.

Jaime woke with a start, her body covered in a cold sweat. Her heart was beating as though she had been sprinting. Bleary-eyed, she glanced at the luminous digital clock on the nightstand: 1:20 a.m. Her nightmare was different, not like the ones of Sarah that had stirred since Kelly Jo's trial. This one seemed to focus not on what had been, but what could be. It unnerved her.

In the dream, Jaime was on the same treadmill at the club she had used hours earlier. It was her favorite. It was positioned in front of a large window. The reflection allowed Jaime to see herself while she ran. In her dream, a great fire burned all around her. What had started as a spark became an inferno it seemed in a matter of minutes.

She began to trot. Wanting to run, to escape the fury. But she did not have the freedom to run fast or effectively. She tried to free herself from her warm-up jacket. As she struggled to pull it off her shoulders, she stumbled but did not fall. Finally she tore the jacket from her body and dropped it at her heels. Her speed increased. She tried to outrun the flames, but they moved with her. They did not retreat. The blaze did not engulf her, but it stayed beside her as though it had become her.

She struggled with the rest of her clothing. First, her shirt, then the sweat pants. They fell from her body with surprising ease. Free of her clothing, she ran faster and faster, as if she was trying to outrun herself.

The fire stayed with her. The heat intense. Almost unbearable. In the window's reflection, her skin began to melt and fall from her body. Bit by bit. Piece by piece. Jaime woke, however, before all that remained of her was her bare bones.

She forced the dream from her mind.

Her hands traveled the length of her body. Her nightshirt and skin, everything, were still intact. She got out of bed. In the bathroom, she splashed cold water on her face and neck. The cold water brought her to her senses. She crawled back into bed and pulled the blanket to her chin. But sleep did not come. She lay there, staring up into the darkness. Time crawled by like a slow moving train until her alarm sounded.

Jaime decided the next time she ran on the treadmill at the club she would use a different one.

Fourteen

Although he could not be called handsome, there was something about Winston Ross that suggested a gracefully aging matinee idol.

Perhaps it was the swept-back thinning gray hair or the glasses that covered eyes the color of a winter day and framed a thinly tanned face. Perhaps it was his sophistication and continental charm. A wiry man with a sparkling sense of humor, he possessed a self-assured persona, one that led many in the Denver legal system to label him arrogant and obnoxious.

Regardless of how co-workers and colleagues viewed the 58-year-old Winston Ross, he was utterly comfortable and consummately in charge when in the courtroom.

Winston was late for his noon appointment with Leigh Roberts. She stood in the center of the large window in his office in an aquamarine-colored glass structure known as the Holy Ghost Building. It sat adjacent to a church on Welton Street bearing the same name. The view from the office window stretched westward to capture a sweeping vista of snow-capped mountains that made up the Front Range. From the window Leigh noticed the mountains took on the same color as the sky and all that prevented them from becoming one were the white tips of snow.

Winston entered the office in a rush. His legal secretary, a trim woman wearing a navy business suit, was at his heels giving him the morning briefing. Winston nodded quickly at Leigh as he removed a black double-breasted suit jacket and put it across the back of his chair. He loosened his yellow silk tie and listened to his secretary.

He stood behind a long ebony desk, perfectly polished. His reflection stared back. Behind him were the degrees of the Ivy-league educated lawyer.

He was rolling up his sleeves as his secretary finished and left the office and Leigh noticed that his white shirt accentuated his tanned face and hands. He turned his attention to Leigh. He smiled, took her hands and kissed her lightly on the cheek.

"How are you?" he asked. "Good to see you. How's Drew?"

Leigh Roberts had met Winston Ross through Alan Andrew Roberts, her ex-husband. Few people called him 'Drew'. The name was reserved for only his closest friends. Winston Ross was one. When Drew and Leigh were married, the two couples spent many long weekends together. Leigh enjoyed their company, but like many of Drew's friends most were at least ten to fifteen years older than she. Leigh often felt out of place, but she had always liked Winston and felt comfortable around him. Despite the years of being divorced from Drew, Leigh and Winston had remained friends.

"You know I don't know anything about Drew," Leigh replied, stepping back from Winston. "I don't know how he is or what he's working on these days."

She moved to a large leather chair in front of his desk.

"Of course you don't," Winston said evenly. "But next time I hear from him, I'll tell him you said hello."

"Don't you dare!" Leigh grinned.

She knew he asked because when Winston and Drew spoke, which was often, Drew always asked about his ex-wife and Ashleigh. Winston never believed Drew had stopped loving Leigh, and he often told her so. He had an inkling that Leigh shared the same feelings about Drew, though he was certain she would never admit to it.

"I didn't come here to talk about Drew," she said.

Winston returned to his chair behind the desk and sat down. "No, of course not. I know why you're here." He paused a moment, then said plainly, "I was taken aback by your call, Leigh. I'm surprised you would want something so detrimental for her."

Her eyes offered no clue to her thoughts.

"Has Ashleigh refused to give her consent for the operation?" Winston asked, but without waiting for her reply, went on, "Because in Colorado even as her legal guardian if she hasn't given consent, you can't substitute your consent to go ahead with the operation."

Leigh frowned. "What does it mean for Ashleigh to give consent if I'm her guardian?"

"Consent," Winston began by saying, "means an informed assent, an agreement if you will, expressed in writing, freely given. It means a fair explanation of the procedures to be followed, a description of the discomforts and risks and an instruction that the resident or other persons giving consent is free to withdraw consent and to stop participation at any time."

He paused, then added, "Ashleigh's been examined by her doctor?"

Leigh nodded.

They both knew that physicians who had been a family's doctor for years often performed such operations. It was done, no questions asked. No one, other than the family and the doctor knew. There were some doctors, however, no matter the family ties, who refused to perform the surgery.

"Your doctor balked and refused to do the operation," Winston said, but it was more of a statement than a question.

Again Leigh nodded.

Winston rubbed a smooth, thin finger over closed lips, thinking in silence. "It's very simple then," he said finally. "No person who has a developmental disability, which includes Ashleigh, who hasn't given voluntary consent can be sterilized."

Winston stopped to exam Leigh's face. Despite her calm and relaxed appearance, he saw the tension that showed around her eyes. He leaned forward, his hands clasped lightly in front of him, a perfect reflection in the desktop. "It's that simple."

She rose from the chair and walked to the window and stared out. Clouds hung like clumps of cotton along the Front Range. "It needs to be done," she said. "Pregnancy is a chance I can't take with Ashleigh. If my doctor won't do it, then we'll find someone who will."

"Do you really want to go through with this?" Winston asked.

"Yes." Leigh replied and her voice was firm. She did not turn to look at him.

Winston's intercom buzzed. A young female paralegal entered, bringing the materials Winston had requested.

"Here it is," he said, nodding his thanks to the paralegal.

"What do we have to do?" Leigh asked, her attention still fixed on the horizon.

Winston took a moment to study the documents and didn't answer immediately. "A hearing on the petition shall be held promptly," he said. "Ashleigh will be physically present through the entire proceeding..."

He stopped abruptly. "Does Ashleigh have an attorney?"

"Yes, she does."

"Who?"

"Jaime Monroe."

Winston nodded with familiarity watching Leigh as she returned to the chair and sat down.

"Yes, I know of her, though I've never met her," he said. "She just won that Kelly Jo Cox murder case. But she's with the DA's…"

Winston's voice faded as Leigh raised her hand.

"Not anymore," she said. "She resigned to take Ashleigh's case."

"She's good, Leigh, and very bright. Can't be more than twenty eight or twenty nine. I've seen her in court. Her husband is a criminal defense lawyer, too, I believe."

"Ex-husband," Leigh added quickly. "She's divorcing him."

"Oh, you know Mitch?"

"I know Jaime."

"Because you covered the trial?" Winston asked.

"Well, sort of. We met the day the jury came back with the verdict. We ended up at the same place for lunch. The tables were full. I was by myself and she asked to join me."

Leigh did not tell Winston about their second encounter at Café Gardenia. Winston seemed taken aback by Leigh's comment. He studied her cautiously.

"I guess I don't need to tell you that's not a good idea."

"Winston, please," she said. "Where were we?"

He paused a moment to find his place. "Ashleigh will be represented by counselor Jaime Monroe-Price…"

"It's just Jaime Monroe," she said. "She's dropping 'Price'."

Winston began again. "Ashleigh will be represented by Jaime Monroe, and will be provided the opportunity to present testimony and cross-examine witnesses. Incidentally, Judge Jessie Gutierrez has been assigned to your case."

"Is that good?"

Winston shrugged. "Could be good, could be bad. With his background, it's good for Jaime and me in that we don't have to spend a lot of time educating him on the issues. However, Jessie might have a soft touch for people like Ashleigh, which may not bode well for us."

Leigh shook her head, disgusted. "This is ridiculous. What does Ashleigh know about being pregnant? What does she know about taking care of anyone? She can barely care for herself."

Winston studied her carefully. "Ashleigh appears able to care for herself, with a little help, and that's no surprise to you. Where's this coming from, Leigh? I know she's been living in a group home for years. Where does she live now?"

"Still at Morningside, but that's going to change."

Winston raised his eyebrows.

"She's moving to an apartment in August," Leigh said. "A host-home."

"Sounds wonderful," he said. "You should be happy. Ashleigh seems to be doing so well. She's come a long way."

"I know she has, but it worries me."

"Why?"

Leigh answered as if she was annoyed. "With less supervision, I'm afraid she'll get lost in the shuffle and people will take advantage of her. This isn't Middle America, Winston."

He laughed. He voice was patient and calm. “It could happen anywhere.”

“That’s not all,” Leigh went on. “Ashleigh’s work arrangements are changing, too.”

Winston looked troubled. “She’s losing her job?”

“She’s getting a new one.”

“That’s great. You should be happy.”

“I am. Of course, I am. But I’m worried about the exposure. There’ll be so much more of it to all kinds of people. She’ll be working in the food court at the Tabor Center. They’ve signed a contract for cleaning services. Ashleigh asked to be part of the team. And she won’t be taking the van that brings her from home to the workshop anymore.”

“She’ll take a regular bus?” Winston asked.

Leigh nodded.

“You should be happy Ashleigh wants to test her limits and that she’s grown tired of stuffing sports bags. She wants to do something more challenging. Seems like she’s really trying, Leigh. It’ll be a wonderful change for her.”

Leigh’s expression turned cloudy. “How many people do you think that place holds at noon, probably a thousand?”

“Leigh, I know how you feel, but this could be good for Ashleigh,” he said. “Who knows? It could help her to blossom. How old is she?”

“Twenty four.”

He caught Leigh’s gaze and held it. “Don’t you think it’s time you cut the ties? Maybe she’s more prepared and ready to go out into the world than you think. She’s lived in a group home, they’re working to prepare her and you know that.”

Leigh stared at Winston, her look incredulous. He ignored her look and continued.

“It’s often hard to tell with people like Ashleigh. Often when they get more exposure in the outside world, like living and working and becoming part of a community, it’s the best thing for them.”

“What makes you such an expert?” Leigh snapped.

Winston raised his eyebrows slightly. “I’m no expert,” he said quietly. “I’m just someone who sees Ashleigh in a different light. I can see where you’re going with this, wanting to have Ashleigh sterilized.

But why don't you wait awhile? Give it six months, maybe through the end of the year to see if this is something you still want to do. Wait and see how Ashleigh does at the new job and living away from the group home before you make any drastic decisions. This is drastic, Leigh. Once it's done…"

His voice trailed off, giving his words time to sink in. The room fell silent and they could hear the telephone ring at the secretary's desk.

"And, if you don't feel comfortable, we can proceed then," he said.

But it was as though Winston spoke into the wind, his words were carried off before they could register any effect. Her voice was firm and unyielding when she spoke.

Almost demanding. "In six months, it could be too late. I know what's best for her."

Winston's eyes narrowed. He smiled thinly and shrugged. "As you wish."

Leigh rested her head against the soft back of the leather chair, closed her eyes and took a deep breath. She realized Winston was trying to help her view the situation from all angles. She was sorry she had been on the defense since she came, but she felt confident about her decision for Ashleigh. When she began speaking again, her voice was gentle. She worked to erase its edge. "Thank you for your concern, Winston. I appreciate it. I know you're trying to help. I just worry that Ashleigh doesn't have the knowledge to understand what all this means."

"She doesn't have to," Winston replied without hesitation. "The capacity to understand, not perfect knowledge, is the key here. She doesn't have to be a scholar. What's more, before a court can consider whether sterilization is medically essential or in Ashleigh's best interest, we have to prove Ashleigh is, in fact, incompetent to make a decision about sterilization. And, furthermore, it has to be an incompetence that won't likely improve the older she gets. If she is incompetent to make a decision today, then she has to remain that way tomorrow or ten years from now." He continued cautiously. "This process isn't going to happen overnight, Leigh. I want you to know that and be prepared for it. It won't be like when Ashleigh turned eighteen."

She glared at him. "You want to talk me out of this, don't you?"

"I'm merely presenting the facts. You make your own decisions. I just want you to be prepared to invest a lot of time, effort and money once we get going. I read about a case that took six years before they reached a decision."

Winston watched for Leigh's reaction, but she remained stoic. He went on. "The case became a war zone between the rights of the mentally disabled and the powers of a parent. The mother said her 25-year-old daughter, who had the mind of a kindergartner and lived in a group home, was a clear target for victimization. She wanted her daughter's tubes tied. The daughter's attorney argued the procedure was too extreme and ignored the rights of the mentally disabled. In various appeals, the judge's ruling was upheld, overturned and reinstated. A real legal struggle."

"Who won?" Leigh asked.

"The mother did, eventually. A United States Supreme Court Justice refused an emergency appeal by the daughter's attorney to block the operation and she was sterilized."

By 1:30 p.m., after they had discussed Ashleigh's case, Leigh left the law offices of Ross, Rosenberg & Klein. She walked from the Holy Ghost Building and into the wind and glare of the midday sun. Despite the sun's warmth, she felt an uncomfortable chill in the wind. Spring was near, but winter still commanded the season. The horizon had grown dark with a dusting of menacing clouds that suggested snow.

The air refreshed her and the walk would clear her mind. She needed that. She waited for a light rail train to pass before she crossed the street and headed for the Dominion Plaza—two three-tiered buildings on 17th Street that housed the *News-Dispatch.*

She was angry with herself and shook her head in disgust over the comment she had made after Winston spoke of the sterilization case that took more than a half decade to reach a decision.

Who won?

With all that's involved in such cases, personally and professionally, medically and ethically, did anyone ever really win? She returned to the office, but had trouble concentrating the rest of the day.

Fifteen

It was well into the evening at Walker & Associates and Jaime was still concentrating on a case history about sterilization. Her eyes burned. She put the file aside and rubbed them lightly with the tips of her fingers. She glanced at her watch. Nearly 8:30 p.m. She was still getting used to her new job and the surroundings, especially her spacious corner office.

Her first two weeks in private practice were a blur. When she had time to think, she remembered her last few days at the DA's office. When she started to pack the last of the personal belongings she had brought to the job more than three years ago, it was harder than she expected. Her colleagues wished her well and gave her a custom pair of boxing gloves with a note saying, *"keep up the good fight."* And she was honored when the District Attorney stopped by her office the evening before her last day.

"Jaime," he had said, half startling her because, given the hour, she didn't expect to see her boss standing in her doorway.

"Yes, sir," she said.

"I just wanted to say good-bye and good-luck."

"Thank you, sir."

He stayed at the doorway and asked about Ashleigh's case. She spent a few minutes telling him. He nodded occasionally as she spoke.

"You and Dan will make a great team, Jaime, but you know the door here is always open if you ever want to come back. And Tia, too. I hate to lose both of you, but you're both welcome back anytime."

"Thank you, sir," Jaime said. "When I see Tia, I'll let her know."

Neither Jaime nor Tia had second thoughts about their decision to leave.

Jaime resumed reading the file, glad she had run this morning. She was supposed to run with Frank at Wash Park, but once more he didn't show. She read until her eyes started to burn again. She closed the file and was gathering her things to leave when she thought she heard a noise in the outer office. She paused and listened. Nothing.

The only light in her office came from a small desk lamp, which she used after hours. She liked turning the overhead lights off after the sun had set and the city had descended into darkness. It was her favorite time to stand at the window and reflect. She would let her mind wander as she watched city lights flicker.

Sometimes her parents came to mind and she wondered what they would think of her being an attorney. She was grateful they had not taken everything from her after what had happened with Sarah. Their love was gone, as was her sense of family, but they did allow her to keep the trust fund that they had established for both their daughters for college. Jaime had used every penny of hers.

She often thought about writing to tell them about college, but talked herself out of the idea. Jaime learned quickly in graduate school when her letters were returned unopened that her parents had little interest in the career she had selected.

She wondered what Sarah would be like if she were still alive. At twenty four, if everything had gone according to plan, she would have been traveling the world playing professional tennis. Jaime felt herself imagining Sarah returning from London, where she would have played on the grass courts of Wimbledon. Or Paris and the clay courts at Roland Garros. Jaime imagined they would play catch up on all that had happened in their lives since they had been apart.

Jaime was filling her briefcase when she did hear something by Tia's desk.

"Tia?" she called. She waited a moment for a response. Seconds passed. Nothing. "Tia, is that you?"

Jaime rose from her chair, and keeping her eyes fixed on the doorway, began to move toward the reception area. "Tia?"

She spoke hesitantly as she looked around the doorway. Then she smiled with relief. "Frank, what're you doing here?"

He had stumbled into the office and over to the couch. He looked like a chiseled stone colossus. She was surprised a man his size could slip inside without being heard. He was sprawled on the sofa. His eyes were closed and his head was resting against the back of the couch. One arm was draped heavily over the side of the couch, his hand dangling lifelessly. His suit was rumpled, and his tie loosened at an open shirt collar.

Her smile fell from her face when she realized he was drunk. She could smell the alcohol from her doorway. "Frank," Jaime said, her voice more sad than angry.

She sat beside him. Frank opened his eyes and lifted his head. Jaime saw that his eyes were red and watery. She could tell he was trying to remember where he was. She watched as he squinted and scanned the room. His eyes stopped and settled on her.

"Hey, big guy, you all right?" she asked.

He blinked several times, as though the glare from the lights hurt his eyes. He sat forward on the couch, covered his face with both hands and then ran them through his hair several times before he looked at Jaime. The look in her eyes was guarded. She wondered how he knew to find her here. They hadn't talked much since she started the new job. She looked at him and waited for him to speak.

"What time is it?" Frank's voice was hoarse and gravelly.

They looked at the brass clock that hung behind Tia's new desk. They watched as the gold second hand made a full sweep around the blackened face.

"Sorry I missed our run this morning."

Jaime nodded, her eyes still on the clock.

"I've had a little too much to drink," Frank said and looked at Jaime, his glassy eyes full of regret and embarrassment. "And I screwed up."

"I guess you'll get around to telling me what happened."

Frank reached into the breast pocket of his suit and, with two fingers pulled out a folded slip of paper. Without looking at Jaime, he handed it to her. She pulled the paper through the grasp of his hand.

"Go ahead," he said. "Open it and see what it says."

She unfolded the paper slowly and, holding it lightly between the tips of her fingers, read every word.

"Frank, I'm sorry."

Frank shook his head and mumbled something Jaime did not understand. Then he said, "So, I don't have to tell you where I've been all day. It's been a shitty miserable day, and I've been out getting reacquainted with all my old bar buddies. I finally had to quit about an hour ago. Ran out of money. I called in sick today. It was no lie, Jaime, I am sick. I'm sick and tired of everything. And now Carol's filing for divorce."

Frank's face flushed a bright red. Jaime thought he was on the verge of tears, but he managed to compose himself. He leaned his head back against the couch and closed his eyes. He had not shaven and Jaime could see the wisps of gray in his stubble.

"She took Rachael. My little girl..." Frank could not retain his composure. He leaned his bulky body forward and buried his face in the hollow of his hands. He cried so hard his entire frame shook.

"Come on," Jaime said." Let's go back to your place. I'll fix you something to eat and you can take a hot shower. You'll feel better."

They stepped from the office into a light rain. She managed to get Frank into her car and before long, they were in front of a high-rise condominium near Larimer Square. They managed to reach the door, but not before the rain had dampened their overcoats and hair. They rode the elevator in silence. Jaime kept her eyes on Frank. He rested his head against the side of the elevator as they rode. The bell chimed slightly out of tune as the elevator door opened on his floor.

Jaime fumbled in Frank's coat pocket for his keys. When she opened the door and turned on the light, she was taken aback by the shambles that greeted her. She walked ahead of Frank and into the living room. She shook her head at the sight in the room. Empty cartons of Chinese food, pizza boxes and soda cans were piled on and around the sofa and coffee table.

Jaime shook her head. "Damn, Frank," she said.

Sweat pants and dirty sport socks lay in a heap near a pair of running shoes by the foot of the couch. A dated *News-Dispatch* and a *Sports Illustrated* littered the floor near an easy chair, positioned in front of a large-screen television.

Frank moved quietly from the hallway into the living room. He collected a pile of ties and suit jackets from the couch and let them fall in a tangled pile to the floor. He sat down heavily.

Jaime walked into the kitchen. Mail remained unopened and scattered on the table. Dirty dishes were piled in the sink. Opened soup cans stood neatly on a counter. A frying pan with a spatula sticking out of it remained on the stove. She looked inside the pan. The grease had hardened around the tip of the spatula and had turned an ugly shade of yellow.

Jaime walked from the kitchen and started down the long hallway toward Frank's bedroom. The bed was a mess of blankets, pillows and sheets. Towels and clothes littered the floor around the bed. She returned to the living room. He studied her intently.

"How can you live like this?" she asked, placing her hands on her hips. "Come on," she said, moving toward the couch. "Time to get up."

She grabbed him by both hands and pulled him to his feet. He caught sight of her in a hallway mirror. She was slim and pretty, dressed in dark gray wool slacks. A matching vest covered a white silk blouse. Her brown hair was pulled away from her face and the light fell on her hair in such a way that it brought out some of the red highlights.

"I'll clean up while you shower," she said.

Frank nodded as she began to push him gently down the hallway.

"I'll fix you something to eat. When's the last time you had something besides pop and pizza?"

He did not answer.

She heard him start the shower as she opened two cans of vegetable beef soup. She waited for the soup to heat and rummaged in the refrigerator for fresh vegetables. There was nothing but a stale onion. She found crackers and placed them in a dish, along with slices of cheddar cheese.

The shower had stopped and Jaime could hear Frank moving around in the bedroom. She filled the sink with soapy water and began to put the dirty dishes in, watching them disappear beneath the suds. She was cleaning, expecting him to walk into the kitchen. After a few minutes, she realized she no longer heard noise coming from the bedroom. She stopped and listened. Silence. She walked to the bedroom and stuck her head around the doorway.

Her gaze settled on him. Frank, freshly showered, his hair still damp, was asleep on the bed. He was shirtless and wearing a pair of black sweats. His bulky chest kept a slow, steady pace going up and down. A small, sad smile spread slowly over her lips. She walked quietly into the room and covered him.

Jaime spent the next hour cleaning his apartment. She put the soup in the refrigerator and picked up the suit jackets and ties from the floor and hung them. She stacked the mail neatly on the table. When she finished, at least some order had been restored. Jaime walked down the hall to check on Frank before she left. He hadn't moved.

She walked to the bedroom window, pushed the curtain aside and stared out.

No snow yet.

Jaime found Mitchell in her thoughts. When she had entered Frank's apartment tonight and saw the mess she started to think about him. She tried to stop her thoughts, but the memories were too strong. In the quiet of Frank's bedroom, she allowed herself the pain of remembering what she had been trying since October to forget. They were still together then and Jaime had come home early, unexpectedly, from a conference. She didn't call Mitchell to tell him she was coming home. She wanted to surprise him.

Mitchell was there. And so was someone else. Someone Jaime didn't expect to see. She could see herself walking into their bedroom, unbuttoning her raincoat and lifting her wet hair off her coat collar to relieve the dampness around her neck. She heard herself calling Mitchell's name. She saw him, shirtless, sitting in bed.

At the same instant, Molly Gibson was coming out of their bathroom. A towel covered her silky, smooth skin. Another towel was draped around her head, hiding a blonde mane of hair.

Jaime and Molly's surprise at seeing one another turned quickly to animosity and the two women exchanged icy stares. Jaime remembered Molly well from college. Jaime started to date Mitchell soon after he had stopped seeing Molly. Too soon. Jaime knew Mitchell had never gotten over Molly. It was clear that she hadn't gotten over him.

Molly dressed quickly and left, as if that would help. Jaime remembered the turmoil within her. Not knowing what else to do, she started to clean their apartment. Mitchell was close on her heels, pleading for forgiveness. She was exhausted when she arrived home that evening, but a burning rage restored her. An anger she hadn't felt since the days of sitting through Sarah's rape trial welled within her.

When she finished cleaning, she didn't bother to unpack. She grabbed her suitcase and left the apartment, but had forgotten her coat. When she walked from their apartment, snow fell on her and turned her shoulders white. But she was too stubborn and too angry to go back for it. She spent two nights in a hotel.

Jaime laughed quietly to herself now and shook her head, pushing thoughts from that evening from her mind. She was putting on her overcoat when a picture of Frank's family in New York City captured her attention, and she glanced at it briefly. She turned out the light and stepped into the hallway. She locked the door and put the key in her pocket.

It was near midnight when she stepped out into the open air.

The rain had since turned to snow.

Jaime watched the snowflakes swirl down and disappear as they fell into the path of light from the street lamps. Turning her coat collar against the cold March air, she looked in both directions and crossed the street, quiet and deserted. The snow was heavy and thick, falling so slowly the flakes seemed to be suspended in air.

Jaime thought her car looked lopsided. When she reached it, she saw the front tire was flat. "Damn," she said, looking again up and down the empty street.

She turned around and looked at the building's entrance. The elegant interior of the lobby beckoned. She considered going back upstairs to sleep on Frank's couch, but thought better of the idea.

Jaime decided to walk to the convenience store on the corner to call for help. It was cold and she was getting wet. She hadn't eaten since noon and was as hungry as she was tired. As she began to walk, she hoped, with a little luck, a taxi would turn the corner. At that moment, one did. She raised her hand, hoping he would stop.

He did. It was the best thing that had happened to her all day.

Sixteen

Jaime was winding down from a difficult day at work when her telephone rang. The last thing she wanted to do was answer it. It was 4:30 p.m. and she had planned to leave the office at a decent time. She had been looking forward to a workout with Frank.

On impulse, she answered it.

"Oh, Jaime, glad you're still there. It's Erin Greene."

Panic gripped her. "Is everything all right?" Jaime asked quickly, fearing the worst about Ashleigh.

"Sure, sure. Everything's fine," Erin said in a reassuring voice.

"What's up?"

"When Ashleigh came home this afternoon she had her mother's laptop with her. Ashleigh said Leigh came to the food court for lunch and forgot it. Can you imagine her leaving something like that just lying around? Goodness. Anyway when Ashleigh left the food court, she brought it home with her. Ashleigh called her mother a little while ago. I spoke with Leigh and she was a little frantic. Said she had no idea where she'd left it. She told me she needs it to finish a story before tomorrow."

Erin stopped a moment, distracted. Jaime listened as Erin answered a question for someone who must have been standing next to her.

"Sorry, Jaime. So, here's the problem, Leigh can't leave her house because she's waiting for a phone call so she can finish another story she's writing. And I'm on duty and I can't leave to go all the way to Evergreen."

"How can I help?"

"If you don't mind, could you possibly bring Leigh her laptop?"

Jaime was hesitant.

"Jaime? Jaime, are you there?"

"Yes, sorry, Erin, I got distracted."

"Can you go? Ashleigh says Leigh really needs the laptop."

Jaime knew she should not agree to return the computer, but she heard herself saying yes before the stronger, wiser part of her emotions could prevail. "Sure. I'll come pick it up."

By 5:15 p.m., Jaime was heading west on Interstate 70 to Evergreen as she pushed the accelerator of her Mazda RX7 to the floor. The car moved without effort, passing others as the highway began to make its gradual climb toward the mountains. The radio blared and the rushing wind blowing in through the car windows invigorated her. The eminent view of the Rocky Mountains began to spread out before her, rolling westward in vast, rhythmic grandeur. On both sides of the highway looming mountainsides of Ponderosa pine and cedar trees surrounded her. Spring was drawing closer and the rolling hillsides and valleys were beginning to thaw and wake from winter sleep.

Leigh's house was on a hill, away from the others in the area. A dark wall of mature trees and pines shielded the rambling old English home from the road. It was painted a pastel gray and white, with a two-car garage. A redwood deck overlooked a rolling hillside. Jaime guessed the house sat on about three acres as she walked up the steps leading to the front door, the laptop in her right hand. She rang the bell. Moments passed. No one came. She rang again. She had just stepped away from the door when Leigh opened it.

"Jaime?" Leigh's voice matched her quizzical look.

Leigh looked relaxed and comfortable in Levi's and scuffed leather boots. The collar to her black corduroy shirt was scrunched up and her hair fell freely about her shoulders. Her sleeves were rolled to her elbows and a pair of wire reading glasses was folded in the center of her shirt.

"Come in," Leigh said, stepping away from the door and opening it further.

Jaime entered and they stopped inside the foyer. Smells of chicken and onion came from the kitchen.

"I'm surprised to see you," Leigh said.

"I came straight from work."

"I guessed that. You look great."

Jaime took a quick inventory of what she wore, a white button-down cardigan and olive-green slacks lined with delicate pinstripes. Her long hair was pinned loosely away from her face.

"Is everything all right, Jaime?"

"Sure, everything's fine." Jaime handed her laptop to Leigh. "I think this belongs to you."

"Oh, God. You didn't have to do that."

"Erin called and said you needed it tonight."

"Well, I do. Thanks for bringing it. I was so relieved after Erin called. I had no idea where I'd left that damn thing. I can't remember the last time I've done something so foolish. I guess I'm a little flustered now that Ashleigh has her new job. But Erin did say someone would bring it to me, but I had no idea they had you for a courier."

Jaime adjusted the smile on her face as though it were a mask. "Erin called and said you needed it and couldn't come because you were waiting on a phone call. Did you get it?"

"I got off the phone just as you rang the bell."

Leigh started to walk toward the kitchen. "Can I get you something to drink, Jaime? It's the least I can do."

Jaime knew at that moment she should refuse. Say no, turn around and leave. Instead, something stronger within her made her turn and follow Leigh. Unveiled through the stone-faced entry was a magnificent iron staircase with an overlooking balcony that suspended over a spacious sun and music room and gave a generous view of a baby grand piano.

"Water, club soda if you have it, would be great. Thanks," Jaime said, as she reached the kitchen.

The gourmet kitchen was accented with almond painted wood cabinets and handcrafted custom tiles, each an individual work of art. Windowed walls and a breakfast nook added an airy, open feel. Jaime stood at the end of a long wet bar that also served as a table.

"When I'm not at work or writing in the study, I spend most of my time in here." Leigh, standing in front of the cooking area, watched as Jaime eyed the bronze-colored pots and pans that hung over the stove. The area was a small island unto itself.

"I love to cook," she said. "It helps me unwind and relax."

Leigh took two large glasses and filled them with ice and club soda. She sliced fresh lemon and squeezed it into the glass and gave it to Jaime. She motioned for Jaime to follow her to the study. From somewhere in the house came the soft sounds of piano music.

"I was just finishing a story. It'll take a minute and we can go outside on the deck. It's a little too cool to be out, but I want you to see the view."

They passed by an oblong window in the hallway and Leigh looked outside. "This is a beautiful time of day," she said. "It's always been my favorite. Seems like I do my best writing by the setting sun. I love the colors on the horizon. Wait 'til you see it."

Leigh's home office looked as immaculate as the kitchen. The cherry and walnut paneling gave the room a darker, smaller look. The glow from a small desk lamp added softness. A large oak desk was positioned parallel to an oblong window and took up most of the space. On top of the desk another computer sat, humming softly. The screen-saver on the color monitor showed a vivid display of fireworks. Leigh set her laptop beside it and opened it. Behind the chair, a bookcase lined the wall from floor to ceiling. Beyond the window, Jaime could see a postcard view of hills and valleys and the town below.

"Must be a great view at night with the lights," Jaime said.

"It is." Leigh's voice sounded distracted and faraway. she was preoccupied by the laptop.

Jaime waited, looked out the window and listened to the click, click as Leigh's fingertips moved rapidly and lightly over the keyboard. Jaime turned her attention to Leigh and, while she wrote, took the time to study her. She seemed to have an air of elegance about her, a sense of sophistication.

"I had to finish that and I didn't want to lose my train of thought," Leigh said.

She met Jaime at the window, taking in the view.

"I love the city," Leigh said. "Always have. I lived in Manhattan for a few years, but I needed a little more room than those tight streets could give me. I could never live in the city. Work, yes. To live, no."

"How long have you been out here?"

"We bought this house about twenty years ago. But it's a very old house and has its own personality. Whoever built it must've had someone like me in mind."

"Why's that?"

"The space is perfect. I can handle the proximity of the people and the buildings and the traffic for only so long, then that's it. After that, I'm ready to get out of there. I need the space."

Leigh watched with Jaime a moment more. "Let's go outside," she said.

Jaime followed Leigh through the living room to the French double doors. The room had an elegance about it that matched Leigh's personality. It was a black and oyster white contemporary setting of well-defined curves and lines that caught Jaime's eye and took it on a pleasing and aesthetic journey from the chair, the table, to the sofa. An 18th-century armoire and the Art Nouveau chair harmonized the room. She would have been happy just to sit in the living room.

Once outside they were greeted by a gentle breeze off the hillside. They walked until they reached the end of the yard and stopped. All around them, it was empty, vast and open. They saw no one. Jaime felt as though they were the only two souls alive on earth. They looked on in silence.

The light from the evening sun splintered the tops of the trees that framed the yard. Beyond them, the sun shimmered on the water of a distant Evergreen lake. Along the horizon, hues of china blue skies and dull, dusty pink, white and gray clouds mixed to an even blend. The breeze picked up, shifting Leigh's hair across her forehead. She brushed it away and looked from the skyline to Jaime.

"I don't understand how anyone can live without some small place of enhancement to turn to," Leigh said in a voice that suggested she regretted disturbing the silence.

They looked on a moment more. The stillness loomed. The only sounds came from the breathing of the earth. They turned and walked toward the house. The ground was hard, then rocky, then soft.

"I want to feel the earth beneath my feet, not just concrete all the time," Leigh said in the same quiet voice.

As they reached the lawn, they passed a large marble sculpture of a lioness and her two cubs. Jaime stopped to study the work of art. The mother was licking one of the cubs along the side of the face. The other waited its turn.

"This is beautiful," Jaime said.

Leigh, her arms crossed over her body, looked on as Jaime walked around each side of the sculpture. She finally looked at Leigh.

"I know what this is. That sculptor did this work. I can't think of his name right now. But he's really famous. I read an article about him in the New York Times Magazine not too long ago. He has permanent collections all over the world."

Jaime frowned as she tried to remember the sculptor's name.

"Could you be thinking of Alan Andrew Roberts?" Leigh asked, looking from the sculpture to Jaime.

Recognition flashed in Jaime's eyes. "That's the one." She walked around the piece a second time. "Is this a replica?"

"No. It's the original."

Jaime looked at her astonished. "They must pay you really well at the Dispatch. Maybe I'm in the wrong profession. This piece had to cost five, six figures."

"I didn't have to pay a thing for it," Leigh volunteered.

"Nothing? Wait. Don't tell me. I know, you did a story on him. He liked it so well, he either gave you a good deal on it, or he gave it to you for doing the story."

"Something like that," Leigh said and there was a playful smirk on her face. She turned from the sculpture and headed for the lawn table and chairs. Jaime followed. She sat down in a chair facing Leigh.

"Actually, see that big building over there that looks like a garage, the one with the skylights."

Jaime looked to where Leigh was pointing and nodded.

"There's more work just like that in there. Most of them are the ones that didn't make the grade," Leigh said.

Jaime looked at Leigh confused. Leigh knew it.

"That used to be his studio," she said softly. "That's what he liked to call it. It's where he did all of his work for years."

"You mean Alan Andrew Roberts used to live here?" Then Jaime's face went smooth, the way it does when something suddenly becomes clear. She looked at Leigh. "Leigh Roberts ... Ashleigh Roberts ... Alan Andrew Roberts..." Jaime spoke slowly. After a moment she spoke again. "So, there's more to it than just having the same last name. Right?"

Leigh smiled as she nodded. "Drew and I were married. I've never called him Alan, not even from the first time I met him. He's only Alan to acquaintances and people he doesn't know. To anyone close to him, it's always been Drew."

Leigh looked again at the lioness and her cubs, then to Jaime. "In a way he gave me that sculpture. He named it A Mother's Love. He names all of his works with three words."

"The name fits," Jaime said, looking at the sculpture that depicted how deeply and thoroughly the lioness cared for her young.

"When he was commissioned to do it, for the right effect, he knew he had to observe a lion and her cubs. But he didn't want to watch them at a zoo. He wanted the real thing. For Drew, it was the only way. We went together. Africa's a beautiful place."

Jaime leaned forward.

"Well, I did do a story on him, so you're right in a way," Leigh went on. "That's how we met. I was a senior at Dartmouth College and editor of the literary/arts magazine. I had already read so much about him. He was just getting started then. And I knew he lived in New York. He intrigued me so I called and asked if he'd be interested in being featured in a profile for the magazine. A regional up-and-coming talent sort of article." Leigh stopped. Her expression was happy as she thought back on her first meeting with Alan Andrew Roberts.

"He said, 'depends on who's doing the article.' When I said me, he agreed. He told me later that he agreed to the interview because he liked the sound of my voice."

Leigh grew quiet as though she was thinking back to the first time they had met. "The first thing he ever said to me was 'wildlife has always been my main interest. I am fonder of it and know it better than anything else.' It's all he's ever done. He was working on a bronze sculpture of a hippopotamus at the time. It was one of the few works he ever did in bronze. He works mostly in marble."

"I've always admired his work..." Jaime hesitated. She wanted to choose her words carefully before continuing. "I take it you're not married anymore?"

"We've been divorced for years. Fourteen to be exact."

"I've read so much about him but nothing about ever having a family."

"I doubt you ever will. He's a very private person. Loves to talk about his work, but never about his private life."

"Isn't he older than you?"

"Twelve years. We met when I was twenty two. We were married in six months and Ashleigh came two years later."

Leigh looked toward the lake. The water expanded and changed from shades of blue, green, and gray depending on the setting sun's reflection and how the wind moved it. It seemed to go on forever. The breeze picked up and blew a few strands of Leigh's hair in her eyes. She brushed it aside with the sweep of her hand.

"We weren't even divorced when he left Denver. I haven't seen him since." Leigh spoke so softly that Jaime almost did not hear her.

"He lets me know from time to time he's still out there."

Leigh leaned forward and took the glass from the table. She swirled the lemon around with her finger, watching as bubbles rose to the surface. "Every so often he'll send me a photocopy of one of my columns with a comment. He lets me know whether he liked it or not. And that's how I know where he is. The last time I heard from him, the postmark said Seattle."

"Has he ever remarried?" Jaime asked.

"I'm not sure. I've never asked."

"What happened?"

"I'm not sure, really," Leigh rested the glass on the table and fell back lightly against the chair. She folded her arms across her chest, deep in thought. "We loved each other, I know. But I think we both just ended up wanting different things. There were times in the marriage when we both wanted to be married. We were so utterly happy together that I think we invented the word."

Leigh stopped for a moment. She seemed to go somewhere deep inside where Jaime could not follow. Jaime stayed silent, waiting for her to return and wondering what had become of them and their marriage.

"Then there were other times when we couldn't stand each other," she went on. "He needed his solitude most of the time, more than he needed me, or whatever it was he needed to have so he could create what it was that lived inside of him. It got to be more what was normal than not. I could not reach him no matter what I did. So I stopped trying."

"And he left you?"

"One Friday night he had a big show for a client opening that weekend in Cherry Creek. I lost track of how much time he spent working to prepare for that show. The hours were endless. We were supposed to go to a gala opening for the exhibit. Drew left home that Friday morning. Friday night he did not come home. By three o'clock Saturday afternoon I called the gallery looking for him."

Leigh's silence gave Jaime the chance to study her. Her pool blue eyes that seemed so friendly and inviting when Jaime first arrived, had turned the thick color of iron. Her energy and vitality had faded.

"Something in me knew when Drew came to the phone it was over for us. He asked if I could make it over all right without him having to come get me. I said of course. He hardly said two words to me the entire night. Of course, we put on a big front for everyone, admirers, investors, collectors, everyone, and no one knew. It was one of the hardest nights of my life, acting happy and smiling for everyone when I was falling apart inside. I went home alone that night. Later that next week, I came home from work and all his clothes and a picture he liked so much of Ashleigh were gone. He left a note on the refrigerator saying the house was mine and he wasn't sure where he was going, but he'd call."

Leigh shrugged. "He never did call. I guess he forgot. All those years summed up in a post-it note on the fridge. Ashleigh was six when her father left."

"Do you think it was because of Ashleigh?"

"What? That he left? I doubt it. That may have something to do with it, Jaime, but very little, I think. Drew loves Ashleigh deeply. He just couldn't show it in a physical way. Never could. He sends money for her all the time. I make sure she gets it and I tell her to spend it on whatever she wants."

Her smile was bittersweet. "I think it had to do more with him. He was a man who lived better alone without the world to bother him, invading on his precious, personal time. When he's alone, he creates. That's why he is what he is today. He has more money than he knows what to do with and is recognized by his work everywhere he goes."

"When did you finally hear from him?"

"About a year later I got a letter from Mexico. There was no return address. I didn't know anyone in Mexico. It was Drew. He wrote to say he'd been there since he left. He wrote that it was a good place to look out over the sea and think."

"Do you still love him?" Jaime asked

Leigh's lips became a thin line. It was the closest she could come to a smile. "Sometimes I think I do. I know I do. There are times I'll be walking through the house and the scent of him will fill the core of me. It was the way he used to smell when he had been working fervently on something."

Leigh made a tight fist with her hand as she spoke. "He'd come through the house looking for me. His body would be hot, pulsating and shimmering with sweat. Radiating with heat. All that intensity would be just surging through every vein in his body. He was like a live wire. You'd think after fourteen years I wouldn't remember those things. But it's funny what you remember. Sometimes the feeling of him is so strong I have to stop and hold onto something to steady myself."

Her last words sent them into a long silence.

"I'm sorry, Jaime, I don't know why I'm telling you this," Leigh said finally, her voice sounding weary.

Jaime's smile was reassuring. "Sometimes it's just good to talk."

"It's getting cold," Leigh said and rose from her chair. She turned on an overhead heater. "You hungry? How about some wine? I have cheese and crackers, too."

Suddenly Jaime felt starved. She hadn't eaten since noon. "Sounds great," she said, watching as Leigh disappeared into the house.

Leigh returned and put a carafe of white wine and a tray of assorted cheese and crackers on the table. She poured Jaime a glass and handed it to her.

"What about the rest of your family? Is there anyone else?" Jaime asked.

"I was an only child. My parents wanted to have more children, but after having me, the doctor told my mother it would be best if she didn't have anymore."

Jaime had asked too many personal questions and decided to let this one slide, but Leigh volunteered the reason.

"She had diabetes. She was insulin-dependent."

Leigh studied Jaime for a reaction. But the even, calm look on Jaime's face did not change.

"Do your parents live in the area?" Jaime asked.

"My father died when I was in the seventh grade. It was good and bad."

Jaime looked at her, puzzled.

"He'd been sick for a long time. It was good when he finally let go. His dying devastated my mother and me. But good things came from it. My father never let my mother do a thing. He owned a clothing store and even when he could no longer handle the affairs, he still refused to let her help. After he died, my mother had to do something. She took over the store. It was a struggle at first, but mother was a resourceful and resilient woman. I knew she'd make it."

"Is she still alive?"

"She died six years ago."

"You were close?"

"Very much. More so after my father died." She took a sip of wine and a piece of cheese and a cracker from the tray. "A good thing happened the year my father died."

"You began to write?"

She nodded. "First thing I ever wrote was a short story." Leigh laughed, almost to herself. When she did the dimple in her right cheek deepened. Jaime thought of Ashleigh. She had a dimple in the same place and when she smiled, it deepened in the same way.

"I still have that story. It's pretty bad. Mother thought it was great. She read it to everyone who came to visit. It embarrassed me terribly, but it made her happy."

Leigh had grown tired of talking about herself and shifted the spotlight to Jaime. "What about you? Still thinking about dropping 'Price' from your last name?"

Jaime's laugh did not hide her discontent about Mitchell. "What your mother said about people being made for each other, does not apply to Mitchell and me."

"What happened between you two?"

"Let's just say I came home unexpectedly and someone else was there with him, keeping my side of the bed warm." Jaime intended not to take the conversation any further. "I don't want to talk about it," she said flatly.

"What about your family?" Leigh asked. "Brothers? Sisters?"

Jaime felt an instant, empty pang in her heart. "One," she said quietly. "I had a sister."

Had.

"She's been dead about as long as your mother has."

Jaime's disposition changed instantly, darkened like a storm, deepened like distant rolling thunder.

"What happened?" Leigh asked softly.

"You got an hour?" Jaime said, half joking.

"I've got as long as you need."

Jaime didn't want to, but she told Leigh everything. They talked until their images turned to silhouettes and the air coming off the hillside had turned cold. Spring was not more than two weeks old, and the night air cooled quickly in the mountains when the sun disappeared.

Jaime finally looked at her watch. "I need to go, I've still got work to do tonight."

"Why don't you stay for dinner? I made bistro chicken with spinach. It's one of my best recipes and I'd love the company."

Jaime wanted to stay. She, too, would love the company. But she had already stayed longer than she had intended. Her plan had been to give Leigh the laptop and leave. She heard herself thanking Leigh, but refusing the offer.

Leigh walked Jaime to the door. Within minutes she was back on the interstate on her way back to Denver. The mountain air was brisk, but she was determined to leave the car windows down. Before her, daylight had long since faded. Night had begun to sweep the landscape. As she made her way toward Denver, the city and the skyscrapers were a dazzling circuit board of lights.

Jaime thought of Ashleigh.

One of those lights was hers.

Seventeen

"*I do not understand how anyone can live without some small place of enhancement to turn to.*"

Jaime had lost track of how long she had been standing and staring out from her apartment balcony. The view offered a sweeping vista of downtown Denver and just enough of the mountains looking west. But tonight with it all staring back at her, she saw nothing.

A week had passed since her trip to Evergreen. What Leigh had said while they stood at the edge of the yard stayed with her, despite what she did to push it away. When she arrived home that night, her apartment seemed different and it had not been the same since.

Jaime remembered how natural and complete Leigh looked in her home. Content to remain where she was and never leave Evergreen. Her possessions made the house her home. Everything in it and its place overlooking the hillside and Evergreen Lake played a part in making her who and what she was.

Jaime's apartment had a balcony. She had always felt happy to come home to this place. Or so she thought. Or at least until a few months ago. She listened as a low rumble of thunder faded into the distance. The rain was tapering off. Finally. It had fallen much of the last two days, leaving the city under a soggy wet blanket continuously renewed from sullen skies. The streets, shiny and slick with rain, were deserted, devoid of people. Denver's dark and sunless days had sent Jaime into a fog she could not shake.

She left the balcony and went back inside. A vase of flowers on the kitchen table caught her attention. The house had been so dull and flat over the last few days that she stopped on the way home from work to buy the cheeriest bunch of flowers she could find.

Jaime surveyed the living room. The furniture, what little of it was hers, was contemporary, with a mixture of brass and glass and the usual hi-fi equipment. Most everything in the house belonged to Mitchell. Since his departure, Jaime had expected to come home on a number of occasions to find nothing but a nail in the wall. She held her breath each time she opened the front door, expecting to see only the indentations in the beige carpet where the furniture once had been.

Her kitchen was plain and simple—the place where she spent the least amount of time. She tried to remember the last time they had eaten dinner together. Nothing came to mind.

She walked down the hallway toward the bedrooms. The spare bedroom held a queen-size bed, a small dresser and nightstand. There were no pictures on the wall and only a single small lamp sat on the nightstand near the bed. She closed the door and stood in the hallway.

Going to Evergreen made her realize she was not happy here. If she ever had. She walked toward her bedroom. She stopped at the door. She hated to go in there anymore. An unpleasant memory, a hurtful image filled her mind.

I came home early. Unexpectedly. He was in there and she was with him. Halloween really was a nightmare. No. Stop thinking about it.

She wanted to have a place like Leigh's. A place, a castle, to leave the world and everything in it behind. A place where a bad day at the office suddenly got better when she closed the front door. A new home would not erase the painful memories this place held, but it would help not to have to enter her bedroom each night.

Convalescence would have to begin somewhere.

Jaime looked around her bedroom. The furniture reminded her of a cardboard cutout—presenting a void only made deeper by the memories the room held. Was there some small place in this world where she could find enhancement? Fulfillment? A place to belong? She shook her head.

I am not happy here.

I am going to move.

I am going to find a new place.

Leigh's familiar words filtered through her muddled thoughts. *"I do not understand how anyone can live without some small place of enhancement to turn to."*

"Neither can I," Jaime said aloud, looking around the room.

She grabbed a pillow and blanket from the closet. She turned and left the bedroom, closing the door behind her.

Eighteen

Winston Ross was looking westward from his large office window when Leigh arrived at noon. A strong wind had kicked up a dusting of snow along the mountains, sending a plume of dark clouds high into the air.

He greeted her at the door. They walked toward his desk holding hands lightly.

"I spoke with Drew last week," Winston said, as he sat down on the edge of the desk facing Leigh. "He asked about you."

"When doesn't he?" Leigh said.

"He asked about Ashleigh."

Winston took a long look at Leigh. It was hard to imagine she had a 24-year-old daughter. In the fifteen years he had known her, she still looked as youthful and vibrant as the day Drew first introduced them.

Today, she looked comfortable and casual, dressed in Levi's tucked inside black leather boots. She wore a thin western-style leather belt with silver tone hardware. The black knit turtleneck she wore accentuated the darkness in her blonde hair.

Winston never knew how Leigh handled Drew's leaving. She never appeared bitter or upset about that or the divorce. She had seemingly accepted it. She married briefly a second time, but it didn't last. He had handled her divorce. He knew she dated on occasion. Mostly in spurts. She would date the same man for a brief period of time before she grew tired of the relationship and ended it. But it had been several years now since she had dated at all.

"I haven't said anything to Drew about your plans for Ashleigh. But it won't be long before it comes up in some conversation," he said.

"Why should you?"

"You know very well why."

"Drew hasn't been in her life for years, why should it be any different now?" she asked. "You know Drew is only concerned about himself. When it's convenient for him, then he worries about others. I can tell you from experience it wasn't often." Leigh began to trace an index finger along the ridge of the leather chair where she sat. When she spoke again, she directed her comments toward it. "Ashleigh is my responsibility, Winston. Not Drew's. And just like last time I was here, I didn't come to talk about what's best for Drew. I came here to talk about Ashleigh."

Winston nodded as he moved from the desk to his chair.

"Here's what we've come up with. I have a mother, who's been in your situation, coming today. She'll tell you her side of the story and what it's like." Winston leaned back in his chair and folded his hands lightly across his chest. He was silent for a moment to collect his thoughts. "What you told me about Ashleigh's medical condition strengthens our case. It may and I'm using the word, may, get the ruling you want, at least in the beginning."

Leigh raised her eyebrows slightly. Winston could tell she was interested and relieved. "That's good to hear."

He nodded. "I thought you might think so."

Winston grew quiet as he shuffled through several stacks of paper on his desk. Finding the ones he was looking for, he spread several sheets out in front of Leigh. She moved closer to the front of the desk. He spoke as she studied them.

"The medical experts I've spoken to have told me that a diabetic condition in addition to a pregnancy isn't the best combination. It's dangerous. In fact, very dangerous. It would require constant blood sugar monitoring and appropriate insulin, if needed, and proper dietary regulations. Everyone said the same thing."

They studied each other a moment.

Winston went on. "It would even be ill-advised and risky for a woman with a normal IQ and diabetes to handle a pregnancy through a full term."

Leigh responded quickly, "But Ashleigh isn't a young woman with diabetes with an average intelligence. She has an IQ of seventy-five. It doesn't matter how you look at it, Winston, Ashleigh is a young woman who has a low IQ. Oh, I know what people are going to think. Once they read about this in the newspaper, I'll be the old witch. I can hear them now, 'Oh, she's just worried her daughter will become pregnant, have the kid and she'll be the one who ends up taking care of it. Why, she's just a cruel, heartless bitch wanting to do such a horrible, unthinkable thing to her daughter."

Her voice was mocking. She looked unmercifully at Winston, her blue eyes icy, narrowed slits. Leigh pushed herself up from the chair and walked around it. She rested her hands on top of the chair and squeezed it until there were indentations in the leather.

When she spoke, moments later, her voice had softened. "Well, they can say whatever they want. I really don't care. The bottom line is pregnancy could and almost certainly will kill Ashleigh. Her health is already fragile. And I won't have it."

Winston tried to read the look in her eyes, but they were unreadable.

"You don't know if that'll ever happen," he said quietly.

"What if it does? I have to think like that because I know Ashleigh won't. Ashleigh would need constant supervision. And then there's the risk the baby would be born prematurely, or have other complications or problems because of the diabetes. People on the outside with all their politically correct ideals, they don't have to live with it. They won't be the ones visiting her grave every day for the rest of their lives."

Leigh could feel herself beginning to ramble, but she couldn't help it. She glanced quickly at Winston. He was a captive audience, focusing intently on her. "Don't you think I want my daughter to have a normal, healthy life? Do you think I want to be sitting in this office contemplating a decision that would destroy a part of her social and biological identity? Don't you think I want Ashleigh to have a long, happy life filled with love and the good things it has to offer? Don't you think I want Ashleigh to have a husband, children and a nice home? I've watched Ashleigh around younger children. I know how she is. She'd be a wonderful mother, but at what cost? Her life…"

Her voice trailed. It was agony for her to say such things about her daughter.

To realize the reality of it.

Leigh continued, now quietly and firmly. "She has a love within her I've never seen or experienced in anyone else. It's the kind of love that children desperately need. Children, hell, we all need it. Don't you think I ache for Ashleigh to be able to give that love freely to her children? I do, Winston, more than anything else in this world."

Leigh stopped. She laughed quietly to herself. She shook her head slowly. "Maybe that's old fashioned. But how else can I say it? It's what I've wanted for Ashleigh from the very beginning, to give her love. She has so much of it and it's so deep."

Leigh stopped to study Winston. She sighed heavily.

"Leigh, come and sit down."

Leigh returned to the chair and rested her head against the palm of her hand. She was depleted. Wounded and drained by what she had laid on the table before him. She sat in silence, waiting for her strength to return.

"I'm not a fool," she said and her voice was weary.

"I know. I know," Winston said.

The angry look in her eyes faded and Winston noticed something else in them. They seemed to harbor sorrow. What she had just finished saying surprised him. He knew Leigh must love Ashleigh. Yet, a part of him had never been totally convinced. He had heard it often before in her words, but saw little in her actions. It appeared she took her responsibilities as a mother as though they had been assigned to her at random, as though it was a duty she had to fulfill until the allotted time was completed. It seemed she accepted those responsibilities begrudgingly. As though they were expected of her, not because she wanted them.

As he listened to Leigh now, he was beginning to see her in a different light. For the first time, he started to think his ideas were wrong. Leigh loved and cared for Ashleigh very much. He saw that now and felt ashamed for the way he thought. It was Winston who was the fool. His gaze stayed on Leigh and grew soft. He hesitated to speak, as if to select his words.

"Leigh, I may have to question Ashleigh when she gets on the witness stand. You won't like what you'll hear. I'm telling you now, so you will know."

She looked at Winston and blinked several times, as though this was something she had not considered. She wasn't sure she liked the idea, but she had to trust that he would not intentionally hurt Ashleigh. She cleared her throat before she spoke.

"I understand," she said.

A soft, almost hesitant knock came at the door. Winston's secretary poked her head inside the room. She smiled quickly at Leigh, then looked to Winston.

"Mr. Ross, there's a Maryanne Lash here to see you."

Winston nodded and said, "Make her comfortable and I'll bring her in after a few minutes. Thanks."

The secretary nodded and closed the door.

"That's the woman I was telling you about," Winston said. "Do you need a few minutes before I bring her in?"

Leigh shook her head.

He rose from the chair and left the office without another word. He returned several minutes later followed by a thickly set woman wearing a dark brown dress that stopped just below her knees. She was plump with a round, pudgy face, rosy cheeks and curly gray hair. Maryanne Lash had a wide, happy grin on her face. She offered her hand and greeted Leigh with a respectful hello. Leigh extended hers and the woman took it. She continued to shake Leigh's hand as she spoke.

"You write wonderfully," she said looking at Leigh politely with large eyes that were more hazel than green. "I read your columns whenever I can. I can't afford to buy the paper often, but I enjoy reading it. When I can buy it, I check to see if your column is inside first. And then if it is, I buy it. If not, I don't."

Leigh smiled, somewhat embarrassed, but grateful to receive such praise. "That's very flattering, Mrs. Lash. Thank you."

"Oh, call me Maryanne." She had a sweet voice and an almost apologetic laugh.

"Thank you, Maryanne."

"Maryanne, why don't you sit next to Leigh," Winston said, gesturing toward the empty chair.

"All right."

An awkward silence filled the room momentarily as Winston returned to his chair.

"Thanks so much for coming, Mrs. Lash," Winston said. "I appreciate your giving us some of your time today. I hope it wasn't too much of a bother for you to come all the way downtown."

Maryanne looked at her dress. She smoothed out the material as though it was wrinkled. "Oh, really, it's no bother," she said. "In fact, I wanted to come. I need to get out of the house a little more often. Now that Jody has moved, there's no one there but me and it sure gets empty sometimes." She stopped and began directing her comments to Leigh. "I took the RTD. It lets me off just a few blocks from here and all I had to do was walk a little ways. I enjoy riding the bus. Always have. Isn't that silly?"

Leigh smiled, searching for something to say. "Some people do," she said. "It's the easiest way to get around the city."

Maryanne returned her attention to Winston and waited for him to speak.

Winston took the cue. "Mrs. Lash, I thought you could start by telling Leigh a little about Jody and your husband."

Maryanne Lash's disposition clouded over almost at once. "My husband left Jody and me thirteen years ago. He said he just didn't want to live with a handicapped child anymore," she said. "I can tell you it was pretty tough for a while after that. Raising her and all. He never sent us a dime. I finally got Jody into a group home in February and now it's just been me at home for a little over a month now. I didn't really want to put my Jody in a group home, but common sense told me the time was now."

She smiled quickly at Leigh. "And I'm not getting any younger, you know. I turned the double nickel last month. Besides, if I would've passed on this opportunity to place Jody, the Lord only knows when I would've gotten another one. Cost was a factor, you know. Anyway, I know a woman who's been waiting to get her daughter into a group home for almost eight years. I miss having my Jody at home, but I'm determined to get used to it."

"Jody had been on a waiting list for six years to get into a group home before an opening finally came," Winston said looking from Maryanne to Leigh.

"I had a hard time making up my mind to let go and put her in there. But six years is a long time and I didn't want to wait any longer. And I have a lot of health problems. Always had."

"What is your daughter's IQ?" Leigh asked.

"About thirty, I guess. She functions at a three-year-old level on some things and a five-year-old on others," Maryanne said. She studied Leigh for a moment. "And your daughter?"

"She's been tested at seventy, seventy-five."

"Oh, my, you're lucky. She can do so much for herself and by herself."

Leigh nodded. "Yes, she can."

"Maryanne didn't have to go to court to have her daughter sterilized," Winston said, glancing at Leigh. She nodded thoughtfully.

"It was easy for me and I sure was lucky, I guess, to have the doctor I did. Jody was twenty-one when her doctor did her surgery. He said he didn't see any sense in having Jody go around and run the risk of getting pregnant."

"Why did you have the procedure done, Mrs. Lash?" Leigh asked.

"I noticed the older Jody got the more aggressive toward men she became. Kissing and hugging and climbing all over them. First time I saw her we were at a picnic and I nearly fell out of my chair! Shocked me to death!"

Leigh tried to suppress a laugh using a hand to cover the grin that had crept over her face. She glanced to Winston, but the gaze behind his glasses was unwavering.

"'Course she doesn't know the difference, but who knows how

they'll react to her when she starts huggin' them like that? I don't think she had any idea what she was doing, but I couldn't let it go on. All she had to do was get with the wrong guy and who knows what would've happened next. I tried other measures before going that route."

Leigh leaned forward. "What, for example?"

"Every kind of birth control imaginable. But that was a disaster."

"How come?" Leigh asked.

"Well, Jody didn't understand how the devices worked or how to use them. What's more, my Jody doesn't understand that sexual intercourse means she could get pregnant. And I know my daughter. There's not a doubt in my mind, she could not be an adequate parent for any child when she still has the mind of a child herself." Maryanne stopped for a moment and look around the office. "Could I get a glass of water, please? My throat's so dry," she said, patting it.

Winston immediately left his chair and went to a small wet bar across the room. He returned with a tall glass filled with water and ice. He handed it to Maryanne. She took several quick swallows.

"Thank you. Oh, my, that's much better. Anyway, that leaves just me. But like I said, at my age and with my health problems, I'm in no condition to be a mother again and raise a child. Oh, I've wanted grandchildren, for sure. Love my sister's grandchildren to death. But never under these conditions would I consider it with Jody."

She took another swallow and looked from Winston to Leigh. "Of course, they tell me that women with a mental disability like Jody probably couldn't get pregnant anyway, but who's going to take that chance?"

Maryanne went on to tell Leigh she felt lucky in some ways. Life was hard raising a handicapped child. Constantly demanding. At least her doctor didn't refuse to do Jody's operation.

"Thank goodness. If I had to go your way, I don't know where I would've come up with the money to pay the lawyer fees and all," Maryanne said, looking directly at Winston.

He smiled calmly at her.

"You know, sometimes I find myself wondering if I did the right thing, especially at night when it's quiet and when the house gets so still. I know I feel a lot better about Jody being in a group home now than I would've before she had the operation."

Winston leaned forward and rested his elbows on his desk. "Do you think she's happier for having the surgery, Mrs. Lash?"

She thought a moment before answering. "I've often thought about that. I do think she's happier for it. I used to never let that child out of my sight ... Now it's easier. There's something else I always think about when the house is so empty and quiet."

"What's that, Mrs. Lash?" Leigh asked, leaning closer to Maryanne.

Leigh felt a sudden sadness for this woman. She seemed terribly alone now, as she probably always had been. Now with Jody gone, her loneliness had magnified, becoming more pronounced as if it pressed itself against her. Leigh could not help wondering how burdensome it was for Maryanne to make such a decision without some kind of guidance. She smiled gently at her.

"I know Jody does not know now, or will she ever know enough to choose between having children, or not having children. It hurts me sometimes when I think about it. But I've always thought of myself as being a very realistic person. I've accepted the way Jody is and will always be."

The room fell silent as Maryanne took another sip of water.

"Do you feel like you've done the right thing?" Winston asked.

"Yes." Maryanne replied without hesitation, but kept her attention focused on the water left in her glass.

"No regrets?" he asked.

"None," she said.

After Winston walked Maryanne from his office, he returned to find Leigh sitting, resting her head against the tips of her fingers.

"Are you all right?" he asked.

Leigh looked up and smiled briefly at him. "I'm fine. Thanks."

Winston rested a hand gently over her shoulder. "She's a strong woman."

"Yes. Yes, she really is." Leigh took a shallow breath. "Sometimes when my house is quiet and empty, I wonder if I did the right thing."

"By putting Ashleigh in a group home when you did?"

"She was only twelve then, Winston."

"Yes, I know," he said.

"Did I do the right thing?"

"Did you think then, at the time, it was the right thing?" he asked.

"Yes."

"Then you've answered your own question."

Leigh retreated somewhere deep inside. Then she blinked several times as though she were trying to clear a memory and return to the present. She glanced at her watch.

"It's late. I've got to get back to the office. I've still got a story to file."

She stood. Winston took her hands and held them lightly. They were limp in his. He felt her weariness. Her frustration.

"Thank you, Winston," she said. "I'll be in touch."

When she reached the door, he called out to her. She stopped. Framed in the doorway, she turned to him. He was still standing near her chair, resting a hand lightly on top. Their eyes met. She waited for him to speak.

"You're not cruel. You're not heartless. And you're not a bitch."

NINETEEN

From Walker & Associates, Jaime walked to the 16th Street Mall, and took the shuttle to the Tabor Center, planning to watch Ashleigh work. She had been employed at the food court for a month, enough time to become familiar with her work and the surroundings. Ashleigh did not know she was coming.

It was Saturday. Jaime had been at the health club by 7 a.m. before heading to the office, where she had spent the last few hours doing paperwork. It was noon and her stomach was growling.

She went to the food court on the second floor, brightly lit by the late morning sun streaming in through windowed walls and ceilings. She took the time to walk around to get the feel of the atmosphere and how the place looked. The food court occupied the entire floor, and there were plenty of places to eat. Tables and chairs were situated closely together. Numerous plants of all sizes and shapes gave the large room a fresh, healthy look.

Jaime surveyed a bedlam of people in line, ordering from menus above their heads and carrying trays to open tables. Everywhere she looked bobbing heads filled her vision. Yet it took her only a moment to spot Ashleigh with her familiar gait, moving easily through the crowd and between tables and chairs. Ashleigh had a gray dishtowel in one hand. She carried a red plastic tray in her other hand as though it were a book.

Despite the look of determination on Ashleigh's face, her lips were traced in a smile. Her eyes were wide and curious under the burgundy visor she wore and seemed to be regarding everything and everyone. Her hair was pulled back from her face. Some strands had pulled away from the rubber tie and had fallen loosely about her shirt collar. Jaime saw Ashleigh's wristwatch and couldn't help the smile that spread over her face.

Ashleigh looked natural and at ease as she moved quietly about her setting. She wore a white short-sleeved cotton top, tan chinos and clean white tennis shoes. A burgundy apron covered her shirt, stopping at her knees. The name Tabor Center Food Court was written in white script on the front of her apron.

From a distance, Jaime watched Ashleigh put the tray in a holder above a wastebasket. She put her hands on her hips and looked around. She watched as a family of four finished their meal and left the table without clearing it. Ashleigh waited until they left the area and then cleaned it immediately. She took the empty glasses and dishes and stacked them on one of the trays. Carefully, she set the tray on a chair. She took the squirt bottle she had clipped to her apron pocket, and sprayed the table with water. She cleaned the table, then the chairs. She brought the trash to the waste basket.

Watching Ashleigh work gave Jaime hope. Those in the food court did not realize she was there, it was as though she had become part of the furniture, another employee.

Jaime could no longer ignore her hunger. She wanted Ashleigh to spot her and selected a table in her section. She bought a Caesar salad and found a table near a window that overlooked the 16th Street Mall. Street corners were thick with people. Since the street was closed to other traffic, only shuttle buses and an occasional police cruiser went up and down the roadway.

"Jaime! What're you doing here?"

Ashleigh pulled Jaime's attention from the window. She returned the wide, bright smile Ashleigh was giving her.

"Hi, Ashleigh. I came to watch to you work."

"Have you been here a long time?"

"About an hour."

"How'd I do?"

"You're doing great. The place keeps you busy, doesn't it?"

"Yeah, but I like it. I like bein' busy. It makes me feel like I'm workin' hard."

Jaime nodded. "You have been. You've hardly stopped since I came."

Ashleigh studied her watch, trying to determine the time.

"Let's see, it looks like it's almost two o'clock. Is that right?"

Ashleigh held out her wrist and Jaime looked and nodded.

"That's means I get off in one more hour."

"Then I'll wait for you here and we'll leave together."

Jaime finished her lunch and waited for Ashleigh. It was 3:30 p.m. before she was ready to go. On the way out, they passed in front of a sporting goods store. The window display advertised a sale on tennis racquets. Jaime stopped a moment to look. There was a Prince racquet on the other side of the glass. Sarah had used Prince equipment. She had tried all the others, Wilson, Head, Yonex, but Prince was her favorite.

Ashleigh was tapping lightly on Jaime's arm, pulling her away from her thoughts.

"Are you okay?" Ashleigh asked, eyeing Jaime with innocent curiosity.

She smiled and nodded. "I'm fine, Ashleigh, just a little distracted. Let's go."

They left the building in silence and walked until they reached Broadway where Ashleigh would take the bus back to Morningside Heights.

"Are you sure you don't want me to drive you home?" Jaime asked.

Ashleigh shook her head. "I like taking the bus. I've been taking it since I started. I used to ride a van from the workshop every day. Now I take the bus. It almost stops right in front of my house. I just have to walk up the street."

Ashleigh's bus arrived a few minutes later. She waved at Jaime as she boarded the bus and found a seat near the back. By the time Jaime arrived at her apartment, a smooth band of thin, gray clouds had covered the sky, casting the city into a premature darkness. She stared unseeing out the apartment window in her living room. Minutes passed before the weather and her view of the city came into focus. The sun that had been shining brightly earlier was gone, taking with it the warmth. The gray skies and naked trees made winter seem real again. The sheer walls of the tall brick, stone and glass buildings that lined the streets only enhanced the cold, gray color.

She thought about the Prince tennis racquet on sale at the Tabor Center. And of Sarah. Suddenly Jaime missed her sister so deeply, she shivered involuntarily. Jaime was nine when she picked up a tennis racquet for the first time. Sarah was almost five. They had been on courts near their home when their father began hitting tennis balls to Jaime. From outside the chain link fence, Sarah watched with an immediate and intense interest.

Her father began to hit Sarah tennis balls. It was as though the little girl had played forever. Her movements were smooth, natural and effortless, the way the sun moves over the landscape. John Monroe would later tell their mother if he had not witnessed Sarah hitting the tennis ball so well and effortlessly, he would not have believed it was their daughter. From then on, Sarah became the focus of the family.

The more Sarah played, the better she became. Jaime was her support. When she was playing well, Jaime's encouragement helped her to maintain her level of play. When she had difficulty finding her rhythm and her pace, Jaime helped her get back on course. It was a role she had played well and settled into with ease.

But that was a long, long time ago. Too long to seem real anymore.

TWENTY

Erin Greene had finished arranging folding chairs into a semicircle when Jaime and Tia entered the living room at Morningside Heights.

"Hi. Over here," Erin said, waving a hand in their direction.

The three women greeted each other as they shook hands.

"Erin, I'm Jaime Monroe and this is Tia Ranch," Jaime said, glancing in Tia's direction.

"Good to finally meet you," Tia said, as she nodded, taking Erin's hands.

"Thanks for allowing us to come tonight," Jaime said.

"We're happy to have you," Erin said. "When Pearl called and said you'd like to attend one of our parenting sessions for our mothers here at Morningside, Bennet May, he's Ashleigh's case manager, and I were thrilled you wanted to come."

Erin grinned, but not broadly, in a way that would draw one to her. Jaime guessed Erin was in her early forties. Wispy streaks of gray ran through her brown hair. It was thick and short, curling naturally about her round face. Brown eyes were framed behind a large pair of round red-rimmed glasses that rested on a small, pug nose. Her nose looked red and sore, as though she had a cold.

A beige pantsuit hung unceremoniously on her slender frame and she wore sensible brown loafers. Jaime and Tia had come straight from work. They wore tailored jackets and skirts with matching heels. Tia's suit was olive-green and Jaime's, a navy-blue pinstripe.

"I thought Pearl Priestly said she'd be coming with you?" Erin said.

"She is," Jaime replied. "But she'll be late."

"Ashleigh so enjoyed meeting Pearl when she was kind enough to come out to meet her. I hope I have Pearl's energy and enthusiasm when I'm her age! Goodness!" Erin said. Another grin revealed a set of small white teeth.

Erin started back toward the semi-circle of chairs. "Come on, if you ladies don't mind, you can give me a hand and we'll finish setting up."

The room also doubled as the kitchen. It was plain and dark paneling covered the walls. With the exception of the usual kitchen appliances and a window along the kitchen table that held enough chairs for eight people, the large room held little else.

"Our mothers learn a lot from these parenting classes," Erin said. "We tell them everything that a mother could possibly face when raising her children. Bennet and I call it the 'Everything You Wanted to Know About Being a Parent but Were Afraid to Ask Your Mom, Dad, Aunt, Uncle and Grandparents' class."

Erin seemed amused by the unofficial title.

"But seriously," she went on, "'Understanding Parenthood' is an intensive class. What the mothers learn here is crucial in the care of their babies. Do either of you have kids?" She looked from Jaime to Tia.

Tia touched her hand lightly to her chest. "I do. Boys. Eight and ten."

"I bet they're a handful," Erin said.

"I can vouch for that," Jaime added quickly.

"Tell us about the class, Erin," Tia said.

"It's a hands-on, twelve-week course. The mothers come here once a week."

"Do the mothers also work?" Jaime asked.

"Oh, yes and they're all married, too, except for one. Three of them clean office buildings and one works with Ashleigh at the food court," Erin said.

"What do they learn in class?" Tia asked.

"Well, everything, everything we can teach them," Erin said. "We show them how to tell if their babies are hungry and what to feed them at the different stages of infancy. One of the mothers wanted to give her son, he's barely six months old, a bite of her pepperoni pizza the other night. We tell them that's a no-no. We also teach them how to tell if their baby is sick and whether the little one needs medical care."

"Sounds pretty comprehensive," Tia said.

"We hope so," Erin said. "We also teach the mothers the kinds of games to play with their children that will keep them stimulated. And we teach safety. Of course, nothing takes the place of experience. But the mothers have to learn that on their own, just as any mother would. Here, we give them the basics and supervision. And over time, they'll catch on."

"Do they learn?" Tia asked.

"You bet they do," Erin said, nodding her head. "They're not any different than any other mother, Tia. They don't want to lose that child any more than you would want to lose your boys."

The mothers began to file in and helped to finish setting up. Erin was putting new chalk in the chalkboard holder when she saw a tall, lanky woman enter the room. Erin noticed Jaime and Tia also watching her.

"That's Joy. She works with Ashleigh. She's twenty-four and the mother of a healthy 15-month-old son named Peter. Cute little thing. Happy. Oh, I've never seen a child look so happy. He coos and giggles every time you pick him up. He's such a delight to have around. Joy is getting so good at handling him now, too. She's a single mom, but I have no doubt she'll be a good mother."

Joy walked across the room and stopped just short of the chairs and the women, seeming uncertain whether to go further. Erin's smile encouraged Joy to join them.

"Come on, Joy," she said. "These are the women I told you were coming to class tonight."

Joy smiled widely when Erin introduced her.

"Joy, tell these ladies about Peter."

"He's mine."

Laughter filled the room like falling coins.

"Erin tells me that I'm good with Peter," Joy went on. "Because when I lived at home, I used to baby-sit kids littler than me all the time. Except they always went back home. When I first had Peter, I kept thinking he'd be going back home somewhere else. Then Erin told me that his home was with me, so I didn't look for him to leave no more."

Erin smiled and exchanged glances with Tia and Jaime. "I told her that wherever she went from now on, that most of the time, Peter would go, too."

Three more mothers entered the room and Erin introduced Jaime and Tia to everyone. Jaime watched as Bennet May followed them in and closed the door. Bennet was a stocky man of medium height with a full head of thick reddish-orange hair. His heavy beard was a shade darker than his hair.

"Okay, ladies," Erin said, clapping her hands lightly. "We're all here so let's get started. We've got a lot to cover tonight."

Within minutes, the room had grown quiet.

"First, let's review a little from last week," Bennet said in a soft-spoken voice.

He looked at each of the young mothers. "Who remembers what happened last week?"

Alice, a 25-year-old mother who had given birth to a son ten months ago, raised her hand. She had skin the color of creamed tea.

Bennet acknowledged her with a nod. "Go ahead, Alice."

"My baby threw up."

"Tell the class and these ladies what made Joseph so sick, Alice. Do you remember?" he asked.

Alice nodded. "Well, his formula wouldn't stay down. I just kept giving him more and more hoping he'd keep some of the food down. But it kept coming up and he just kept crying and he was so hot. Touching him was like fire. But comin' here helped me to know what I was doing wrong..."

Alice looked at Jaime and then the others. "Joseph's much better now."

Erin leaned over and whispered to Tia and Jaime. "Joseph was having an allergic reaction to his baby formula. But until this class, Alice didn't know that someone who has a fever meant a sign of some kind of illness. She thought if she gave him more formula, some might stay down. She's come a long way and I'm proud of her."

Everyone looked over their shoulder as the door opened. It was Pearl. She slipped in silently and nodded quietly to acknowledge everyone. Not bothering to take off her long, tweed coat, she took the chair next to Tia.

When Bennet finished the review of last week's session, Erin took over and the discussion switched to bathroom safety.

"All right, ladies, here's an example, let's say you're giving your child a bath and the telephone rings…" Erin stopped and glanced around the group, their rapt attention on her. "What do you do?"

"You go answer the phone and see who it is," Kathy, a 22-year-old mother with a one-year-old son, answered quickly and with confidence.

Erin raised her eyebrows and inhaled deeply. She shook her head slowly, looking devastated. She removed her glasses and slowly cleaned them with a tissue she had pulled from her pocket.

Christine, a heavy-set, pear-shaped woman, laughed out loud. "No sir, Kathy, you silly fool! That's not right!" she said. "You never, never, never leave your baby alone in the tub, not to answer the phone, the doorbell, or nothin'!"

"You can too answer the phone, if you got one of them cordless ones! You can take those things anywhere. They're cool!" Joy interjected.

Erin looked at Christine. She was twenty-five with an 18-month-old daughter. "Christine, you told Bennet and me that you've learned a lot from these classes. But what did you know before coming here about giving your daughter a bath?"

Christine looked intently from Jaime and Tia to Pearl. With the spotlight beaming on her, her assertiveness faded. She seemed to shrink in her chair. Christine looked down at her hands and began to fold and unfold them nervously. She cleared her throat several times before she could speak.

"Well, at least I knew that I was supposed to keep her little head out of the water, or she'd drown," she said.

Her voice was so low and soft everyone had to lean forward to hear her.

"That wasn't the case for one mother who was here last year," Pearl said speaking softly to Tia and Jaime, as the discussion continued around them. "Erin told me that one mother had put her youngest daughter in the bathtub. The radio was playing and her favorite song came on and she left the bathroom to turn up the volume. She forgot about her baby in the tub. The television was also on in the same room and she apparently got distracted watching it."

Tia looked wide-eyed at Pearl. "Oh, my God. What happened?"

"The baby drowned. Now the mother's parents have custody of the other two children," Pearl said.

"Oh, Lord, what a tragedy," Tia said, shaking her head.

As Bennet continued teaching, Erin and Jaime left the group and walked to a table with cookies and coffee.

"The class seems helpful for the mothers," Jaime said as they walked.

Erin nodded. "It is. We also have an extensive sex education awareness class they've all gone through."

"Has Ashleigh been through it yet?" Jaime asked.

Erin shook her head. "She's taking the next session."

"What about Leigh? Has she attended the class in anticipation of Ashleigh attending?"

"Oh yes," Erin said. "Leigh has always been very much involved in everything that concerns her daughter and she's very active with all the activities here. She's always been a great volunteer. Ashleigh does spend holidays with her mother, but Leigh's always here to help decorate before the holiday."

"What about a boyfriend, Erin? Ashleigh says she's not interested."

"She's not. What's important to Ashleigh right now is her new job and eventually having a place of her own. She's very determined about that, Jaime. She has priorities just as we do. Someday maybe, she'll be interested in boys, but not now."

They walked in silence for a moment.

"It's wonderful you're going to take Ashleigh's case, Jaime. I can't believe you left the DA's office to do it."

Jaime's smile and a slight shrug were her response.

"Ashleigh will be leaving us soon," Erin went on. "And going to live in a more independent setting. She's ready for it and she's excited."

"I know. She talks about it every time we get together."

"It'll be the best thing for her. It can only help. Like her working with Joy at the food court. I've already noticed a big change in her. And so has Bennet."

They reached the table and Erin poured coffee into white Styrofoam cups.

"Cream or sugar?" she asked handing a cup to Jaime.

Jaime shook her head and she took a small sip.

Erin said, "You know, a lot of times the chance for people like Ashleigh to get out in the community is the best thing to happen to them. They begin to blossom and Ashleigh really has. I knew she had outgrown her job at the workshop. She can do more than stuff sport bags. For some, it's the only work they can do.

"Don't get me wrong, it sure beats staying at home sitting on the sofa staring at the tube all day, but it's all they'll ever be able to do. Now with those like Ashleigh, working in a sheltered setting is a good place to start. But once they get the experience they're ready for other things. Ashleigh was ready."

Erin put cream and two teaspoons of sugar in her coffee and began to stir. "When the contract came through for the food court, I told Bennet I wanted Ashleigh on that list. He agreed just as I did. He thought it would be the best thing for her..." Erin stopped to eye the cookies before she took a chocolate one. "For some, working in the community is a disaster. It's definitely the wrong thing for them. They just can't handle the added stress and really shy away. But for people like Ashleigh, it's just what the doctor ordered. Getting out to experience what everyday life is like is the best thing for them."

"Like learning how to take the bus," Jaime said.

"Exactly. When Ashleigh worked at the workshop, she rode the same blue van. It picked her up here at the group home the same time every morning and took her to work. She didn't have to think about anything. Everything was done for her. Now riding the bus forces her to have some independence."

Erin thought a moment before she continued. "Just like when

Ashleigh first came to see you, Jaime. She insisted on going alone." Erin put her hand against her chest. "I wanted to go with her so badly I could hardly stand it. But it was something Ashleigh had to do on her own. I knew she had to start sometime and it might as well have been then."

Erin smiled. But Jaime noticed it was not the bright, cheery smile she had been using during the parenting class. It seemed to take effort and held more sadness than joy.

"Ashleigh's been living here almost twelve years," Erin said quietly. "I came just a month before she did. Sometimes I feel like I've raised her like my own. I almost couldn't handle the thought of her getting on that bus alone to come see you, but she insisted."

"She did a marvelous job," Jaime said.

There were tears in Erin's eyes she immediately blinked away. She nodded quickly, clearing her throat. "Yes, she did."

They looked toward the group in silence, watching Bennet gesture with his hands as he spoke to the women.

"What exactly are Ashleigh's abilities to reason and to understand?" Jaime asked.

"You mean how competent is she?"

Jaime looked from the group to Erin. "I appreciate your directness. Yes, how competent is she?"

Erin pushed her glasses up on her nose and finished the last of her cookie. "Ashleigh's disability is considered mild."

Jaime nodded. "That much I know. But before Ashleigh and Kelly Jo, I didn't know anyone with a mental disability. I'm probably like many people when it comes to that. When you think of it, you think of people who can't do a thing for themselves. Meeting Ashleigh was a pleasant surprise."

Erin's laugh sounded as tinny as a wind-up toy machine. "That's the way I was," she said. "And people are surprised for the most part when it comes to learning about types of mental retardation. We fear and are uncomfortable around the unknown. Especially around people who have some type of a mental disability."

Erin looked into her coffee cup, mesmerized. "Have you ever gone into a restaurant and a family comes and someone in the group has some type of mental obstacle or a noticeable disability? You do what's natural.

You stare. You don't mean to, but you can't help it. You just stare. So, should the family hide at home and not go out because they have a child who has some type of a delay?"

"How do you get beyond that?" Jaime asked.

"By looking beyond the person's handicap," Erin said. "Because there really is a person inside. They have feelings, too. They feel happiness and sadness. Don't think for a moment just because some can't express themselves, they don't have feelings. What we need to do as non-handicapped people is look deeper. And we need to learn to just be ourselves."

Erin turned to the table for another chocolate cookie. She took a bite of it before she spoke. "Anyway, back to Ashleigh. Part of the concern comes from the lack of understanding. Just like the rest of us, people with some type of mental retardation continue to develop mentally and physically as they grow. On a cognitive level, however, that's where the difference begins. Their thinking and reasoning skills differ. They become much slower than people with an average intelligence. And the ability to think logically decreases with the severity of the disability." Erin sipped from her coffee cup. "But someone like Ashleigh has the reasoning ability of a ten or twelve year old."

Jaime looked with Erin at the group. The four mothers, each of their heads in a jaunty tilt to one side and holding their babies, listened as Bennet spoke.

"If anyone walked in this room right now and saw that, they'd think they were normal," Erin said, keeping her eyes on the group. She shifted her attention to Jaime. "No one ever said the rites to motherhood were an easy path to follow, Jaime, even for the best mothers. And for people like Joy, Kathy and Alice and Christine, motherhood is like working a puzzle, more like a thousand-piece puzzle. They just have to keep trying for the right piece."

Erin turned and patted Jaime gently on the forearm. She went on. "But that doesn't mean they don't want to try and do what's best for their child. Take Joy as an example. When she first came here, she couldn't even read something like See Spot Run. When she learned she was pregnant with Peter she told me "pretty soon Peter will know how to read and who's gonna read to him? I'd better learn to read so it can be me. I want to read him a nursery rhyme."

"What happened?" Jaime asked.

"We got her working with a literacy volunteer. By the time Peter is old enough to read, Joy will be able to read Mother Goose to her son. But I've lost track of how many times we've had that bathroom discussion. And I can tell you we'll have it over and over."

Erin studied the group a minute longer. "In some ways they can make the best mothers, and in others, you can't leave them alone for a second."

"What makes Ashleigh a good candidate to work at the food court?"

Erin set her coffee cup on the table. "There are two main categories people with moderate and mild mental retardation fall into, trainable and educable. But thankfully those classifications are no longer used." Erin touched Jaime lightly on the arm. "And it's about time. Anyway, so you can have an idea, the classification system is based on intelligence quotients and relates, but does not conform precisely, to the scheme advocated by the American Association of Mental Deficiency. Ashleigh's considered educable."

Erin used her fingers to put the word "educable" in quotations. "This means those who are educable have IQ's between about fifty and seventy-five. Ashleigh's is around seventy-five."

"How does that differ from..." Jaime's voice trailed off, she had forgotten the word. Erin finished her sentence.

"Trainable? Or TMR as we like to say. Well, those who are considered trainable have IQ's between twenty-five and fifty-five. And for EMR, or educable, individuals, they typically are able to achieve academic work to at least a third-grade level. By the end of their education, at age twenty-one, in a public school setting, some can do work at about a sixth-grade level. That's Ashleigh's level.

"What about those considered trainable?" Jaime asked.

"TMR people typically do not achieve very useful academic skills. In school, they are taught basic living skills mostly, how to set the table and how to wash clothes, and good work habits, good communication and social skills, cleanliness, health and good eating and leisure behaviors."

"Ashleigh's been here since she was twelve. That seems so young," Jaime said.

"Oh, heavens, that's not unusual at all, given the extensive waiting lists to get into places like this. In fact, the waiting lists for all types of services for the handicapped have become atrocious. Don't look at Leigh Roberts as the bad, heartless mother, Jaime. She did the right thing. It's only part of many reasons why she put Ashleigh in so young. Many mothers with children like Ashleigh do the same thing."

Erin turned her attention to the group. "Oh, looks like they're through," she said, watching as everyone began to collect the chairs.

A few moments later, Tia and Pearl joined Jaime and Erin.

"That was a wonderful class, Erin," Pearl said. "Those young mothers are so lucky they can have a place like this to come and learn."

Erin thanked Pearl and then invited her and Tia to help themselves to the coffee and cookies. Favorites for both, they each poured coffee and took two cookies.

They left the group home and walked out into an early spring evening with Jaime feeling happy. Spring had a way of doing that to her. Jaime and Tia refused Pearl's invitation for Italian food. Tia had to get her sons and Jaime was meeting Frank to box.

At the club, Scott McIntyre pushed Jaime hard while they waited for Frank. He made her run two miles of interval training—sprint then jog, sprint then jog. She put on her boxing gloves and started to hit the heavy bag. Scott braced himself against the far side of the bag to steady it as she let go with a barrage of left-right combinations.

"You OK?" Scott asked as she stopped and stepped away from the bag.

She nodded, too out of breath to speak.

"Look here," he said, pointing at the bag. "You're getting better. You can see the dent in the bag where you've hit it right."

Jaime smiled broadly and wiped her forehead. She had just finished her work out and was ready to leave when Frank finally showed, an hour late. She eyed him skeptically. But she didn't ask why he was late, or where he had been. She did not want to know.

Jaime also refused Frank's offer for dinner. She just wanted to go home. As she put the key into the lock of her apartment door, she found Ashleigh and Sarah in her thoughts. The workout left her muscles as loose as rubber bands. She felt weak from hunger. She settled on a banana and a handful of almonds. She would fix something later. She went through the mail, but nothing interested her enough to open it. She threw the junk mail and sale catalogs in the trash and put the rest on the table.

She went to the bathroom and turned on the shower. She went back to the bedroom to undress. She frowned at the sight of some of her laundry, several bras, panties and pairs of sport socks, out on the bed. She put her hands on her hips and looked from the bed to the dresser, absolutely certain she had folded and put the clothes away the night before. She shook her head and grabbed the lingerie and socks and put them away.

As she undressed, the picture on the nightstand of Sarah hitting a tennis ball caught her attention. She picked it up and ran a finger along the frame.

Thoughts shifted like clouds ...

"Mom? Dad?" Sarah called to them from the kitchen doorway.

They had finished dinner and were sitting at the table. They looked at Sarah, startled.

"Did you change your mind about dinner, dear?" Nora asked.

"Yeah. I'd like to eat something," Sarah said, coming into the kitchen.

Nora and John exchanged curious glances as she rose from the table to fix Sarah a plate.

"We have your favorite tonight, dear, pork loin and oven-roasted potatoes," Nora said. Her back was to Sarah and John. "You know how much you like that."

"That's great mom, thanks," Sarah said, but her voice was lifeless.

Nora set the plate in front of Sarah. She stared at it for several minutes before she slowly started to eat. Nora returned to her chair. They watched as Sarah ate.

"Mom, dad, I've been thinking. Now that Jaime has started college and I'll be starting high school in a few days, maybe it's time I get on with things. You know…"

Sarah pushed her dish away from the front of her and folded her arms on the table. Her parents remained silent and waited.

"I've been thinking that it's time I start acting like the high school student I'm gonna be ... I'd better start acting like a grown-up. And I'm sorry for all the trouble I've caused you guys since … you know..."

Sarah rose and stood beside the chair. She looked at her mother, as though waiting for an answer.

Nora nodded, tears clouding her vision. "Of course, dear. That would be wonderful. Anything you want to do."

Sarah gave them a delicate, scanty smile, put her dish in the sink and left the kitchen. At that moment, she thought of Jaime.

"I've got to call Jaime," she said, looking from John to the phone on the wall.

Jaime picked up the phone in her college dorm room on the end of the fourth ring. She was returning from the library and was coming down the hall when she heard her phone start to ring. She dashed off in a dead run to answer it. She gave an out-of-breath hello, one that did not sound like her.

"Jaime? Sweetheart, it's me," her mother said.

"Hi mom," Jaime said and couldn't help sounding hesitant.

"I have wonderful news."

Jaime listened, the joy in her heart growing, the longer her mother spoke. But their rapture was short lived.

Sarah began attending high school. But the erstwhile Sarah had vanished long ago. The shell of her was the ghost that moved on through the darkness of her life. She became involved with the wrong crowd. Drinking and drugs would be with her through school and on the night she died.

The telephone rang in Jaime's apartment, tearing her away from the laden memory of long ago.

She stared at the phone as it rang, as if she were trying to figure out where she was. She answered it and listened as the caller spoke.

"No, sorry," she said. "You have the wrong number."

The voice on the other end was not her mother's. Just as Jaime knew it would not be. She tried to think of the last time she had heard from her mother. Birthdays, Mother's Day, Christmas, all had come and gone. There were no cards. There were no calls.

How long had it been? It made her sad to remember.

Six years since she had last heard the sound of her mother's voice.

Jaime thought how involved Leigh was in Ashleigh's life. How much she loved her.

She looked at the receiver. She dialed her mother's number, but hung up the moment it started to ring.

Twenty-one

Jaime made the short walk from her new office to the Denver Public Library on Broadway with a biting wind nipping at her heels. It sent a chill through her as she entered the newly remodeled library. It was warm and inviting. This was a perfect day to be inside a place where she did some of her best thinking amid the hushed, but bustling, silence.

The Denver Public Library, an architectural masterpiece, offered a sacred stillness that reminded Jaime of a great cathedral. The remodeled central library was triple the size of the old one with seven levels above ground and three below.

She settled at a table in General Reference Center and Reading Room to work the rest of the afternoon. Two hours into her work,

Jaime's attention was distracted when a young girl sat at the table next to her. A library clerk had followed the girl to the table. Jaime kept part of her attention fixed on the girl who whispered to the librarian what she needed. Jaime watched as the clerk handed her the book and pointed to a section. Satisfied the girl had found what she was looking for, Jaime became absorbed again in her own research.

A few moments later Jaime felt a slight tug on her sleeve. She could smell bubble gum. She found herself looking into the eyes of the young girl.

"Excuse me," the girl said, smiling shyly over a full set of braces.

Jaime put her pen down.

"Could you help me?"

"What're you looking for?" Jaime asked.

"I'm trying to finish my homework and I can't find the right books. This one is not going to work," the girl said, pointing to the book the librarian had given her.

"Can't they help you over there?" Jaime asked, as she looked beyond the girl to the library clerks behind a desk.

The girl looked and pointed to the woman who had helped her. "Well, she gave me this book, but I can't read any of the words," she said.

Jaime guessed the girl to be in the sixth grade. Her smooth fresh, face was full and round. Her loosely curled brown hair reached to her shirt collar. Her bangs hung just below her eyebrows, which she continually batted away with her hand. Her body was pudgy and round. The white shirt, green and blue plaid pleated skirt and blue socks she wore suggested a private school. A small smile spread over Jaime's face. An image of Sarah, then Ashleigh, flashed before her.

The girl handed Jaime the book. She opened it and flipped through the pages. The words were in Arabic. "Well," Jaime said. "It's all Greek to me, too. Why don't you move your things over here."

The girl smiled widely at Jaime, showing braces and a large wad of bright pink bubble gum. "My homework assignment is social studies. It's on the Middle East."

The girl pushed her bangs away from her eyes, pointed to her paper and then looked at Jaime. "I have fill-in-the-blank, true or false and multiple choice questions and I have to find definitions for these words."

Jaime took the paper and studied it. The few hours' work she had left would have to wait. “All right,” she said. “I’ll help you, but, here’s the deal, you don’t get off easy. You have to do the work and write the answers down.”

“It’s a deal,” the girl said, smiling.

Jaime and her student left to get the other books they needed. On their way back to the table, Jaime looked down at the girl who walked beside her carrying a stack of books that weighed more than she. She grinned widely at Jaime. Jaime grinned back.

For the next two hours, Jaime did the kind of work she hadn’t done since college, schoolwork. While looking through history, encyclopedias, dictionaries and reference books, they found answers to the homework questions. They were looking at a map of Middle Eastern countries when Jaime noticed the girl’s name written in large block letters at the top of her homework papers, GEORGIA.

“Were you born in Georgia?” Jaime asked.

“Three hours from it,” Georgia replied happily. “But we live here now and have for three years. But my mom hates it here and wants to go back. But I don’t. I want to stay. I have really cool friends and I want to live here all my life. What’s your name?”

Jaime told her.

“Are you married?”

Jaime’s laugh was small. “Well, sort of. I’m separated right now.”

Georgia looked at Jaime’s left hand. She saw her watch, but no wedding ring.

“Where’s your ring?” Georgia asked. “My mom always wore hers ’til she and my dad got a divorce. Then she sold it to a pawn shop so we could buy a TV.”

Jaime thought of her marquis-cut solitaire ring that had spent more time in her jewelry case in the past eight months than on her finger.

“It’s at home,” Jaime volunteered.

“Does that mean you’re gonna get a divorce?”

“Probably,” Jaime said nodding slightly.

“That’s what happened to my mom and dad, well I mean Rick, ’cause he’s not my real dad either, my first dad moved away before I was big enough to know him. I never even met him. Well, I guess that’s kinda a lie, ’cause my mom said I met him when I was a little baby, but I don't remember him. First my dad, I mean Rick, moved out of the house, well, actually, my mom threw him out, and then she said he's never coming back and that she's gonna divorce him. That's how it happened."

"It happens like that sometimes," Jaime said.

Georgia sat up high in her chair. "But my new daddy's really nice. He takes us to all kinds of places. We're going to the zoo tomorrow and I can hardly wait."

The girl studied Jaime with curious innocence. "Are you a reporter or something?"

"Something like that," Jaime replied. "I'm a lawyer."

"Really! Wow!" Georgia's brown eyes grew wide. "You must be really smart if you know this stuff."

"You'll know it with time too, Georgia."

"My mom doesn't really like lawyers very much," Georgia volunteered.

"Neither does mine," Jaime added.

"She says they're only out to make a fast buck."

Jaime nodded with a half-smile. "Some are, but not all of them."

"Are you like that, Jaime?"

She grinned and shook her head. "There are some attorneys who want to help people overcome what's happened to them so they can get on with their lives." She touched the tip of her fingers to her chest. "That's the kind of attorney I am."

"You make pretty good money?" Georgia asked.

"Pretty good."

"A million dollars?"

"No, not that much, but some."

Georgia returned her attention to her homework and studied the next fill-in-the-blank question: What is the sacred book of the Muslims called? She looked to Jaime. They had the World Book Encyclopedia open and began to scan the pages. Georgia's eyes beamed with excitement when they found the word, Koran. The final fill-in-the-blank question asked the student to define the word *nomad.*

"What's a nomad?" Georgia asked, turning from the assignment to Jaime.

They studied their choices: herdsman, sultan, soldier, wanderer.

"You tell me," Jaime said. "A nomad is someone, a group of people, who don't have a permanent home, who move about constantly in search of a place to live."

She watched as Georgia frowned and scrutinized the choices, then circled the one that came closest to matching nomad.

"It's someone who doesn't have a home. Someone who's always wandering around," Georgia said, looking to Jaime for approval. Jaime smiled and nodded.

"Is that it, Georgia?" Jaime asked.

"Yep, thanks a whole bunch. You really helped me a lot. I'm gonna tell all my friends at school that a really nice lawyer helped me with my homework."

"You're welcome."

Georgia looked at Jaime's pile of paperwork. "Do you have lots to do?"

She reorganized the papers on her table. "It's not that much. It shouldn't take much longer. Besides, I needed the break anyway and I was glad to help you, Georgia."

The girl looked at Jaime. When she smiled Jaime saw that some of her bubble gum had become stuck in her braces.

"You could be my big sister," Georgia said.

Jaime's laugh was sad, like the murmur of the sea. Georgia's words caught her off guard, but she held her composure. Georgia caught sight of her mother, who had entered the library.

"Uh oh, there's my mom, I gotta go." She started to collect the books to return them, but Jaime rested her hand over hers and she stopped.

"Go on," she said. "I'll return them."

"Thanks, Jaime, for helping me! Bye!"

With a quick wave Georgia was gone. Jaime watched smiling as she greeted her mother and pointed in her direction. They left hand in hand through the library doors. When they were gone, Jaime's smile disappeared slowly, like dew off a rose.

Jaime studied the work on the table, her enthusiasm gone. She shook her head sadly. "Sarah," she whispered. "What did I do to you? What would you be like today?"

She looked where Georgia had gone through the door with her mother. Now only strangers walked quietly in that direction. Jaime thought of the immense size of the Denver Public Library. Out of the entire area she had selected to do her work, how did Georgia manage to find her here?

Twenty-two

Tia stuck her head inside Jaime's office and waited patiently for her to finish her telephone conversation. Jaime hung up and looked to Tia.

"Pearl called while you were on the phone to cancel lunch. She said she can't get away and owes you a hotdog."

Jaime protruded her bottom lip and smiled mischievously at Tia. "Too bad," she said, "I was really looking forward to a hotdog and chips!"

Jaime decided she would go to Café Gardenia and left the office. She was seconds from entering the café when she noticed Leigh in line at the deli, studying the overhead menu. Jaime stopped, weighing whether to go in. She glanced to the table where they sat the first afternoon they met and remembered their conversation. She thought of their second encounter and decided to find another place to eat. Before she could walk a block, however, she thought of Ashleigh. Jaime glanced at her watch. Ashleigh would be working. She decided to make a quick return to Café Gardenia to see if Leigh would accept her invitation to join her for lunch at the food court. She was next in line to order.

Jaime called to Leigh above the din of the crowd.

She turned, saw Jaime and waved. "Want to join me?"

Jaime nodded her head and then met her in line. "I'm on my way to have lunch at the food court. Why don't you come with me?"

Leigh looked at Jaime for a moment, considering the invitation. She smiled apologetically at the deli clerk and stepped out of line. She followed Jaime out of the cafe and they walked in silence until they reached the mall.

"Ashleigh says you've only been to the food court one time since she started."

Leigh nodded. "That was the day I left my laptop."

They walked the rest of the way to the Tabor Center without another word. The food court was as busy and crammed as always. They looked for Ashleigh for several minutes before spotting her about to reach a dirty table. She carried a dishcloth in one hand and a spray bottle in the other.

"There she is," Leigh said and pointed in Ashleigh's direction. "I'd recognize that walk anywhere."

Jaime looked to where Leigh pointed and saw Ashleigh. Jaime had a wide smile on her face, feeling as though she was the proud sister of Ashleigh Roberts. Leigh looked on impassively, but the expression on her face began to change to a softer, gentler radiance the longer she watched Ashleigh work.

"Come on," Leigh said, taking Jaime by the forearm. "I don't want Ashleigh to see us. Let's watch her work and we'll talk to her later."

Jaime purchased a slice of pizza with tomato and broccoli, and Leigh bought a spinach salad. They found a table near Ashleigh's section, inconspicuous enough so that she would not easily notice them. They ate in silence watching Ashleigh. She looked as content to be there as the day Jaime first saw her and worked just as hard. The moment people left a table in her section, Ashleigh moved to clean it so it would be ready for others.

It started out innocently enough.

Four teenaged boys, with sodas, pizza and hamburgers and fries on their trays, were looking for a place to sit when they saw Ashleigh finish clearing a table with four chairs. She was hardly out of the way when they clambered into the section, sliding their trays on the table. They noticed how quickly Ashleigh cleaned tables. The table next to them was empty. An open target.

It started with a spoon. When they made sure Ashleigh was looking in their direction, one of the boys set a spoon covered with ketchup on the empty table. She saw the spoon. She went to the table, picked it up and then cleaned the area with her dishcloth.

She had no sooner left the table than one boy called to her.

"Hey, stupid, you missed a spot!"

Ashleigh turned and saw soda all over the table. The look on Ashleigh's face did not show anger or frustration as she returned to the table. She picked up the cup as some of the dark liquid dripped from the table to the floor. She cleaned the table, then the floor.

One of the other boys spoke. "Better get your mop, retard, or you'll miss a spot."

One of them dropped a handful of napkins. They landed near Ashleigh's feet.

"Here, use these that'll help. You probably don't know what a mop looks like!"

Amused with themselves, they poked and slapped each other on the shoulders, while struggling not to roar with laughter.

Ashleigh kept her attention focused on cleaning the floor. She did not look at them. When she finished, she collected the napkins and wadded them into a tight ball. The boys watched Ashleigh and waited for her to put the cup and napkins into a trash can. They called her again.

"Hey, you're falling down on the job!" one of them yelled. "Are you blind, too?! You missed something!"

Ashleigh looked over her shoulder to where she had just cleaned and saw that a slice of pizza had landed topping-side down. The expression on Ashleigh's face did not change. She avoided looking at the boys as she picked up the pizza and cleaned the floor.

Leigh and Jaime had stopped eating and were watching intently. Jaime noticed that Leigh was flexing the muscles in her jaw and had swallowed hard several times. Her face had turned crimson.

"Those little bastards," Leigh said. "I'm going to put a stop to this now. They won't do that to Ashleigh. I told Erin this was a bad idea from the beginning."

She started to leave the table, but Jaime put a firm hand around her wrist. They looked directly at each other, eyes flaming. A look of anger mounted in Leigh's eyes, turning dark like an approaching storm.

Jaime's voice was firm. "Don't."

"Are you blind, Jaime? Look what they're doing to Ashleigh. They're making her look like a fool. I'm not going to sit here and let it continue."

Jaime did not remove her hand. Her voice was unyielding as she spoke. "Ashleigh can handle it. Let her go. She's doing fine. Can't you see they just want to get a rise out of her? Leave Ashleigh alone. Let her do her job. She's doing fine." Jaime emphasized the word fine. "You won't help her by intervening. Please, Leigh, sit down."

Reluctantly, she did.

Jaime was working to control her own anger. She removed her hand from Leigh's wrist and firmly gripped the sides of the table. She continued to hold on as though she was on a sled speeding down a steep hill. Her grip was the only thing that kept her from falling over the edge. The women, fighting with all their strength and control not to intervene, kept their attention focused on what was happening to Ashleigh.

And, it just so happens, a security guard was also watching.

He was a tall, burly man, hairless as a statue. The look on his face was severe. He had witnessed the entire scene and saw all he wanted or cared to see. He sauntered over to Ashleigh's section, his jaw clenched. His arms were firmly grasping his security belt and his chest was perfectly still as though he wasn't breathing. He got to the table and crossed his arms over his chest. It made him appear even more broad-shouldered, and he easily towered over Ashleigh and the boys by more than a foot. He didn't have to say a word. The boys took one look at him and scattered out of the area as quickly as mice.

They left the table looking like a tempest had passed through. French-fries, pizza and half-eaten hamburgers were all over the table. Some of the French fries had fallen on the floor. Trays, napkins and empty soda glasses littered the top of the table and the chairs.

Ashleigh came and stood beside him. He looked down at her and his hard face softened.

Ashleigh smiled. He almost did. "I was watching you, young lady, you did a fine job with those boys," he said in a thick, deep voice. "A fine job."

Ashleigh's grin widened. He waited at the table until she cleaned it. The security guard helped her carry the items to the trash.

Leigh had seen enough. "Let's go."

They left the food court without talking to Ashleigh. They did not speak again until they reached the street. Leigh's anger fueled her steps and Jaime had to quicken hers to keep up. They crossed Larimer Street with a crowd of others.

"Slow down!" Jaime said and grabbed Leigh by the arm. "You can't outrun what just happened. And where the hell are you going? The *Dispatch* is that way!" Jaime jerked a thumb over her shoulder.

Leigh turned and looked at Jaime. The anger in her eyes still flaming. People continued to pass between them. Jaime moved closer to a building and pulled Leigh along with her. Leigh folded her arms and squeezed them tightly across her chest. She was trying to take small, deep breaths to calm herself. She glanced in the direction of the blue glass windows of the Tabor Center.

"I knew that was a damn ridiculous idea from the first moment Ashleigh told me she was going to do it," Leigh said roughly. "It's all Erin's fault! She put Ashleigh up to this."

Jaime looked at Leigh unmercifully, shaking her head. "It's not a bad idea and it's not Erin's fault, Leigh. No matter how much you want to believe it is. You want Ashleigh to work in a workshop and stuff sport bags with newspaper the rest of her life? You of anyone should know she can do so much more. What you just saw proved that. Ashleigh should be doing exactly what she's doing."

Leigh's laugh was short and harsh. "And have things like that happen? I can't believe you feel that way. You're crazy."

Jaime ignored Leigh's comment. "I can't believe you want your daughter to do something she's outgrown." Jaime touched the tips of her fingers angrily against her chest. "Ashleigh needs to be stuffing sport bags about as much as I do."

"Maybe if she were, that wouldn't have happened," Leigh said, and pointed angrily toward the food court.

An elderly couple getting into a cab across the street captured Leigh's attention. Jaime felt Leigh's hurt and anger ooze from her skin, like a deep, festering wound.

"This is just another step toward a life of more independence for Ashleigh," Jaime said, her voice even and smooth. "Don't you want that for her? Don't you think Ashleigh wants that? Don't you think she wants to be more on her own, to be free to experience the same things you and I do in life? What we just saw is something that just happens in life. And it could've happened to us, to anyone."

Leigh looked at Jaime through eyes that had become narrowed slits. Her lips formed a thin line. "I'm not a fool, Jaime," she said firmly.

Jaime traced a pattern with the tip of her shoe in the sidewalk. She went on, "I'm sorry. You know what I'm telling you. Ashleigh needs experiences like that. It was rough, who's denying that? It was just as unpleasant for me as it was for you. It was just as tough for Ashleigh to experience, but still it happens. Every day can't be a good day."

Jaime looked at Leigh earnestly and continued softly. "And she did the right thing to ignore them. That should tell you Ashleigh knew how to handle the situation."

But it was as though Leigh had not heard Jaime. "It wouldn't have happened at all if she were still at the workshop."

Jaime laughed in disbelief. She shook her head in disgust and her voice had a hint of sarcasm when she spoke. "No, I guess not. Sports bags don't talk back. You're right. Yeah, I guess that's definitely what Ashleigh should do with the rest of her life. Next bag, please."

Leigh responded crisply, without hesitation. "You're *not* me, Jaime. When this hearing is over *your* life will go on. I have to deal with what happens to Ashleigh *every day* of *my* life."

For a long, loud moment, only the blaring noise from the traffic stood between them.

"I don't intend to be just a fleeting figure in your daughter's life," Jaime said finally. "She's come to mean a lot to me. I want to help her, even after this is over. But just as I can't be there always to protect her, you can't either. It wouldn't be fair to her, or you. Will you be there at every shift Ashleigh works from now on to stop things like that from happening? Who's not thinking logically here?"

Jaime looked with Leigh at the older couple who had finally managed to get in the cab. She mumbled something Jaime could not understand.

"I should've stopped it." Leigh said in a voice so low Jaime hardly heard her above the traffic.

"Is that why you didn't want Ashleigh to work in a public place like the Tabor Center? Because of what just happened?" Jaime asked.

Leigh watched the cab drive away. When it became one with the other traffic, she turned her attention to Jaime. She opened her mouth to speak, but closed it without commenting. She began walking slowly along the 16th Street Mall. Jaime followed, but it wasn't until they passed the Tabor Center that she spoke again.

"Ashleigh did not waver once," Jaime said. "You saw that. She didn't let them get the better of her. She could've gone to her supervisor and asked to go to a different section or make them leave. But she held her ground." Jaime eyed Leigh quickly. "I suspect she has some of her mother's stubbornness."

Leigh smiled in spite of herself. She kept her attention fixed straight ahead as she walked. Jaime could tell the incident had drained her. She looked as limp as a shoestring.

They stopped at Welton Street for their paths to separate.

"I'm sorry this had to happen," Jaime said.

"Why are you apologizing? You had nothing to do with it."

They parted without saying good-bye. As she returned to work, Jaime remembered the boys taunting Ashleigh. She heard their snickering and their jeers and what they said.

Stupid. Retard.

When they said those words all their other words had turned to whispers. Those words stood out and echoed in a deep chasm in Jaime's mind, moaning like a distant sea.

The words sickened her. She wanted to attack their ignorance and cruelty like a rabid dog. She wondered how Ashleigh felt being subject to their badgering and teasing, or if she had even noticed. Jaime felt as though someone had stabbed her with a dull knife. She could only imagine Leigh's disappointment. Her distress.

Or could she? Jaime wasn't a mother. She had no idea what it was like to watch as her child endured pain and embarrassment at the cruel, insensitive hands of others. Was Leigh feeling disappointment? Anger? Fear? Grief? Jaime knew she would never fully know the depths of Leigh's pain. Her secret sorrow.

Stupid.

The food court scene only deepened her belief in Ashleigh. Ashleigh had limitations, but she would prevail. Jaime was not foolish enough to think Ashleigh would become a lawyer, or a doctor, or that she would become a professor, or president of a corporation. Now she was working in the food court. Someday she would go on. Perhaps she could work delivering mail within a large company, maybe even the district attorney's office. She would do what it took to succeed, despite her limitations.

That thought lifted Jaime's spirit, but when she tried to recall another time she felt as defeated as she did witnessing the incident at the food court, one thing came to mind: reading Sarah's obituary.

Jaime had always felt reading her sister's death notice was the lowest, darkest moment in her life. And nothing would ever take the place of that.

Twenty-three

It had been a particularly frustrating day at work.

Jaime spilled coffee on her new suit and she was still angry over the incident with Ashleigh and Leigh at the food court. To top everything, she had left most of the paperwork for a deposition on her kitchen table.

However, it was Wednesday and that made her feel better. She would have Ashleigh for the night and she would box with Frank. When Jaime hit the heavy bag in warm ups, she would remember the four boys at the food court. She looked forward to hitting the bag. After boxing she had planned to take Ashleigh for pizza and then rent a movie. Ashleigh had been looking forward to the evening with abandon.

Barry Winters and Frank were standing together when Jaime and Ashleigh entered the gym. Barry's expression grew soft at the sight of Jaime and he walked over to greet them. Barry had been working the front desk for about a month when he met Jaime Monroe for the first time. He thought often of the first night he saw her standing at the desk waiting to give her card to get into the club. She had been smiling and talking to someone standing beside her. When he greeted her, she gave him a soft smile and said hello. From then on, he thought of her.

Jaime introduced Ashleigh and they shook hands.

"Mind if I stay and watch?" Barry asked.

"Sure," Jaime said.

"Hey, Jaime!" Frank called.

"Frank, this is Ashleigh," Jaime said introducing them.

"Hi," Ashleigh said.

She put Jaime's gym bag on the floor and shook Frank's hand.

"I've heard a lot about you from Jaime. She says you're quite a gal."

Ashleigh beamed when she looked at Jaime who returned the wide smile.

"Ready?" Frank said, looking again to Jaime.

She pointed to her gloves. "As soon as Ashleigh helps me put on my gloves."

Jaime was surprised to see her estranged husband Mitchell when she entered the gym. He watched as Ashleigh helped with her gloves, but didn't acknowledge them. Jaime hadn't seen him at the club in weeks and wondered why he was here tonight. She looked in his direction. Mitchell Price was a lean, muscular man who stood six-foot-one. His dark hair was short. His sideburns shaved. A mustache and beard framed his lip and chin. A dimple in his lower left cheek formed a deep canyon when he smiled. She remembered it was his dimple that first attracted her to him.

Mitchell stood with his back against a wall holding a basketball loosely in his hands. He stared at them the entire time Ashleigh helped Jaime with her gloves.

"Who's that?" Ashleigh asked looking with Jaime at Mitchell.

"It's Mitchell, someone I don't want you to meet."

Twenty minutes into the workout, Jaime, her skin gleaming under rivulets of sweat, landed a few good punches, but the impact was minimal against Frank's bulky body. Frank had never intentionally hit Jaime when they sparred together. When they boxed and Jaime lowered her guard, Frank would give her a tap to her body—a sign to show her what he could do to her if he wanted. When Jaime got sloppy, Frank would remind her of the time he had tapped her to the solar plexus and how she had bent over, struggling to hold back her tears. She had never let on how much his 'tap' had hurt, but she didn't have to. He had gotten her attention.

It was a good sparing session. Then Frank's opening came. The first punch landed hard and firm against Jaime's right side. Her knees buckled from the blow. A clamorous gasp of pain burst from her lungs that turned the heads of everyone in the gym, their attention glued on the boxers.

Ashleigh and Barry were among them, transfixed by what was taking place before them on the mat, a short distance away.

Jaime looked at Frank, the amazement wide in her eyes that he had struck her and at the force of his blow. She stumbled and then scrambled, trying quickly to regain her composure. Frank pummeled a second, harder blow straight into her mid-section, grunting as he made the connection. The force lifted her slightly off the mat as her body folded into his fist. He followed with another thunderous blow to her side. She groaned with pain, the air gone from her body. She struggled for breath. She did what Frank was waiting for. She dropped her glove slightly to protect her body, just enough away from her face.

Frank saw his opening.

Jaime never saw Frank's glove as it blurred before her and connected against the left side of her face. It was his favorite punch. He had worked on it for years before finally mastering it. It was the Larry Holmes hallmark punch, an overhand right. He had learned to use it from watching the former champion. Frank used it effectively, but only when he sparred against men. He knew its power, its devastation.

Jaime fell like stone, slamming face first to the canvas. Blood and saliva covered the mat.

Frank stood over her and watched as she lay lifeless. "Didn't I always tell you not to drop your stupid guard," he whispered as anger began to ricochet around in him like a bullet. He stepped silently away from the mat as Barry rushed to Jaime's side.

Frank and Barry locked eyes for a fleeting moment. "You son of a bitch. Get the hell out of here, loser, before I throw you out," he growled at Frank as he brushed by him.

Frank looked to Mitchell and swallowed hard. Mitchell's small smug smile showed satisfaction. Frank walked toward him, pulling off his gloves. He stopped a foot away and threw the boxing gloves at Mitchell. One missed, the other bounced off his right shoulder.

"I hope you're fucking happy," Frank said.

Frank had almost talked himself out of the plan when he saw Ashleigh enter the gym with Jaime. But it was too late. He was already committed. He had told Mitchell it went against his beliefs, but his financial situation was so desperate he didn't know what else to do. His gambling habit was the only reason he agreed. It was the money. He needed the money.

As Frank headed for the stairs, Mitchell called out to him, "Hey, buddy, I believe you now. You really were a contender!"

He ignored Mitchell's comment as he glanced over his shoulder and watched as Barry gently eased Jaime over and lifted her upper body into his arms. Her arms lifeless at her side, were resting in her lap, the palms of the gloves turned upward. Her head fell loosely like a rag doll over his arm. Blood covered the front of her shirt. Ashleigh was kneeling next to them. She had one hand on Jaime's shoulder. The other held a towel Barry had given her. She was cleaning the blood away from Jaime's cheek.

Frank turned and left. By the time Mitchell reached the small group, he heard Jaime choking from the odor of the smelling salts Barry had passed under her nose. He did not move closer.

Jaime opened her eyes and blinked slowly. She remembered nothing about going down. The dull, throbbing pain in her mid-section and the ringing in her ears commanded her full attention. She tried shaking her head to stop the ringing, but it didn't help. Blood continued to ooze from her upper lip. She could taste sweat and blood in her mouth. She swallowed several times trying to fight her queasiness.

"Jaime?" Barry waited for her to respond. "Jaime?" he said again, "It's Barry. Are you all right?"

Jaime could hear his voice, but as she tried to get her bearings she could not answer him. Suddenly everything was clear when she thought of Ashleigh.

"Ashleigh! Where's Ashleigh?" Jaime said and tried to move, but stopped quickly as a gripping pain shot through her torso. She winced and fell back against Barry's arm.

"It's okay, Jaime, I'm right here," Ashleigh said and patted her shoulder.

Jaime's eyelids fluttered then closed.

Barry said, "We need to get you to a doctor, Jaime. The lip looks bad. You're going to need stitches and you probably have some broken ribs and a concussion too. I saw those blows."

"No ... really ... that's okay. I'll be fine. Let me just sit here a few more minutes," Jaime said in a foggy voice.

After several minutes, she tried to stand, but the pain and sudden dizziness caused her knees to buckle. As she sank to the floor, Mitchell moved to take her arm. Barry reluctantly let go.

"Let me help. I'll take her to the hospital," Mitchell said, looking at Barry. He avoided looking into Ashleigh's eyes.

Jaime tried to pull her arm away to resist Mitchell's help, but she didn't have the strength. Her head was spinning and she was in no condition to object, or to get herself home. Blood was still oozing from her lip and falling on her clothes and arm. She decided a hospital might be a good idea. Mitchell's grip was strong and firm around her shoulders as he helped her to her feet.

"Get your things," Mitchell said. "I'll wait for you and Ashleigh upstairs."

Barry and Ashleigh helped Jaime remove her gloves and then they helped her to the locker room. Barry stopped at the door and released Jaime's arm.

"Make sure they take good care of her, Ashleigh," he said.

Ashleigh nodded. "I will."

Barry watched as they disappeared into the locker room, feeling his temples beginning to throb. He clenched his fists and wanted to find Frank and kill him for what he had done to Jaime. Instead, he took the stairs two at time and dashed outside where he sprinted several long blocks until his lungs burned and the cool night air calmed him.

Ashleigh and Jaime did not come upstairs immediately. The walk had left Jaime nauseous and unsteady on her feet. She left her car at the club and they rode with Mitchell to the hospital. They were silent in the car, but Mitchell glanced at Jaime every few minutes during the drive, her head resting against the car window, eyes closed.

"You didn't have to take me," Jaime said when they reached the hospital. Her voice sounded fragile. It hurt to breathe. All she thought about was why Frank had hit her. And so hard.

Jaime had a slight concussion and several deeply bruised ribs. The emergency room doctor put four stitches in her upper lip. Expect to be uncomfortable for the next several days, he told her.

It was near midnight when Mitchell brought Jaime and Ashleigh to the apartment. He helped her up the stairs and stood next to her until the elevator reached their floor. Ashleigh followed carrying Jaime's gym bag. Mitchell got as far as the front door, but Jaime refused his offer to stay the night. With much effort Ashleigh managed to help Jaime get undressed and into a nightshirt. Jaime was sitting on the edge of the bed trying to stop the room from spinning when Ashleigh brought her ibuprofen and a glass of water.

"Here, Jaime, the doctor said to take these. They'll help."

Jaime took the pills and water Ashleigh offered. She swallowed them and handed the glass to Ashleigh. She put her head against the pillow as fast as the pain would allow. Ashleigh softly sat on the bed next to Jaime, studying her. For a moment, the only sound in the room came from the short breaths Jaime was attempting to take because it hurt too much to breathe.

"Ashleigh, you haven't eaten anything," she said. "You know it's not good for you. I'm sorry we couldn't go for pizza."

"It's all right. I had a banana and some juice in my bag and ate that while you were in the hospital, I'll find something to eat pretty soon," Ashleigh said and she continued to stare at Jaime, who had her eyes closed.

"Does your lip hurt, Jaime?"

Jaime ran her tongue lightly back and forth over the stitches. Everything hurt. "A little."

Jaime could sense Ashleigh probing at her and opened her eyes. She was disoriented, but she knew enough to know that Ashleigh had been wounded by what she had witnessed. She wasn't sure what hurt more, Frank's blows, or the look in Ashleigh's eyes. Jaime's hands had been resting lightly on her stomach. She raised her right hand and extended it toward Ashleigh, and she took it.

"I'm sorry you had to see this tonight, Ashleigh. I never meant for you to see something so ugly."

"Why did Frank hurt you?"

Jaime was quiet for a moment. She couldn't answer a question she didn't know. "I wish I knew."

"You'd better go to sleep, Jaime, maybe in the morning you'll feel better and then your lip will be better. Erin always says that there's nothin' so bad in the world that a good night's sleep won't fix. I'm gonna find something to eat and then I'm going to sleep on the couch."

Ashleigh waited for Jaime's response, but instead heard only shallow breathing.

The next morning Ashleigh poked her head in the bedroom. Jaime had rolled to her side and was still asleep. She walked into the bedroom and sat down lightly on the bed. "Jaime?" she called softly.

Jaime did not move. Ashleigh waited a minute and then rested her hand on Jaime's shoulder and called again. "Jaime? Jaime, wake up."

She stirred slightly. She had forgotten the events of the previous evening and turned over as she heard Ashleigh call her name. She moaned deeply as a sharp, stabbing pain pierced through her mid-section. She grimaced and thought of Frank. She blinked waiting for the pain to subside. She looked at Ashleigh and managed a small smile. Ashleigh looked fresh. She had showered and had pulled her hair back in a ponytail. She had her uniform on and was ready for work.

"Have you eaten?" Jaime asked, still groggy from a restless sleep.

Ashleigh nodded. "I had a bowl of cereal."

"What time is it?" Jaime asked.

Ashleigh looked from Jaime to her wristwatch and began to study it intently. "It's uh ... uh ... It's…" She looked at Jaime wanting to extend her wrist in her direction so she could see the hands on the dial, but Jaime had closed her eyes. She looked back at her watch. "Uh, it's uh ... ten o'clock! Jaime, it's ten o'clock," Ashleigh said in a triumphant voice and then smiled.

Jaime nodded slightly.

"Mitchell's here. He brought your car back. He wants to leave the car keys, but he wants to talk to you."

"Tell him to give me a minute," Jaime said.

Ashleigh nodded and left the room.

Jaime rose from the bed slowly and looked at herself in the mirror, to an unforgiving reflection. Her lip was puffy around the stitches and she had a raspberry rash across her swollen and bruised left cheekbone. She tried touching her cheek, but it was too tender. Her eye was black and blue, on its way to becoming a brilliant purple. The white in her eye was a deep red.

"I'm a mess," Jaime said and turned away from the mirror.

She tried putting on her robe, but it hurt too much to expand her rib cage. She tossed it on the bed. Mitchell entered the bedroom and Ashleigh followed. He stood behind Jaime. She looked at his image in the mirror before her. He studied the features on her face.

"You were really out of it last night," he said.

"What would you expect?" she said sharply. "It's not every day that someone you know beats the crap out of you."

"Why weren't you wearing any head gear?"

Jaime shrugged, ignoring his question.

"She should go into the other room," Mitchell said, jerking his thumb over his shoulder, referring to Ashleigh without looking at her.

Their eyes met in the mirror. She winced slightly as she turned to face him.

"She can stay right here," Jaime said and Ashleigh moved to stand closer to her.

Mitchell turned, brushed by Ashleigh and walked to the bedroom window and stared out. The wind was whipping and he felt the chill against the glass. Jaime came and stood behind him. Waiting. Mitchell finally turned to face her.

"Ashleigh said you wanted to tell me something before you left the keys," she said.

He looked at her, examining the bruises on her face, she was still so pretty, even now. He wanted to touch her.

"I've missed you, Jaime. I miss being with you."

Jaime frowned and shook her head. "That's what you wanted to tell me?"

"You've pulled away from me," Mitchell added.

Her laugh was incredulous. "You should've thought about that the night Molly Gibson was in this room. Besides, it doesn't matter anymore."

Jaime stopped and looked at Mitchell with a cold, icy stare.

"We're separated, but I guess that hasn't sunk in yet," she said.

He looked at her, his lips set angrily in a thin slash. After a long moment he spoke. "I thought you would need someone to help you. And I wanted to help you. You were always so independent, so distant, off in some other world, still worried about your sister, I guess, but there have been times when you've needed me ... and ... I just wanted you to need me again."

Jaime ran her tongue over the stitches in her lip, studying Mitchell. Her eyes narrowed and her hurt at what happened last night, at least for the moment, had turned to anger. Ashleigh came and stood beside her.

"As you can see, Mitchell, I have all the help I need right here."

Mitchell looked at Ashleigh and their eyes locked until Jaime's words brought his attention back to her.

"Don't forget the only reason you took me to the hospital last night is because Ashleigh can't drive. I don't have the strength to throw you out now so I hope you have sense enough to leave on your own."

She turned, leaving him at the window to watch her walk away. Her voice was crisp when she spoke again. "I have to shower. I'm late for work."

Mitchell left the bedroom without saying a word to Ashleigh.

Jaime had showered. Her long brown hair was wrapped in a thick white towel. Ashleigh was watching her put on makeup, what makeup she could, in the bathroom mirror. Jaime winced slightly as she grabbed a hand towel.

"Does it still hurt, Jaime?" Ashleigh asked.

Jaime nodded, and thought a moment before she answered. "It's not so much getting hit that hurts," she said looking at Ashleigh in the mirror.

"What then?"

Jaime sighed, a small sound. "What hurts more is why Frank did what he did rather than the hurt that came from getting hit by him."

"'Cause that kind of pain will go away pretty soon, huh," Ashleigh said.

Jaime smiled and nodded slightly and hoped Ashleigh did not sense her surprise. "Yes, Ashleigh, because this kind of pain," Jaime said and pointed to her bruises. "Will go away eventually. The other pain, why Frank did what he did, will take longer to heal."

"Then why did he do it?

Jaime shook her head and shrugged her shoulders. She couldn't answer.

"I thought he liked you. I mean, you told me he did," Ashleigh said.

"I thought he did and he does, but Frank just has lots of problems, that's all."

"What kind of problems?"

"Problems that you would never understand." She leaned into the mirror to examine her stitches. "Ashleigh, even I don't understand Frank's problem."

Jaime drove Ashleigh to work.

"I'm sorry about last night," Jaime said as they reached the Tabor Center.

"It's all right, I understand."

And Jaime knew she did. "We'll do it again. The works, pizza and a movie. Deal?" she asked.

"Deal!"

After a quick, gentle hug, Ashleigh got out of the car. As Jaime waved and watched her disappear into the building, her smile came from within, one that came with the sense of wellbeing. She knew they would be closer now because of what they had experienced. Jaime knew she could not fully explain to Ashleigh why Frank had hit her and would not attempt to try. She would just tell Ashleigh that sometimes foolish people do desperate things, simply and very often for reasons they're never able to fully explain.

She drove to the office. Tia Ranch was the first person she saw. Her eyes grew as round as the moon at the sight of Jaime.

"Oh my!" Tia said, speaking through her hand that covered her mouth. "Lordy, Lordy, girl, what on earth happened to you?!"

Jaime tried to make light of the situation. "You should see the other guy," she said and did her best to grin at Tia.

TWENTY-FOUR

Two weeks had passed since the boxing incident with Frank. The pain Jaime felt from his blows and most of the bruises were gone, but the hurt over why still lingered, just as she told Ashleigh it would. She had not seen Frank since and wondered if she ever would again.

From her office window she watched the busy streets of the city below. There were people on every corner and cabs, buses and cars at every light, which was normal for a Denver rush hour. She rested her hand against the glass. It was warm where the sun had touched it. But the sun had dipped low enough behind tall buildings, leaving the streets in heavy shadows. Pain stabbed at her heart and she knew it had nothing to do with what happened that night at the gym with Frank. In a few days it would be May twenty-four, the six-year anniversary of her sister's death.

She knew why this time bothered her. She had gone back to Boston to attend a wedding of a college friend on May twenty-four two years ago. Jaime left the wedding reception that afternoon and walked through the hundred-acre urban campus until she found herself standing near her old apartment building.

At that moment it was as if she had been propelled back in time. Memories played out before her like a home movie.

Jaime had gone home to Denver to attend Sarah's high school graduation, but left that same day to return to Boston to study for finals. She could still hear the telephone ringing in her apartment the day she received the call on May twenty-four that Sarah had died. The emptiness made the shrill of the ring fill every corner of the room.

It was her mother. She was trying to speak and control hysterical sobs simultaneously. Jaime could not understand her. She heard herself trying to tell her mother to calm down. Her parents had called rarely during her four years at college, unless it was necessary, and they had hardly spoken to her during the few days she was home for Sarah's graduation. She had an inkling why her mother had called. Of course, Jaime wanted to deny it, but it was a phone call she had long come to expect. There was a silence and Jaime could tell her mother had passed the phone to her father. He cleared his throat, the way he always did before he started any telephone conversation. Her father's words were clear and precise.

"Jaime?"

"Yes, dad," she said in a meek voice.

He wasted no time coming to the point. "Your sister's dead."

Jaime clutched the phone tightly. Her eyes narrowed at the clock radio on her nightstand. It showed 5:41 p.m. She felt as though someone had pushed down on her shoulders with tremendous force.

"When?" Her voice was barely audible. She leaned against the wall for support.

"Last night. This morning, really, about 1:30, maybe it was two o'clock ... I don't know ... it was the state patrol ... I can't remember what they said. She was in her car with that rowdy group of friends of hers and she was driving. They'd been drinking."

Sarah had asked Jaime to stay and go to the graduation parties with her, but Jaime had refused. She said she had to return to Boston to study for finals. Sarah had promised to come out in a week and they were planning to drive back to Denver together.

Maybe if I would have stayed...

Jaime remembered having her own satisfaction, however small, when Ryan McKenna was convicted of raping Sarah Renee Monroe a few months following her ordeal with the ectopic pregnancy.

"Have the ladies and gentlemen of the jury reached a decision?"

"Yes, your honor, we have."

The bailiff walked from the jury to hand the judge the written verdict. When the judge read the verdict, he glanced to the jury, then nodded at Ryan.

"Will the defendant please rise."

Ryan and his lawyer rose slowly.

"We find the defendant, Ryan McKenna, guilty."

Jaime turned her attention to her sister, who was visibly relieved. Jaime wanted to go to Sarah's table to embrace her, but she was already surrounded by a group of well-wishers. Her mother and father were already smothering her with hugs and kisses. So she remained seated alone and watched from the distance.

With a start, Jaime realized her father was crying on the phone.

"Where was the accident?" Jaime asked.

He cleared his throat and began again. "At the cottonwood tree ... the one near the house."

"Dad, I'm coming home," Jaime said, remembering the many times she and Sarah had run to that cottonwood tree and home again.

Her father's voice interrupted her. "I don't want you near this place," he said and his voice was firm.

His words and tone of voice sent a chill through her. She swallowed hard as her mouth went dry. She tried licking her lips to moisten them, but her tongue only stuck to them. She had known that someday it would come to this. Somewhere inside her, she was certain her parents were looking for the chance, something, any kind of excuse, to blame everything that had happened to Sarah on her.

"Dad, you can't do this to me. Please. Sarah was my sister ... She forgave me for what happened ... even if you and mom never could."

Jaime felt herself on the edge of tears. It took all she had to keep them from coming. She was defeated, but determined that no one would see her cry again. It was a silent promise she made to herself on the telephone.

"Jaime, you're not to come near this home again," her father said. "Do you hear me? You're not welcome to come to Sarah's funeral or back here for any reason."

"What about my things?" My clothes? My bedroom furniture? What about that?"

Material things. Her clothes. The bedroom furniture. They were trivial, but Jaime felt herself groping for a last sense of family to hold onto.

"I'll have them removed and placed in storage and send you the key."

On the other end, Jaime heard the clicking sound in her ear.

A broken connection. The last of it.

Just as well, she thought.

Jaime had no longer felt part of the family. She felt as if she had been there on loan, subject to change, just biding her time until asked to move on. Without ever having to say a word, it was the message Jaime knew her parents were trying to convey. It wasn't long before she began to think of herself like an unwelcome guest, on the outside looking in, a songbird on a migratory path.

She slid down the wall until her stomach rested against the front of her thighs. Jaime stared straight ahead, but saw nothing. Nothing except the only photograph that remained on the nightstand. It was the picture of Sarah playing tennis the summer before she was raped. She beamed in the photo, much the way Jaime remembered her smiling at graduation.

It amazed Jaime whenever she looked at her sister. Sarah was so precocious, in looks as well as mannerisms. After she was raped and then had the ectopic pregnancy, it wasn't long before Sarah began to fade, like a summer storm. All of her thunder gone.

Jaime closed her eyes and waited for the tears to come. But nothing came. She had cried so much, she was certain no tears were left within her. It would not be hard to keep her promise now. Jaime smiled to herself. She was good at keeping promises. Always had been.

She rested her head against her forearms and closed her eyes. When she woke, the apartment was dark. In a haze, she tried to remember where she was. The telephone was poking her in the side. Then she remembered the phone call. Her knees ached from their awkward position. She pulled herself to a standing position and put the phone back in the receiver. The clock radio showed 8:15 p.m.

Jaime found Sarah's obituary in the Denver newspapers a few days later. A photo taken of Sarah that Christmas accompanied the notice. Jaime wondered why her parents had selected that photo. Sarah wasn't smiling and it had been a lousy Christmas.

The paper said the funeral would be Saturday, one week after Sarah's graduation. That meant it would be at least another week before Jaime could return to Colorado to visit her sister's grave.

Time would simply trickle by. A knot formed deep in the pit of her stomach. It made her so physically ill she almost did not make it to the bathroom.

A few days after the funeral, Jaime had stopped to pick up her mail. Among the junk mail, a small neatly typed white envelope attracted her attention. There was no handwriting on the outside of the envelope, no return address. It didn't matter. Jaime did not have to look at the postmark to know who sent the letter. She opened it.

Inside was the key to a Boulder storage facility.

Twenty-five

There was something about the way the cream-colored-brick Tudor looked at the corner of Virginia Avenue and Corona Street near Wash Park that struck a certain, silent chord in Jaime. She had mentally moved in the same afternoon she saw the For Sale sign looming in the yard overgrown with weeds.

The house, with its pinnacle gables and carved finials, was her favorite style. The exterior was lined with a combination of brick, stone, and wood. The red-brick steps lined with two mature birch trees seemed to invite her to the door and offer her to come inside. She felt immediately attached to the home, as though arms had reached out, taken hold of her and pulled her toward it. She could not believe her luck in finding it.

It also helped that the Tudor faced east and west, which would allow for plenty of sun. That's how the home looked the first afternoon she saw it. She had opened the door and, after walking through a small entryway, was struck by an open and inviting spacious living room. A large bay window provided a cozy alcove and an abundance of natural light. Sunlight streamed in a southern window. The barrel-vaulted ceilings, descending to scalloped arches with niched peaks, added drama and gave the room an airy look. The stone hearth and mantel would bring welcome warmth on lifeless winter days.

Stairs ascended to a formal dining room, accompanied by a domed vaulted ceiling accented by detailed plaster, where a majestic lattice window rose like a half-moon above the dome's curves. In the kitchen, the large window over the sink would catch most of the afternoon sun. A sliding glass door opened to a small redwood deck, where a grove of trees loomed just beyond.

Jaime made an offer on the house during her first visit. She would move over Memorial Day. She had outgrown the apartment on Arapahoe Street. She could not enter her bedroom anymore without seeing Molly Gibson coming out of her bathroom, wearing her bathrobe. And she had grown tired of the endless noise that life in the city had provided and looked forward to quiet evenings on the deck of her new home.

The move almost started in disaster, when Tia pulled out at the last moment. Derrick had broken his leg so badly at the park that it required surgery. Jaime thought she would be on her own, had she not met Leigh by chance downtown that same day. When she mentioned the incident, Leigh quickly volunteered to help. Jaime was grateful for the offer. Other than paid help, she had no one else to call on such short notice. It went against her better judgment to accept Leigh's offer, but she agreed.

The weekend finally gave Jaime the chance to sample Leigh's cooking and test her claim that she was famous for it. Cooking was not Jaime's forte. Cooking for her was more like a utilitarian exercise than something she enjoyed. For Leigh, however, cooking was different. It was her outlet, her way of easing into an evening after work. She loved to follow recipes and create her own dishes.

On Friday they unpacked the kitchen and Leigh brought asparagus risotto she had prepared at home. Saturday night she fixed pasta with sun-dried tomatoes, fresh herbs and fresh baked bread. The only thing Jaime had to do was purchase the wine. Sunday night they enjoyed chicken in a creamy mustard sauce.

By late Monday afternoon everything had been moved from Jaime's apartment to the Tudor. With her hair pulled back in a ponytail and wearing faded jeans and a football jersey, Jaime finished unpacking her office.

"That about does it," she said, looking at a gathering of empty boxes around her feet. Leigh came from the living room and stood in the doorway, arms folded. Her hair was piled on the top of her head. Strands of it had fallen and hung loosely around the nape of her neck. She looked comfortable dressed in a dark-blue denim shirt and Levi's.

"You're probably glad to be gone from there," Leigh said, meeting Jaime's eyes.

Jaime nodded. "I am. With Mitchell, I just felt like I never knew what I was going to find when I came home."

Leigh looked at Jaime and tilted her head as if to ask what she meant.

Jaime shrugged, taking the cue. "I don't know. It's probably nothing. It's probably just me and all the stress since Kelly Jo's trial."

Jaime paused to collect newspaper from the floor and stuff it in a box. She stood and looked at Leigh, who was still studying her intently, waiting for her to continue.

"It's like I'd come home and it would just feel like someone had been in the house. Things just seemed out of place. But like I said, it was probably just me. It's been a tough few months. Mitchell left before Thanksgiving and the only time he's been back was the night he took Ashleigh and me home from the hospital."

"What did you do with your apartment key?" Leigh asked.

"I left it on the kitchen counter with a note," Jaime replied. "Then I called and left a message at his office. I knew I wouldn't have to talk to him there, because he never answers his phone at work. The place was in his name, anyway. So he can take care of it. I just took what was mine. The furniture was all his. Now he can deal with it."

Leigh looked over her shoulder to the living room surveying the new furniture. "That's right," she said. "Let him deal with it."

They worked the rest of Monday afternoon with a gentle rain falling outside, little conversation between them and Leigh's homemade chicken soup simmering on the stove. When the last of the work was done, they feasted on soup. They stayed in front of the fireplace long after their meal was over. They talked of random things and both were careful not to mention Ashleigh. Sarah, of course, had found her way into their conversation. The bond that was forming between them relaxed Jaime. It made her feel as though she could trust herself to talk at length with Leigh. The wine helped, too.

Through, tiny, desperate breaths, Jaime managed to tell Leigh a story she had told only once, to Pearl.

"It was all she could do to keep from screaming..." The words Sarah had used in telling Jaime about the night she was raped tumbled from her mouth, filling the space between them. Jaime sat, captured by the rise and fall of the flames in the fireplace. Leigh's comforting hand on her shoulder prompted her to continue.

A tear fell on Jaime's hand. It formed a small pool. She forced the rest of them back inside. Just as she always had.

"He … he held his hand over her mouth. Sarah told me a thousand times that the strength of his grip had squeezed her inside lower lip into her teeth, cutting it. She could taste the salty blood in her mouth.

"When everything was over, Sarah focused on the shelf above her and fixed her attention on the tennis trophy she had won in a tournament last weekend serving an ace. She said it was the trophy that had kept her from screaming."

Jaime's laugh was fragile and she continued. "And that's when I think everything started to happen."

Leigh frowned. "What happened?"

"She just stopped thinking about everything. One by one, the frames went out of focus. Her mind went black," Jaime said. "Sarah told me so many times about that night. She said she lifted herself up slowly off the floor and started the shower. The water ran until it was hot and the bathroom filled with steam. She stepped inside. The scalding water hit her face, her body. She flinched slightly as the water peppered her body. It was too hot to bear, but it didn't matter. She needed to be clean. She needed to wash away the evidence. Wash away the memory. Wash away the pain."

Jaime buried her face in her hands.

The fire in the stone hearth leapt and crackled, but the shadows that rose and fell on the wall were silent. Leigh watched a moment, mesmerized. She went to the kitchen for coffee in an attempt to break the unsettling mood. She returned and handed a cup to Jaime. The fresh aroma mixed with wood and heat. Jaime had put another log in and stoked the fire, and Leigh noticed her face was flushed from the heat.

Jaime stared at the black liquid and, for what seemed a long time, the room was silent. She finally ended by saying, "And in a few years she would die in a car wreck." She continued to trace the rim absentmindedly and, when she spoke again, directed her comments toward the cup. "Sarah lost the will to live. She just didn't have the strength to get beyond what had happened to her. That happens to people sometimes."

Leigh shrugged. "Couldn't your parents get Sarah professional help? A psychiatrist or something? Something could've been done to help her, both of you."

Jaime shook her head. "My parents did try professional assistance, but it didn't work." Jaime felt a sudden coldness as a shiver crawled up her spine. She cupped her hands around her coffee mug and leaned closer to the fire. "I always thought Sarah was a strong person, but everyone has their limits," she went on, still staring at the fire. "She wanted to die. I really believe that."

Leigh had been enchanted by the flames, but looked at Jaime, transfixed. "What makes you think Sarah wanted to kill herself? I can't believe that, not with the others in her car."

Without another word, Jaime rose and left the room. She returned moments later holding a small, white envelope. She looked at Leigh, studying her. The look was unwavering. She handed Leigh the envelope. Jaime's name and her Boston address were typed neatly in the center of the letter. There was no return address.

Leigh pulled the card slowly from the envelope and studied it. On the front, large, cheerful and delicate flowers were packed into a thickly cut vase. Another lay on its side near the vase. She ran her hand lightly over the top. It looked as though the picture had been drawn with love. Leigh looked to Jaime and she nodded as if to give her permission to open the card. Leigh opened it and read the words written neatly in the center.

Jaime, I may not always be beside you.

But I'll always be with you. Always.

There was no signature. When Leigh finished she looked to Jaime. Their eyes met. Leigh's despairing look almost reduced Jaime to tears, but she managed to hold her composure.

Jaime raised her eyebrows slightly as if to say, *see I told you so*. "That's Sarah's handwriting."

An extended silence filled the room. From the open window Jaime could hear the far off rumble of a jet airliner. There had always been something about that sound that pulled at her. It often filled her with a deep sense of longing she was sure she could never fill. She felt as lonely tonight as she ever had hearing it.

"Sarah knew what she was doing," Jaime said. "The letter came a few days after she died. She must've mailed it the morning she graduated. No wonder she was happy at graduation. She knew that night it would be all over. She never intended to go on."

"What about the others with Sarah in the car that night?" Leigh asked. "Surely Sarah wouldn't do something like that with others in the car with her?"

Jaime looked at Leigh for one, long penetrating moment. When she spoke, she sounded like a frightened child. "The old Sarah never would, but who knows how skewed her thinking had become and how truly deep she had gone. Ryan had hurt her, hurt her terribly. I don't know, maybe she felt like hurting someone back? She sure hurt me. No one will ever know of the darkness that lived inside of Sarah after what had happened. We were as close as twins and even I couldn't comprehend that darkness. It was buried with her."

Leigh read the card again before she closed it and gave it back to Jaime.

"I don't know why I've saved this," Jaime said, taking the card. "It destroys me every time I read it. I feel like it's some kind of punishment, keeping it, but it's the only piece of Sarah I feel like I have left. It was the last thing she ever gave me."

Jaime left the room putting the card inside the envelope. When she returned she went to the bay window. Rain fell evenly from the sky. It landed lightly against the glass in long, silver streaks. The smell of the rich, wet earth entered through the open window.

Leigh stood quietly behind Jaime. She rested her hands on Jaime's shoulders and felt them weaken at her touch. It was all Leigh had to do for Jaime, show comfort and compassion. Jaime struggled to keep from crying. It had been so easy to keep the tears at bay these past few years.

Kelly Jo Cox's trial, however, made everything resurface. She was like a storm cloud about to burst.

Leigh felt Jaime's struggle. "It's all right to cry, Jaime."

It was all she had to say. Her words were like opening a door and letting air into a room on fire. Jaime could no longer hold it inside. She left the window and sat down at the kitchen table, clutching the sides of it with her hands. She squeezed until they hurt. Jaime did everything she could to stop the tears from coming. But it was a fight she could not win. The masquerade was over. She felt her eyes begin to moisten. It almost surprised her. Leigh's voice echoed.

"It's okay to cry, Jaime..."

She blinked once. A second time. Tears welled until they had nowhere else to go. They spilled over her lids and fell freely down her cheeks and onto her football jersey. She did not struggle to stop them from coming, or raise her hand to clear them away. She cried because she wanted to. She cried for everything she had ever lost. Her heaving sobs finally began to quiet. Before long they turned to a whimper. Leigh didn't move. Finally there was silence. Jaime put her head down on her arms, physically and emotionally drained.

Leigh spoke quietly. "Go and lie down, get some rest. Try to sleep if you can."

"I don't want to sleep anymore," Jaime said quietly, her voice muffled. "If I could get away without sleeping at all, I'd do it. I hate sleeping anymore."

Silence surrounded them. Jaime did not have the strength to move. She lifted her head and glanced around the kitchen. Leigh studied her. Her eyes were red and puffy, her face splotched with tiny red circles.

"You probably think I'm a fool don't you?" Jaime said.

"What? For crying? For being human, to accept what happened to your sister and try to make the best of a crappy situation at home and with your parents? No, Jaime, I don't think you're a fool. It takes courage to accept your mistakes and then try to go on with life. I wish I could say the same for your parents."

Leigh hesitated a moment and stared at Jaime. The tormented look in her eyes welled like a tempest. "It takes a lot of courage to deal with a pair of sanctimonious parents, who fail to accept the blame for what happened to Sarah and instead dump everything on you. Instead of doing everything they could to help the both of you get through what happened, they did nothing. It's disgusting."

"My parents know I'm an attorney," Jaime said.

"How?"

"My aunt. My mother's sister. She's the only one I've kept in touch with over the years. I talk to her a few times a year. She told my parents."

"Did they attend your graduation?"

Jaime shook her head. "Besides, they hate lawyers," she said with a small laugh.

"Why on earth?"

"The parents of the others in the car with Sarah sued for wrongful death and pain and suffering. My parents finally settled with the last of them a year or so ago." Jaime pursed her lips. It was her best attempt at a smile.

"Will you go lie down? Please." Leigh glanced at her watch. It was after 10 p.m. "Start fresh tomorrow. I'll clean up here."

Jaime scanned the kitchen, eyeing the dirty dishes on the table and counters and pans on the stove. Leigh read her mind. "Don't worry," she said with a smile. "I know where everything goes."

Without another word, Jaime pushed herself away from the table and left the kitchen. Walking toward her bedroom, she remembered the night she had done the same for Frank, cleaned his place while he slept in a drunken stupor.

She looked at her new bed. The dreams would come, but she needed sleep. If the running dream and dreams about Sarah weren't bad enough, the ones with Frank lately were equally bad. She had dreamt Frank was running after her, wearing an oversized pair of boxing gloves. She always managed to wake just as he was about to grab her. She could feel his hot, labored breathing against her neck. Hear him growling like an animal. Jaime pushed the dream from her mind as she pulled off her clothes. She slipped on a nightshirt. She didn't bother to pull down the bedspread. Instead, she lay down on top. She felt her eyelids grow heavy. She did everything she could to keep them from closing. But in the settling darkness, the longer she lay still and the quieter the room became, the closer she moved toward that floating feeling that comes before sleep. She could hear Leigh moving about in the kitchen. The sound soothed her. She turned on her side and in minutes had fallen into a deep sleep.

An hour later, Leigh finished cleaning. She looked around the kitchen and the living room. Jaime still had much work to do. But that was good. As time went on, she would shape and form it into a home, a place that would become her own.

Framed in the doorway of Jaime's bedroom, Leigh listened for a moment. The only sound came from Jaime's soft and steady breathing. She walked quietly into the room and turned on a soft light that illuminated from the nightstand. She saw a blanket folded at the foot of the bed. She covered Jaime. She turned off the light and darkness surrounded her.

She thought of what Jaime had said when she had finally stopped crying.

"What a way to start living in your new home. Crying like a baby."

There was nothing Leigh could say. She felt differently about crying than Jaime. She would tell Jaime someday that crying was not a sign of weakness. But Leigh knew she wouldn't have to tell her, she would come to the realization on her own.

Crying cleanses the soul.

As Leigh locked the front door to Jaime's home, she thought of her daughter Ashleigh as a little girl. A child of fire and ice. She thought often of the times after Drew had left them. She remembered the loneliness that had been her frequent companion in those early days. Ashleigh could not understand. Leigh had no brothers and sisters, her mother and father were gone. She felt as lonely and isolated from the world and everyone in it as she ever had.

There were many empty days. Her only comfort came in crying. And many times she did. It seemed the tears came mostly when she was driving. Since it was in the car that she did her best thinking, it seemed only natural that her tears would fall then. The tears were often so deep and heavy she could not see to drive and had to pull over.

It was not long before she began to welcome those moments. When she was ready to continue, she felt better, lighter, as though a mooring had been lifted from her soul. A good cry was like the gentle rain that had washed the earth clean this Memorial Day weekend. She stepped into the night. The rain had stopped. The earth smelled pure and sweet. The clouds had parted, giving way to the slip of a quarter moon. The velvet ceiling of the sky was alive with a wash of stars.

Before her, the neighborhood was empty and deserted, the houses quiet and dark. The moon was her only companion as she walked to her car. It took her a moment to lower the ragtop of her Volkswagen Cabrio. The night was cool, but she wanted to drive with the top down, to feel the air. She almost hated to start the Cabrio and break the comforting silence that surrounded her. She started her car, interrupting the stillness. She headed for Interstate Twenty-five and then Interstate Seventy would take her home to Evergreen.

It was calling her.

Twenty-six

The Corinthian-columned Denver City and County Building sat like a massive temple looking east at the gold dome of the state capitol building across Broadway.

Jaime was heading to the city and county building after a light boxing workout with Scott through the noon hour. It was the first time she had boxed since Frank had knocked her out. She had felt apprehensive when she first stepped on the sparring mat with Scott, but she'd refused to let her fear get in the way. The incident would not stop her from doing a sport she loved.

At least it wasn't taking much effort adjusting to her new home. For that, she was thankful. She had been living in Wash Park for three weeks and she already felt a part of her home and the area, like a tree in the forest.

Jamie continued her walk toward the courthouse. The unflinching glare from the mid-morning July sun baked down on her face and arms. The heat from the past week had been relentless, a cruel form of punishment, as temperatures even failed to cool down during the night. As she walked, heat rose from the pavement in hazy images and she felt the warmth seep through her heels. Jaime removed her suit jacket and picked up the pace toward the courthouse.

As she entered the building's entrance off Bannock Street, Mitchell had just stepped off an elevator with a group of attorneys from his firm. He noticed her immediately. But she did not see him. Mitchell watched, taking in every detail of her appearance as she headed down the hallway. It was the first time he had seen her since the boxing incident. Her hair was pulled away from her face. She wore a white sleeveless silk blouse that deepened the tan on her shoulders and arms. The wide belt she wore over a camel-colored linen skirt accentuated her slender waist. She looked elegant and refined as she always had.

As Jaime moved deeper into the building, she stopped suddenly, feeling as though someone was watching her. Mitchell stepped away from her view. He waited until she passed him, then he followed her.

It was the ninth of July. Ashleigh's hearing was tomorrow and Jaime had received permission to enter one of the empty courtrooms. She let the door close quietly behind her as she slipped inside. Paneling the color of cinnamon covered the walls. The desks and chairs matched the color of the walls. She set her blazer over the arm of a chair and began to scan the perimeter of the courtroom, taking in every detail. She studied the room intently and began to do what she always did before one of her cases was set for trial. In an empty courtroom, she would spend some time imagining the upcoming events.

She stood near the back of the room. As though she was a movie director, she stretched out her hands before her, palms forward. She brought her thumbs together to form the bottom of a frame, as though she was about to see the courtroom using a camera's viewfinder. As she moved her arms left to right, right to left, Jaime could produce a wide angle or telephoto effect, depending on where she wanted to focus. She imagined how the courtroom scenes would play out.

Despite an icy tentacle of uneasiness that had wrapped itself around her when she entered the empty courtroom, she felt surprisingly calm.

The seats for the audience would most likely remain empty. Ashleigh's case, at least for the initial hearing, would not generate any media attention. That would, of course, change during the appeals process. Jaime panned right until her view came to the table where she, Ashleigh and Tia would sit.

She moved the frame slowly to the left and along the wooden railing, the threshold that separated the audience from the attorneys, judge and jury. She continued to pan left until the desk where Leigh and Winston would sit came to view. She held the frame steady on the empty desk.

She walked to the railing. The viewfinder stopped when Jaime put her hand on the railing and stepped from the audience area to where she would sit. She took her place and set her palms on the table, lightly at first, then firmly. Returning her hands to the frame, Jaime panned until the judge's bench came into view. Jessie Gutierrez would preside, nodding slightly, interjecting when appropriate, and keeping his attention fixed on the activity in his courtroom.

She panned and stopped at the witness stand. Jaime thought of Ashleigh taking the stand. Then she thought of Erin Greene and the others who would give their expert opinions regarding Ashleigh's medical condition and competency.

Jaime lowered her arms and rested them in her lap. She looked to the juror's box. The chairs would remain empty. The decision on Ashleigh's case would remain with Judge Jessie Gutierrez.

She rose and ran the tips of her fingers along the top of the desk. It was smooth, even to the touch. She did not linger in the area long and turned to leave. She looked to the back of the courtroom and gasped at the sight of Mitchell sitting in the last row. His elbows were resting against his sides, hands entwined. His index fingers, resting lightly against his lips, formed a steeple. She noticed he still wore his wedding ring. She felt his eyes on her and hoped he had not sensed her surprise at seeing him. But feared he probably had.

She reached him and stopped. He looked trim and was symmetrically dressed in a navy, herringbone suit, starched white shirt and a yellow print tie. He had shaved the mustache and beard that had framed his lip and chin, making him look younger now than his thirty-two years.

She gave him a cool, detached look. "Shouldn't you be getting a murderer off?"

Mitchell did not answer.

"What are you doing here?" she asked.

"I came to watch," he said mildly. "I see you got someone to let you in."

She nodded slightly and folded her arms across her chest. They stared at each other in silence.

"Doing a little imagery, Jaime?"

She didn't answer, he knew what she came to do.

Mental images. Jaime had learned about imagery when Sarah's tennis coach told Sarah it was a great way to prepare mentally for a match, without ever picking up a racquet. When Jaime began to box she also started to use imagery to help her learn a demanding and physical sport. She would visualize hitting the bag and working at it until her punches became a smooth, even rhythm. Imagery became especially helpful for Jaime when she became an attorney.

"Why do you have to do this every time?" Mitchell asked.

"Why does it matter to you?"

He chuckled and looked beyond her to the jury box. "I hear you bailed on the DA's office."

Jaime nodded.

"How's old Dan Walker treating you these days?"

Jaime chose not to answer.

"Your eye looks better than the last time I saw you."

Mitchell's remark caught her off guard. She stepped back and subconsciously raised her hand to her eye. She rubbed it lightly and remembered the bruises. She thought of the man who had bruised her and why. The emptiness of loss and hurt she had felt toward Frank that night deepened a little, as it did each time she recalled that evening.

"I need to go," Jaime said, determined not to give Mitchell the satisfaction of seeing her upset. She grabbed her blazer and moved quickly from the courtroom before giving him the chance to say another word.

When Jaime entered Walker & Associates fifteen minutes later, Tia greeted her as she opened the door. Tia had eaten most of her lunch at her desk, a quarter pounder with cheese, large fries and a medium diet soda.

"Sorry I'm late," Jaime said stopping at her desk.

"Where've you been?"

"Down at the city and county building."

"Got the feel for it?" Tia asked. She handed Jaime her lunch bag. Jamie nodded as she opened it and pulled out a bagel sandwich with cream cheese, avocado and tomatoes. Jaime pulled up a chair and then took a quick inventory of what Tia was eating.

Tia raised her drink in Jaime's direction. "It's diet. Does that count?"

Jaime grinned as she took a bite from her bagel.

Later that afternoon they met with Erin and Ashleigh for final preparations for the hearing. After Ashleigh and Erin left, Jaime and Tia continued to work. Tia looked from her document and fixed her eyes directly on Jaime, perplexed.

"Girl, you know what I can't figure out is why Leigh wouldn't just be satisfied that if Ashleigh were to have a boyfriend and become sexually active, why couldn't it be enough that Ashleigh use birth control?" She was silent as she thought and then went on. "You know the disability rights group will say eliminating sexual assault is the most humane way to avoid pregnancy. Not what Leigh and mothers like her have in mind, tying the fallopian tubes of a person who is incapable, or capable for that matter, of making a sound decision."

Jaime tossed her pen on the desk. She raised her right eyebrow slightly and nodded her head in agreement. "I wish it were that easy for Ashleigh," she said.

Jaime scanned her cluttered desk. "But you've read the doctor's reports. Birth control pills may not be compatible with Ashleigh's diabetic condition. That's already hard enough for her to manage effectively without daily intervention. Their reports show it could increase her potential of cardiovascular disease and high blood pressure. It doesn't leave room for many options if Ashleigh can't take the pill."

Jaime closed her eyes and leaned her head against the back of the chair. When she opened her eyes, Tia stared directly at her. They both felt the same.

"This is going to be a challenge," Jaime said quietly.

Tia looked thoughtfully at Jaime. "What about other birth control devices? There's got to be something else that could work for Ashleigh without going to such extremes as sterilization."

Jaime shrugged. "When the pill came on the market in 1960, it became America's most popular form of birth control, but it doesn't work for everyone and probably won't for Ashleigh. For that matter, sterilization is just about as popular."

"When a woman makes that choice on her own."

Jaime pointed at Tia. "Exactly."

Tia went on. "Of course, it doesn't help matters much now that AIDS has changed the course of practically every type of research. The trends seem to move toward improving the old barrier methods, condoms and diaphragms that at least offer protection against AIDS and other sexually transmitted diseases."

Jaime nodded. "That in itself is doing as much to drive contraceptive research as is the prevention of pregnancy. And it doesn't help that in the past few years, contraception has become entangled with abortion." She shook her head and looked as dejected she felt. "The problem seems almost simple for us to solve, Tia, but the point here for Ashleigh is not whether she has the choice of using a diaphragm, or her partner wearing a condom. The point is, her choice remains whether she wants to be sterilized and we know from the many conversations we've had with Ashleigh that is not her desire. We both know if that happens, other choices become moot. What does it matter after that? Leigh has her life to live, her own choices to make. Ashleigh should have the same."

Jaime rubbed a finger over her lips as she thought. "Look, it's simple," she said. "This whole case comes down to this: Being human is not necessarily about making the right choices, it's about the right to make them. We think Ashleigh should have that right. And Leigh doesn't."

It was 6:30 p.m. when they had reached a stopping point. Jaime set her pen on the desk and rubbed her eyes as Tia watched.

"You look exhausted, Jaime. Go home and get some rest. Come on, let's walk out together."

Jaime scanned the documents and files that covered her desk. She shook her head. "I just have a few more things to do here. Besides, Scott and I are going to box again tonight." She looked gingerly at Tia. "You'd better go though. The boys are going to wonder what happened to you."

By the time Tia had collected her things and returned to say goodnight, Jaime had turned on her lamp. It shed a soft light over her desk. Jaime was so absorbed in reading that Tia did not disturb her. She looked on in silence, admiring Jaime's depth and persistence.

"Hey, Jaime, take it easy!" Scott McIntyre stood behind the black heavy bag and used what strength he had to hold it steady while Jaime pounded with a flurry of solid punches. She stopped hitting the bag, lowered her arms and stared at Scott. Perspiration covered her brow and strands of her wet hair clung to the sides of her neck. Her heart hammered and her breathing was rapid.

"Am I doing something wrong?" she asked.

"Are you kidding! You're doing great! I've never felt you hit the bag like you are tonight."

Scott and Jaime completed their workout with a slow mile run around the indoor track and she headed to the locker room, ready for a shower and steam. On the way out of the club, Emily, a small slender woman, was standing at the front desk to greet her. Her dark hair pulled back in a ponytail accentuated her pretty, oval face.

"Here's your card, Jaime."

"Thanks, Emily, see you later."

As Jaime turned to leave, Emily called to her. "Oh, wait, Jaime! Barry said he wanted to talk with you before you left tonight. He's outside by the pool."

Jaime found Barry Winters stacking a fresh set of towels into a rack near the pool. When he saw her coming toward him, his smile reached to his eyes. As he set the towels on the shelf and went to meet Jaime, he tried not to think of the night Frank had knocked her unconscious, but it had a nasty way of forcing itself in. Barry had lifted Jaime into his arms and he remembered having to let her go when Mitchell stepped in to take her to the hospital.

Jaime did not come to the club for nearly two weeks after that incident. He tried several times to call her at home, but the answering machine always took his call. He left one message. "Hey, Jaime, it's Barry," he said quietly into the phone. "I'm just calling to see how you're doing. If you need anything, anything at all, you can call me and I'll get you whatever you need."

He left his number, but she never called.

"I'm glad Emily caught you before you left, Jaime," Barry said.

"She said you were out here. What's up?"

Barry smiled softly and his eyes grew tender, almost affectionate in the short time he took to study her. She looked refreshed and casual. She had only towel-dried her hair and it was still damp against her shoulders. The plum-colored top she wore deepened the brown in her eyes. She wore no makeup and Barry detected a soft scent of her body lotion.

"Nothing really," he said, suddenly feeling his face flush. "I wanted to wish you good luck tomorrow. I know you have the Ashleigh Roberts' hearing."

Jaime smiled. "Thanks for remembering. I'll need it."

"Let me know how it goes will you? Please, Jaime, I'd like to know."

"Barry!" Emily called to him from the door. "Phone call!"

Barry waved to Emily and he and Jaime walked toward the door together. Jaime said good-bye to them both and turned to leave. Emily kept an eye on Barry as he watched Jaime until she disappeared. When he turned to take the phone from Emily, his eyes met hers. He only smiled at her. Emily's smile was in her eyes. He knew what she was thinking and she was right.

Barry took the phone. "This is Barry," he said, glancing in the direction he last saw Jaime.

It was nearly midnight by the time Jaime had eaten and cleaned up after dinner. She felt exhausted and ready for bed. She was asleep the moment her head hit the pillow.

"Not again," she muttered, and rolled over to glance at the digital clock. The luminous red numbers showed 3:23 a.m. "Damn. Leave me alone."

The running dream again. It was the same as it always was, from the first night the dream invaded her sleep. The fire surrounded her, but did not consume her. She ran for her life, but on the treadmill, she went nowhere. She just ran and ran and ran. Her clothes, and this time more of her skin, fell from her body. Each time she had the dream, she came closer and closer to becoming a skeleton. An empty shell.

Her thoughts were the same and they frightened her.

Am I going to die? Like Sarah did? Is my life spinning out of control? Is that what this dream means? Nowhere to run, nowhere to hide.

The thoughts unnerved her, but no matter what she did, she could not push them from her mind. It was the first time she had the dream since moving into her new home. She hoped she had left the nightmares behind, but they had followed her here.

An old phrase her grandmother had often said stirred within Jaime, from the farthest reaches of her mind … *"Wherever you go, there you are."*

Twenty-seven

When Jaime entered the courtroom, Leigh and Winston were already sitting at their table. Jaime was sorry now for every moment she had spent with Leigh. She stopped at the doorway, immobilized as if this moment suddenly revealed Leigh's true intentions. The woman sitting with Winston Ross seemed like a different person, not the one who had helped her move. Not the one who listened to every word about the night Sarah was raped and the day she died. Not the one who finally gave her permission to cry.

What had she been thinking? Did she jeopardize Ashleigh's hearing because of her association with her mother? She could hear Pearl's gentle, but firm warnings about getting too close. Advice she had selfishly and blatantly ignored.

It was an effort to push air through her lungs, as though someone was standing on her chest, but Jaime willed herself to move through the gallery. She kept her eyes on Winston's table. He studied a legal pad and Leigh faced the judge's bench, her elbows resting on the tabletop, hands folded lightly. She was studying her hands and looked deep in thought. Leigh was wearing a sleeveless, linen sheath, with the long sleeves of a cardigan looped around her shoulders. Her hair was pulled away from her face. If she heard Jaime enter the courtroom, she gave no indication.

Tia and Ashleigh were already seated. Jaime looked at them and smiled to herself as she neared the table. Tia looked sophisticated and confident dressed in a gold and cream colored jacket with matching skirt. With her hair in a chignon, Jaime matched Tia's style wearing a navy and white suit and matching heels. Ashleigh sat quietly beside Tia, her hands resting in her lap. Her hair fell softly and loosely across her shoulders. She was dressed simply in a white blouse and red crepe jumper.

Tia looked up when Jaime reached the table. With a quick nod to Tia, Jaime sat down. She put her hand on Ashleigh's forearm and squeezed lightly.

"Ready, everyone?" Jaime asked, her voice low.

"We're all set," Tia answered. Ashleigh nodded.

The room was silent except for the rustling of papers. Leigh and Winston were bent toward each other talking, their voices whispers. They stopped talking as Judge Jessie Gutierrez entered the courtroom. Everyone stood and waited until he reached the bench and sat down. The judge adjusted his glasses on the end of his short nose and he glanced briefly at everyone.

"Good afternoon. Are we ready?"

Winston Ross rose from his chair. He looked briefly at Jaime and then to Jessie.

"Yes, your honor," he said.

"Very well, Mr. Ross, you may proceed."

Jaime watched as Winston smoothed his crimson-colored tie against his starched-white shirt. He wore gray, tony trousers with chiseled lines that created a kind of powerful elegance. He looked relaxed and at ease as he began to address the judge. She wished she felt the same way. She had managed to drift back to sleep after the running dream, but woke feeling jittery. Her nerves were taut and she felt like a rubber band ready to snap.

"Thank you, your honor," Winston said. "A petition filed by my client, Leigh Roberts, in early January, seeks the sterilization of her daughter,

Ashleigh Roberts, who has mental retardation. Leigh is Ashleigh's mother and legal guardian. You will hear evidence presented by three expert witnesses including an internist, who specializes specifically in the treatment of diabetes, a psychologist and a professional in the field of developmental disabilities. Your honor…"

Winston paused before continuing. He looked earnestly at Leigh and then to Ashleigh, who held his gaze only a moment before she averted her attention and looked to Jaime.

"Your honor," he went on, "Leigh Roberts loves her daughter very much, a love that manifests itself in many ways. Her love for Ashleigh is one of the very reasons why we are in this courtroom today…" Winston's voice trailed off as he walked behind Leigh and rested his hands lightly over her shoulders.

"And, out of a deep, abiding love for her daughter and concern for her physical health and well-being, Leigh has elected to seek the court's approval to have her daughter sterilized. Not an easy decision for any mother to make.

"But Leigh Roberts is a pragmatic person, your honor, realistic to the point that she knows this isn't something she wants to do, but, rather, something she must do. A hard and unpleasant reality that her only daughter has a form of mental retardation and has diabetes, offers her the grim outlook that a pregnancy would not only be detrimental for Ashleigh's baby, but also for Ashleigh. Results could be deadly for both of them."

Winston grew quiet for a moment. He looked thoughtfully at the judge. "Not a pleasant thought for a mother to have to live with, your honor. With a deep love for her daughter, Leigh has come to recognize that the best and only option for Ashleigh to avoid the consequences of becoming pregnant is to have her fallopian tubes tied.

"What you will hear is evidence to support that Ashleigh's poor health and her mental disability, albeit mild, mean that a pregnancy would not be advantageous to her and, therefore, not in her best interest. You will hear evidence in this hearing, your honor, which will show why, because of Ashleigh's diabetic condition, it is medically essential and necessary that she be sterilized."

Winston returned to his chair and sat down.

"Is that all, Mr. Ross?" Jessie asked.

"Yes, your honor, thank you."

The judge looked to Jaime. "Counselor?"

As Jaime stood, she pushed her feelings of uneasiness aside and replaced them with a quiet, but forceful determination and confidence. She took a deep breath and willed the heavy feeling in her chest to go away. Ashleigh was depending on her and she would not let her down.

"Thank you, your honor. We prefer to give opening statements when we call our first witness, if it pleases the court."

Jessie rubbed a thick finger across his lips as he thought, then looked at Winston. "Mr. Ross?" the judge said.

Winston rose slightly, holding his tie against his shirt. "We have no objections, your honor."

"Very well then," he said, looking from Jaime to Winston. "Mr. Ross, call your first witness."

Winston stood and spoke in an even, firm voice. "Our first witness is Dr. Steven Richie."

Silence settled over the courtroom as Dr. Steven Richie walked to the witness stand. He was in his late fifties, a thin man of medium height. His dark hair, peppered with gray, was cropped closely to his head and beginning to thin on top. He wore wire-rimmed glasses that encircled deep-set brown eyes. An aquiline nose and a thin mouth that turned down at the corners gave his already slender, clean-shaven face a hawk-like appearance.

"Dr. Richie, would you tell the court how long you've been practicing medicine."

"I've been an internist for nearly thirty years. Much of my practice has been devoted to treating diabetes."

"Could you explain for the court, Dr. Richie, what diabetes is?"

Steven Richie nodded thoughtfully and paused before he answered. "Stated simply, diabetes is a physical problem that causes a person to have too much sugar in their blood. Medically, it is called diabetes mellitus. To put it in layman's terms, the cells in our bodies can't run without a fuel called glucose. It is manufactured by our bodies through the foods we eat, which, in turn, is carried to the cells via the bloodstream. But glucose can't get into and be absorbed by the cells in a person who has diabetes.

Basically the cells are locked up tighter than a Manhattan apartment."

Sounds of quiet laughter filled the courtroom.

Dr. Richie smiled briefly and continued to address Winston Ross. "Consider insulin the key that unlocks those tiny apartments. Insulin is produced by beta cells from a gland called the pancreas." Dr. Richie stopped a moment and pushed his glasses up on his nose as he considered what to say next. "Diabetes can be broken down into types one and two. In Type I diabetes, also called juvenile diabetes, the pancreas no longer produces insulin, therefore making the patient dependent upon daily insulin. If left untreated, the disease will progress rapidly.

"Type II diabetes is generally a milder form of the disease and affects about 90 percent of the diabetic population. The beta cells are still present and making plenty of insulin, however, it's not being utilized effectively by the body's cells. Type II, or maturity-onset diabetes as it was once commonly called, refers to patients who are typically non-insulin dependent. Patients with this type of diabetes need to modify their diet, lose weight and exercise to control their diabetes.

"Only 30 percent of people with diabetes of this type are insulin dependent. In either case, the end result is that sugar remains in the blood, causing high blood sugar. I should state, however, that both types of the disease need maintenance by proper diet and exercise."

"Could you please tell the court what are some of the long-term complications associated with diabetes, doctor." Winston said.

"Well, a number of things. Normally the body relies on the hormone insulin to break down sugar and starch into fuel for the cells. When the system malfunctions as with diabetes, sugar accumulates in the blood. Untreated, it could eventually lead to blindness, heart disease, kidney failure and nerve and vessel damage that makes amputation necessary, and in some cases, death. But, as with any disease, medical professionals can occasionally go overboard when explaining to a patient for the first time that they have diabetes."

Dr. Richie suppressed a chuckle. "I knew a case once where a nurse had a patient absolutely convinced that she would eventually go blind, become a bilateral amputee and would need dialysis three times a week. You can imagine the emotional fallout that woman must've felt when she heard the news. Diabetes can be properly controlled and does not have to go to such extremes. It is, however, not a disease to be taken lightly. It's serious and should be treated that way."

"Thank you, doctor," Winston said. "Does heredity play a role in diabetes?"

"Yes, very much. Diabetes is not only classified by type, but also by degree of carbohydrate abnormality." Dr. Richie began to count on his fingers to make his point. "In order of increasing severity these are prediabetes, subclinical diabetes, latent diabetes and overt diabetes. A patient may progress through all four stages, remain in one stage, or even revert to a less severe stage. A patient with prediabetes has no signs of abnormal sugar metabolism, but has certain characteristics that predispose him or her to the future onset of diabetes. Functional hypoglycemia is associated with early and mild maturity-onset diabetes. About 30 percent of patients with functional hypoglycemia eventually go on to develop diabetes."

"And such could be the case with Ashleigh, who has functional hypoglycemia," Winston said, extending an open hand in Ashleigh's direction. "Is that not correct?"

Dr. Richie paused and looked carefully at Ashleigh. Her hands were folded and resting in her lap. Tia and Jaime were on each side of her like bookends. Ashleigh's attention was fixed evenly on him.

Dr. Richie said, "Yes, Mr. Ross, that's correct. This group includes patients whose parents, one or both of them, or other blood relatives have diabetes. Diabetes is considered a recessive inheritance."

Winston walked to the witness stand. "Which means?"

"Which means an individual may carry the gene but does not develop the disease, but can pass it on to the next generation. But diabetes is imminent, especially when the disease runs in the family."

"And you treated Leigh Robert's mother who was an insulin-dependent diabetic until her death six years ago. Is that not correct, doctor?"

Dr. Richie nodded. "Yes, that's correct. She was my patient for several years. She had juvenile, or Type I diabetes, which required daily use of insulin."

"And you treated Ashleigh on her initial visit and several thereafter?"

Dr. Richie nodded looking at Leigh. "That's correct."

"What can Ashleigh expect from her functional hypoglycemia condition. Dr. Richie?"

"As I said earlier, she could advance through each of the four stages, or remain where she is now, or she stands a 30 percent chance of developing Type II diabetes."

"So, in other words, doctor, Ashleigh will never be completely free of the disease?"

"That's correct. Once a person has a form of diabetes, it will be with them for the rest of their natural life."

"So they will never be symptom-free, is that correct, doctor?" Winston asked.

"Yes, that's correct."

Winston nodded and stroked his chin thoughtfully. "I would imagine in your practice, Dr. Richie, you must treat a number of women whose pregnancies have been complicated by diabetes."

"I have."

"What is your expert opinion, doctor?"

"Pregnancy creates additional stress for diabetics, no doubt. Many things can go wrong with the mother and the baby."

"Such as?"

"Diabetic women do have risks of miscarriages in the early stages of pregnancy. There's the chance of malformation occurring in the first trimester of fetal development and babies can be abnormally large at birth, weighing in excess of nine pounds. If the mother has severe complications, her physician may also consider terminating the pregnancy to avoid health risks to the mother."

"What would some of those health risks be, doctor?"

"Retinopathy, kidney disease or high blood pressure."

Dr. Richie thought quickly, then added. "A pregnant woman is dependent upon a team of physicians to help her through the pregnancy and to have a healthy baby. In addition to an obstetrician and a pediatrician, an internist is also important. Someone like me is responsible for helping the mother not only during a pregnancy, but during and after delivery as well."

"Why is that so important, doctor?" Winston asked.

"Insulin needs will typically decrease abruptly on the day of delivery.

In some cases they have been known to drop as much as 60 percent. If the fetus and the mother are both healthy, however, the doctor may let the pregnancy take its course. But many babies born to diabetic mothers are born early and by cesarean section, typically by the 37th week. And the infant's survival then becomes paramount."

"Is it impossible for a woman who has diabetes to have a healthy pregnancy, Dr. Richie?"

"It's not impossible, Mr. Ross, just a lot more complicated. The minute that baby is conceived is the minute those blood sugars need to be under control. And it has to be checked and monitored several times each day throughout the pregnancy. That is absolutely essential. Diet and caloric intake will also change, making it necessary for the mother to follow strict diets planned for her by a dietitian, and she has to be certain that her blood sugar remains in control. Pregnant women with diabetes should make more visits to their doctor during their pregnancy."

"Dr. Richie, given Ashleigh's diabetic condition and her mental disability, by what percentage would you say a pregnancy for her would be destructive?"

Dr. Richie considered his words carefully. "Virtually 100 percent. The probability of problems and complications to Ashleigh Roberts' health, if she were to become pregnant, would be significant, Mr. Ross. A pregnancy would be very destructive for Ashleigh. Given her functional hypoglycemia, there would be a quite high probability of episodes of hypoglycemic shock. Pregnancy for someone with Ashleigh's condition may even bring on Type II diabetes."

Winston returned to his table. He slipped his hands partially into his pant pockets, then turned to face the doctor. "Based on your assumption of Ashleigh's intelligence level and her ability to think abstractly, to understand and to comprehend, do you believe Ashleigh would understand and be able to do what's necessary to carry her baby to a healthy term?"

Dr. Richie pushed his glasses up on his nose and shook his head. "No, I do not believe so. Not only does Ashleigh run the risk of passing the potential of diabetes and mental disabilities along to her baby, but given her IQ, she may not be able to care for herself or the baby. Especially with her lack of sound mental abilities, that would be a disaster for her and the infant and for society."

"Thank you, Dr. Richie." Winston looked at Jessie. "I have no further questions for this witness, your honor."

Jessie nodded and looked to Jaime.

"Counselor, do you wish to question Dr. Richie?"

"Yes. More a point of clarification, your honor," she said.

She stood and walked to the witness stand. "Dr. Richie, isn't it true that there are more than 400 types of mental retardation and, of that number, only about half have known causes?"

"Yes, I believe that's correct."

"So children don't get mental retardation simply by having a mother who has a mental disability."

"No."

"So women with normal or above average IQ's, and who have diabetes, can have children who are mentally disabled?"

"Yes."

"And women with mental disabilities, or who have below-level intelligence, and who have diabetes, can also have normal children."

"That's correct."

"In other words, Dr. Richie, unlike diabetes which is a disease that can be passed on through family generations, mental retardation is not hereditary."

"Yes, that's correct."

"So, your statement earlier about the threat, if you will, of Ashleigh passing along her mental disability to a child, were she to have one, is inaccurate. Is it not, doctor?"

Dr. Richie nodded slowly and shifted slightly in his chair. He offered an anemic response. "Well, yes. Actually, what I meant to say was that there might be the chance that the child may be environmentally disabled."

Jaime's eyes narrowed slightly, but the look on her face remained tempered. She was working to keep her voice level, devoid of any emotion. "Well, what you meant to say and what you actually said, doctor, are two different things."

Jaime returned to her table and then looked at Dr. Richie. "Just one more question, doctor. You stated there is a 30 percent chance that Ashleigh may develop Type I or II diabetes is that correct?

"Yes, that's correct."

"So is the court to take it that there is then a 70 percent chance that Ashleigh will never develop Type I or type II diabetes?"

Dr. Richer shifted in his chair and cleared his throat before he spoke. "Well, yes."

Jaime looked at the judge. "Thank you. I have no further questions for this witness, your honor."

"You may step down, doctor," Judge Gutierrez said, turning his attention from Dr. Richie to Winston. "Mr. Ross, call your next witness, please."

Twenty-eight

Winston stood, resting his fingertips lightly on the table. "Thank you, your honor. We call Dr. Paul Anderson."

Tall, bald and rotund, Dr. Paul Anderson had features that evoked the image of Hoss Cartwright in late middle age. As he took the oath, his rich baritone voice filled the courtroom. When he was seated, Winston walked to the witness stand.

"Dr. Anderson, you are a psychologist who has been practicing for a number of years, is that correct?"

"Thirty-two to be exact."

"And how do you know Ashleigh Roberts?"

"I'm the staff psychologist with the Denver County Community Center for Developmental Disabilities. Ashleigh's work and residential programs were set up through the Community Center. Ashleigh and I have also had a few visits with each other this year."

"And what was the nature of those sessions, Dr. Anderson?"

"The sessions were designed to help Ashleigh come to terms with and adjust to the new changes in her life."

"Meaning her new home and job?" Winston clarified.

"Yes, those were the issues."

"How would you say Ashleigh responded to those impending changes?"

"Quite well, actually. She said she was ready and eager for the change."

Winston stroked his chin thoughtfully and nodded. "Dr. Anderson, you were appointed by the court as a mental health professional to testify in this hearing regarding Ashleigh's mental and physical health. Medically speaking, doctor, do you think Leigh Roberts is right to petition the court to order that her daughter be sterilized?"

"Yes. It is my opinion that Ashleigh should undergo the procedure."

"Could you tell the court why, Dr. Anderson?"

"Ashleigh would live a much happier life if she were to have the surgery."

"How so, sir?" Winston asked.

"Well, for one thing, that would allow her to broaden her social activities without the health risks of an unwanted pregnancy. Granted, Ashleigh is a high functioning young woman, yet she still needs supervision, albeit very little, in doing some daily tasks such as when it comes to controlling her diabetes. That leads me to believe Ashleigh could not act as an adequate parent for a child when she still needs to have daily care herself.

"Additionally, I don't think Ashleigh could tolerate the stresses of a pregnancy, mentally or physically. Even if she did manage to get through the pregnancy on the physical aspect, which given her condition, I find highly unlikely, I think mentally, the possibility of caring for the baby is next to none."

Winston looked thoughtfully from Ashleigh to Dr. Anderson. "If Ashleigh failed to be able to take care of the baby that would mean she would lose it, is that not correct, Dr. Anderson?"

The doctor nodded. "That's correct, Mr. Ross. Neither Ashleigh, nor her guardian, nor society at large should be forced to assume the financial and psychological burden of an unwanted child. It is my opinion that, let's say, for example, Ashleigh makes it through a physically demanding pregnancy, if she were not able to take care of the baby, as we're speculating here, for her to lose that baby would be equally traumatic."

The courtroom was silent for a moment as Winston thought. "Could Ashleigh, perhaps, become depressed over the loss of having to give up her baby?"

"Most definitely," Dr. Anderson said. "Women suffer from depression if the pregnancy terminates at any stage, but to carry the baby to term, deliver, only to have the baby taken away from her because she has failed to care for it adequately would be absolutely devastating."

"How do you think Ashleigh would be able to handle a situation such as you've described, doctor?"

"She wouldn't," Dr. Anderson said firmly. "The situation would be almost too much for her. I don't think Ashleigh could go through something like that and remain mentally sound."

"What are you suggesting, doctor? Suicide?"

Jaime held up her hand. "Objection! Your honor, this is complete speculation."

Winston glanced from the judge to Jaime. "May I remind Ms. Monroe that Dr. Anderson is a court-approved expert in exactly this field. Who better to assess the mental stability of Miss Roberts than him?"

The judge considered both attorneys. "He's right, counselor. Your objection is overruled."

Winston repeated his question. "Are you suggesting suicide, doctor?"

"Possibly. Particularly with postpartum depression. With depression comes the risk of suicide. Or Ashleigh could attempt to change her life in passive ways."

"How so, doctor?"

"Well, for example, changes in her job performance, or in her diet, which we know, given her functional hypoglycemia, would be detrimental to her health."

"Percentage-wise, Dr. Anderson, and in your expert opinion, how certain are you Ashleigh would have significant complications, mentally and physically, with a pregnancy?"

Dr. Anderson ran a hand over his smooth, baldhead, hesitating, as though he were weighing Winston's question in his mind. "Virtually,

100 percent. Complications would be significant. It is extremely likely Ashleigh's physical health, as well her mental health, would be placed in serious jeopardy by becoming pregnant."

Satisfied with the doctor's answer, Winston smiled slightly and nodded at the doctor. He returned to his table.

"Thank you, Dr. Anderson. Nothing further, your honor."

"Very well," the judge said, looking to Jaime. "Do you wish to cross examine this witness, counselor?"

Jaime rose halfway from her chair.

"No, your honor, I have no questions for this witness."

"You may step down, Dr. Anderson. Mr. Ross, your next witness," Jessie said to Winston.

As the doctor left the witness stand, Jaime cast a sideways glance in Leigh's direction, remembering their conversation about Sarah's suicide. She was unable to stop the thought in her head that perhaps Leigh had suggested to Winston to push that line of questioning. She didn't want to believe that Leigh had pursued a friendship with her only to manipulate her.

Jaime turned toward Tia, who was tapping her lightly on her arm.

"Are you okay?" Tia asked. "You look like you're unhappy about something and wanted to object."

Jaime shook her head. "No, no. I'm fine. I have nothing to ask him."

Winston stood and called Raymond Smith, a tall, wiry man in his late forties. Thick and loosely curled hair covered his head. A hard life seemed to be etched in a tired, fleshy face. There were deep creases in his forehead. Deep laugh lines framed his eyes and mouth and a thick graying mustache covered his lip. Winston went to the front of his table. He centered his tie and folded his arms lightly across his chest.

"Mr. Smith, please tell the court your occupation."

"I'm a case manager with the Denver County Community Center for Developmental Disabilities."

"And how long have you been with the agency?"

"About eleven years."

"And how long as Ashleigh's case manager?"

"Almost three years."

Winston tapped his index finger lightly against his chin. "Mr. Smith, a recent study has suggested that abuse and neglect may be common among children born to parents who are significantly mentally limited. And the study showed that society is somewhat ill-prepared to help with the situation."

"That's correct. The question, with regard to parenting failure of significantly mentally disabled adults, is not *whether* they would abuse their children but *when*," Smith said.

Tia immediately tugged on Jaime's arm. When Jaime leaned toward her, she spoke in an urgent whisper, "Are you going to let him get away with saying that?! We both know Ashleigh would never do *anything* to hurt a child."

Jaime turned from Tia without saying a word. She felt herself struggling to stop thinking about the intimate details she had shared with Leigh about the day Sarah died and stay focused on the questioning.

"Are you familiar with the study?" Winston asked.

Smith nodded. "I am. The study suggested that children who were born to mentally disabled parents and who are cognitively brighter and had better speech skills than their parents, ran a greater risk of being abused by their parents. A child who had a significantly higher IQ would clash continually with their parents who had a lower IQ."

"What do the findings suggest?" Winston asked.

"Well, they are of major concern, given the fact that a survey also conducted along with the study, showed that adults with mental delays are having just as many children as normal adults. According to the study, mothers and couples with mental impairment had an average of three children and some were having as many as nine."

"Which fuels the issue that mentally disabled parents would not be able to properly and adequately maintain and run the family and, as a result, physical abuse and neglect could run rampant in such a family?" Winston asked.

Raymond nodded. "That's correct."

Tia and Jaime exchanged glances, but Jaime did not raise an objection.

"What causes that abuse?" Winston asked.

"Well, it comes as a result of the parent's frustration at not knowing what to do in difficult situations, where the parent's ability to think abstractly is greatly diminished. The lower the parent's IQ, the more difficult it is for them to think abstractly. Parents who have, and I'll use the word here, mental retardation, rarely, if ever, sexually abuse their children. Wherein lies the problem. While they themselves do not sexually abuse their children, for the most part, the parents are unable to protect their children from being abused, sexually or otherwise, by others."

Winston cast an open hand in Ashleigh's direction. "And how would you classify, Ms. Roberts?"

Raymond glanced toward Ashleigh and briefly held her gaze. "Well, I'd have to classify her as a very likely candidate to abuse a baby, especially if things got to be too much for her which of course they likely would—"

Jaime stood immediately and shouted her objection. "This is nothing but hearsay! Your honor, there's simply no way of knowing that."

"Sustained," the judge said and looked at Winston. "Counselor, move on."

"What were some of the other findings in the study?" Winston asked.

Raymond twisted and pulled at a corner of his mustache as he thought. "Neglect seemed to be one of the biggest problems that the children of mentally limited parents faced. The study showed that, on occasion, the parents had difficulty remembering their children's names, or when their birthdays were, and you know how some children are about their birthdays. It's a very important day to them and they want their parents and siblings to remember such a special occasion. In addition, the study showed there were even some instances where parents had a difficult time distinguishing their children from other children."

Winston nodded thoughtfully. "Some of your former clients who are now living in the Denver community and who are now mothers participate in the center's parenting classes. Is that not correct?"

Raymond nodded. "Yes, sir, that's correct."

"What is your opinion of such classes, Mr. Smith?"

"The success is limited. The classes work well when the mother's child is quite young, through about preschool age, I'd estimate. Though the child continues to grow and learn and his cognitive level begins to broaden and expand, the mother stays at the same level, and, as I said, therein lies the problem.

"A mentally delayed adult can babysit a small child with virtually no problems. But as her children continue to grow and reach the age of six and start to attend school, the abilities of the mother to respond in an adequate, intelligent manner becomes increasingly difficult, if not impossible. The problem becomes even more chronic as her child reaches adolescence. By that time, a mentally delayed parent's ability to respond to her child as an adult is almost nil."

"You're aware of the constitutional laws in regard to sterilization, Mr. Smith?"

"Of course."

"What is your expert opinion?"

"The intent behind many of these safeguards allows the limited or the incompetent person to lead a life with more independence and the freedom from the hindrance of parental obligations. Its intent is also to help prevent procreation from parents, because of limited mental capacity, who could not adequately care for their children."

"Do you think that, given Ashleigh Roberts' limited mental capacity and medical condition, such laws would be applicable in her case?"

"I do."

"Thank you, Mr. Smith."

Winston returned to his table and, after studying a legal pad for several moments, looked at the judge.

"I have no further questions for this witness, your honor."

The judge extended an open hand in Jaime's direction. "Your witness, Ms. Monroe."

"Yes, your honor, thank you, I have several questions for Mr. Smith."

Jaime took her time walking to the witness stand, her heels tapping lightly against the polished floor. She studied Raymond Smith for a moment before she started to speak. Up close, Jaime noticed his skin had a transparent look that reminded her of wax paper. She could see faint tiny blue veins in his nose.

"It's not a revelation to anyone here in this courtroom today, Mr. Smith, that marriage and procreation has been typically discouraged among people with mental retardation."

Smith nodded. "Yes. It is an age-old debate."

"But it becomes a question of civil rights when we began to say that a woman, or a couple with mental impedance, cannot have children and start a family, just because they are mentally disadvantaged." She thought a moment more before she continued. "How many years ago did deinstitutionalization begin, Mr. Smith?"

"More than twenty, twenty-five years ago."

"And wasn't it also about that time that sterilization could no longer be performed on a woman without her informed consent, which she, herself, must express?"

"Yes, that's correct."

"We've come a long way since the turn of the 20th century when most states enacted laws that provided for the compulsory sterilization for myriad misfits, if you will, the mentally ill, the mentally deficient, and in some states, people with epilepsy, sexual perverts and habitual criminals. If this were fifty years ago, even twenty years ago, we wouldn't be in this courtroom today, because the choice to sterilize Ashleigh Roberts would not be her decision to make. The decision would have already been made for her..."

Jaime paused and looked at Ashleigh. She was leaning forward, arms resting lightly on the table. She turned her attention back to the witness stand. "In other words, sterilization today is no longer a convenient option for families of developmentally delayed women. Which means today, unless a court were to grant a guardian of a delayed woman permission to have her sterilized, the choice is hers. How do you feel about those laws, Mr. Smith?"

Raymond Smith twisted a corner of his mustache. He hesitated, as if to select his words, and then looked levelly at Jaime. "I have my reservations, but I support those laws."

Jaime cocked her head. "And what are those reservations, sir?"

"I could easily give you a number of examples of why it troubles me, counselor, but I will cite only one. My wife is good friends with a mother with four children who live in the Springs."

"Colorado Springs?" Jaime confirmed.

"Yes. Two of her children have mental limitations. One of them is sixteen and is severely disabled. Mostly non-verbal. She appears to have no interest whatsoever in motherhood or sex. However, her older sister, with Down's syndrome, is quite the opposite. And, needless to say, the mother is having a difficult time with her.

"The young woman, as you might expect any 18-year-old to be, is interested in what many her age are, getting her own apartment someday, going to the mall, having a boyfriend. She wants to have children at some point and has even gone to the extreme of giving her would-be children names. She's given the yet-to-be-born children girl's names only, because she has told her mother little girls are the only thing she's going to have.

"It is the mother's desire that her daughter not bear children for the very reason that she simply would not know the first thing about how to care for them, since much of the time, she still has problems caring for her herself. The dilemma is quite typical of what many mothers face who have daughters who are developmentally delayed."

Jaime nodded briefly as she scanned a legal pad. "I would like to go back to something you said earlier, Mr. Smith, if I may, regarding the recent study on abuse to children of significantly mentally delayed parents."

"Certainly."

"Ashleigh's classification of mental delay is considered mild, is that correct?"

Raymond nodded.

"You'll have to answer the question verbally for the record, Mr. Smith," the judge said.

"Sorry, your honor. Yes, that's correct. Significantly sub average intellectual functioning is defined as an IQ of seventy or below. Seventy was selected because most people with IQ's below that number require special services and care."

Jaime nodded. "And Ashleigh's IQ has been tested at about seventy-five, correct?"

"Around seventy to seventy-five, yes."

"So, given her IQ level, you would consider Ashleigh to be high functioning?"

"I would."

"Then, Mr. Smith, isn't it correct to say that the adaptive functioning in people with mental delays—as well as people without—is also influenced by personality traits and characteristics, motivation, education, and social and vocational opportunities?"

"Yes, that's true."

"And, isn't it also correct to say, the better the adaptive functioning skills in someone who is developmentally delayed, the better it is for someone like Ashleigh Roberts?"

"Yes, that's accurate. Ashleigh has always shown the desire to want to learn and she's always been known to have higher levels of adaptive functioning."

"Then isn't it also accurate to say, after hearing testimony earlier from Dr. Anderson, that Ashleigh was eager and motivated to begin a new job and living arrangements. And that those who know Ashleigh Roberts will tell you, that even with her mental limitations, she's a responsible, personable and likable young woman, who is fit to be a mother and raise children, were that her choice?"

He nodded slightly. "Yes, Ms. Monroe, your assumptions would be accurate. I would also like to add, however, that one cannot be sure how Ms. Roberts would react to the stresses and strains of motherhood."

Jaime continued. "And while the parenting classes may not be the best for mothers and couples with mental delay, at least the classes provide some assistance and direction for them, where otherwise there might be absolutely none. And by attending such classes, the mothers and couples are at least showing the willingness to want to learn to be better parents for their children. Would you say that assumption is also accurate, Mr. Smith?"

"Yes, it would be, but of course as I just stated, it would depend."

"If I recall my visit to one of the parenting groups, the young women attending the class said they had benefited very much from what they were learning. It seems to me we're basing a lot of information here today on just a single study..." Jaime paused to collect her thoughts and allow herself to calm down. Her anger was doing a slow burn, her frustration mounting. She took a deep breath before she began again. "Perhaps we'd be better off not giving that study so much credence, since, is it also not true, Mr. Smith, that a limited amount of research is readily available on child-rearing practices among adults with mental impedance?"

Smith considered the question. "Yes, it's true. Research is limited.

However, I wouldn't necessarily say that. From my experience I would say that the study has proved to be an accurate representation."

Jaime sighed deeply and quietly. She turned and left the witness stand, looking slightly helplessly at Tia. She reached her table and looked squarely at Judge Jessie Gutierrez. "I have no further questions for this witness, your honor, thank you."

The judge looked at Winston. "Mr. Ross?"

Winston spoke as he rose from his chair. "No, your honor, we have nothing further."

"You may step down, sir," judge Gutierrez said to Raymond Smith.

When he had left the witness stand, the judge looked to Jaime. "Your opening statements, counselor?"

Jaime took another deep breath. She felt as though someone was stomping on her chest now.

Twenty-nine

Jaime had remained standing at her table after her questions to Raymond Smith.

"Thank you, your honor," she said and looked down at Ashleigh, who turned and met her gaze and the smile in Jaime's eyes. When Jaime spoke she directed her comments to her client.

"Ashleigh has gone through most of her young life already with two strikes against her, functional hypoglycemia and some obstacles mentally."

Jaime looked at the judge. "But those limiting words, your honor, are not in Ashleigh's vocabulary. She has worked to overcome them. She is striving to become as independent as possible. You will hear evidence today to support that Ashleigh is striving to be like any other young, responsible woman her age. She lives out within the community and has for years. And in a few weeks, she will take another step toward greater independence when she moves into an apartment.

"She now works in a public setting and has worked steadily since she was eighteen. Ashleigh's mental limitations and diabetes have not stopped her from trying to lead the most normal life possible. It has not stopped her from having the same hopes, dreams and desires we all do. What Ashleigh Roberts has done with her life, despite her obstacles, proves she is capable and competent to make her own decisions. It proves she wants to take an active role in managing her own life and that her caregivers don't have to make every decision for her. Ashleigh is not saying she will have a baby, or even that she wants to have a child, just that she should have the right to choose."

Jaime's attention returned to Ashleigh. "Allowing the court to grant her mother's request for sterilization would destroy everything this young woman has worked to achieve."

She focused her gaze squarely on Judge Gutierrez. "Your honor, it will destroy her hopes for the future. It most certainly will make her feel like a second-class citizen. You will hear evidence during this hearing that will show how well Ashleigh has learned to overcome her diabetes and how she has adjusted to living with mental delays. You will hear testimony that will prove Ashleigh is an able, competent young woman, capable of making her own decisions."

Jaime stopped to rest a hand gently on Ashleigh's shoulder. She let the silence carry a moment through the courtroom.

She went on. "As I said, your honor, Ashleigh has always had two strikes against her. Let's not make it three by taking away from her a choice that is rightfully hers to make. You will hear testimony today from Ashleigh's personal physician, her group home supervisor and also from Ashleigh Roberts herself. Thank you, your honor."

The judge nodded, looking from Ashleigh to Jaime. "Call your first witness."

"Thank you, your honor. We call Ms. Erin Greene."

Ashleigh turned in her chair to the gallery to face Erin as she rose from her seat. Their eyes met and, as Erin reached the threshold, she winked at Ashleigh, causing Ashleigh to smile widely. Ashleigh watched Erin walk to the witness stand. Erin wore a loose-fitting navy print dress that stopped just below her knees. She wore the same sensible shoes as on the first day Jaime had met her.

Jaime waited until Erin was seated and then walked toward the witness stand and studied her a moment. When Jaime first met Erin at the parenting class, her nose was red and chapped from a bad cold. Erin's nose was as red today as it was that first evening, but this time it was her allergies that had the better of her.

"Erin, please tell the court what you do professionally."

"I work for the Denver County Community Center for Developmental Disabilities. Presently, I am the Morningside Heights group home supervisor where Ashleigh lives. Prior, I had worked several years as a case manager for the Community Center."

"And how long have you been the group home supervisor where Ashleigh lives?"

"Oh, goodness, let me see. For as long as Ashleigh's been there, going on thirteen years."

"Could you please tell the court a little about the group home? There are many types of these homes, correct, Ms. Greene?"

"Yes, that's correct. There are several different types of homes to accommodate a range of skill levels and needs. Services include intensive twenty-four-hour supervision and behavior development programming and adaptive functional training. And the homes are located within the community, which forces our clients to confront their disabilities. They take on the often daunting daily task of navigating the bus schedules, holding jobs and mingling with other people, just like we do."

Erin leaned forward in the witness stand, pressing her hands firmly on her lap. "You see, we want them to blend in as much as possible," she said. "The goal here is to get them back into the mainstream. We want them to participate in the same things, go through the same daily grind of living as the rest of us."

"What about Ashleigh's group home?" Jaime asked.

Erin eased back in her chair, allowing herself to relax. "Ashleigh lives in a group home with less intensive supervision, where a supportive environment is provided and the training emphasis is directed toward developing better self-management skills. In this type of setting the clients are working to prepare themselves to eventually live in more independent settings. Clients who come into this type of group home setting are capable of eventually living on their own."

"And such is the case with Ashleigh is it not, Ms. Greene?"

Erin nodded. "Yes. Ashleigh will be leaving us soon." Erin looked quickly at Ashleigh. Her approval showed in her eyes. "Next month she'll be moving into an individual apartment setting, or what we call a host home. It will be a semi-independent and even less intensive living arrangement than where she lives right now. The setting will provide Ashleigh more training in the form of guidance, teaching and support."

Jaime paced slowly along the witness stand and rubbed an index finger lightly along the surface.

"How well do you think living in a group home has worked for Ashleigh?"

Erin answered without hesitation. "It was probably the best thing her mother did for her, especially getting her in as early as she did."

Erin felt the weight of Leigh's stare on her, but carefully avoided looking at her. Until Leigh had petitioned the court, the women were good friends and had been since they met at Morningside. Leigh's request, however, had driven a wedge between them. Before her petition, they had talked almost daily. When Erin learned of Leigh's wishes for Ashleigh, their relationship had become distant and strained. They spoke only a few times since Leigh had made her wishes known.

"Leigh did the right thing," Erin went on. "She knew the waiting lists to get Ashleigh into a group home would be extensive. It was a difficult decision, no doubt, for her to put Ashleigh in a group home when she did, she was just a child, but she knew what she had to do. It may have been an unspeakably hard decision for Leigh to make, but it was the best thing for Ashleigh and her mother knew it. I'll be the first to give her credit. It's what any mother would want for their child. The move helped her prepare to work out in the public like she's doing now and move toward more independent living."

Jaime continued to trace her finger along the witness stand. "You also mentioned that you were a case manager early on in your career. Don't you still do that, at least for Ashleigh?"

"Yes. Of course, I help all the clients who live at Morningside..." Her face softened as she looked at Ashleigh. "But I've always been attached to Ashleigh. It's been that way since I came."

"Don't you also work closely with Bennet May, Ashleigh's case manager?" Jaime confirmed.

"I do, yes," Erin replied.

"And what do those duties entail, Ms. Greene?"

"Well, we assess Ashleigh's needs then develop a service plan for her to meet those needs. Case managers provide coordination between the individual and their families, professionals, programs, community agencies and funding sources. We advocate on their behalf and provide supportive counseling and crisis intervention when needed. Case managers function as the hub of the wheel, if you will. Their role is central in accessing and coordinating available resources to meet the client's needs."

"How would you explain your relationship with Ashleigh?"

"Well ... I..." She looked down at her dress and attempted to smooth out a wrinkle. Silence consumed the courtroom. "Well," Erin cleared her throat. "We've always been very close. Ashleigh finished growing up at Morningside, you might as well say. It was her home. And I was there for her, nursing her when she was sick, helping with homework, watching TV together, trying a new recipe, you know, just about anything. We've done all of those things. She did other things that people her age have done, granted a bit slower. Ashleigh attended school until she was twenty-one and then graduated. But I can tell you she didn't wait until then to start working. She began working at the sheltered workshop after school a week after she turned eighteen."

"And Leigh Roberts was very supportive of this was she not?" Jaime asked.

This time Erin looked at Leigh. Their eyes met and locked briefly before Erin looked away and back to Jaime.

"She was, very much. Leigh, Bennet and I worked on getting Ashleigh into the workshop more than a year before it finally happened."

"How was working in the workshop for Ashleigh?"

"It was one of the best things to ever happen to her. She accepted the responsibility of having a part-time job just as any responsible teenager would. She'd come home from school, have a quick snack and go work three hours at the workshop. She held that job for six years before she went to the food court. She blossomed working there. It was a stepping stone for Ashleigh."

"How did Leigh react when you told her Ashleigh would be changing jobs and having a new place to live, which Ashleigh also wanted to do very much?" Jaime asked.

Erin's face clouded. She had felt the constant weight of Leigh's attention on her from the moment she took the witness stand, but she was determined not to look at her. Her answer was firm. "She wasn't as receptive to the idea as she had been previously with the workshop, or as she was about putting Ashleigh into the group home."

"Why was that?" Jaime asked, looking briefly at Winston and back to the witness stand.

Erin squared her shoulders, crossed her left leg and folded her hands firmly over her knee. "Ashleigh had already developed diabetes and it worried her mother that something would happen to her at work or wherever she might be and people might take advantage of her, possibly sexually. She didn't want that to happen to Ashleigh, especially with the hypoglycemia."

Erin paused a moment and then went on. "Leigh had always been progressive with Ashleigh. She was open to Ashleigh trying and learning whatever she could. But when she developed the functional hypoglycemia, Leigh seemed to change almost overnight. It was as though she no longer wanted her daughter to do anything. She started to pull in the reins. Leigh told me she would feel more comfortable if Ashleigh remained at the group home and the workshop."

It was Jaime who looked in Leigh's direction. She had her attention fixed directly on Erin. Her left hand was resting on the table and her body was bent toward the witness stand, as she listened to the exchange.

"Do you remember what Leigh told you?" Jaime asked.

"Well, she never actually said it straight out, but only hinted that she would consider asking her doctor to have Ashleigh's tubes tied so nothing like that would happen and then she'd feel a lot better about her working outside the workshop and living outside the group home."

Leigh averted her gaze from the witness stand. She sat back against her chair. She rested her forehead lightly against her fingertips.

"Which is exactly what Leigh did, was it not?" Jaime confirmed.

Erin nodded slightly, her brow in a tight knot. "Yes. She even told me about the doctor appointment, but he refused to do the operation, thank God. So, it came to this."

Erin's voice had been forceful and firm the entire time she had been speaking, but with her last sentence, her voice softened almost to a whisper. Jaime noticed the slight change in Erin's disposition and returned to her table to allow her the time to adjust. She studied a legal pad for a moment and then turned to face Erin.

"Ms. Greene, has Ashleigh's medical condition affected her life?"

Erin pressed her back firmly against the chair. She cleared her throat and when she spoke again, her voice had returned to its former, secure level. "Well, it has certainly, but we, Leigh and I, have helped Ashleigh to make the adjustment. But Ashleigh deserves the credit, really, because she's the one who has to live with the condition. It's hard sometimes, as it would be for anyone who wants a candy bar or ice cream, but Ashleigh has adjusted and done very well, all things considered."

"How did you and Leigh help Ashleigh?"

Erin answered without hesitation. "After we found out what was wrong with Ashleigh, for several weeks the two of us, Leigh and I, lived the kind of life Ashleigh would have to live from now on."

"You decided to do that?"

"We both did. In fact," Erin extended an open hand toward Winston and Leigh. "It was Leigh's idea."

Jaime followed Erin's open hand until she met Leigh's heavy stare. Jaime held it only a moment before looking back to the witness stand. "Why?"

"So we'd know what it would be like. We thought we'd have a better handle on her disease and could help her learn to adjust and live with it if we did." Erin suppressed a laugh. "We became walking encyclopedias. We knew all about diabetes."

Erin glanced at Leigh. She had a small smile on her face and Erin could not help smiling back.

"What did you do?" Jaime asked.

"Well, we ate like a person with diabetes would, which included snacks at the proper time. We exercised. We tested our blood sugar, which you know means having to poke your finger with a needle. We even went to the point of injecting ourselves using a saline solution. I didn't like that part. But thankfully, the doctor said Ashleigh wouldn't need insulin, but we did it just the same."

"Why?" Jaime asked again.

Erin answered without hesitation. "Because we wanted to know what it would be like. If we were going to do it, we were going to do everything, injections and all."

Erin paused a moment to think before continuing then said, "I think it was good for the both of us to do what we did."

Jaime tilted her head. "Can you explain?"

Erin looked beyond the threshold to the gallery, to where Dr. Steven Richie still remained seated, listening to testimony.

"Well, it helped us to develop a real empathy for what someone with diabetes has to do. It was sort of like getting under their skin. Dr. Richie concurred with our suggestion that we do it. He said it would help us with Ashleigh. And it did, because we wanted Ashleigh to continue to live as normal a life as possible. She'd been going along so well up to that point and Leigh and I didn't want anything to impede on her progress. We learned a lot that's helped the three of us, really."

Jaime was standing parallel to the jury box. She had been doing well to avoid Leigh's gaze. But when she turned to lean against it, she looked directly into her eyes. Jaime remained impassive. She was determined Leigh would read nothing in her eyes, as though she were looking at an opaque window.

"How well do you think Ashleigh has adjusted to her hypoglycemia?" Jaime asked.

"It's been hard for her, but she's done very well, given the circumstances."

After a brief, thoughtful pause Jaime asked, "What does Ashleigh do at home, Erin?"

"Anything anyone else does. She cooks. She cleans. She washes clothes. She goes for groceries. She watches television. She has a hobby, she likes to make beaded necklaces. She made this one for me," Erin said and she looked at Ashleigh as she lifted the necklace off her neck. Ashleigh grinned widely at her.

Erin focused her attention on Jaime. "And she's also just started to learn to paint, something she's always wanted to do. Reading has always been difficult for Ashleigh, but she reads simple books."

Erin stopped and played with the necklace between her fingers to allow herself more time to think. "She and some of the other women go shopping, to the movies, we go out to dinner. We have picnics in Congress Park, near our home. We love the summer for the outdoor concerts in the area parks. And she babysits for the other mothers when they come to the parenting class and bring their children."

"What is your opinion of mothers with developmental delays becoming parents?"

"Parenting is difficult for anyone," Erin said with conviction. "I know mothers with such delays who have a very difficult time with their children. It's a struggle for some, but it's also not without rewards. I know some mothers and couples with developmental disabilities who make very good parents. They love their children, nurture and take care of them better than some normal people I know. It works both ways. It goes without saying that any family worries about vulnerability. But I can't see it being any different than trying to counsel poor women not to have children."

"What about abuse? Do parents with mental impedance abuse their children?"

"A mother's intellectual limitations can lead to abuse or neglect and the under stimulation of their child, but it is unintentional. Most are doing the very best they can to raise their children."

"Has Ashleigh ever expressed an interest to you about becoming a mother?"

"Well, she loves children. We've had many conversations on what it would be like to be a mother and raise a child."

"If Ashleigh were to someday become a mother, could she?" Jaime asked.

Erin pursed her lips and nodded firmly. "Yes. Ashleigh would make a good mother. I am not foolish enough to think that love is all you need to care for and raise your children, but I know it still counts for something. And Ashleigh has more love within her than anyone I've ever known."

"Ashleigh has been classified as mildly delayed. What does that mean?"

Erin shifted slightly in her seat and pushed her large, round glasses up on her nose. She thought a moment before answering. "There are four degrees of severity, reflecting the degree of intellectual impairment. They are mild, moderate, severe and profound. Those with mild mental limitations, such as Ashleigh, make up about 85 percent of the population with some developmental delay.

"They can acquire academic skills up to about the sixth grade by the time they reach their teens. They achieve social and vocational skills well enough to maintain minimum self-support. They can work in unskilled and semiskilled occupations. Of course, they may need assistance when under unusual social or economic stress, but most all people who have some sort of mild mental disability can and do live successfully in the community. They can live in group homes, or in supervised apartments or in some cases, independently."

"Is there a possibility for Ashleigh to live completely on her own someday?"

"Absolutely," Erin answered firmly. "And she's already expressed a desire to do so. That's a ways in the future, but it's a goal she can work toward. Expectations for them should be based on their skills and potentials—not generalizations or stereotypes."

"You feel very close to Ashleigh don't you, Erin?" Jaime asked almost as a whisper.

Erin felt her breath rise and stop in her throat, forcing her to swallow over the sudden constriction. She folded her hands tightly and pulled them toward her body. She fought to keep her tears at bay.

"I've loved her as if she were my own," Erin responded in a soft voice. "And I've often felt that way. Lately with all this unfairness, I've sometimes found myself wishing she was my child."

"Do you think this court should order Ashleigh to undergo sterilization?"

Erin flexed the muscles in her jaw. She hesitated only a moment before she answered in an unyielding voice. "No, I do not."

"Why not?"

"Ashleigh has a constitutional right not to be sterilized, which is as sacred as any constitutional right. The choice should be hers."

Jaime smiled slightly and nodded at Erin. "Thank you, Ms. Greene."

Jaime looked at Judge Gutierrez. "I have no further questions, your honor."

The judge directed his attention to Winston.

"Do you wish to question this witness, Mr. Ross?"

Winston pressed his tie against his shirt as he rose. "No, your honor."

"Very well, thank you, Ms. Greene, you may step down."

Erin rose to leave the witness stand. She was the first to notice Ashleigh. She had slumped down in her chair. She knew exactly what was happening and bolted from the witness stand.

"Orange juice!" Erin yelled. "Orange juice! Quick! Get some orange juice!"

There was a moment of confusion, as everyone watched Erin race across the courtroom floor toward Ashleigh. Erin was at the table before anyone else knew what had happened. She had her arms around Ashleigh.

"What on earth?!" Tia gasped as she jumped back from the table. "Ashleigh was fine a second ago."

"Orange Juice! She's gone into hypoglycemic shock! Quick! We need to get her some orange juice!" Erin said, looking for her large shoulder bag on the other side of the threshold.

The pallor on Ashleigh's face had turned ashen, her breathing rough and labored. Had Erin not been holding Ashleigh's arms, she would have fallen from the chair. Jaime was now standing on the other side of Erin. Her hands were around Ashleigh's shoulders. Leigh was standing next to Jaime, their shoulders only inches apart. Tia, Winston, the judge and the others remained in their places, looking on wide-eyed.

Erin spotted her bag. She pointed to it and looked at Tia.

"Tia, get my bag. There's a small container of orange juice in there." Erin's voice remained cool and collected.

Tia leaned over the railing, grabbed Erin's handbag and set it on the table. She rummaged through it for several seconds before she found the plastic bottle filled with orange liquid. Tia's hand trembled slightly as she tried to open the bottle. Finally she pulled the top off and passed the bottle to Erin. Some of the juice spilled on a legal pad on the table as they exchanged the bottle.

Erin lowered herself to be at eye level with Ashleigh. Her eyes were squeezed shut and her lips were pressed firmly together, making it impossible for Erin to get the juice in her mouth.

"Ashleigh, honey, it's Erin. Please, open your mouth. You need the juice, sweetie. The orange juice will you help you. Just one drink and you'll be fine. Can you do that for me?"

No response.

Leigh motioned to Tia to help her move the table away from the area near Ashleigh. They did and Leigh bent down and rested her hands on Ashleigh's knees.

"Ashleigh, honey, it's mom. Erin has orange juice. Can you drink it for us?"

No response.

Erin tried to give Ashleigh a drink, but her lips were pressed so tightly together she could not get the liquid to pass through. The juice dribbled down the front of her chin and landed on her white blouse.

"Come on, Ashleigh. Open your mouth just a little and drink the orange juice Erin has for you. It'll help you." It was Jaime who spoke.

Ashleigh's lips eased open slightly. Erin was able to get some of the juice in her mouth. Ashleigh choked on the first sip, but swallowed the second one. She took another sip. Finally a big swallow. As the juice hit Ashleigh's stomach, the episode began to subside. She opened her eyes and looked from Erin to her mother and finally to Jaime.

"Doin' OK?" Jaime asked.

Ashleigh nodded. Her breathing slowed and color began to return to her cheeks.

Tia pulled a washcloth from the handbag. "You always carry this stuff with you?" Tia asked as she handed it to Erin.

Erin nodded as she took it and cleaned her hands, then the juice from Ashleigh's chin. Erin sighed deeply as she pushed Ashleigh's hair from her eyes.

"Are you all right?" Leigh wanted to know.

Ashleigh looked at her mother and nodded.

Erin shook her head and positioned her hand on her hips. "What brought that on?"

Tia looked at her watch. She tapped the face with a long, red fingernail. She looked at Jaime.

"It's been right at four hours since we've eaten."

Jaime nodded looking from Erin to Leigh.

"We had lunch just before noon," Jaime confirmed.

"Well, she'll be OK now," Erin said.

Calm returned gradually to the courtroom, as Winston helped Tia put the table back in its place and Jaime and Leigh picked up papers that had scattered to the floor. Ashleigh drank the rest of the orange juice and Erin returned the empty bottle to her bag. When everyone had returned to their place, Judge Gutierrez glanced at his wristwatch.

"There's no reason to continue this hearing today. Will it be better for Ashleigh, since she still needs to testify, if we postponed the remainder of the hearing until tomorrow, Ms. Monroe?" the judge asked in his deep voice that filtered through the courtroom.

"Yes, your honor," Jaime said.

"And what about your last witness, Dr. Martin Stone? Can he also return tomorrow?"

After conferring briefly with Dr. Stone and Erin, Jaime nodded to them and returned her attention to Judge Gutierrez.

"Yes, your honor."

"Very well, this court is adjourned until 9 a.m. tomorrow."

"I'll call you tonight, Ashleigh, honey," Leigh said, as Winston ushered her from the courtroom.

Tia gathered their belongings as Jaime left the city and county building to help Erin get Ashleigh in the car and home. During the drive back to Morningside, Erin glanced in the rearview mirror at Jaime. Jaime was staring straight ahead and her bottom lip was clenched between her teeth. She looked as though she was deep in thought, but the look on her face was vacant, devoid of any emotion.

"Do you think this has done anything to your case, Jaime?" Erin asked.

Jaime looked at Erin in the mirror and shrugged. Uncertainty showed in her eyes. "I don't know," she said quietly.

They rode the rest of the way in silence.

By the time they reached home, Ashleigh had rested her head against Jaime's shoulder and had fallen asleep. And Jaime was holding her hand.

Thirty

The morning air shimmered in desert-like sunshine, preparing to turn another July day into a convection oven.

By 8:55 a.m. all had returned to the courtroom. Ashleigh was sitting between Jaime and Tia. Erin was sitting directly behind them. Leigh and Winston were sitting side by side. There was a hushed quiet in the courtroom as they waited for Judge Gutierrez. At 9 a.m. he walked through the door. After he seated himself and adjusted his glasses, he stroked his pencil-thin mustache that ran the length of his lip. He gave Ashleigh a grandfatherly look and smiled. "How are you today, Ashleigh?" he asked, his voice calm and deep.

Ashleigh smiled shyly at the judge and her voice carried well when she answered. "I'm fine. Thank you."

He nodded and directed his attention to Jaime.

"Counselor, are you ready?"

Jaime took a deep breath as she rose. "Yes, your honor, we are."

"Call your next witness, please."

"Your honor, we call Dr. Martin Stone."

Dr. Martin Stone carried himself with grace and ease to the witness stand. He was a tall, distinguished man. At sixty-one, his thick shock of silver-tinted hair and chiseled features reinforced his impressive presence.

Jaime stood beside her chair with her hand resting casually on top. "Dr. Stone, would you please state your occupation for the court."

"I'm a licensed private gynecologist and my practice also includes obstetrics."

"How long have you been practicing medicine, doctor?"

"Twenty-eight years."

"And how long have you known Ashleigh Roberts?"

"I delivered her."

Dr. Stone glanced briefly at Leigh. There was a small smile on her face. He returned his attention to Jaime when she started to speak.

"How long has Leigh Roberts been your patient?"

"She started coming to me several years before Ashleigh was born."

"And Ashleigh?"

"Ashleigh started coming to me when she turned eighteen."

"And during your years of practice, how many babies could you estimate you have delivered? Give us a ballpark figure if you can, please."

Dr. Stone looked toward the ceiling as he thought for a moment. "I've delivered at least four thousand babies."

Jaime nodded reflectively. "And of that number, Dr. Stone, how many would you say were pregnancies complicated by diabetes?"

"More than two hundred."

"When did you first diagnose Ashleigh as functional hypoglycemic, Dr. Stone?"

"Leigh called one Monday after Ashleigh had spent a weekend with her and said she noticed she seemed nervous all weekend and that she had stumbled quite a bit for no apparent reason. She went on to explain that one minute Ashleigh would be cold and the next, she would be perspiring profusely. She said Ashleigh complained of feeling tired, weak and hungry all weekend. Leigh called my office after talking with Erin Greene, who had called Leigh after Ashleigh's visit that weekend, to compare notes."

"What did Erin say to Leigh, doctor?"

"Erin also confirmed what Leigh had been telling her and added that Ashleigh had been very irritable and cross lately and sometimes spoke incoherently. Erin told Leigh that Ashleigh had a "hollow leg." She couldn't seem to get enough to eat. Erin also told Leigh that Ashleigh had complained frequently of muscle spasms and soreness in her arms and legs. Leigh called me following her conversation with Erin. And because her mother was a diabetic, of course, she was very worried about Ashleigh."

"And Leigh brought Ashleigh in for a checkup?" Jaime asked.

"Yes."

"And then what happened?"

"Given that diabetes runs in Leigh's family, I suspected that it may be the early signs of the disease. Unfortunately, that was the case here. A series of tests confirmed it. After a glucose tolerance test, Ashleigh was diagnosed with functional hypoglycemia."

"How old was Ashleigh when she was diagnosed?"

"Twenty."

"Until yesterday, Dr. Stone, how many times has Ashleigh experienced hypoglycemic shock?"

"Only one other time that I'm aware of. Though sweets must be avoided, I've never known Ashleigh not to be without at least six or seven Lifesavers in her pocket, as she had yesterday."

Dr. Stone paused as though he were replaying the events of Ashleigh's hypoglycemic shock episode in his mind. "Though she did not use the candy, it's best that she always has some with her," he went on. "By knowing the warning signs of hypoglycemic shock, which Ashleigh and those who care for her do quite well, a person can usually prevent an episode from occurring. Unfortunately, as you saw in court yesterday, sometimes the passage from the early to the later stages of hypoglycemic shock happens so rapidly that someone else, such as Erin did yesterday, must administer the proper treatment. We were able to witness that not only did orange juice do the trick, it quickly helped."

"What do you think caused yesterday's episode, doctor?" Jaime asked.

"Well, it could've been one of several things. It had been several hours since Ashleigh had eaten. That could've been a factor. It's been terribly hot these past few weeks. And this hearing has put a lot of stress on her, which may have also triggered it."

Jaime nodded. "This is only the second time since Ashleigh was first diagnosed with functional hypoglycemia four years ago that she has had an episode. What would that lead you to believe, Dr. Stone?"

Martin Stone rubbed his chin thoughtfully between his fingers and took several moments to answer. "Well, it would show me that Ashleigh has learned to maintain and control her condition quite effectively. She knows what she can and can't have in regards to food. She knows that she has to eat right and exercise and knows that checking her blood sugar is essential. Ashleigh also knows that while she carries candy with her, that it is not a treat, but something that would be used to help her, were she to have the time to react to a hypoglycemic episode."

Jaime walked to the front of her table. She carefully avoided Leigh's stare. She studied notes on a legal pad for several minutes. When she looked again to Dr. Stone, her manner was cautious, her expression, alert.

"Dr. Stone, Leigh Roberts visited your office in late December of last year, but she did not come to see you at that time for her annual checkup did she?"

"No, she did not."

"Do you remember her reasons for coming to talk with you?"

Dr. Stone nodded. "She explained that Ashleigh would be changing jobs after the first of the year and moving from the group home. It worried her that Ashleigh, given her medical condition and naiveté, could be taken advantage of. Her concern was that a pregnancy could be the end result. Her biggest concern was the potential health risk it posed for Ashleigh and her baby, but especially to her daughter."

"And what did she ask you to do, doctor?"

"She wanted to have her daughter sterilized to avoid the probability of pregnancy."

"And if you were to sterilize Ashleigh, Dr. Stone, what would that procedure be?"

"A tubal ligation."

"Which means surgery?"

"That's correct. A tubal ligation is an invasive procedure that involves tying the uterine tubes."

"Could you please tell the court, doctor, why you told Leigh Roberts you elected not to do the surgery on Ashleigh."

"First and foremost my objection to Leigh Roberts' request is due to the fact that sterilization is a surgical procedure. It involves body integrity. I've been friends with Leigh for many years. She and Ashleigh have been patients in my practice for years. And, yes, sterilization can be and is done quite often by other doctors as a means of birth control for mothers with daughters who have a cognitive delay, with no questions asked."

"Have you ever done the procedure before, Dr. Stone?"

"I have, many times. But only on women who are considered to have normal intelligence and who have come to me with their husbands because they no longer want to have children. The mothers wanted to have their uterine tubes tied, as opposed to taking an oral contraceptive for birth control and gave their consent. But that was not the case in Ashleigh's situation."

"Why couldn't you do the procedure in Ashleigh's case?" Jaime asked.

"Ethically, it does not sit well with me and never has. It was something I could not bring myself to do. Sterilization procedures are generally irreversible. It destroys an important part of a person's, man or woman, social and biological identity. And, in addition, the long-lasting effects can be traumatic and detrimental."

"Are there any alternatives to the proposed procedure?"

"I would consider the pill for Ashleigh should she come to me and express an interest in becoming sexually active. Though oral contraceptives are the best method for birth control, I would still be hesitant, however. There are some risks for diabetic women who want to take oral contraceptives. I'd consider all the risk factors before I prescribed any type of oral contraceptive for Ashleigh."

"What about other forms of birth control? How would those work for Ashleigh?"

"I would not consider an IUD for Ashleigh. They're less effective and are used with caution with people who have diabetes."

"Why is that?"

"Women who have diabetes and who use IUDs risk infection and danger of perforation of the uterus."

"But despite Ashleigh's diabetic condition, you would be willing to help her through a healthy pregnancy, if she were to become pregnant?" Jaime asked.

"Absolutely. Many women who have diabetes become pregnant. There are precautions and special programs to follow and they follow them with little ill effects on the baby."

"Dr. Stone, knowing what you know about Ashleigh and her intelligence, do you believe, in your expert opinion, if she were to become pregnant, she would be able to follow a special program and carry her baby to a healthy term?"

"With supervision, yes, most definitely."

"And finally, doctor, if Ashleigh were to follow such a program, does she have the competency to do so as well as to understand the consequences and dangers to herself and to her baby should she fail to follow the program?"

"Yes." After a brief, reflective pause Dr. Stone added, "Ashleigh understands the relationship between sexual intercourse and pregnancy."

The doctor looked seriously at Leigh. She returned the glance for only a fleeting moment before she fixed her attention on a non-existent pattern on the wall behind him.

Dr. Stone went on. "She understands that babies do not fall off turnip trucks, nor are they delivered by storks wearing granny glasses."

Jaime covered her mouth inconspicuously to try to hide the smile that was doing its best to form. Tia looked at Ashleigh and stifled her laugh.

"Thank you, doctor."

Jaime looked at the judge. "I have no further questions."

The judge motioned to Winston. "Mr. Ross?"

"Thank you, your honor."

Winston stood and walked slowly to the witness stand. "Dr. Stone, you failed to mention other birth control methods such as diaphragms, condoms, and spermicidal jellies and foams. Are there health risks involved with using these types of birth control for women who have diabetes?"

"No, there are generally no health risks in using them."

Winston nodded carefully, keeping his attention squarely on Dr. Stone. "Yes, I didn't think there was. Couldn't Ashleigh use those? Can you tell the court why you wouldn't consider this type of birth control for Ashleigh? Is there another reason why you did not mention them?"

"Their success relates to proper use."

"Which means you must remember to use them each and every time you have sex if you want to avoid pregnancy, is that not correct, Dr. Stone?"

"Yes, counselor, that's correct."

"How well do you suppose Ashleigh or her partner would think to remember to use such methods of birth control?"

Martin Stone answered firmly, without hesitation. "It would be difficult for me to say, counselor, since I don't know what Ashleigh would do in moments of passion."

"Dr. Stone, pregnancy and diabetes mix about as well as water and oil. Surely, you of all people sitting in this courtroom know of the complications and dangers involved with such a pregnancy."

Winston Ross looked at Dr. Stone as though he expected an answer to his rhetorical question. The doctor made no attempt to answer. Winston stroked his chin for a few moments before continuing.

"We've heard testimony in the last day and a half that has told us the body relies on the hormone insulin to break down sugar and starch into fuel for cells. And, when the system malfunctions in diabetics, sugar accumulates in the blood and can eventually lead to blindness, heart and kidney disease, and in some cases, vascular damage that makes amputation necessary. We've also been told here that babies born to diabetic women are also at greater risk of stillbirth and birth defects. Could you tell us, doctor, what kinds of complications can arise when a woman such as Ashleigh becomes pregnant?"

Dr. Stone shifted in his seat. He cleared his throat before he spoke. "No two pregnancies are alike, Mr. Ross. For every woman the situation is different…"

"Yes, of course it is, doctor," Winston said, interrupting. "But wouldn't you agree that a fetus does not tolerate high blood sugar any better than the mother. It's just as much of a hostile environment for the baby in a mother's womb as it is for the mother carrying it. Wouldn't you agree?"

"Yes, I would."

"Then, wouldn't you also agree, doctor, that even though Ashleigh may follow all the right steps during a pregnancy, and, despite everyone's best intentions, the pregnancy could still be extremely detrimental to her health?"

Dr. Stone responded hesitantly. "Yes, that would be correct."

Winston nodded and smiled with a satisfied grin. "Thank you, Dr. Stone."

Winston looked from the doctor to Judge Gutierrez.

"I have no further questions, your honor."

The judge looked to Jaime. "Counselor?"

"Just one question for Dr. Stone, your honor."

Jaime rose, but stayed at her table to address the witness.

"Dr. Stone, how difficult is it to be pregnant and have diabetes?"

"It is difficult and creates extra worries of course, but if a woman takes care of herself, she can still have a healthy baby. Women with very mild diabetes or functional hypoglycemia, such as in Ashleigh's case, who continue to maintain a proper diet and monitor blood sugar during pregnancy will most likely eliminate the need for any other type of therapy."

"Thank you, Dr. Stone. I have no further questions for this witness, your honor."

The judge nodded at Dr. Stone. "You may step down, doctor."

When Dr. Stone had reached the gallery, the judge directed his attention to Jaime.

"Your last witness, Ms. Monroe."

"Your honor, may I have a moment with my client?"

The judge nodded.

As Jaime sat down, a memory of Beverly Cox taking the witness stand in the Kelly Jo Cox case flashed briefly before her. She huddled with Tia and Ashleigh. "Ashleigh, are you sure you want to go through with testifying? I don't want to put you through something if you don't want to."

Ashleigh shook her head firmly. "I want to and I'm ready."

Tia and Jaime exchanged glances as Jaime rose to her feet. She gently put her hand on Ashleigh's shoulder and squeezed. Jaime's touch brought Ashleigh's eyes to hers.

"Your honor, we call Ashleigh Roberts."

Ashleigh rose slowly and Jaime watched her walk toward the witness stand with the same coltish grace she had become so used to seeing. Ashleigh took the oath, sat down and folded her arms against her body. Jaime kept the look on her face indifferent, but inside everything was coming to a boil. She was trying to keep the images of Beverly crying on the witness stand from clouding her thoughts. She didn't want to have to do this to Ashleigh, too. This courtroom was the last place she wanted them to be. Though they had not known each other long, Ashleigh had filled Jaime with a kind of peacefulness she found hard to explain. Ashleigh was the quiet field that Jaime walked through at sunset. All she wanted to do right now was take Ashleigh and run.

We could be sisters and roam the Earth.

Jaime walked to the witness stand. She met Ashleigh's stare. Jaime was calm and steady and, though wide-eyed, Ashleigh appeared to copy her poise. Jaime studied Ashleigh a moment before she spoke. Ashleigh looked as gentle as a leaf swaying in the breeze.

"Ashleigh, do you know why we've been in this courtroom these past two days to listen to each of these men and Erin talk about you?"

"Yes."

"Could you tell the court why?"

Ashleigh nodded. "I'm here 'cause my mother thinks it's probably a good idea that I don't have kids. She's afraid that something bad will happen to me if I had them."

"And what would that something be, Ashleigh?"

"She's afraid my diabetes would get worse and I'd go into a coma and die if I got pregnant."

"Do you know and understand that your diabetes could get worse?"

Ashleigh nodded. "Yes."

"Ashleigh, have you ever thought about having children someday?"

Again Ashleigh nodded. "When the girls come to class to learn about being a mom, sometimes they bring their babies and I watch them. Sometimes they sleep and that's nice. They look so quiet and peaceful. My mom tells me all the time that's what I used to look like when I was little."

Jaime heard Leigh stifle a small laugh. Jaime glanced toward Leigh and saw that the look she gave her daughter was soft and her smile was rich in warm memory. Her small outburst caused Winston to look in her direction. He put a hand over her arm and patted it.

Ashleigh continued. “And sometimes I hold them and when I hold them that’s when I think about having babies.”

“So maybe someday you think you’d like to have a baby?” Jaime asked.

“Yes, but not all the time.”

“And if you wanted to have a baby would you want that choice to be yours?”

“Yes.”

“You know, Ashleigh, how important it is to take care of yourself now?”

Ashleigh nodded. “Yes, I know. And I do.”

“And do you know that it would be that much harder to take care of yourself if you were to become pregnant since you have functional hypoglycemia?”

Again Ashleigh nodded. “I know.”

“Do you think, Ashleigh, that you could take care of yourself if you were to become pregnant, if the choice was yours to make and care for a baby after it is born?”

“Yes. I could do it because I do now. Lots of people help me. They teach me what I’m supposed to do and I learn that way.”

“Do you understand what your mother wants to do to you?”

“Yes.”

“Can you tell the court?”

“She wants me to have an operation so that I can’t have a baby.”

“Do you want to give your consent for that operation, Ashleigh, to be sterilized?”

Ashleigh shook her head and answered simply. “No.”

“Why not?”

“Because I can make up my own mind. I have about a lot of things. I wanted to take the job at the food court with the others when she didn’t want me to and I want to live on my own someday. I can make a decision on this one, too. And my decision is no. I don’t want to be operated on.”

“Thank you, Ashleigh.”

Jaime sighed silently. She was through. She did not want Ashleigh on the stand any longer than she had to be. She looked at Ashleigh, nodded and gave her a quick wink. As Jaime headed toward her table she gave Winston an uncompromising look. She turned her attention to the judge. "I have no further questions for Ashleigh, your honor."

The judge looked at Winston. "Mr. Ross?"

Winston rose slowly. "Yes, thank you, just a few questions for Ashleigh, your honor."

This was the moment Jaime feared. As she seated herself, she glanced at Tia and they exchanged dismal glances. Jaime and Tia had done everything they could to prepare Ashleigh for whatever questions he might ask, and she prayed they had done their homework. They had told Ashleigh repeatedly what Winston most likely would do, but now Ashleigh was at his mercy.

And that was all Jaime could hope for. His mercy.

As Winston walked toward the witness stand, he casually slipped his right hand into his pant pocket and Ashleigh watched with simplicity as he approached. When he reached the stand, he studied the delicate features on her face. The hazel color of her eyes looked blue today, matching more the blue in the blouse she wore. The softness of her smooth skin reminded him of a young child.

It is, he thought, what she is, a *child*.

Winston directed his attention toward his hand and pulled a small tan-colored package from his pocket. Grasped between his index and middle finger, Winston held it at eye level for Ashleigh to examine. Jaime and Tia could see the package and knew what it was. They leaned forward in their chairs, eyes set squarely on Winston and Ashleigh. All watched as Ashleigh studied the small square package. She looked at him when he spoke.

"Ashleigh, do you know what this is?"

Ashleigh fidgeted and shook her head. "No, sir."

Erin, sitting behind Jaime and Tia, quickly unfolded her arms and leaned toward them. She spoke quietly but urgently under her breath.

"She does too!" Erin said in an exasperated whisper. "She's had the parenting and sexual education courses. She most certainly does know what that is!"

Winston said. "Well, Ashleigh, it's a condom. Do you know what they're used for?"

"No, sir."

Erin was beside herself. "She knows! Ashleigh does know what they're used for and how it's used! Why is she telling him no?!"

Erin's outburst caused Judge Gutierrez to look in their direction. It was a stern look that made Erin blush. Erin looked away and tried in vain to whisper encouragement to Ashleigh. "Answer the question, Ashleigh. You know it. You know it."

Winston continued in an almost condescending air. "Ashleigh, if you don't know what a condom is, then you don't know how to use it, do you?"

Ashleigh's eyebrows drifted toward the top of her head as she looked at Jaime. It only took seeing the expression on Ashleigh's face to know that she was scared and didn't know or remember how to answer the question. From the corner of her eye, Jaime could see Leigh watching the exchange between her attorney and her daughter. She was as still as a statue, the look on her face registering no emotion.

In that moment Jaime knew what it meant to feel hatred toward another human being. She remembered how she felt sitting in the courtroom the day Ryan McKenna was found guilty of raping her sister Sarah. She hadn't hated anyone as much since Ryan as the way she now felt toward Leigh Roberts.

Jaime returned her attention to Ashleigh to see her shake her head no.

"Ashleigh." The judge spoke to her.

Ashleigh looked at him.

"You'll have to answer the question for the court," he said.

Ashleigh looked at Winston and spoke softly. "No, sir."

Erin slumped against her seat. Jaime kept her attention fixed on Ashleigh, careful not to show any emotion.

"Thank you, Ashleigh," Winston said and looked at Judge Gutierrez. "Nothing further."

The judge looked to Ashleigh, smiling slightly. "I also have a few questions for you, Ashleigh," he said and pressed a meaty hand against his robe.

Ashleigh looked at Jaime, as though to ask if it was all right. Jaime smiled slightly and nodded. Jaime had told her to expect that the judge might also want to ask questions. Jaime tried to suppress her sudden fear Ashleigh would exhibit the same timidness she did with Winston's question. But when she saw Ashleigh straighten in the chair, her fears subsided.

"You've told the court you might like to have a child," the judge said.

Ashleigh nodded. "Yes, sir. But not for a long time."

"How much time is a long time?" he asked.

"Maybe about when I'm almost thirty-five or forty."

Tia and Jaime exchanged uneasy glances.

Ashleigh thought a moment more and added. "But that might not be a good idea."

"Why not?" the judge asked.

"'Cause I've seen it on the television where they say it's bad for a girl to wait that long to have a baby. So if I had one, it would have to be a lot sooner than that. I'd still want to be young so that I could play with them in the yard."

Jessie nodded thoughtfully. "The doctors have been explaining here that it would not be a good idea for you to have a baby, Ashleigh. That, in fact, it could be very dangerous for you to have a child. It might mean a threat to your health and possibly even your life. Did you hear that testimony?"

Ashleigh looked to Jaime and back to the judge before she answered. "Yes, sir, I did."

"Did that testimony maybe make you think that perhaps having children would not be a very good idea for you?"

"I might not even ever have one. But if I did, then I want to make my own decision. People don't tell me what clothes to wear in the morning. I pick them all by myself, because I like making my choice on what to wear. I understand lots and lots of things. And when I don't, I try and talk to people who will help me and I learn that way. Sometimes it's hard to understand and I have to ask again. But I ask and I try to learn. I want to learn. I would learn and would have the best baby possible. I want to be able to make up my own mind about having a baby."

"Do you realize, Ashleigh, if you were to become pregnant it could possibly kill you?" he asked.

Ashleigh nodded. "Yes, sir. I know that once you die, you go to Heaven, this place in the sky, and this life down here is over and you don't ever come back."

Judge Jessie Gutierrez sighed as he sat back against his chair and studied Ashleigh. He removed his glasses, studied them for a moment as if to collect his thoughts and returned them to his face. "Thank you, Ashleigh," he said. "You may step down."

There was a fleeting silence as Ashleigh rose and left the witness stand and returned to her place between Tia and Jaime. All had their eyes fixed on Judge Gutierrez.

"That concludes the testimony?" he asked, looking at each counselor.

Jaime rose, and Winston followed, adjusting his tie as he stood.

"Yes, your honor." Winston said.

"Our closing arguments will be submitted to you in writing, your honor," Jaime said.

"Very well," the judge said. "The court has heard testimony and arguments by the parties on the petition and will take the matter under advisement." He nodded to Jaime and Winston. "You both will be notified when I have made my decision. This court is adjourned."

Thirty-one

On the second Monday after Ashleigh's hearing, Jaime Monroe and Winston Ross received their expected call from Judge Jessie Gutierrez's office. They were to meet in his chambers at 10 a.m. Tuesday. Jaime told Pearl she would come to her chambers when she left Judge Gutierrez's chambers.

Winston was in Jessie's outer office when Jaime arrived. Awkward small talk filled the space between them as they waited to be ushered into the judge's chambers.

The judge was seated behind his large mahogany desk when they walked in. He rose and shook hands with Winston, then Jaime. With a thick, stubby hand, he gestured toward two empty chairs by his desk. They sat down in the butter-soft, black leather chairs to face the judge. Gutierrez's bulky frame filled his entire chair as he sat down. And Jaime couldn't help thinking that the Michelin Tire Man so accurately described his soft, full frame. The judge's heavy breathing filled the room as he collected his thoughts. He looked from a wall lined floor to ceiling with law books to the attorneys, who returned his gaze. Jaime's was particularly scrutinizing and held Gutierrez's attention a moment longer.

When the judge spoke, his voice was low and serious. "Counselors, I have spent the last eleven days in deep thought over Ashleigh's case, and the decision I've reached has not come without intense introspection."

He reached for a manila folder on his desk. He opened it and read for several minutes in silence. "Ashleigh appears to be a high functioning young woman and I'm impressed with how much she has done with her life, given her mental and physical limitations. My biggest concern, however, remains the status of her health, or the lack thereof..."

He stopped a moment, his attention captured by the contents in the manila folder.

Smoothing his mustache between his thumb and index finger, he went on: "Ashleigh's health troubles me greatly and I do not think, based on the testimony I heard in court, that she could withstand a pregnancy, mentally or physically."

Jaime felt her breathing stop. She had been clutching the sides of the chair and she kept her attention riveted on Gutierrez.

He closed the folder and folded his hands over the top. He continued in the same low-pitched voice. "Therefore, this court concludes that the sterilization of Ashleigh Roberts is medically essential," Judge Gutierrez said looking first to Jaime, then Winston.

Jaime remained seemingly indifferent to the judge's announcement. To control her emotions, she looked beyond him to the window, to the masonry of tall buildings she could see through the slits in the half-open blinds. She did not want to hear more, but he continued to speak as though he were a wind-up toy.

"This conclusion is based on the opinions from the experts in this case who testified it was clearly necessary that, in order to preserve the life and physical and mental wellbeing of Ashleigh, this procedure would be in her best interest. As I said, this decision has not come without considerable thought and research. I realize Ashleigh objected strongly to having the procedure done, but this court has rejected her wishes and desires because I believe that her very life would be at stake if she were to become pregnant. Therefore, in the best interest of her preserving her life and her mental and physical health, the court concludes that sterilization is the best possible solution for Ms. Roberts."

Jaime felt as if she had been trapped in a rockslide and everything was about to topple on top of her. Hard, fast and heavy. The change in the tenor of the judge's voice recaptured her attention.

"*However*, I want to point out and stress that while the court heard testimony that should Ashleigh give birth to a child, her mother and guardian, Leigh Roberts, may end up raising the child and Dr. Richie testified that should Ashleigh have a baby, it would be a disaster to society..." He stopped a moment and looked from Winston to Jaime. "I want to stress that those comments expressed by those witnesses, were not relevant to the court's decision. My decision to order Ashleigh's sterilization was made purely from a medical standpoint based on the testimony I heard from your witnesses. The court did not base its decision on those other factors."

The judge looked at Winston. "Mr. Ross, your client's request for sterilization is hereby granted. The request for tubal ligation by a qualified physician can be performed on Ashleigh Roberts no earlier than forty-five days, at which time Ashleigh's rights to appeal will have expired."

Winston nodded. There was little emotion in his voice when he spoke. "Thank you, your honor. I will let Leigh Roberts know."

The attorneys rose to leave. Jaime nodded her acknowledgment of the judge's decision without offering a word. Saying something at that moment without collapsing into tears of disappointment and frustration would have been impossible. Jaime followed Winston from the chambers as though she operated on remote control. When they reached the hallway Winston stopped and turned to look at Jaime.

"I'm sorry, counselor. You did a scrupulous job with Ashleigh's case. I'm sure this is just the beginning."

Jaime shrugged her shoulders. She was not feeling especially well at the moment. "It is, Winston," she said.

With a wave of his hand Winston was gone. When he had turned the corner, Jaime closed her eyes and leaned against the wall. She needed a moment to regain her strength before going to Pearl's chambers. For the first time, Jaime wished that she and Pearl weren't such good friends. How much better it would have been had Pearl heard Ashleigh's case. If anyone would have understood, it would have been Pearl.

Jaime knew she would have to tell Ashleigh next, but first she would find Pearl. As she pushed herself away from the wall, she replayed leaving the judge's office and heard herself talking with Winston, but it was as though everything had happened without her permission.

She began to walk toward Pearl's chambers. She entered the outer office and noticed the door to her office was ajar. She knocked hesitantly.

"Hello? Pearl?"

Jaime poked her head inside the office as Pearl looked up. Her face softened at the sight of Jaime.

"Hello, dear," Pearl said and rose from her desk.

She came around to greet Jaime. She took Jaime's hands, but Jaime would not look up. Pearl gently lifted her chin. The gesture brought her eyes to Pearl's. Their eyes met and locked. The tension and hurt showed in Jaime's eyes. Jaime averted her gaze because she knew Pearl could see in them what she did not want her to see.

"Jaime, I'm sorry."

Jaime shrugged. "I failed her, Pearl. Ashleigh was counting on me and I failed her. I couldn't give her something she needed most."

"Hush," Pearl said and she took Jaime by the hand and walked toward the couch. "I'm sure Judge Gutierrez's decision didn't come without a lot of thought."

"Yes, I know" Jaime said, then added quickly. "I wish you were the judge."

Pearl laughed and patted Jaime's hands, which were folded on her lap. "You know that wouldn't have been possible."

"I know, but if you were, things wouldn't have gone this way and I wouldn't dread having to tell Ashleigh."

Pearl stared at Jaime for what seemed a long time. And Jaime fidgeted a little, as she often did under Pearl's unflinching gaze.

"Maybe not," Pearl said with an even tone.

The comment made Jaime gasp slightly.

"What do you mean maybe not?"

Pearl shrugged and removed her hand from Jaime's.

"I don't know if I would have ruled any differently, dear."

Jaime shook her head, confusion showing in her eyes. "What do you mean? You would have ruled the same way Judge Gutierrez did?"

Jaime forced herself to look at Pearl with a sixth sense that made her think something else lurked beneath her statement. "There's more, isn't there," Jaime said and her tone was accusatory.

The question took Pearl by surprise. When she did not respond immediately, Jaime knew she was right.

"You obviously followed the case closely. What else would have influenced your decision?" Jaime asked in a straightforward voice.

Pearl nodded almost expectantly. "I didn't do a very good job of getting by you, did I?"

Jaime pressed her lips together tightly and shook her head slowly. Pearl sighed heavily and leaned back against the couch. She felt Jaime's eyes on her, weighing down on her.

"I've never told you much about my mother, have I?" Pearl said.

"No, you haven't."

"I was eight when she died, you know, and the oldest of three siblings. But I should have been the oldest of four, and probably more for that matter."

Pearl looked directly at Jaime, who remained stoic.

"Mother, God rest her, died from complications due to her fourth pregnancy. She had developed gestational diabetes after my brother was born. She was insulin dependent from that day on. Ten months later, Mother was pregnant again."

Pearl looked to Jaime to measure her reaction. But if Jaime was surprised at the sudden revelation, she did not show it.

"Why didn't you tell me before?" Jaime asked in an even, collected tone.

Pearl shrugged, uncertain how to answer.

"Shortly before my sister was born, Mother lapsed into a diabetic coma. Doctors were monitoring her throughout the pregnancy, but it happened so quickly, it was as if they didn't know what to do when her blood pressure dropped suddenly. By the time they got the baby out it was too late, she wasn't breathing and attempts to revive her failed. We buried them together and seven years later, my father beside them."

Pearl reached for Jaime's hands and held them lightly. They were limp in hers.

"I guess I don't know what to say," Jaime said, without taking her eyes off Pearl's thin hands around hers.

"There's nothing you can say, dear. That was a long, long time ago. Maybe now you'll understand why that would also have been my decision."

"Why did you tell me about Ashleigh's case?"

"Because I thought it would do you good. I thought it would do you both good."

"How?" Jaime asked, struggling to keep hurt and anger from her voice. "I failed in court. I failed Ashleigh. And I have to go back and tell her that now."

"You've helped her in other ways," Pearl responded and her voice was soft.

Jaime looked to Pearl and nodded without speaking.

"Please understand, Jaime."

"Sure, I understand and I respect Judge Gutierrez's decision," Jaime said finally.

"I hope this won't change anything between us," Pearl said.

Jaime forced a weak half smile. "It won't."

Jaime pulled her hands from Pearl's and rose from the sofa. She straightened her skirt and collected her briefcase.

"Let's get together for hotdogs soon, all right, dear?" Pearl asked as Jaime reached the doorway.

Jaime nodded. She opened the door and left Pearl sitting alone on the sofa. Before Jaime could make it to the elevator, she found a restroom and barely made it to a toilet before she threw up.

Tia and Ashleigh were waiting in Jaime's office when she returned. Jaime's shoulders were turned inward, the look on her face sullen. Her color was gone.

"What happened?" Tia asked, more in an effort to break the weighty silence that had fallen over the room.

Jaime sat at her desk and studied her folded hands. She looked at Ashleigh for a silent moment before she spoke. She would keep her voice strong and confident as she spoke, in an effort to mask her disappointment. Jaime wanted to stay positive for Ashleigh and hoped it would not be a weak attempt. She forced a smile.

"The judge, Ashleigh, in your case," Jaime began slowly by saying, "took everything into consideration. Everything you said and everything everyone else said who testified on the witness stand and, based on that testimony, he has made a decision. He has granted your mother's request."

"What does that mean?" Ashleigh asked, her voice sounding confused.

Jaime swallowed slowly and then spoke. "Well, it means that the judge has granted your mother's petition to have an operation to have you sterilized."

Tia's and Jaime's eyes centered on Ashleigh. Ashleigh raised her eyebrows slightly and shrugged her shoulders. She looked with uncertainty and wonder from Tia to Jaime. Jaime desperately wanted to look away, but she forced herself to keep her eyes on Ashleigh.

"Well, our hope lies in the appeals now," Tia said flatly, looking to Jaime.

Jaime looked at Tia and nodded.

"Do we have to go and do the operation tomorrow, Jaime?" Ashleigh asked.

Jaime felt the weight of Ashleigh's words press against her. She smiled. It was a small, sad smile. She shook her head slightly and suddenly felt very tired.

"No, Ashleigh, we don't have to go tomorrow."

Thirty-two

Anger whirled inside Jaime like a hurricane.

Each time a scene from the courtroom, or the judge's office flashed in her mind, she pummeled the heavy bag in a flurry of left-right punches. The bag would swing toward her and she would lunge toward it and knock it away with her shoulder, or push it away with her gloves. Then, as though for good measure, she hit the bag again as it moved away from her. Sweat ran down her back, soaking her shirt as she continually lambasted the heavy bag.

The muscles in her arms and upper body screamed for her to stop. Her eyes burned from sweat. She finally stopped, unlaced her gloves and threw them to the floor. She grabbed the towel and dried her neck and shoulders, muttering to herself as she buried her face deep inside the thick towel. After she rested a few minutes and drank enough water to cool her system, she laced her gloves again and resumed punishing the bag. At least she could take her frustrations out on something that she had some control over, and on something that could not hit her back.

When Barry Winters returned from dinner he checked for Jaime's card. She was there. He hurried up the stairs to the third floor, where he saw Jaime sitting against the wall. From the distance he took everything in about her. Strands of hair had escaped from her ponytail and had fallen loosely about her face. She had a towel around her neck. She seemed focused on the bag swaying lightly before her. Her arms were resting heavily over her knees and she was holding an empty water bottle loosely around its neck. She was so deep in thought she did not notice him approach.

"Mind if I join you?"

His voice startled her back to the present.

"Sorry, Jaime, I didn't mean to scare you."

"You didn't," she said and flashed a half-smile as she patted the empty place beside her. For a few moments they sat in silence.

"Things didn't go so well today, we got the judge's decision."

"I gathered."

"I got your messages last weekend, Barry. Thanks for calling."

"You haven't been at the club much lately and I wanted to see how it went."

"Thanks. Pretty good I thought, at least until this morning. I went to the mountains last weekend. I just didn't want to be home thinking about the hearing. I needed a distraction and I thought an overnight stay would do me good. I did some hiking and being outside helped a lot."

Barry nodded. "You've told me how much you enjoy being outside."

Jaime forced a half-smile. "It definitely helped and work was so busy this week that it helped to keep Ashleigh's hearing from being the first thought on my mind."

"What happened?" Barry asked.

Jaime shrugged. "The judge decided against us." Hurt flowed through her like a small stream. "He said he based his decision on Ashleigh's medical condition. He said a pregnancy would damage her physical health and she shouldn't risk it."

"Isn't she mentally delayed?"

"Well, she is. But that's not what had the judge so concerned. For her level of disability, Ashleigh is high functioning. She does well for herself, she just needs a little more help with certain things."

She stopped to look at him. He listened, his blue eyes intent on her face.

"Ashleigh has functional hypoglycemia."

"That too," Barry said flatly.

"That too. Unfortunately most forms of birth control just don't work well with her type of diabetes. That was, in part, what the judge said he based his decision on." She was quiet for a moment. "You know something else, Barry?"

He looked at her, his eyes wanting to know her thoughts.

"You know what's been bothering me a lot lately? I've been thinking about it hitting that bag."

Barry leaned closer to Jaime.

"I think Leigh Roberts used me."

He wanted to comfort her, but didn't know what to say.

"You'll appeal?" Barry asked.

Jaime nodded. "I have until mid-September. At least Leigh has agreed not to go forward with the sterilization while this appeal is pending. That was sure big of her. Maybe with any luck, we'll all be old and gray by the time this thing gets through the system and then it won't matter anymore."

Barry looked at the heavy punching bag, the indentations where Jaime had left her mark.

"You like boxing don't you, Jaime?"

"I love it. I love beating the crap out of that stupid bag, especially tonight." She thought about his question a minute more. "I'm able to work longer hours and keep my attention span and concentration level on high because of boxing. I feel like my mind is clearer, even though right now I feel as though I'm in a fog."

She looked at him playfully and said, "But don't call me Rocky."

He laughed.

"How do you feel about women who like to box?" she asked, eyeing him earnestly.

Barry raised his eyebrows and looked thoughtfully toward the ceiling as he replied. "Well, I know why you do it. It's a great aerobic workout and a great stress reliever..."

"And," Jaime said, sure more of Barry's opinion was forthcoming.

"And that's exactly what you need for the kind of job you have. I guess what it comes down to is a matter of traditions and attitudes. The way I look at it is that women who box have several obstacles to overcome.

Traditionally, boxing is a male's sport. Then there are those who have an attitude about boxing in general and whatever you say to them, even if you're Mohammed Ali, nothing will change their minds." He stopped to collect his thoughts. "Then you have those people who think that women are supposed to be delicate and tender and shouldn't box at all."

"You don't think that women should box then?" she asked.

"Jaime, I think *women* should do whatever makes them happy. But, personally, no, I don't think boxing is a sport for women."

Jaime countered quickly. "The secret to boxing is movement and timing, Barry. And women can be just as good as any man at that. Besides, I don't spar much, especially anymore. I just like the workout."

He looked gingerly at her, a glimmer in his blue eyes. "Personally, if you really want to know, I think women are to be loved and held and cared for."

Jaime rolled her eyes at him. "Oh, Barry, you're such a romantic."

Barry studied Jaime. Her complexion was ruddy from the workout. Her large and usually expressive eyes seemed diminished and the tension showed within them. He remembered she had smiled at him when they first spoke tonight, but it held weariness. Barry never remembered seeing her look so defeated and exhausted.

"Go home, Jaime," he said. "Get some rest. Things will work out for you and Ashleigh."

She looked from the empty water bottle she had been turning over in her hands to Barry. She gave him a faint smile. He rose to his feet and offered her his hand to help her up, but she waved off his gesture.

"I'm going to sit here another few minutes, then go another round with that bag. Then I'm going to take a steam and shower and *then*, that's exactly what I'm going to do, Barry, go home."

By the time Jaime made it home, she was exhausted physically and emotionally drained. She felt weak from hunger, but too tired to fix something to eat. She stared for several minutes into an open refrigerator. Nothing looked appealing. She grabbed an apple from the fruit basket, took a big bite and then smeared it with peanut butter.

She glanced through the mail, eating a handful of almonds, but stopped half way through. She threw the rest of the mail on the kitchen table. Nothing she read registered anyway. Jaime let out a deep sigh as she stretched her body on top of her bed. She had not bothered to undress. She did not want to sleep, because she was certain the nightmares would come. Bad dreams about running, cottonwood trees and becoming a skeleton. Terrible dreams about Frank chasing her. Horrible dreams about Molly Gibson and Mitchell.

It was inevitable. She was asleep within moments.

And the dream came.

It was raining the day Jaime finally made it to the cemetery, more than a week after Sarah's funeral. The downpour was relentless. From the car window, Jaime saw that the dirt had not yet settled over her sister's grave. The rain pounding down on the dirt made the running water dark, muddy and loose. It ran in all directions.

There were no flowers. She was sure the stormy weather from the last several days had washed them away from the temporary marker they once adorned. It was hard for her to imagine all that remained of Sarah was a temporary marker.

Jaime opened the car door, stuck the umbrella outside and opened it. Rain landed against it in a continual monotonous thud. Water splashed around the bottom of her Levi's and boots. She reached the grave and stared at the temporary marker.

She lowered herself to her knees and placed a hand lightly over the top of Sarah's grave. Dirt quickly covered the tips of her fingers as the rain fell down around them. Jaime set the flowers on the mud. The steady rain began to press the petals into the dirt almost immediately. She stood and stayed only a few minutes more before she turned to leave. For reasons she did not know, she closed the umbrella. The rain quickly fell on her and flattened her hair against her head, neck and shoulders. She was soaked by the time she reached the car.

Jaime woke from the dream with a start.

She lifted herself to her elbows and looked around the bedroom. The lamp near her bed was still on. The shadows in the room were long and silent. Her mind returned unwillingly to the dream that woke her. Jaime turned out the light. Darkness surrounded her. She settled against the pillows. Jaime stayed awake until the dawn made her closed curtains bright.

When her alarm sounded, she did not want to get up to face the day.

Thirty-three

Leigh woke in a hotel room in Vail, drained and empty.

She woke long before her alarm sounded. As tired as she felt, she was certain going back to sleep wouldn't be a problem. Her mind, however, was crowded with thoughts, and she couldn't fall back to sleep. She had felt depleted and weary since Ashleigh's hearing. Though she had spoken to her daughter every day since the hearing, she had only seen her once. Ashleigh had come home to Evergreen and stayed overnight. They did what they had always done in their time together, Ashleigh helped Leigh cook and they stayed up late watching movies. They did not mention the hearing.

Leigh had learned of the judge's decision a week ago. She had her wish, but did not especially feel like celebrating. She accepted the worn-out feeling as part of the process of going through the ordeal. She had expected it would pass after a few days' rest, but each day she only grew more tired.

Leigh was in the mountain town on a newspaper assignment and had considered asking her editor to postpone the interviews set for today. However, since getting the people together to be interviewed for the story was a story in itself, postponing it was not the best idea. So she traveled to Vail to interview people who were part of a federal witness protection program. The angle was why they had gone into the program and how their lives had changed. Leigh was thrilled to get the assignment. This morning, however, Vail was the last place she wanted to be.

She had driven to Vail in her Volkswagen Cabrio, hoping the fresh air and breeze would clear her mind. But this drive had not helped. It wasn't until she left Georgetown on Interstate 70 that the rain finally stopped and she could put the top down. By the time she arrived, her mood still had not improved. She checked into the hotel and went straight to the room.

Leigh wanted to finish the interviews by 4 p.m. She needed to get back to Denver to get Ashleigh. The Morningside Heights group home was going to be remodeled and residents had to make other living arrangements during construction. Since Ashleigh's new living arrangements were still not finalized, Leigh had made plans for Ashleigh to stay with her while the group home was being remodeled.

Leigh told Erin Greene she would collect Ashleigh by 7 p.m. At roughly hundred miles to Denver, she wanted to leave Vail in plenty of time. She didn't finish until almost 5:30 p.m. She should have known the interviews would take longer than planned. Whenever she did these kinds of interviews it took extra time. In order to write the best story, she let the interview go as long as her subjects were willing to talk. She had not become an award-winning journalist because she limited her interviews to an hour.

Leigh called Erin as she was leaving Vail. "Tell Ashleigh I'll be there before bedtime," she had told her.

By the time she reached Georgetown, roughly forty-five miles from Denver, she met the rain she had left behind the day before. She stopped to put the top up on the Cabrio. Just beyond Georgetown the rain intensified, hitting the window in a torrent. Leigh could see that many cars had pulled to the side of the road to wait out the storm. She wanted to stop. She wanted to pull off the road, find a place to eat, to relax and wait out the storm. She had eaten breakfast, but nothing since.

A tremendous headache had settled deep in her skull. Her hunger only added to her fatigue and the throbbing in her head.

But she had to keep going. She was going to get Ashleigh. Ashleigh needed her.

Just beyond Idaho Springs, she approached a semi-trailer. It sprayed a heavy volume of water against her windshield, momentarily blinding her as she passed alongside the 18-wheeler. The Cabrio's windshield wipers worked feverishly, but she could not see again until she had pulled well in front of the rig. With the semi behind her, she relaxed slightly, loosening her grip around the steering wheel.

She had reached the part of I-70 she dreaded to drive — an area called Dead Man's Curve, which had been affectionately dubbed "Fatal Alley." The stretch of road earned its recognition for the numerous accidents that occurred there, many of them fatal, due to the sharp curves and steep grades truckers and motorists were forced to navigate during their descent from the mountains into the outskirts of Denver. She always breathed a sigh of relief when she left Dead Man's Curve in her rearview mirror.

Leigh was approaching the area when she saw a cluster of red taillights in the distance. The brake lights from each of the cars were illuminated, shining in the rain. She leaned closer to the steering wheel, as though moving the few extra inches would provide a better look at what was ahead. She slowed, giving herself the time and the distance to stop. She had turned off the radio to concentrate on the drive. That made it easier to hear the sound of the air horn coming from the semi behind her.

She glanced in the rearview mirror. The headlights of the truck she had left in the distance in Idaho Springs were getting closer. The horn sounded louder.

My God, he's not going to stop! He can't stop!

She looked again to the cars in front of her. Still not moving. One more glance in the mirror. The lights from the rig were so close they were starting to form one light. Panic surged within her. She quickly counted the cars in front of her. Five. Maybe six. Not one of them moving. She slammed her hand down on her horn, letting it stay there. None of the cars moved. Her heart was beating wildly in her chest like the rain on the windshield. The rig's air horn sounded as if it were in her backseat.

Another glance in the mirror. Eyes wide in panic.

Headlights framed in the mirror.

Impact.

Metal upon metal.

The tiny Cabrio began to buckle as the semi pushed its way into it. The airbag exploded, slapping Leigh in the face. She screamed as the semi pushed her car off the roadway and sent it barreling into the barricades. Ashleigh walking toward the witness stand consumed her last moments of consciousness as the Cabrio went airborne, then tumbled once, then twice. The semi struck another car before the trucker finally gained control.

First silence. Then yelling. Followed by confusion. None of the other motorists was badly injured. The semi driver and some of the others ran from their cars toward the Cabrio. It had landed in the median on the right side of the road, right at Dead Man's Curve. There was rain, relentless rain, and mud everywhere.

Along the way the motorists collected an overnight bag and a purse that had been thrown from the car. There was a briefcase. Papers, soaked limp by heavy rain, were scattered everywhere. The ground looked white as snow. There was a shoe. A high heel. The tan leather turned dark by the downpour.

They reached the Cabrio.

It was resting on its top. The ragtop torn. A tire still spinning. There was a woman inside. The seatbelt kept her from being thrown from the car. She was unconscious and bleeding. The car was positioned at an odd, unbalanced angle, making it nearly impossible for them to reach her.

No one could get close enough to the Cabrio to see if she was still alive.

Thirty-four

Jaime's telephone rang, rousing her from a deep sleep.

In the darkness, she fumbled to find the switch for the lamp near the bed. She squeezed her eyes tightly as she turned on the light. She answered on the fifth ring, mumbling hello.

"Jaime?"

"Speaking," she said in a groggy voice. She rubbed her eyes, trying to clear the cobwebs from her mind.

"It's Erin. Leigh's been in a car accident."

She woke instantly. "What?"

"Leigh's been in a car accident," Erin repeated.

Jaime sat up in bed and looked at the time, 5:10 a.m. "When?"

"I got the call from the hospital about thirty minutes ago. She was taken to Wheat Ridge General Hospital around midnight, I think. The hospital called here."

"What happened?"

"Well, details are sketchy. Leigh had just come out of surgery. From what I was told it was raining and several cars, including Leigh's, were involved in a wreck with a semi on I-70, near Evergreen."

Jaime knew of the stretch of road to which Erin was referring. She thought of Leigh's tiny Cabrio, a slick car, as black as the night.

"How badly was she hurt?" she asked.

"Pretty bad. There were some internal injuries. She broke her radius and ulna. The doctor said it was an open fracture on her forearm and during surgery they put plates and screws in her arm so it could heal. He said she'll be OK."

"What was she doing on the highway so late? Ashleigh told me Leigh was supposed to be at Morningside before seven."

"Well, she was," Erin said, "but she called and said her interviews ran long and she'd be late. By 10 o'clock, I started to get worried because she hadn't arrived and she didn't answer when I called her cell phone. Everyone else here has found other living arrangements. Ashleigh and I are here for now but we have to be out by noon today."

There was a moment of silence.

"It's no problem, Jaime, Ashleigh can stay with me."

"Erin, I'd really like Ashleigh to stay with me, if it's OK."

Erin hesitated only briefly before responding. When Ashleigh returned to Morningside Heights after her first visit with Jaime, she was the only thing Ashleigh talked about. "Ashleigh would like that," Erin said, smiling into the phone.

"We'll work it out later. Maybe I can pick her up after work. What about Leigh?"

"She's in ICU. The hospital said she's in serious condition and lucky to be alive."

"Does Ashleigh know?"

"Not yet. She's still asleep. It'll upset her for sure."

"No doubt."

"I know it's probably the last thing you'd want to do, Jaime, but I don't know who else to call for Leigh. Would you be willing to go to the hospital?"

Jaime spoke without hesitation. "I'm on my way."

Within the hour Jaime had dressed and was out the door. It was just after 7 a.m. when Jaime entered the hospital, remembering her own visit a few months ago. She remembered regaining consciousness at the club and seeing Barry and Ashleigh as they huddled over her, faces clouded in concern. She thought about being in the emergency room and having to have stitches sewn into her lip. She remembered she did not flinch when she felt the keen prick of the needle as it entered just above her upper lip to deaden the wound. She pushed the thoughts of that evening from her mind as she took the elevator to ICU.

Leigh's room was dimly lit by a fluorescent light positioned at the top of her bed. It cast an eerie glow into the room, the way light looks submerged in murky water. The only sound in the room came from the machines clustered around Leigh's bed.

Jaime hardly recognized her. Her face was badly bruised and swollen. There were several large gashes, including one above her left eye. There was a cast on her right arm, tubes coming out her left arm and an oxygen tube over her nose. She looked limp like a rag and her body seemed dwarfed by her bed. Jaime stayed near the door and looked at Leigh for several moments before she could bring herself to enter. What dislike Jaime felt toward her vanished when she saw how wounded and bruised she was.

She walked softly into the room and stopped at the foot of the bed. Leigh's head was turned slightly toward Jaime. Her eyes were not fully closed, but she did not appear to be awake. There were deep creases in her forehead and Jaime wondered if she was feeling the effect of her pain. She moved slowly along the side of the bed, keeping her eyes on Leigh. Then she looked for Leigh's hand. It was resting lifelessly on her stomach. Jaime hesitated a moment before taking it, then she slipped hers gingerly inside.

It was warm to the touch. Leigh stirred slightly. She opened her eyes slowly. It seemed to take all the strength she had. She fixed them blankly on the wall.

"Leigh?"

Leigh shifted her eyes slowly toward the figure that had taken her hand. The image was blurred. She squinted, but could not make out who it was.

She spoke with effort. "Hospital?"

"Yes. You're in the hospital. Wheat Ridge General."

"Am I going to be all right?"

"Yes. You're going to be fine."

"Jaime?"

"Yes, it's me. I ... Erin called and I came as soon as I could."

Leigh sighed heavily. "I … I was in an accident?"

"Yes, you were, but you're going to be all right."

Silence.

"Do you remember what happened?" Jaime asked.

Jaime saw Leigh squint and she wasn't certain if the grimace came from the pain, or if she was trying to remember the accident. Leigh spoke with effort. "I was on I-70 … coming home ... It was raining. Raining really hard ... It was dark ... I was supposed to pick up Ashleigh. I, I was late already ... I had to keep going. She needs me..."

Leigh stopped talking and moved her eyes toward the ceiling. She swallowed hard, as though she were trying to push down pain that appeared to be so intense even moving her eyes from side to side was agony. Her discomfort made Jaime wince.

"Ashleigh ... She was supposed to stay with me..." Leigh managed to say.

"Yes, I know, I know all that. But don't worry about Ashleigh. She'll be fine. We've taken care of everything. She has a place to stay. You need to be quiet now and rest. Your condition needs to stabilize. Please. I can only stay a few minutes right now."

Leigh tightened her grip around Jaime's hand. Her strength had not deserted her, despite her injuries. In her grip, Jaime could feel her fear, the apprehension that lay ahead.

"Jaime, please, don't leave … please."

Jaime spoke quickly and quietly. "Only for a little while. You're in ICU and I can only stay a few minutes, but I'll be in the waiting area. I won't go anywhere. I'll come back when it's time. You need to rest."

Jaime eased her hand free of Leigh's grip. By the time she reached the door, Leigh had slipped back into unconsciousness. Jaime left the room and walked by the nurse's station. It was empty. Jaime looked around for someone to talk to about Leigh's condition. She saw no one and turned to leave. Jaime was almost to the ICU doors when she heard a male voice calling out.

"Miss! Excuse me! Miss! Do you have a moment?"

Jaime stopped when she realized the man was talking to her. She turned to look at him. He was dark skinned, medium height and slender. His thick, dark hair was short and combed away from his face. A thick mustache covered his upper lip. The name tag clipped to his white coat read: Dr. Azar.

"I saw you coming out of Ms. Roberts' room. Are you a family member?"

"No, no, I'm just a friend. Are you her doctor?"

"I was on duty when she came in."

"How is she?"

"She's serious, but her condition should stabilize eventually. She had some internal damage and bleeding, but came out of surgery all right. But she's got a concussion, four broken ribs and the others are badly bruised. She has a broken collarbone and a badly broken arm and lots of cuts and bruises, as you saw. Once she stabilizes, we can move her out of ICU. We didn't know who to contact when she came in. We couldn't find any next of kin listed for her."

Jaime shook her head to confirm. "No. Her parents are dead and she's an only child. I don't know who else you would've contacted, other than Morningside Heights."

"We didn't know if she was married," Dr. Azar said. "We found a card in her wallet. It said she had a daughter who is developmentally delayed who lives in a group home in Denver. She's probably not capable of understanding or comprehending what's happened, so I didn't want to call there, but we had no other alternatives."

Jaime swallowed hard and her eyes narrowed. She stared at him and anger began to coil like a snake in her stomach. She flexed the muscles in her jaw. It was all she could do to control her anger. When she spoke, it took everything she had to keep the tone of her voice civil.

"Leigh's been married, twice. Her first husband's name is Alan Andrew Roberts. He lives in Seattle, but I don't how to reach him. I don't know a thing about her second husband, not even his name. And, if you must know, doctor, her daughter, Ashleigh, is *quite* capable of understanding what she's being told and of taking care of herself. Yes, she has some delay, but it's mild."

Jaime stopped talking. She felt her pulse pumping rapidly as she took a pen and a piece of paper from the counter. She scribbled her home and work phone numbers on the paper and handed it to the doctor. He accepted the note without a word.

"I'll be here another couple of hours and then I'll be at work. I can be reached at that number should anything with Leigh's condition change. I appreciate your time, doctor. Have a good day."

Jaime's voice was ice when she finished speaking. She abruptly turned and walked away, leaving the doctor standing speechless in the middle of ICU. Jaime headed for the cafeteria for coffee and something to eat.

An hour later Jaime returned to Leigh's room. She went to the bed and touched her lightly on the shoulder. "It's Jaime."

Leigh opened her eyes and looked at her. When she spoke her voice was weak. It was almost hard for Jaime to hear her.

"Where's Ashleigh?"

"Ashleigh's with Erin. But she's fine."

"Wasn't she hurt badly in the accident?"

"No, Leigh. Ashleigh wasn't in the car when the accident happened. You were alone and going to get her when the semi hit you."

"She doesn't have a place to stay … she needs me."

Jaime gently placed her hand on Leigh's shoulder. "You're not going anywhere. You've been badly injured and you're in a lot of pain. You need to stabilize before you can even get out of here."

"Do you like the name Ashleigh?"

Jaime looked at Leigh, puzzled by her sudden change of the subject. It was the pain and the medication talking. If she wanted to talk about Ashleigh now, Jaime would listen.

"Yes, Ashleigh is a very nice name," Jaime said softly. "It fits everything about her."

"Ashleigh ... was born on Christmas Eve. I knew the baby was going to be a girl and that she was going to be born on Christmas Eve ... I already had her name, Ashleigh, picked out. I always told Drew that Ashleigh was my Christmas present to him."

Leigh tried to smile, but she did not have the strength. "She was the joy in everyone's eye, especially to my mother ... But my mother's gone now, too. Drew's gone ... Everyone's gone."

Leigh fell silent and Jaime thought she had slipped into unconsciousness. She stayed by the bed without speaking.

"Jaime? Are you still here?" Leigh asked.

"Yes, I'm here."

"If something happens to me, I don't know what I'd do about Ashleigh ... I was going to get her ... She won't have a place to stay. I can't leave her now, she … she needs me ... I have to be here for her. I'm her mother."

Jaime sensed Leigh's fear rising. Using a soft, even voice, she worked to quiet her. She hoped her words would bring some comfort.

"Leigh, listen to me, Ashleigh's fine. She wasn't with you in the car when you had the accident. She hasn't been hurt and she has a place to stay until you get better. When I come back this afternoon I'll bring Ashleigh. Please believe me. You'll be out in no time and then Ashleigh can stay with you until she gets ready to move to her new place."

Jaime's voice was confident and steady. Leigh exhaled a long, deep sigh and closed her eyes. Jaime waited but she did not open them again. Satisfied that Leigh had lost the fight to stay conscious, Jaime left her room.

Jaime looked at her watch. She was late for work.

She left Wheat Ridge General Hospital and stepped out into a fine, pearl-gray drizzle.

THIRTY-FIVE

It was nearly midnight when Jaime heard the sharp knock at her front door. Her heart started to drum in her chest as she headed for the door. When she saw who it was, she breathed a sigh of relief.

He was standing alone on the doorstep in a circle of wan light. Beyond his body, a sable darkness surrounded him. He had his hands stuffed deep into a long black raincoat and his shoulders were turned in against the cold night air. It had been a raw and windy day, as every day had been since the court's decision. The heat wave of those few weeks had since snapped, leaving the region draped under a continual, steady blanket of soggy, cold weather. Unseasonable for midsummer.

A fog had rolled in and Jaime could see faint wisps of it curling around the murky light where he stood. She took the chain off the door and opened it.

"Hello, Jaime. I'm sorry to come at such a late hour. I came straight from the airport. I hope it's not too much of a bother, but I'd love to come in for a few minutes, if I could."

His voice was deep and thick. So rich that Jaime could have scooped it up with a spoon.

"It's no bother at all," she said, as she opened the door. She extended her hand toward the living room.

"I saw your light on. I was hoping you weren't asleep."

Jaime's nightshirt was covered by a short, nylon robe tied at the waist and she was barefoot. She shook her head. "I was in the study finishing some paperwork. Let me take your coat."

His scent was thick with the outdoors, rain and earth. He removed his raincoat and handed it to her. She opened a hall closet and hung it inside.

"I wasn't sure you'd recognize me in the dim porch light. It's nothing but shadows out there. I probably should've waited until morning to come, but I didn't want to wait that long. I came as soon as I could. Thanks for letting me come in."

"I'm glad you came, Alan."

"It's Drew."

His request made her smile.

"How is she?" Drew asked.

Jaime motioned for Drew to follow her into the kitchen. They stopped at the bar that served as a casual kitchen table and separated the kitchen from the living room. She stood on one side, he faced her on the opposite. They pulled out the bar stools and sat down.

"She's going to make it, but it'll be a while before she can really do anything."

"Is she in her own room?" he asked.

Jaime shook her head. "Not yet. She's still in intensive care. The doctor told me they'll probably move her tomorrow. Can I get you something to drink? I just made a fresh pot of coffee."

Drew looked around the kitchen. "On a night like this, coffee would be great," he said "And sugar please."

"How did you hear about the accident?" Jaime asked, as she left the table. She took two large mugs from a rack and began to pour coffee into them.

"Winston called me. He gave me what details he could. I got on a plane as soon as I heard. I was lucky to be back in Seattle. I got back a few days ago from Vienna. I was getting ready for another engagement when Winston called."

Jaime set a cup of steaming hot coffee in front of him, along with a spoon and bowl of sugar.

"Winston must've told you where to find me, too," Jaime said.

He nodded slightly as he sipped from the mug. "Yes. That and a column Leigh wrote about a month ago about this friend of hers with a new home in Washington Park."

She looked at him, the expression on her face observant and interested. "How did you know it was me?" she asked and her face brightened as she smiled.

"I didn't really, until Winston gave me your address."

"So Leigh was right, you do read her columns."

"Whenever I get the chance. I did send her a little note about that one. I've been doing that for years, just to let her know where I am. She knows I could be anywhere. The postmark is the clue. That one, as the last few have been, was from Seattle."

Drew put three teaspoons of sugar into his cup. Jaime was quiet and watched this world-famous sculptor, whose work she had long admired, stir his coffee.

He was as she envisioned, with a handsome profile and deep-set eyes. Jaime knew now where Ashleigh got the color of her eyes. And their intensity. His face was exquisite, his features finely chiseled. He was clean shaven with a full mouth that curved into dimpled cheeks. His curly, coal-black hair had a permanent tousled look and skimmed the top of his shirt collar. It was thick and rich, with gray showing evenly along the temples and at the crown of his head. She wondered how much he had changed in appearance from the days when he and Leigh were together.

It was difficult to tell that Alan Andrew Roberts was four years shy of 60. He wore an ebony polo shirt and black corduroy jeans. He was a big man, broad shouldered and deep chested, with muscles spread out evenly over his 6-foot frame. His short-sleeved shirt showed forearms that were beefy and covered with thick hair. He wore a heavy gold bracelet on his right wrist and a thickly set sports watch on the other.

His hands, the million-dollar part of his body, were short, but wide and compressed. They were craggy and scarred, indicative of the nature of his work. His right index finger was slightly swollen and the entire fingernail was black and blue.

"When are you planning to see Leigh?" Jaime asked.

"Tomorrow. I don't know how she'll react. But I'll cross that bridge when I'm outside her door in the morning."

"Erin Greene called me at five o'clock yesterday morning," Jaime said. "She said the hospital called and told her what had happened. She asked if I could go. For some reason, Drew, I thought about you when I was driving to the hospital. I don't know why really, but I had a feeling this would bring you back."

He smiled slightly and the lines around his eyes deepened.

"I couldn't stay away," he said and shrugged his big shoulders slightly.

Drew ran his bruised finger around the rim of the coffee cup. He stared at the cup to avoid looking at Jaime. His manner seemed polished and relaxed, but Jaime wondered if something more like ice and flint lurked just beneath the surface.

"I've been thinking about coming back for a long time now, most of this year anyway. I guess this was my opportunity. I hate the thought of her lying in that hospital bed as the reason for my return, but it got me here and that was the hardest part, just getting here."

He stopped a moment. His facial features seemed to soften and yield to more pleasant thoughts. "Just as she has always done for me, she made it easy for me, almost effortless. I wanted to come back to Evergreen, to see her and to see Ashleigh again, but there wasn't the opening, or the opportunity for me just to come ... But Leigh always made everything easy for me. When we were together she did everything for me. Loved to cook for me. She took care of all my business affairs, everything. All I ever had to do was know what time I had to be where."

"Why did you leave her, Drew?"

The big man shrugged his shoulders. His eyebrows drifted upward as he looked at Jaime, his deep-set hazel eyes penetrating. His voice was reflective, almost pensive when he spoke. "You want different things when you're young, at least you think you do. What you don't realize when you're young, twenty-five, thirty, thirty-five, is that you really don't know what you want until you've lived a few decades more."

Drew held up his mug for more coffee and Jaime brought the glass pot to the table and poured him a second cup. He scooped three more teaspoons of sugar into the mug.

"Each piece of work I do takes a little more out of me. I shave another piece from my soul with every piece I finish. I've been doing this kind of work since I was young. It's always been in me and I can see myself doing it for the rest of my life."

Drew looked from the mug to Jaime. Her eyes fixed on him. Her body forward, her head tilted slightly to one side. He went on. "I'm to the point and have been for several years, maybe a good twenty years, where I can be more selective about the work I do. Don't you think I'm at the point now, Jaime, where I can do less, but ask for more?"

She nodded and smiled. "I should think you've been there for years."

"Perhaps I have," he said and his voice was thoughtful. "But I haven't allowed myself to see that. I still work as though I'm the starving artist I was 30 years ago."

Jaime laughed quietly.

"Hard to believe isn't it?" he continued and his face somewhat softened. "Harder still to accept when you're a driven man, driven to the point of obsession as Leigh used to tell me, anyway. I've had to tell myself it's all right now that I can be more selective, to do less until I don't want to do anymore. And what I'll choose then is to do no more."

"Do you want to come back to Denver?"

"I've traveled all over the world, been to some places four and five times. I've seen it all, and I've been everywhere. Most of it has been on my own. Alone, Jaime. The older I get, the more the aloneness gets to me. I still want to travel, but it's the aloneness I want to change. I want someone beside me to share the place where I am and everything that comes with it. Does that answer your question?"

"Do you think Leigh will want to change her life now, back to the way it was for you? Her life is different now. Do you think she'll want you back? It's been so long."

Drew responded with silence and a fragmented look in her direction. "I've been a selfish man for many, many years, Jaime and I know what a real bastard, an asshole I've been to Leigh, and I can't change any of that now. It won't ever be the way it was, but we could start again."

"Do you still love her, Drew?"

He did not have to answer. It was in his eyes. "When I'm doing a sculpture, Leigh's all that fills my mind. It's almost as if she's the fire, the passion that burns inside of me. I feel her everywhere around me as I work. She's on every layer of my skin." He stopped talking and studied the palms of his thick hands. "When I finish, the feeling of her inside of me is gone. And I don't know what exhausts me more, the work I've finished, or the feeling of her that's vanished."

He looked from his hands to Jaime.

"I've come back because I want to be with them. Now when I travel I want Leigh with me ... And Ashleigh ... It's been so long since I've seen her. I've often wondered if I passed her on the street, if I would know her."

Jaime's gaze traveled the length of his face. She smiled almost sadly. "Of course you would, Drew. She came from you and is a part of you. You'll always recognize her." She hesitated a moment before she spoke again. "Ashleigh's here."

"I know."

"I don't want to wake her, but I want to see her, Jaime. It's one of the reasons I came here tonight. I want to look in on her."

Jaime rose from the chair and motioned for him to follow her. "Come on, she's in the spare bedroom."

They walked the length of the darkened hall in silence. Jaime stayed at the door as Drew walked into the bedroom. He turned on the light on the nightstand. It shed a delicate, small light into the room and fell softly on Ashleigh's face.

Jaime watched as Drew did not move. He watched Ashleigh sleep. Captured by her innocence. Seized by her very presence.

It was not the same Drew Roberts Jaime had seen at her front door less than an hour ago. His large frame and features seemed diminished, somehow shrunken.

He moved closer and sat down lightly on the bed. Ashleigh was lying on her side, facing him. Bangs were covering her eyes. He gently brushed them to one side. He rested a hand lightly on her shoulder. Ashleigh did not move or open her eyes. For a long time, Drew stayed at the bed, his hand resting against his daughter's arm.

Drew spoke finally, but he did not turn to face Jaime. "You know, Jaime, when Ashleigh was a little girl, I used to carry her upstairs to bed and she never moved a muscle. She never woke up ... We, Leigh and I, would be on the couch watching a movie or something and she'd get right between us and curl herself into a little ball. She looked like a kitten. Then she'd fall asleep and I'd carry up her to bed. She'd come down to breakfast in the morning and say 'Daddy, did you carry me upstairs to bed last night'?"

For a time, only Ashleigh's soft, even breathing filled the room.

"It's been so long since I've seen her. But you know..." His voice trailed off and he turned to face Jaime. "You're right. I'd recognize her anywhere I'd go."

Her voice was nearly a whisper when she spoke. "Yes, Drew, you would."

He rose from the bed and turned off the light. He met Jaime at the bedroom door and followed her back to the kitchen.

"Why did you leave Denver?" Jaime asked quietly.

The words seemed to catch him off guard. He looked at Jaime. The expression on his face seemed pained, almost distant. He sighed heavily before he spoke.

"After all these years of being away I have finally learned what it is I need to know ... I could live and get along fine without someone I love, but it's a completely different story when it comes to learning to live without someone you need."

Jaime frowned and shook her head.

He smiled at her. A patient smile. "I love Leigh and have from the moment I saw her get out of the car the day she came to do that first interview. She has a rare beauty I've never been able to capture with words or with any of the work I've done."

Jaime nodded in familiarity. "Leigh told me all about the day you two met."

"A week or so before I left her and Ashleigh, we were lying in bed. Then I told her what I had been thinking."

They were standing at the bar. Jaime leaned forward with interest.

"I said 'Leigh I love you. I always have. So please don't take this wrong, but I don't need you. I can live with your love from a distance, but there's something in me I can't explain, I don't always need to be with you. I can't.' I waited, expecting her body to tighten and for her to withdraw and pull away from me. But she didn't ... It was dark and I could feel her slender body as she turned toward me. I knew she was studying what she could see of me in the dark, but she said nothing."

Drew put his hand on the back of the chair. The gold bracelet dangled lightly. "I think she knew, at that moment, probably even before, that I was preparing to leave, but she never said a word."

"What about Ashleigh? What about your need for her and her need for you? Wasn't that strong enough to make you want to stay?"

He looked away from Jaime, his eyes full of remorse. He shook his head slowly, sadly. "I don't know, Jaime. I was wrong to leave and I see that now. Sometimes you don't know what people really mean to you until you've lived a few good years away from them ... In their absence, you see what you love most in them. In their absence it becomes clear ... Perhaps it's too late to change anything, but I hope not. If Ashleigh will let me, I'll work to make it up to her. I can't change what's happened, but I can work to make her future better."

Drew looked at his watch. "I'd better get going. You've got to go to work in the morning."

She walked him to the front door. She took his raincoat from the closet and handed it to him. He placed it over his right forearm.

"You said Winston called you about Leigh?"

"Yes. He's my attorney and takes care of everything for me, but we've been close friends for years. He's probably the best friend I've ever had. I've often thought we are more like brothers, than friends. He's always been there for me."

"He's kept you up to date with what's gone on with Leigh all these years?"

"Yes. And Ashleigh, too. He called me when this sterilization stuff became known. Winston told me he wanted to talk Leigh out of it, but she was insistent. He said she told him it was the only way she could have any peace of mind. Winston called about the outcome of Ashleigh's hearing. There's not much I can do, Jaime, Leigh is Ashleigh's legal guardian."

"Yes, I understand. I know she is."

"You're appealing the court's decision?"

"Of course. We've already started the process."

Drew nodded thoughtfully. "I don't know of anything that's worth having, Jaime, that isn't worth fighting for."

She watched in silence as Drew put on his raincoat.

"Drew, you're welcome to stay the night."

"Thanks, Jaime. But I don't want to be here in the morning when Ashleigh wakes. I want to deal with seeing her for the first time in own way and in my own time. I'd rather it be just the two of us."

Jaime nodded. "I understand."

"Your hospitality has been gracious. But it's been a long, long time since I've been to the house in Evergreen. That's where I'm headed."

"I've got court in the morning," Jaime said. "But I want to know how Leigh is doing. Please let me know. Call me at the office. I'll be there the rest of the day after court."

Drew nodded. "I've always loved a Tudor," he said, as they walked toward the front door. "They're rich in character."

Jaime nodded, taking a quick inventory of her new home. "This home is me," she said and smiled. "I loved it the second I saw it."

She opened the door and Drew stepped out into the night.

"Thanks for the coffee, Jaime."

He stood on the brick porch and listened for a moment. "Nice neighborhood," he said, finally. "Quiet."

Jaime nodded, then watched until he disappeared into the deepening fog that began at the edge of the yard.

Thirty-six

Drew called her name.

Leigh's eyelids fluttered open. She stared at the ceiling, unsure what she heard.

She spoke faintly. "Drew?"

It was painful to turn her head, but she forced herself to turn toward the voice. The image of the tall man standing over her bed was hazy. Her mind was foggy and seemed thick with clouds. Her vision faded in and out. Voices sounded muffled. It must be the medication playing tricks on her. It couldn't be Drew. He was so far away.

Seattle, the postmark showed. Wasn't it?

But it sounded so much like him. It had to be. She closed her eyes again.

She had heard the resonant sound of his voice calling her name for years. Even after he had gone, the sound of his voice stayed with her. It seemed to call to her from every corner, every crevice of the house. It seemed to be alive and thriving in every room. She would pass the garage where he worked and could hear him call to her.

It had been years since she had last seen him. She slowly opened her eyes. She tried to focus on the figure that stood before her. It was no use. The image of him blurred like rippling water. She did not have the strength to keep her eyes open for any length of time, let alone to keep them focused.

Then he touched her. Softly, like a gentle mist, on her shoulder.

His touch left no mistake.

She stared at him. "Drew? Am … am I dreaming?"

"I hope not."

She knew it was Drew's touch. It was gentle yet firm. She remembered that sensation. She could feel within his touch its power, its energy. At the same time, she could feel its grace, its caress. There was flexibility, a dexterity and strength in his hands that allowed him to grab and hold marble and shape it into works of art. Yet, his hands could be as gentle as if he were to grasp a child by the hand, or hold a kitten. With his bruised index finger, he gently stroked her arm, traveling the length of it several times.

"You really are here," she said.

He nodded. "I am."

She forced herself to concentrate on him. In her haziness and pain, Drew seemed untouched by the years.

"You've hardly changed at all."

He laughed gently as he patted both hands against his mid-section. "Maybe it's a good thing you can't get a good look at anyone right now, or else you'd noticed I'm getting pretty thick around the middle."

"I ... I never expected you to come." Leigh's voice was fragile, almost inaudible. It took all her strength to keep her eyes open and speak to him.

"Winston called. I came as soon as I could. I … I had to be here with you."

Leigh smiled weakly. "I'm glad you're here, Drew, I ... I was afraid. I still am. And I don't want to be alone."

"I had no idea what to expect this morning, if you'd want to see me or not. You won't be alone now, if you want me to stay."

"I would've been disappointed if I were just dreaming it was you. I don't know what I would've done if I woke and you were just a dream and it was just the pain medication playing tricks on me."

Leigh's comment brought a smile to his face, but she had closed her eyes and did not see it.

"Are you still in Seattle?"

"Yes," Drew spoke quietly. "It's nice. Not as much rain as everyone says there is, but still a bit too much."

"You never liked rain."

"You're right. I never have liked too much rain."

They were quiet until the hospital paging system broke their silence.

"What happened, Leigh? Do you remember what caused the accident?"

Leigh blinked several times and then stared blankly at the ceiling. "I was coming back from Vail ... I was exhausted. I ... I was going to get Ashleigh. She was going to stay with me and ... I was so exhausted, Drew. Ashleigh's hearing drained me. What they did to her ... What I let them do to her..."

Her voice trailed off and she closed her eyes. Drew thought she had slipped into unconsciousness, but she opened her eyes again. She continued to speak, but her feeble voice faltered.

"I think I fell asleep at the wheel, but I don't know for sure. I don't remember anything after that except when I came to in the emergency room ... They told me what happened, I think, but I don't know. I don't know if I've done the right thing, Drew, with Ashleigh, with anything. I don't know ... I don't know ... I don't want Ashleigh to be without me. I don't want to hurt her, and make her angry with me. But I have, haven't I? She hates me, I know she does."

He put the tips of his fingers gently against her lips. "Rest now," he said. "Don't worry about Ashleigh, she'll be fine. Everything's being worked out."

An elderly, thin nurse came and stood at the door. "Mr. Roberts, time's up."

Drew smiled and waved an acknowledgment to the nurse. "I'm on my way out." He turned his attention back to Leigh, and when he took her hand, she noticed his bruised finger.

"What did you do to your finger?" she asked.

"My hammer attacked me. Better move over."

Leigh laughed, but she stopped quickly. The pain made her grimace. "Oh, Drew, don't make me laugh. It hurts so much."

"You're still in ICU. I can only be with you a short time, but you're going to be fine. Remember that. The doctor says you're going to be fine."

"I hurt all over," she said weakly.

"I know. But that'll pass."

Drew studied her bruised face. Her face and neck were covered with lacerations, as Jaime said they were. There was a large gash above her left eye, which was blue and purple and nearly swollen closed.

"And you're beautiful," he said quietly.

She made a weak attempt to form a smile.

He put the tips of his fingers gently against her forehead and stroked her lightly.

She closed her eyes when he touched her.

It was just after noon when Jaime entered Wheat Ridge General and took the elevator to ICU. She looked for Drew in the waiting area, but he wasn't there. She went to Leigh's room and saw him. She stood at an angle so he could not see her. Drew was leaning his stocky arms over the bed railing and holding Leigh's hand. She could not tell if Leigh was awake. She backed away from the door and went to the cafeteria.

Jaime was eating a salad when Drew entered the cafeteria. They looked at each other simultaneously. Jaime waved to him and he motioned to the buffet counter. She waited for him before she finished the rest of her lunch.

"How's it going?" she asked when he set his tray down and took the chair across the table from her.

He had selected the same lunch as Jaime, a mixed salad of red lettuce, black beans, broccoli, peppers, with hard-boiled eggs sprinkled over the top, mineral water and an apple. Drew had also added coffee and a slice of apple pie. He unfolded his napkin and placed it across his lap. He eyes rested on Jaime.

"You look great for just the few hours of sleep you must've gotten after I left this morning," he said.

Jaime wore a red wool pique jacket with silk jersey slacks. She had not had time to pull her hair back in the morning, the way she usually wore it when she would be in court. It looked rich and silky as it fell freely against her shoulders.

"Red's a striking color for you," he said.

Jaime was silent, but smiled, embarrassed by the compliment. She had never received such a gracious compliment, not even from Mitchell and it flattered her.

"Thank you," she said, finally.

She wanted to return the compliment. Drew looked handsome dressed in a black short-sleeved cashmere sweater and matching tony trousers, but decided to keep the compliment to herself.

"I thought you were going to be in court," he said.

"It ended early. I thought I'd make a quick stop here and try to see Leigh before going back to the office. I don't know if I can come after work. I'm picking up Ashleigh. We need to get some of her clothes to bring to the house."

They ate for a time in silence. Jaime finished her salad and took a small bite from her apple.

"How's she doing today?" Jaime asked.

"Still in a lot of pain. And she's in and out of consciousness."

"How did she react to seeing you?"

Drew finished the last of his salad and took a long drink from his mineral water. He looked levelly at Jaime. "Well, she didn't object to me being there. In fact, she seemed pleased, even happy I was there. But I wonder, Jaime, just how much of it was Leigh talking and reacting to me and how much of it was the pain medication and her state of mind. I honestly can't say yet how she feels about seeing me."

Jaime nodded carefully.

Drew went on. "I asked her about what caused the accident. She told me she had fallen asleep at the wheel, but that's impossible."

"Why?"

"It was raining like crazy. You know what it's like when hard rain hits the ragtop on a convertible. The sound inside is almost deafening. There's no way she could've fallen asleep with that kind of noise going on overhead. It's obvious her thinking is fragmented and distorted right now. I'll just have to wait and see how she'll react to seeing me when her pain isn't so intense, and she's thinking more clearly and has had some time to recover."

Again Jaime nodded.

"She mentioned Ashleigh several times. Seems worried about what's going to happen with her since she can't take care of her."

Jaime leaned back in her chair. She looked thoughtfully at Drew before she spoke. "There's so much to Ashleigh that it seems even her own mother doesn't know or understand. She can do so much, more than Leigh realizes."

"I didn't tell her Ashleigh would be staying with you," Drew said. "I figured it should come from you."

"I'd planned to tell her today."

Jaime watched as Drew removed the plastic wrap from the apple pie and began to pick at it.

"I'm glad we were able to talk last night, Jaime. I felt comfortable telling you a little about Leigh and me. You seem like someone who absorbs deeply what she's being told. Do you understand what I was telling you about love and need?"

"I understand what you were telling me only in the way that I feel about it, Drew. Everyone looks and feels toward love and need differently."

He nodded. "I thought about that driving to Evergreen."

Drew cut into the apple pie with his fork, but then without taking a bite, put the fork down on the plate. As he rested his elbows on the table and folded his hands, the heavy, gold bracelet slid down his arm. He looked at Jaime over the tops of his hands.

"My love for Leigh has changed in only that I love her more than the first day I saw her. What's changed is the need. I need to be with her now more than ever ... Imagine that my life is like a tapestry. It's made up of many thousand colorful strands, which, at some point, after a lot of time and skill and effort, are eventually made into a vivid pattern."

With his fingers, Drew outlined the shape of an imaginary rug on the table. He pretended to remove a single strand from the rug. His manner was dignified, precise and exact. Jaime watched with interest.

"I've removed a piece of the pattern. Alone, this single strand means nothing. It could never hold up on its own. By removing it, it not only makes the whole pattern of this tapestry incomplete, but this single strand no longer has meaning. Its intrinsic value is lost."

His watchful, straightforward look settled on Jaime. "It's useless."

She found him to be as intriguing, as captivating as the work he did.

He touched the tips of his fingers to his broad chest. "I've lost track of how long, but all I've felt like for some time is nothing more than a mere strand. I need to be part of something, someone beautiful, to be made whole again, to feel whole again."

"That someone is Leigh," Jaime said.

"Yes."

It was only a single word, but Drew's deep voice seemed to fill the entire room.

"Wasn't it Einstein who said that the past still exists and that time is like a road on which we are traveling?" Jaime said.

Drew nodded and added without hesitation. "And are the first days of our lives together still out there on that road, even though we've passed it years ago? And can we go back again?"

"What brought this on, Drew?"

He grew quiet to collect his thoughts. "Age mostly. And life. Just living life."

"I would think someone like you already has everything figured out."

Drew laughed. It was patient and forgiving. "You never really ever figure everything out, Jaime. If you did, life would be dull. That's what fuels us. What keeps us going. The need to know. The answers are out there, but they won't fall in our laps. We need to search to find them. But I think, though, if I had it to do over again, I'd do it differently."

"How?"

"I wouldn't leave them."

Jaime shook her head in disagreement. "No, you wouldn't, Drew. You'd probably do the same all over again. You're just talking now like a man who's lived almost sixty years and the person he still cares deeply about struggles for life in the ICU. It's easy to look back at the past and say I'd do this or I'd do that differently if we were given that chance. But that doesn't count, because we can't do that. What counts is the here and now. There are consequences with every decision and we have to deal with them."

Her words did not leave him with a smile.

"We'd better get going," she said, glancing quickly at her watch. "We can only visit Leigh a little while and I need to get back to the office."

They left the table in silence and headed back to intensive care.

Drew had not touched his apple pie and the coffee was cold.

Thirty-seven

By the end of the week, Leigh's condition had improved and she had been moved to a private room. Drew still had not had contact with Ashleigh. But Jaime and Ashleigh spent every free moment together that they could.

Ashleigh had made several visits with Jaime to her health club and became enthralled watching Jaime box, especially when she used the speed bag. Jaime made it look so easy and Ashleigh was eager to try. Jaime wasn't as receptive to the idea, but Ashleigh was insistent, so Jaime strapped a pair of gloves on her new boxing partner.

Ashleigh was about as coordinated as a rag doll when she tried to use the heavy bag. It was worse when she attempted the speed bag. Ashleigh quickly removed the gloves when the speed bag came back one time before she was ready and hit her in the nose. Jaime had to turn away. It was all she could do not to laugh and avoid saying "I told you so."

One noon during lunch, they walked along the 16th Street Mall, bought hotdogs and looked longingly into store windows. One evening,

Jaime made a picnic and they went to a concert outdoors at City Park. Another evening, they spent watching the New York Mets play the Colorado Rockies at Coors Field. They spent an entire Saturday with Tia and her sons at Elitch Gardens amusement park. Ashleigh and the boys rode nearly every ride, some of them twice. Another evening, Tia, the boys and Jaime and Ashleigh went swimming. Derrick and Darryl swam, but Ashleigh only got her feet wet. She didn't know how to swim.

One Sunday afternoon, Jaime and Ashleigh walked at Washington Park. In the distance, as they neared the tennis courts at the south end of the park, Jaime could hear the dull popping sound of balls being hit off racquets. As they neared, the sound also attracted Ashleigh's attention and she looked in that direction.

"What's that game called?" Ashleigh asked. "I watch it on TV sometimes."

Jaime's smile was more of a grimace. "It's called tennis."

Ashleigh looked at Jaime. "Have you ever played?"

What smile there was on Jaime's face slowly faded. "Yeah, a few times. I played a lot when I was growing up, but I haven't picked up a racquet in a long, long time."

"How long?"

Jaime shrugged her shoulders. "I don't know, Ashleigh, but a long time. Maybe like almost ten years."

Ashleigh's eyes widened. "That long!"

They took the path that led to the courts and watched, their fingers gripping through the chain link fence, as players hit the ball back and forth.

"They're good," Ashleigh said, as her head moved left to right, right to left, as she tried to follow the ball.

"They're pretty good, but I knew someone who could play a lot better."

Ashleigh looked at Jaime. "You?"

Jaime shook her head.

"Then who?"

"Someone I knew. Someday I'll tell you about her, but not today."

Ashleigh considered Jaime a moment before she turned her attention back to the tennis players. "Why does watching this make you sad?"

Jaime squeezed her grip on the fence a little harder. "I'm not sad," she said, trying to mask her true feelings. "I'm just thinking of someone who used to play and she was very good. Her life changed and her life ended differently than either of us had hoped or planned."

"She was close to you, like a sister or something?"

Jaime turned away from the tennis courts and rested her back against the fence. She looked to the sky. The weather had become more like the season it was. The summer sky was a clear, deep blue and the sun a brilliant, gleaming yellow. A slight breeze and the park's tall, shady trees kept the afternoon pleasant and cool. "Yes, Ashleigh. She was my sister and she was a very good tennis player."

Ashleigh copied Jaime's position against the fence. "How come she didn't keep playing?"

"She died six years ago," Jaime said, trying to keep her voice level. "And didn't get the chance to become a professional tennis player like the ones you see on TV."

"They're really good."

"That's how my sister played. Just like that."

Jaime sensed Ashleigh's next question would be about Sarah's death and she had no intention of going into detail, at least not here and not today. She turned abruptly to the courts. "How 'bout if I make good on that promise to rent a movie and you and I go back to the house? I'll call for pizza later and we can make popcorn."

"That'd be cool!"

But as they walked toward Downing Street, Ashleigh turned and looked back over her shoulder at the players on the courts and then to Jaime. "Will you teach me how to play, Jaime?"

Jaime had a deep, dull feeling in the pit of her stomach. She did not want to refuse Ashleigh anything, even though she had no desire to watch or play tennis again.

"Jaime?"

Jaime looked at Ashleigh and realized she had not answered her.

"Sure, Ashleigh. We'll play. We'll pick a night next week, find a court and we'll play. How's that?"

"That'd be swell!"

Jaime had planned to spend a quiet Sunday evening at home and decided what had happened at Wash Park would not dominate the rest of their day. In fact, she felt odd that the encounter had left her feeling surprisingly happy. Jaime rented a movie, ordered a cheese and mushroom pizza and made popcorn. She wanted it to be just the two of them.

The movie credits from “Fried Green Tomatoes” were rolling when Ashleigh spoke, breaking the two-hour silence that had been between them. “This has been lots and lots of fun even though the movie made you cry, Jaime,” she said, picking the last few good kernels of popcorn from the bottom of a large bowl.

They were sitting next to each other on the couch, their shoulders touching. Jaime turned to Ashleigh. Her hair had been in her eyes and Jaime brushed it gently to the side. “I’ve enjoyed it, too. I cry every time I watch that movie.”

“I liked that ride at Elitch Gardens,” Ashleigh said. “The one that looked like a big wheel and went round and round.”

“The Ferris wheel?”

“Yeah, that was great. And that other ride, where we got into those squishy, little seats and went up the hills really slow and down really, really fast.”

“The roller coaster? That’s always been my favorite.”

Jaime’s gaze settled on Ashleigh, and her eyes grew soft. “Haven’t you ever been to Elitches before?”

Ashleigh shook her head. “And I’ve never been to a baseball game either. Those hotdogs were really good, but I wish the Rockies would’ve won.”

“Hasn’t your mother ever taken you to places like that?”

Again Ashleigh shook her head. “She comes to visit me all the time at my house and we usually go to eat somewhere and sometimes I stay at my old house on the weekends, and we do some stuff there, but we don’t do stuff like me and you have.”

Jaime only nodded slightly, she didn’t know what to say. She wanted to ask why, but Ashleigh was not the one to ask.

“But I hope my mom’s gonna be OK.”

Jaime nodded reassuringly. “Don’t worry, Ashleigh. She’s going to be fine. She’ll be out of the hospital in a few days. And then you can stay with her.”

"Can I stay here with you instead?"

Jaime's face broke into an incandescent grin. "I'd like that, but let's see how your mom does," Jaime said. She put her hand on Ashleigh's shoulder and squeezed it gently. "Ashleigh, do you understand what it is your mother's really trying to do?"

Ashleigh nodded thoughtfully. "I think so."

"Can you tell me?"

Ashleigh looked toward the ceiling as she thought over her answer. "She wants me to have an operation so that I can't have a baby like when she had me."

"And do you want that? Would you want to go through with the operation?"

Ashleigh shook her head. "No. But most people don't think I know too much of anything. But I know lots and lots of things. They just never ask me. But I'd tell them if they'd ask. Just like I did when we were in that room with that judge."

Jaime laughed. "You're right, Ashleigh. You did very well in that room with the judge." The look in Jaime's eyes became calm, collected. "There's going to be a lot more of that, Ashleigh, if the case comes back for another hearing. Rooms you're going to have to sit in and answer questions again from judges and people like me. The next part of this process might take a while before we get through."

"I can wait."

Jaime responded only with a small smile and a slight nod. Though their relationship was rudimentary, Jaime was learning quickly to appreciate Ashleigh's simplicity, her calm, composed approach to life. She was quietly self-confident and, despite her disability, had the ability to express herself clearly. She had a disposition that was centered and even-tempered.

"Come on," Jaime said rising from the couch. "You need to brush your teeth and get ready for bed."

Within the hour Ashleigh was in bed and Jaime was sitting next to her.

"If your sister were still living now, would she be as old as you?"

Jaime shook her head slightly. "No, Ashleigh, my sister was younger than me. In fact, if she were still alive she would be the exact same age as you."

"Twenty-four?"

"Twenty-four."

"How old are you?"

"Twenty-eight."

"How much older is that than me?"

"Four years."

"What's her name?"

After Jaime told her, she also decided it was time to change the subject.

"Ashleigh, I have something to tell you."

Ashleigh looked at Jaime, her eyes wide. It was a soft look of wonder.

"Your father is in Denver. Do you remember him?"

"Is he the man that sends me money all the time?"

Jaime grinned. "Yes, that's the one."

"I've seen pictures of him. There's one of mom and him that she keeps in her bedroom. They went to a place faraway, I can't remember the name of it, to have their picture taken there."

The place was Africa. Jaime remembered Leigh telling her about their trip. It had been magical.

"When I was little and still living there with mom, sometimes I'd go in her bedroom and I'd see her and she'd have that picture in her hand like she was looking at it. Sometimes, and she didn't know I was there, she'd rub her hand over the frame. She still misses him a lot, huh."

"She misses your father more than either of us will ever realize."

"Maybe she still likes him?"

"Maybe."

Jaime pulled the sheet up to cover Ashleigh's arms.

"Your father came back to Denver to be with your mother and to help her get better after the car accident." Jaime hesitated before continuing, careful to weigh her words. "He wants to see you, Ashleigh. I'm going to your mother's house tomorrow to see him. What would you like for me to tell him?"

"What should I say?"

Jaime regarded Ashleigh with a sisterly kind of love. It was here, too, they both shared a common and deepening bond. It had been six years since Jaime had last seen and spoken to her own father. She had often wondered what she would do if given the same circumstances. Their connection made Jaime feel a surge of love so strong for Ashleigh she almost could not breathe. Her response was simple. "You say what your heart feels, Ashleigh. I can't tell you what to say."

Ashleigh thought for only a moment. "I say yes." There was a sense of anticipation, of eagerness in her voice.

Jaime touched Ashleigh lightly on the arm and rose from the bed. She turned off the lamp and when she reached the door, Ashleigh called to her. "Jaime."

She turned to study a near-darkened image of Ashleigh that came from the small amount of light that had slipped in from the hall.

"Do you like me because I remind you of Sarah?"

Her words wounded Jaime. She returned to the bed and sat beside Ashleigh. She looked at Ashleigh for a long time before she spoke. "Some things about you remind me of Sarah. But I like *you*, Ashleigh, because you are Ashleigh. And more than anything else, I hope you'll remember that."

Jaime stayed at the bed until Ashleigh's eyelids grew heavy. At the door, Jaime turned to look at Ashleigh. "Good night, Ashleigh," she whispered.

The only sound that came back was Ashleigh's soft breathing.

Morning came quickly, and by ten o'clock Ashleigh was at the Tabor Center, ready to start her shift. Jaime was driving to Evergreen, a place she had not been since the evening she had returned the laptop to Leigh. But she still did not know why Drew wanted her to come to the house, instead of the hospital.

When she arrived, she noticed the door to the garage was open. She poked her head inside the open and spacious garage and was instantly hit by the smell of stale air and lingering dust. The garage had the dank feel of an ancient tomb and she guessed it had been years since the doors had last been opened to let fresh air in.

"Drew?"

No answer. She called more loudly a second time.

"I'm back here," came his deep voice from a place Jaime could not see.

Jaime glanced in the direction she heard his voice and began to walk toward the back of the garage. As she made her way deeper into the building, dust motes hung in the balance before her. They drifted in and out of shafts of sunlight streaming in from the skylights. Along the way she passed a half-finished, large marble sculpture of a leopard feasting on a small zebra. The broad modeling of the leopard's head and shoulders suggested an almost impressionistic quality.

"Hi. Glad you could make it," Drew said, as he stepped out from behind what Jaime guessed was a piece of sculpture. She could not tell because it was fully covered by a large white canvas tarp.

"How's it going?" she asked.

Jaime could tell by the way he had dressed that he had planned to work on whatever was concealed beneath the tarp. He had on tattered tennis shoes with no socks and a black sweat top and pants. The legs and sleeves were cut away. A pair of plastic goggles hung around his neck. She looked from him to the life-sized object that lay hidden beneath the canvas.

"I think I know now why you wanted me to come here instead of the hospital."

Drew's smile was luminous. Jaime noticed the features of his face were more strongly carved than at any other time since his arrival in Denver. She felt she was looking at the core of him. He was nervous energy about to explode. He had a brightness about him that shone like light from heaven. Yet, he seemed almost humble, a great artist placid about the kind of work he did.

"I wanted you to see this, Jaime," he said.

Drew lifted and pulled the tarp away. Jaime looked on with eagerness as the marble sculpture came into view. It looked perfect.

"That's beautiful," she said.

"It's not finished."

Jaime looked at Drew, unable to contain her puzzlement. "I don't understand."

Drew walked the full length of the marble sculpture without uttering a word. When he reached Jaime, they looked at the piece, studying it intently.

It was a five-foot high marble sculpture of a mother and child. The mother was sitting with one leg tucked beneath her and the other up and bent at the knee. The infant rested on her folded leg and she held the baby close to her breasts. The mother's head was bent to the sight of the infant. Her hair was long and flowing against her back.

"Leigh said you name all your work in three words."

Drew nodded, as he looked from Jaime to the sculpture.

"It's called A Mother's Love. The one you saw out front," Drew said, pointing to the leopard and zebra, "is called Feast After Famine."

Drew studied the mother and child before he spoke again. "I work in stone. I always have. Marble has been around since the beginning of time. Marble was the favorite of the Greeks, as it is for me. It has beauty. It has durability. It's one of the easiest stones to work with and I like the way it feels against my hands."

Silence filled the space between them. It was so quiet Jaime thought she could hear the sound of the dust motes as they settled on the sculptures.

Drew went on. "I started this piece when Leigh and I were still married and I was still living here. The first time I saw Ashleigh, Leigh was holding her that close. She looked down on her with a love so deep I couldn't describe it then and I can't describe it now, except maybe through this."

Drew looked from the pure white silence of the mother and child to Jaime. He narrowed his eyes and the hazel color in them became cloudy. He crossed his arms tightly across his chest. "I never finished it. It deeply disappointed Leigh and I've never forgotten that. I even finished the pedestal for it. It's right over there."

Jaime followed Drew's finger across the garage, where another tarp covered what she knew now was the pedestal.

"I did it especially for this piece. I knew it would enhance the piece enormously ... This is the only work I've ever done that doesn't have anything to do with wildlife. Long after I left, there'd be days I'd be working on something else and this piece would pop into my mind just like that."

Drew snapped his fingers. "Then it'd be with me for days before I'd eventually forget about it again."

"I don't understand, what's missing?" Jaime asked looking at the piece.

He left her standing where she was and moved closer to the sculpture. He examined it and then motioned for her to come. He did not say a word, but allowed her to study the sculpture up close. She rubbed her hands over the woman's face. Then she saw what was missing.

The intimacy of details.

The ones that would bring the sculpture to life, into existence, had not yet been carved. The eyes, the curvature of their noses and mouths, the veins in their arms and on the back of their hands, their fingernails. They were the precise attention to details that needed time and effort and skill to shape and form.

Drew ran his hand along the contours of the woman's hair.

"Until I can finish those, Jaime, the work isn't complete."

Jaime looked to her right. Every sculptor's tool used during the various stages of the shaping process, sat on a large, hand-crafted workbench. There were rock hammers made of forged steel and metal-head mallets that were used to make rugged blows against large, rough stone. He saw her looking at the hardwood hammers that were used to strike the chisels.

"I preferred hardwood hammers to metal," he told her, "because it eases the shock on me, the tools and the stone."

There were rasps and files, from fine to coarse-toothed, which were used to round and smooth surfaces. Finally, Jaime saw bushing hammers and bushing chisels and flat-edged chisels that were used to cut away areas close to the stone. On the floor next to the wood bench were many pairs of eye shields and plastic glasses and a Roto hammer, an electric tool used for carving and roughing-out edges. The machine saved a sculptor countless hours of hard-hand chiseling.

"Is this what you'll do when Leigh comes home from the hospital?" Jaime asked.

"Yes. But I'm not telling her about it until I've finished. It will be a surprise. I want to care for her. I'm hoping it'll help the healing process."

She looked at Drew and thought of Leigh. Their love for each other had never died. It did not come to an end, the way a season does or fade away like a summer storm. Their love was perpetual. Jaime felt sad that they had been away from each other for so many years. So much time lost.

"It'll be exactly what she needs, Drew," she said.

They walked from the garage into the light of the late morning sun. Drew looked to the sky, shielding his eyes against the glare.

"I'm fascinated by light, Jaime. But not the light of midday, when shadows fade, and they are all but beneath us, but of long, late afternoon shadows and the light of the early morning. Leigh is most beautiful then, in the morning when the light is young."

They walked for a moment in silence. Drew kept his attention fixed on the mature trees that shielded the old English home. They were still sentinels, guarding the fortress.

"You've talked to Ashleigh?" Drew asked.

"Yes."

Drew looked over his shoulder to Jaime, his eyes asking the question.

"She's excited to come see you, to meet 'the man who sends her money.'"

He laughed out loud. It was friendly and contagious and Jaime laughed, too.

"When she comes we'll go look for rocks," Drew said.

"Rocks?"

"Ashleigh was fascinated by rocks when she was a little girl. We spent hours searching the backyard and along endless countrysides and beaches looking for them. There's a lot of pleasure in discovering a dramatically shaped stone."

"What would you do with them?"

"Nothing. Just look at them and hold them, maybe take some home. They are so pure in their natural state, it'd be a sin to put a chisel to them."

"Ashleigh would like that."

They reached the RX7 and Drew opened the car door for her.

"Thank you for coming, Jaime. And thank you for everything you've done to help Ashleigh. I appreciate that you want to go the distance with her and the case. I know the bond between you two has been set and will continue to deepen."

His words almost brought tears to her eyes.

Drew watched until the RX7 turned the corner and disappeared from sight. With the summer sun beating down on him, he turned and walked toward the garage, where he would work to bring the mother and child to life.

The following afternoon, Jaime returned from court and had just set her briefcase on her desk when Tia poked her head in the office. "Ashleigh on line one for you, Jaime."

"Thanks," Jaime said and grinned widely at Tia.

Jaime had been in court all day physically, but mentally, she had been thinking of Drew and Ashleigh. It would be their first time together in years. She simply ached for it to go well.

"Hey, Ashleigh, what's up?"

"Jaime, guess what I found today!"

"What?"

"A really cool rock!"

Jaime swallowed back her tears. "That's great, Ashleigh! I can hardly wait to see it."

"It's here at home, you can see it when you come, 'kay?"

"I'll be there soon."

When Jaime hung up the phone she looked at the clock. There would be no workout this evening. It was the last thing she wanted to do. In one hour, she was going home.

Where Ashleigh and precious stones were waiting.

Thirty-eight

After twelve days, Leigh was released from Wheat Ridge General Hospital and Drew took her home to Evergreen. When she walked slowly into the kitchen, a large vase of flowers, filled with the bright colors of summer, was sitting on the island counter where she did her cooking.

"They're beautiful," she said.

Drew stayed at the kitchen entrance, his arms crossed over his chest and watched as Leigh cupped her hand around the flowers and moved closer and let the sweet fragrance fill her.

"They're from your flower garden," he said. "Ashleigh and I picked them. We thought it would be a nice way to welcome you home. Ashleigh is very excited to see you home. She didn't like seeing you lying in that hospital bed."

Leigh nodded. "I know. I didn't like that she had to see that either. She's been through enough these last few months."

"Ashleigh will have the next two weeks off from the food court to be here to care for you. We thought the kitchen was the best place for the flowers, since next to writing, cooking is what you do best," Drew said and walked into the kitchen. He stopped only inches from her. He patted the stovetop easily with his hand. "'Course, it'll be a while before you can actually use this, but I can wait."

She turned to look at him and then back to the flowers. There was a grin on her face. "You know, Drew Roberts, if anyone would've told me at the beginning of this year I'd be standing in my own kitchen smelling flowers given to me by my ex-husband and daughter, neither of whom he has seen in years, I would've told them they were absolutely out of their minds."

He took a daisy from the bunch and handed it to her. He looked at her seriously. "I don't know if I would've believed them either," he said.

It was early evening when she had finally walked through the front door of her home. The sun had dipped low in the sky and the day had cooled to a comfortable level. It was the time of day they both enjoyed. Beyond the window, another vase full of flowers had been set on the lawn table.

"Look out there," he said.

She followed Drew's gaze out the window and smiled when she saw the flowers.

"I was hoping the evening would be beautiful like this when you finally came home," he said. "Let's go outside and get some fresh air. That hospital air gets to a person after a while."

He took two bottles of mineral water from the refrigerator and glasses and followed her outside. Before she went to the table, she took a brief tour of the yard to inspect her vegetable garden and flower patches. Drew watched from the table. She lowered herself slowly to the ground. With her hand, she pulled at several small weeds that had grown among a patch of Sweet Williams.

"You've done a great job of keeping everything weeded and alive," she said to him.

"Don't give me any of the credit, since it wasn't me. It was Ashleigh."

Leigh straightened up, turned and looked at Drew. "Ashleigh did all this?"

"Yes. She knew you'd be happy to see that your flower garden is doing so well. She did a great job didn't she?"

"Yes, she did."

She returned to the table.

"You sound so surprised," he said.

"It's just that…"

"It's just what?"

"It sounds so strange for you to say Ashleigh and I did this, that's all."

"It sounds strange to me, too. I didn't think it would happen the way it did, but in the short time we've been together, it's like we've never been apart ... I expected Ashleigh to hate me."

Leigh laughed quietly. "Ashleigh doesn't know the meaning of the word, and never has, and it has nothing to do with the fact that she doesn't know what love means."

She looked at him and studied him as though she were committing his facial features to memory, as though it were her first good look at him since she had been in the accident. His tanned skin made the white in his eyes and his teeth look like snow. He looked calm and relaxed. Her color was much the opposite. She looked drawn and pale. She was still in pain and every step took effort and drained what little reserve of energy she had managed to build. She looked over the flower garden.

"Ashleigh's been out here with me before, but we've never worked in the garden, or weeded together," Leigh said. "It's just that I didn't think it would be something she'd like to do. But I'm glad, in fact, very happy she wanted to. When my shoulder gets better and I get the cast off, we'll do it together."

"It's my guess Ashleigh would like that very much."

She looked again to the flowers and the garden. "When did Ashleigh do this?"

"She was out here Saturday and spent the night. She even dusted and cleaned the entire house."

They sat down and Drew opened the water and poured until the glasses were full. Then he squeezed in fresh lemon. He handed Leigh a glass and said, "In fact, Ashleigh's coming tomorrow and the rest of the week. She said she wants to stay at Jaime's at night, but wants to help take care of you during the day while I work."

"You've been commissioned to do a sculpture in Denver?"

There was a lilt to her voice. It deepened his belief in what he hoped would happen over the next few weeks. Now he faced his toughest challenge, whether she would accept his return, or tell him to go back to Seattle. He remembered the conversation with Jaime in the hospital cafeteria.

It can never be like it was.

It doesn't have to be. It can be different. It can be better. Now that Leigh's concussion had cleared and some of her pain was gone, he would know if she was happy he had come, or if it had been only her fear and pain talking. The lacerations and bruises on her face were healing. It would take extra effort for her to get around for the next few weeks, with her collarbone and ribs healing, but she would recuperate faster now that she was home.

"I'll be working in the garage," Drew said. "I've been working in there since I came. Will that be all right?"

The look she gave him bordered on the absurd. "Of course it's all right. I haven't been inside in years, though."

"You could hardly tell. When I opened the garage again, it was like I hadn't been gone more than a day."

She momentarily forgot her pain. Her blue eyes radiated and grew round in wonder. She seemed happy, pleased by what he had told her. "What type of wildlife will it be this time?"

"Well, it's one that I've been meaning to complete for some time."

He was vague. With her, he knew he could be. It was not unusual for them when they spoke of his work. He talked little about the piece he had been commissioned to do until the project was near completion.

They drank their water for a time in silence.

"While I'm working, Ashleigh wants to come help take care of you until you're able to do things on your own again. She'll be cooking some light meals and helping you with whatever else you need."

His comment caught her off guard and he knew what she was thinking.

"Ashleigh wants to come, Leigh."

She flashed him a skeptical look. "After what happened in court, I can't see Ashleigh wanting to do anything with me, let alone come here and care for me. I'm sure she has better things to do than be with her mother, a heartless bitch, whose only goal in life is to have her sterilized."

He ignored her comment. "I talked with her and Jaime has, Leigh. It's what Ashleigh wants to do. Ashleigh said you're her mother and she wants to help you."

The look on her face softened. "Do you think she wants to come, Drew?"

"Of course. You of all people should know Ashleigh doesn't say or do anything unless she really means it. She wants to be here."

The expression on her face told him she believed it was Ashleigh's idea to come and not something Drew or Jaime or Erin had talked her into.

"Are you hungry?" Drew asked, changing the subject.

Suddenly the hunger that had been gnawing at her all afternoon grew insatiable.

"Starved," she said.

"Me too. I'm going for Chinese, be back in thirty minutes."

They drank white wine with their dinner and the evening was pleasant and warm enough to eat outside. Drew did not want to overdo their first evening together by doing too much too soon, but he couldn't resist. On his way home, he bought two long, tapered white candles. After he put the plates and cartons of Chinese food on the table, he placed the candles in a pair of silver holders.

The candlelight softened her facial features. The light made traces of her bruises. Some of her color had returned and her cheeks seemed to glow. The blue in her eyes had turned almost violet. They were soft and searching and seemed to take in his every move.

When they finished eating, Drew looked into the empty bag. He took out two fortune cookies and handed one to Leigh. He watched while she opened hers and read it.

"What does your fortune say?" he asked.

"Yes. Go ahead with confidence."

"And yours?" she asked.

He opened the cookie and read it.

"The length of your distant days will be filled with companionship."

He looked for a moment at the wax that had melted and collected into the silver holders. He looked at the flames. They were on the edge of burning out.

"Thank you," she said in a soft voice.

He looked at her with tender hopefulness over the dying candlelight. It danced in her eyes. He wanted to reach for her hand. It took every ounce of his strength not to. It was too soon.

"You've got to be exhausted," he said.

"A little."

"Go on to bed. I'll clean up."

Within the hour he had cleared the table and loaded the dishwasher. Freshly showered, he was shirtless and dressed in running shorts. He stood at the edge of the bed, towel drying his hair watching Leigh as she slept soundly. She had not stirred or moved since he had entered the bedroom and started the shower.

He gently eased into bed and pulled himself close to her. Their bodies were only inches apart. He ran his finger along her smooth skin. She sensed him and moved closer. He let her tuck her head between his chin and chest. Her fine hair was loose and silky. Drew ran his fingers lightly through it.

Had they ever been apart?

He thought of Seattle and how alone he had felt there and how empty the nights were. Sometimes the clock never seemed to move. He could hear her breathing lightly. The warm air from her breath rose and fell against his chest. He could learn to like this again. He could feel his own eyelids grow heavy. The last time he looked at the clock, it was near midnight. He drifted off to sleep, holding her in his arms.

When she woke the following morning, she slid her hand across the bed, hoping to feel Drew lying there. When she felt nothing, she looked to his side of the bed. It had been cold for hours. That's how it was whenever he worked. Up before dawn and to the garage. She would not see him again until early evening. She heard the sound of dishes and pots and pans being rustled in the kitchen. Suddenly she remembered Ashleigh was coming.

How long have I been asleep?

She grimaced as she turned over to look at the clock. She was still in a lot of pain, but couldn't think of any place she wanted to be other than in her own bed. The clock showed 11:45 a.m. She had been asleep for almost thirteen hours. Except for the pain in her shoulder, arm and ribs, she felt rested.

Moments later she felt the presence of someone standing at the door. It was Ashleigh. Her hair was pulled back in a ponytail and she wore a mint green polo shirt, khaki shorts and clean, white tennis shoes. She was grinning widely at her mother. Leigh returned the smile and patted the side of the bed. Ashleigh came and sat beside her.

"What time did you get here?"

"Dad came to get me at Jaime's and we were back here by 10."

"Where's your father?"

"In the garage. He told me he'd see you tonight. Does that mean he's gonna be out there all day, mom?"

She nodded. "That's what it means, Ashleigh. It's the way he works."

"Are you hungry?"

"I'm starved. I haven't eaten a thing since your father stuffed me with Chinese food last night."

Ashleigh's eyes widened. "Great! I've got your meals all planned out."

They sat together at the kitchen table and ate eggs scrambled with Swiss cheese, bacon and wheat toast. Ashleigh drank juice and Leigh drank coffee. It was the first meal they had ever eaten together that Ashleigh had cooked.

"Everything was delicious," Leigh said as they cleared the table together. "Where did you learn to cook eggs like that?"

"Erin showed me."

Leigh watched Ashleigh load the dishwasher.

"We're gonna have a light lunch of tuna fish sandwiches and tonight, it's meatloaf," Ashleigh said. "See, I have everything I need to cook it right over there."

She looked to where Ashleigh was pointing. Hamburger, breadcrumbs, ketchup and eggs and bottles of spices and seasonings were sitting next to a large mixing bowl.

"Where's your recipe?" Leigh asked.

"Don't need one. Erin showed me this recipe. Besides, I know it by heart, anyway. When it's my turn to cook at home, this is one of the recipes I like to make."

"Are there others?"

"Yeah, I like to make macaroni and cheese."

"From a box?"

"Mom. No, don't be silly. Did you use a box when you made me macaroni and cheese?"

Leigh could not help her smile. Ashleigh's favorite food growing up had always been macaroni and cheese. But she refused to eat it if Leigh had prepared it from a box.

"I make it the way you did when I was little," Ashleigh said. "Remember? With fresh tomatoes on top and baked in the oven so everything gets nice and crunchy."

Leigh watched Ashleigh finish loading the rest of the dirty dishes. It had been a long time since she had made macaroni and cheese. She did not remember how she made it, but she was glad Ashleigh did.

"Do you need help making the meatloaf this afternoon?" Leigh asked.

Ashleigh shook her head. "Dad left strict instructions you weren't supposed to do anything but rest. He said if you felt better later on this week, then you could help me. 'Kay, mom?"

Leigh nodded, not about to argue. Just getting out of bed, eating breakfast and helping Ashleigh clear the table had exhausted her. She spent the next few hours asleep on the couch in the sunroom. She woke the instant Ashleigh touched her arm.

"Mom. It's time for lunch. Are you hungry?"

On the table next to the sofa was a silver tray. Her lunch was tuna fish with lettuce on toasted wheat bread. The sandwich had been cut in half. A mixture of grapes and apples, pears, peaches and nectarines had been cubed and placed in a small bowl. There was a tall glass of iced tea with fresh lemon.

"It looks delicious, Ashleigh. Are you going to join me?"

"It's not time for me to eat yet and I'm bringing dad a plate. I told him I'd bring him one when I fixed yours. Hope you like it. And then I'm going to finish the meatloaf."

"Who taught you how to make tuna fish sandwiches?"

"Erin showed me," Ashleigh said to her mother as she left the room.

By 7:30 p.m., less than a mouthful of meatloaf remained. The table in the dining room was being used for the first time in many years and the chairs were being occupied by three people who had been apart equally as long, but who were quickly easing back into being with one another. By eight o'clock Drew was taking Ashleigh back to Jaime's. Leigh walked with them to the door. She watched as they walked down the steps and disappeared behind a grove of pine trees that shielded the house. She stared at the trees until her eyes grew tired.

Can this be happening?

She felt foolish for wondering if she should pinch herself. But she did not want to, because if she was dreaming, she did not want to wake up.

Thirty-nine

By the end of the week Ashleigh and her mother had been together every day and did things with each other they had not done in years, or had ever done. Ashleigh washed clothes and cleaned the house. What meals she didn't make, Drew went to get.

Leigh worked to regain her strength. She slept long and late and when she woke, her breakfast was ready and waiting. In the afternoons, early in her recovery, she did little except sleep and read and listen to piano music, which Ashleigh played softly on the stereo so that every time Leigh woke, she could hear the music.

Leigh's strength gradually returned. By the end of the second week, she was strong enough that she no longer wanted to spend entire afternoons on the couch in the sunroom. She would sit at the table outside and watch Ashleigh work to weed the garden and flower patches. She pointed to weeds her daughter missed.

Ashleigh helped Leigh wash her hair, since she still could not lift her arm above her head. Whenever Leigh asked Ashleigh where she had learned to do so much, Ashleigh always replied, "Erin showed me." They would sit together at the table and drink iced tea. Leigh read to Ashleigh. Sometimes it was poetry. Sometimes it was from the newspapers, other times it was from books that told of the sea, or Africa. They looked at coffee-table books filled with photographs taken from all over the world. They would talk about the places.

It was now Sunday and Ashleigh had stayed the weekend in Evergreen. Leigh decided she was well enough to make dinner and had just returned to the house from picking zucchini. As she opened the sliding glass door, she heard the sound of piano music. It sounded like someone was playing on the baby grand in the sunroom. She listened a moment more. Nothing. As she started to walk toward the kitchen, the music began again. It wasn't the piano music she heard when she woke in the morning. Someone was playing, or at least trying to play, her piano.

It was a crude version of Chopsticks. It was clumsy, but she knew the melody. She listened. It could only be one person. A small smile formed.

She brought the zucchini into the kitchen and went to the sunroom. She watched from the doorway as Ashleigh continued her attempt to play Chopsticks. She was bent fully into the piano, her long hair falling in front of her. When she made a mistake on a note, she would stop to study the keys before she started again.

Leigh loved the piano. When they were young, Drew taught her to play, and after he taught her, she began to use the piano to help her write. When she wrote and wanted to drive home a point, or deepen the impact of what she was saying in a column, she would stop writing to play the piano. The music relaxed her and cleared her mind. It made writing a column or a story, easier. When she returned to the computer to write again, words would flow as easily as the musical notes she had played.

After Drew left her, she would spend entire evenings in the sunroom playing the piano. It became her solace. The notes and music became her companions and helped her ease and pass many empty and lonely hours. On the piano The Last Thing on My Mind was the song she played often:

"Well, I could have loved you better,

I didn't mean to be unkind.

You know, it was the last thing on my mind."

Leigh came and stood behind Ashleigh. Her daughter looked up when her mother put her hand on her shoulder. She grinned widely.

"Did Erin teach you to play Chopsticks, too?"

Ashleigh shook her head. "Erin doesn't know how to play the piano, mom. Dad showed me."

"But you were so little then and you still remember?"

Ashleigh shot her mother a silly look. "Mom, of course, I remember. Joy, the one I work with at the food court, her mother has a piano, too. When I go with Joy to her parent's home on Sundays, I play it over and over."

Ashleigh started to play again, but missed a note.

"Shoot," she said, disappointed with herself.

"You almost have it, Ashleigh."

Leigh sat on the piano bench next to her daughter. "Here, let me show you."

It was still painful for her to move and lift her shoulder, but Chopsticks was a song two could play. Her arm was still in its cast, but could use her fingers and she rested her hand on the keys.

"You play there and I'll play here," Leigh said.

For the next hour mother and daughter stayed at the piano and played. They giggled like children and pointed at each other when the other made a mistake. Finally, they made it through the entire song without making a mistake. They hugged each other in triumph.

The last of the music had faded away before a word was spoken.

"Mom," Ashleigh said quietly. "When I saw you lying in the hospital, I thought you were gonna die and it scared me really bad. Don't leave me, 'kay."

Ashleigh had been looking at the piano keys when she spoke. Leigh lightly put her hand under Ashleigh's chin. She turned toward her mother. Tears welled in Leigh's eyes, but she blinked them back and tried to keep her voice from breaking as she spoke. "I'm sorry you had to see me like that, sweetie, but I don't want you to worry, I won't ever leave you." She pulled Ashleigh into her and hugged her tightly.

"I love you, mom."

Leigh closed her eyes and pressed her lips tightly together. She shook her head.

How could she love me after what I'm trying to do to her? "And I love you ... Ashleigh, I never meant to hurt you. I hope you know that. Somewhere inside of you, I hope you know that. I ... I only want what's best for you. Please understand that. Please don't hate me for it."

Ashleigh pulled away from her. Their eyes met. It was a deep, searching look.

"I know, mom. I understand. I don't hate you."

Leigh ran her hand lightly through Ashleigh's hair. It was soft and shiny. "If we could all love like you," she said quietly.

It was nearly nine o'clock when Drew returned home from taking Ashleigh to Jaime's. Leigh was in bed.

"Exhausted?" Drew asked as he came in the bedroom.

Leigh nodded without speaking. Drew left to take a shower. He was in the bathroom combing freshly washed hair when Leigh spoke to him. "Ashleigh and I played Chopsticks on the piano today."

He came from the bathroom and sat next to her on the bed.

"She's learning to play and doing well. I had no idea she could play the piano that well," she said. "We're always doing other things when she comes for the weekend."

"Seems like these past few weeks have been full of surprises for you," he said.

She had been lying on her side. She rolled to her back for a better look at him. "You and Jaime put her up to this, didn't you? Just so I could see all of this, so Ashleigh could prove to me that she's capable and competent enough to live all right on her own and make her own decisions."

His answer was simple. When he spoke, it was nearly a whisper. "No."

"If you want to know the truth, Leigh, I had planned to hire someone to come here and help take care of you, but Ashleigh wouldn't hear of it. She told Jaime and me that she wanted to take care of you. What her reasons were for wanting to do that, I'm afraid I don't know. That's something you'll have to ask her."

He took her hand and rubbed it lightly between his thumb and index finger. "And I don't think what you've seen Ashleigh do these last few weeks is anything you didn't already suspect or know she could do anyway. I think that you've just gotten so caught up in all this sterilization stuff that it has clouded your thinking."

She looked deeply into his eyes. Pulled in by their grasp on her, she felt immediately and completely contained by them, as though she were being pulled into a black hole. The look in his eyes could utterly absorb her as fully and thoroughly now as it could twenty years ago.

"I sat in court, Drew, and listened to those men testify about Ashleigh. I listened to every word they said. They said she couldn't do this and she couldn't do that and this would happen and that would happen. But if they could've been here this last week, they'd take back everything they said about her. Everything."

There was silence for a time between them.

"Ashleigh was only a few feet from me in that courtroom, but I felt like she was a million miles away. I felt like I couldn't talk to her, or comfort her when she needed me. It was as though there was this concrete barrier blocking us and I couldn't get to her, no matter what I did. I hated it and I don't want to ever feel it again."

"What you're doing to Ashleigh now may just do that."

"I know. I know," she said, quietly.

He laughed a small, patient laugh.

"She doesn't hate me," she said.

He studied her, his expression muddled.

"This afternoon, when we were playing the piano, she said she loved me. I asked her to understand that I never meant to hurt her."

"Ashleigh knows that."

"I needed to hear it from her."

"Maybe I need to hear from you then. It's hard for me to understand why you would want to do something like this to her ... I know the core of you, Leigh, and have since the day we met. You've always been permissive with Ashleigh. Now isn't the time to start pulling back ... Let Ashleigh be free. Let her continue to learn ... It may not have been the easiest decision you ever made by yourself to put Ashleigh into a group home when she was twelve, but it was the right thing."

"If I didn't do it then, who knows when the opportunity would've come along again," Leigh said. "I didn't want to take that chance. Putting her in when I did has helped her. How was I to know her health would change?"

"Ashleigh's health is no reason to suddenly start thinking that she shouldn't be doing anything or can't do anything. She needs to continue to live."

"The waiting lists to get into a group home these days can be eight years…" Leigh went on as though she had not heard him.

Drew looked at her long and softly. It stopped her from talking.

"Leigh, I understand," he said. "You don't have to defend yourself or justify anything. You did the right thing."

She blinked several times and nodded. "I didn't want Ashleigh to think I was abandoning her ... It was my biggest fear ... I was only trying to do what was right for her. I only wanted her to go forward. It seemed the only way. I never meant to hurt her."

"I know."

"How could you possibly know, Drew, you weren't here."

Her voice sounded dark and irritated. He stayed silent at her remark. He could not deny that and could not change what had been between them. There was nothing he could say to Leigh to make her realize he wanted their lives to be different and better, if it was what she wanted. He felt it was. He would work for it to become that way. He would do in actions, what he could not say in words.

"My mistake was not doing more with her then," she said softly. "Maybe now I would've seen everything she could do and it wouldn't have taken a car accident for me to see everything Ashleigh's capable of doing."

"Mistakes are only mistakes if you don't learn from them. You can do more with Ashleigh now. Make the time, take the time to be with her. You'll both be better for it. You can learn from each other."

"Am I doing the right thing now, Drew, wanting Ashleigh to have the operation?"

He rose from the bed and went to the window. A velvety darkness had descended and covered the hillside and home lights twinkled like stars in the distance.

"I can tell you only what I feel," he said. "But that would do little good to help you. You decide and make up your own mind. It'll mean nothing coming from me."

He stared out the window for a time before returning to the bed to lie beside her. She turned on her side, away from him. He rested his chin lightly on her bare shoulder. His chin was rough from a day's beard growth. "Think of everything Ashleigh has done in the last few months. She's gone from working in the workshop to the food court. Someday she will go on from there. Within a few weeks, she'll be moving. That doesn't mean she's going to rush out and find the first guy she meets, hop in the sack and get pregnant. She may need help to get her through some days, Leigh, but Ashleigh is capable of doing very much for herself, including having a child."

"It's Ashleigh's diabetes. The diabetes. It could destroy her, even kill her. The judge saw that. What's the matter with everyone else? Can't the rest of you see that too?"

"I'm not denying that's a factor. But what're you saying? Does that mean we sterilize every child-bearing woman who has diabetes just because of the dangers and complications of giving birth to a child? This isn't the Dark Ages. What's happened to your thinking? There are nutritionists and programs that pregnant women with diabetes can and do follow. They give birth to healthy, happy normal babies. If it ever comes to that, then we'll find a program for Ashleigh. We'll hire a nutritionist. We'll hire a slew of them. We'll do whatever we have to do to keep Ashleigh and the baby healthy."

He was silent. He wanted his words to sink into her thoughts.

"That's the choice we can make, Leigh. But I think it can be up to Ashleigh whether or not she wants to have a child. The choice should remain hers. If she decides to someday be a mother, then our choice would be to help her."

"We can do all we want to protect her from the outside, Drew, but what about from within? What about the damage that could be done from within her own body? It's not about finding the best program, or hiring the best nutritionist, I worry about. This is about what will happen within Ashleigh, if she gets pregnant. That's what worries me."

"You're not in this alone anymore," he said. "I'll be with you. It'll be our choice together."

Leigh turned with effort to look at him. She studied him with intense scrutiny, taking in every detail of his face. That's what it was. Suddenly he knew. He could tell by the desperate look in her eyes. She feared having to deal with Ashleigh's mental disability, along with a pregnancy and diabetes by herself. It was a fear, an apprehension so strong, so deep-seated, it almost made her tremble.

She pulled away from him, her voice fragile and hurt when she spoke. "I believed you would always be with me ... And then you left. Every decision I made for Ashleigh after that was on my own. You sent her money, I know. But it was not the only thing ... I needed support. I needed help with her needs. People aren't exactly breaking down the door offering help when you have a child like Ashleigh."

"I know."

She was on the edge of tears. She wanted to hold them back, to stop them from coming, but it was useless. They spilled over and rolled down her cheeks. Having Drew near her again had been like a dream. Scenes she only once imagined were now playing out vividly before her. She had felt more complete, more fulfilled again in these past weeks with him near, than she had felt in years. She wanted to go forward with him, but she hesitated. The only place she wanted to be was in his arms. But her fear of being hurt and abandoned again overshadowed everything.

"I know what you're feeling, Leigh."

"How can you possibly know what I'm feeling?"

When Drew spoke his voice was even. It contained a richness that she was certain she had never heard before.

"I can feel your aloneness, your insecurities and your fear of me leaving you again. There was a time when I could only love you, and I've never stopped loving you, but my need for you was a different story." He stroked her bare shoulder gently. His touch was downy and she closed her eyes. He went on. "It is the need that has changed. I need you. I need to know you're with me and I need to know you want to be with me ... I have no right to be here. I know that. I know what kind of a jerk I was. No one knows that better than I do. You could kick me out and tell me to go the hell back to Seattle and get the hell out of your life, but I hope you won't. I hope you want me to stay because you need me and because you want me here."

"What about love, Drew? Do you think I could still love you even after what happened between us? You take off after that show and leave me here. For days after you left I kept thinking you would return ... Every time the phone rang, each time someone knocked at the front door, I hoped it would be you. Every time I went to the mailbox, I ached to see something in your handwriting ... I'd lay in this bed the nights after you left, knowing you were gone ... Do you think I could still love you after that?"

Drew's answer was simple. He answered her in a whisper. "Yes."

She turned into him, hiding her face between his chin and chest, as she had done the first night they had been together. He could smell the fragrance from her freshly washed hair. It was soft against his skin.

He held her and after a long time, he spoke. "The first morning I came to see you after the accident, I felt it in your touch that you were glad I had come back. I knew then I could be in your life again, if you wanted me to be."

He did not have to say another word. Everything he said was true. For what seemed a long, long time, the only noise came from the tick, tick of the clock on the nightstand. He reached to turn out the light. In the dark, she tried to read his mind.

"What should I do about Ashleigh?" she asked.

But the darkness was silent.

Drew thought about their first evening together after she came home from the hospital. And their dinner. He looked to her in the darkness and spoke in a whisper.

"What does your fortune say?"

Forty

From the stairs, Frank Powers watched Jaime attack the heavy black bag. Slim and pretty, with her hair pulled back, she had never fit his image of a boxer.

He looked around the gym. It was empty, save for Jaime.

He had not been back to the club in four months, since the evening he had knocked her unconscious. When he remembered that exact moment, the blank, deserted look that washed over her face after he hit her the fourth and final time and he knew she was going down, he hated himself for what he had done.

Sometimes he would play back the scene that seared him the most over in his mind: looking back over his shoulder and watching as Barry Winters gently turned her over and seeing that the blood staining the front of her white T-shirt, was hers. It was her blood because he had hit her—something he promised himself he would never do. To any woman. Let alone Jaime.

He thought about the first time he met Jaime. She was in full swing into an intense workout while her trainer Scott shouted words of encouragement. When she finally stopped, Frank introduced himself as her new sparring partner. He could tell from the moment that he looked at her, with her sweeping smile and those wide, brown eyes, that there was something special about her. He would have done anything for her and often told her so.

He thought about the implications of what he had lost. Their three-year friendship. He thought about the look on her face, the determination and the glimmer in her eyes when they sparred. He thought of the countless nights of long conversations over dinner. He thought of Sunday afternoon runs, whatever the weather, at Wash Park, along the Platte River and at Red Rocks Park, her favorite place to run.

One afternoon, shortly after he had hit Jaime, he saw her at a downtown deli. He watched her study the menu. She had an index finger pressed against her lips, tapping lightly as she scanned the menu. She looked beautiful. Her hair was unconfined and free, covering her shoulders. He looked in from the outside window, catching sight of her before she saw him. He stepped away from the door to a place where she could not see him, in order to study her. She was facing his direction in such a way that he could see the bruise under her eye was beginning to turn and lose its color.

He had often wrestled with calling her to apologize and had spoken with Scott to see how she might react. Scott shrugged his indifference, telling him Jaime hadn't mentioned his name since the evening he hit her. She hadn't sparred at all, not even with Scott. Her boxing workouts now consisted of aerobics, hitting the heavy bag, the speed bag and shadow boxing.

Maybe he would tell Jaime what had occurred a few days after the incident with her in the gym when he saw Barry, the club's desk manager, leaving the grocery store he was about to enter. Their eyes locked. Barry dropped his grocery bags and came at him in a fury.

"So, you think you're such a big man, Frank?! Huh! Why don't you have the balls to go against someone your own size instead of hitting women!"

Barry raised his fists. Frank kept his arms by his sides.

"Come on, you asshole! Raise your fists and let's have it out right here! I'll show you what it's like to really fight!" Barry was yelling now and shoppers in the parking lot had stopped to stare. "Or are you just going to stand there and let me knock the shit out of you!"

Barry punched Frank hard in the face. He stumbled backward and fell heavily into his car. Barry charged Frank and hit him a second then a third time. Frank grunted deeply from the force of Barry's blows.

"You're a sorry son-of-a-bitch, Powers! I never want to see your miserable face at the club again." Barry spoke through clenched teeth as he backed away from Frank, his fists still at the ready.

Frank remembered that encounter as he watched Jaime hitting the heavy bag with a final flurry of solid punches.

She stepped away, wiping her forehead. He had come to see her tonight for several reasons. She was right; everything had caught up with him. He hoped she would accept his apologies and what else he had come to say. He was certain given the kind of person he knew her to be, she would. Things would never be the same between them, but he could accept it better, knowing she had forgiven him.

Jaime was working to unlace her glove when Frank walked up behind her. She was so deep in thought she did not hear him approach or feel him standing there.

"Jaime?"

Her shoulders stiffened.

"Jaime." Frank called again, his voice soft and hesitant.

She did not want to turn to face him, but when she finally did, it was the first thing he saw. It was there just above her lip, as he knew it would be.

The scar.

Shaped like a crescent moon, on her upper lip. Every time she would look in the mirror, it would be one of the first things she saw.

That's how she'll remember me.

For a moment they stared at each other. Jaime felt him looking at her scar. She rubbed a gloved hand over it, to take his attention from it. She looked away from him and turned to leave, but he caught her arm and held it. Gently.

"Wait," he said. "Please."

He held it for only a second before he let go. "Jaime, don't. Stay a minute and talk to me. There are some things I have to say to you. Please." He was trying, but failing, to keep the tone of his voice from sounding as though he was pleading.

Jaime had thoughts about what it would be like to see Frank at the club again after what had happened. She wasn't sure how she would have reacted. There was something inside her that hoped he had come to apologize, but she couldn't be sure. After he had hit her, she was no longer sure what to believe about him.

She stayed. He felt a sense of relief that she was willing to listen to him. They did not move from the heavy bag. Jaime wrapped her arm around it. She did not look at Frank, but kept her eyes on two men who had just entered the gym and headed toward the speed bag. The sound of Frank's voice brought her eyes back to his. His looked weary and bloodshot.

"Jaime, can we talk for a few minutes?"

She leaned toward him. Her facial expression seemed positive. That was the Jaime he knew. He never knew her to be unwilling to at least listen to anyone, no matter what the reasons were.

Frank realized he had not rehearsed this part. He wasn't sure how to begin, so he started with Ashleigh. "How'd the hearing go?"

Jaime only hinted at her true dissatisfaction at the outcome of the hearing. She spoke matter-of-factly. "Not very well. The judge granted Leigh Roberts her petition. We're appealing."

He nodded and an awkward silence fell between them. Frank studied the palms of his hands, unsure of what to say next. "Jaime, I ... I did something to you that I never dreamed in my life I'd ever do..."

He looked down to her. Her eyes seemed soft and searching. He half expected her to bolt from the room, but she did not. It gave him courage to continue. "I can't expect you to forgive me for what I've done, but I hope you will at least try. I've thought of this moment between us a hundred times and wondered what I'd say to you. I kept telling myself if I got the chance to talk to you again, what to say would come to me then." He paused, then flashed a quick, half smile. "Well, the moment is here and I still don't know what to say ... I want to say I'm sorry, because I am, but I know it's not enough. I ... I haven't put on a pair of boxing gloves since and won't ever again, if that's any consolation ... And I…"

"Frank."

He stopped fidgeting with a towel he was holding and looked at her.

"That's enough," she said. "If you want to apologize, then I accept."

"I want to apologize."

"I accept."

Jaime began to unlace her gloves and Frank, out of instinct, moved to help. He hesitated, but was surprised when she let him continue. When he finished unlacing the first glove, he pulled it off her hand and gave it to her. He watched saying nothing while she did the other one.

They walked in silence toward her towel and gym bag. When they reached her equipment, Frank went for Jaime's water bottle and handed it to her. She leaned back against the wall and took a long drink.

"There's more to what happened that night than I think you know," Frank said.

Jaime felt a bubble of apprehension stir in her. But she stared straight ahead, not giving him the satisfaction of seeing her expression.

Frank cleared his throat. "You shouldn't just blame me for everything that happened that night."

This time he had her attention. She looked at him intently, trying to figure out what he was saying.

"Mitch had something to do with that little altercation," he said.

"Mitchell? I don't understand. What … what do you mean Mitchell?"

Frank had to avoid Jaime's eyes when he spoke again. "Mitch … Mitchell, he, well, he paid me. He paid me to hit you."

She stared at him in disbelief. Her eyes widened and she felt her heart drop as though she had been standing on a trap door. Her face flushed as heat rose in her body. Her voice was hollow and, as she spoke, she stammered. "P … paid?" Jaime shook her head slightly. She took a small sip of water. She swallowed slowly and looked at Frank, her face forlorn. "I … I don't understand, Frank. What do you mean p … paid?"

"What it sounds like, Jaime. Mitchell paid me to knock you out."

She swallowed hard, afraid to ask how much. She didn't have to. Frank volunteered the information.

"He … a … he paid me a thousand dollars."

"A thousand dollars," Jaime echoed.

She felt as though a pair of invisible hands had taken hold of her lungs and squeezed out the air. "But … but why?" she managed.

Frank shrugged his shoulders and looked away.

She spoke in a hollow voice. "Is that all our friendship meant to you, a thousand dollars?"

"Jaime, I couldn't put a price tag on our friendship."

She burst out laughing. "Well, you sure could that night."

Frank looked from the large window to the city. Above and below him were lights that blinked from tall buildings squeezed together. Amber streetlights glowed along near-empty streets. People were wearing raincoats and carrying briefcases and umbrellas, moving on from one destination to the next. The air had turned cold. Summer was over. It would be fall soon, maybe an early winter.

"There's something else," he said.

She took the towel and put it behind her neck. She looked at Frank as though to give him the permission to continue.

"I've resigned. My days as an investment banker are over."

He looked at her intently to study her reaction, but she offered nothing.

"After Carol and Rachael left, I didn't care anymore and ... I slipped up and got caught bouncing some checks to pay off a debt."

Jaime remained impassive. "How much of a debt?'

"Hundred thousand."

"Maybe if you would've hit me a little bit harder, Mitchell would've paid that debt for you as well." This time pain showed deeply in her eyes. "Except I don't know how much harder you could've hit me."

"Jaime, please. I was so far under with that debt I didn't know what else to do. I didn't have anywhere else to turn. Any amount would've helped. Mitchell heard me on the phone in the locker room a few nights before I hit ... before it happened and he approached me."

"What did he tell you?"

"He said he'd help me, if I'd help him ... He asked how much I needed and I told him a grand would get them off my back. But I said I needed it right away and couldn't wait. He said he'd help me if I agreed to..."

Frank's voice trailed off. To talk about what happened now while looking at her was almost too much.

"If you agreed to do what?" she asked.

"You know, if I agreed to hit you hard enough so you would need help. Mitchell said he wanted to be the one to help you."

"Mitchell is a fool," Jaime said and there was a rise of anger in her voice. "And you were, too, for agreeing to help him. He didn't want to help me, Frank. He just wanted to get back at me for telling him to leave and wanting a divorce. It just wouldn't have looked so good for him to slap me around, so what better person than my sparring partner? That wouldn't be so obvious to others, would it? Why it was just Jaime and Frank boxing and Frank got a little carried away and didn't realize he was beating the shit out of a girl."

He looked away, nodding. She was right. He began to fidget with the towel again. "You've always said foolish people do foolish things, Jaime," was all he could say.

Her laugh was callous. She shook her head in disbelief. "If money was all you needed, Frank, and that badly, you could've come to me. It would have been a lot less painful for both of us."

"We agreed when we first met that no matter how desperate my situation got, I would never ask you for money," he said.

"Oh, I see. But it was all right to take money from the man I'm about to be divorced from and then hit me so hard that I had to depend on him for help to get me home that night." She looked at him incredulously. "That's what I don't understand, but enough of that, that's an evening in my life I'm trying to forget. Let's change the subject."

"It's just going from bad to worse," he said.

"I don't see how," Jaime said.

He hesitated, thinking. "Would you like to go for coffee to finish this conversation?"

Jaime shook her head and somehow Frank already knew she would not want to go. He blurted out the last of his news.

"I'm going to prison." He stuffed his big hands deep into the pocket of his overcoat. "I've agreed to a plea bargain. My attorney thinks it's best."

She raised her eyebrows slightly and her lips became a thin, straight line. "How much time?" she asked, her voice shallow.

He answered without hesitation. "Two years, at the very least, eighteen months. Who knows?" Frank said with a harsh laugh. "Maybe jail will be the best thing for me."

Jaime held up her hands. "That's enough, Frank. I don't want to hear anything else. You came here to apologize and I accepted. Now you need to go."

He studied her and thought about how it would be to never see her again. The thought made his heart feel heavy and hard as granite. A lump formed in his throat, forcing him to swallow over the sudden constriction.

"This will be a lot easier for me if I know one thing from you."

Jaime was silent and closed her eyes. When she opened them he was looking at her.

"What," she said matter-of-factly.

"I'm sorry for hurting you. It's earnest. You know that don't you?"

She nodded slightly. "I know."

He offered his hand. But she turned away and fixed her attention on the heavy bag and began to move toward it.

Frank watched her go. "So long, Jaime."

She nodded without looking at him. He turned and headed for the stairs.

Jaime started to gather her things to leave.

Of course. It all made sense now. About Mitchell.

She was right when she told Leigh the weekend she moved into her new house. It wasn't stress at all. She hadn't imagined any of it. Frank's confession made everything clear. The snowy night her tire was flat. And the day she saw Mitchell in the courtroom before Ashleigh's hearing. The times she came home and found mail she thought she had thrown away the night before sitting on the counter. The lingerie she was certain she had folded and put away, out on her bed. Mitchell was behind all of it. Since she had moved and he didn't have a key, nothing else had happened. She nodded now, knowing all she needed to know.

Jaime grabbed her gym bag at her feet and put it over her shoulder. She turned to face the window. Beyond her reflection, she could see clouds moving across the night sky. Traffic lights on the streets below blinked from green to yellow to red. Cars moved north and south, east to west. People hurried to get in out of the rain. Watching and with her mind busy in thought, she was reminded that nothing in life was ever completely still.

Before Frank took the stairs to leave, he turned to look at Jaime one last time. She was still looking out the window. Her arms were crossed lightly over her body and she looked reflective. It would be his last image of her. He turned and headed down the stairs.

"Is that it, Frank?" Emily said, as she handed him his card a final time.

"Yeah. I guess. Time to move on."

With a wave of his hand, Frank turned and left the counter as Emily watched. Barry did, too, from the back room, but he did not come out. In a moment of memory and longing, Barry recalled a Friday evening Jaime came to the club. Jaime seldom came to the club on Fridays, but she surprised him by showing up for a late workout. He remembered how his heart started to drum in his chest when she came around the corner.

After Jaime had been at the club an hour, Barry left the other attendants in charge of the desk and he walked through the club and found her alone on the third floor. She was having trouble trying to wrap her hand for boxing.

She needs my help. Before he went to her, he took a minute to study her. Her long slender frame belied the power she could pack in a punch. The indirect light was slanted enough to accentuate her features, creating a shadow on her face that revealed the high cheek bones, her wide, sensitive mouth and luminous brown eyes.

"Hi," he said. "Need some help?"

The moment she looked up to him, she seemed so vulnerable. Without a word she held out her hand for his help. He never wanted to let go. It took only minutes to wrap her hand. When he finished, she looked up, smiled and thanked him. He wanted to hold her in his arms, but he settled for touching her lightly, gently, on her shoulder.

"You're welcome," he said and then moved on.

When Barry was certain Frank was gone, he came out and stood beside Emily, his arms crossed tightly over his chest. They caught the last glimpse of Frank as he walk down the steps and disappeared into a mid-September rain.

"Is he gone for good?" Barry asked.

He could see Emily's reflection in the window. She nodded.

"Good riddance," he said.

Forty-one

"Dad? Dad, can I go get a hotdog?"

Ashleigh was tugging on Drew's shirtsleeve trying to get his attention, as he watched baseball action between the Colorado Rockies and the San Diego Padres. Leigh's recovery was nearly complete and she had always been a Rockies fan, with season tickets nine rows up from the third base line at Coors Field. It was a beautiful, calm late summer afternoon and Drew, Leigh and Ashleigh were doing something they had done only rarely, spending a Sunday afternoon at a baseball game.

With her father's attention still captured by the game, Ashleigh asked a second time.

"Dad, can I go get a hotdog?"

Drew slipped his hand into his pant pocket and pulled out a fifty-dollar bill, handing it to Ashleigh without looking at her. But when he realized she was getting up and going for the hotdog by herself, he turned to look at Leigh. "Should Ashleigh go by herself?" he asked.

"There are all kinds of people here. Maybe I'd better go with her."

Leigh took her attention from the pitcher's mound to look at Drew. She looked from him to Ashleigh who was now excusing herself as she passed along the others sitting in her row. Leigh's first instinct was to go with her, or let Drew accompany her, but something told her Ashleigh could go on her own. She looked again to Drew.

"Let her do it by herself, she'll be fine," Leigh said.

They went back to watching the game.

When nearly twenty-five minutes had passed Drew looked over his shoulder to see if Ashleigh was returning, but all he saw were strangers coming down the stairs. "Ashleigh's still not back yet," he said glancing at his watch and then at Leigh. "It shouldn't take this long to get a hotdog. Come on, let's go see if something's wrong."

They left their seats to find Ashleigh.

When they reached the top of the steps, they were met by a sea of people moving in all directions. They weaved in and out of traffic looking for the food stand where Drew had told Ashleigh to buy her hotdog. Leigh saw Ashleigh first and a wave of relief swept over her. Ashleigh was standing in line, waiting her turn along with everyone else.

"Look, Drew, there she is," Leigh said, pointing Ashleigh out to him in the line.

He looked in her direction and saw Ashleigh standing between an elderly couple who had just reached the cash register and two couples of teen-agers. Ashleigh was holding her hotdog in one hand and a soda and the money in the other, waiting patiently to make her purchase. He could not help his smile.

Ashleigh may have been waiting patiently for her turn to come, but the two young couples behind her were not. When Leigh and Drew got within earshot of Ashleigh they stopped. They would wait here to let her make the purchase. She had come this far, navigating her way through crowds to get a hotdog, and she could do the rest.

Drew and Leigh could hear the voices of four teenagers behind Ashleigh complaining rudely that the line was too long and the clerk was too slow ringing up the food purchases. Their comments were falling on deaf ears, but their exchange and their closeness to Ashleigh made Drew uncomfortable. He glanced quickly at Leigh to see how she was responding to the situation, but the look on her face was calm. He dismissed his apprehension and returned his attention to Ashleigh just in time to hear one of the girls ask her a question. The question came just as Ashleigh was about to set her hotdog on the stainless steel counter to pay for it.

"Hey, what time is it?" she asked pointing to Ashleigh's wristwatch.

Ashleigh became distracted at the girl's question and set only part of her hotdog on the counter to look at her watch. The hotdog teetered a moment and fell to the ground. Sauerkraut and wiener landed partially on Ashleigh's clean white tennis shoe. The teen-agers behind her whooped with laughter. Even the clerk couldn't help chuckling. But Ashleigh didn't notice that her hotdog had become part of her wardrobe, she was too busy trying to determine the time.

The teens standing behind Ashleigh realized they were on to something.

"What's the matter, your watch stopped?" the same girl asked.

"Hey! What's the holdup? Hurry up, up there, would ya! We're missin' the game!" Another voice shouted from the back of the line.

The girl yelled back. "We're trying to! But this girl up here's a retard! She doesn't know how to tell time and she dropped her hotdog on the ground!"

The motley crew began to laugh again. The cheers coming from the fans in the stadium seats behind them seemed to quiet down as Drew and Leigh focused their full attention on their daughter.

"I'm going to help her," Drew said and started in Ashleigh's direction.

The memory of the day at the food court bubbled up in Leigh and Jaime's words came tumbling down on her as if she were caught in an avalanche.

"No," she said, grabbing Drew and holding him firmly by the arm. "Leave Ashleigh alone, she's fine. She'll handle this."

For the first time in Leigh's life, she felt certain she was right about Ashleigh's competence.

Something inside her she could not explain said that Ashleigh could and would handle it. And for the first time, she now realized how Jaime had felt the day at the food court when they were reluctant witnesses to the painful exchange between Ashleigh and the boys who had taunted and teased her. What had stayed with Leigh was how well Ashleigh had handled it.

Drew returned his attention to Ashleigh, watching her as she studied her wristwatch, trying to tell the time as the line behind her continued to build.

"Leigh, look what's happening," he said. "Are you blind? They're teasing Ashleigh, but they're not going to keep doing that if I'm standing there."

She managed to conceal her smile. Those were almost her words exactly the day at the food court. They resounded within her as clear as a bell. As she tightened her grip around Drew's arm, she remembered how firm Jaime's hand had been around her wrist when she wanted to intervene at the food court.

"Drew," Leigh spoke softly enough that he had to bend into her to hear her. "Ashleigh's fine. You're the one who said she could get the hotdog. You can't intervene now."

Drew and Leigh heard the clerk tell the teens the time and then ask Ashleigh to step out of line so that the people behind her could make their purchases and get back to the game. Ashleigh stepped away from the cash register, but she did not move to get another hotdog. Instead she continued to stare at her wristwatch.

Then the sound of Erin's voice filled her mind.

When the big hand is on the six and the little hand is on the two, it's 2:30.

Ashleigh looked up to the teens who were nearly finished paying. "It's 2:30," she announced proudly.

But they ignored her. Her mother and father watched as the teens collected their drinks and hotdogs, moved out of line and disappeared into the thick of the crowd. They never gave Ashleigh another glance. Ashleigh looked from the crowd to her shoe and then to the hotdog still on the ground beneath the register. As she moved to begin to clean up the mess, the clerk waved her off.

Drew and Leigh stayed in their places and watched as Ashleigh ordered another hotdog and this time passed through the line and paid without incident. They watched as she went to the condiments area for relish, ketchup and mustard. But before placing the items on her hotdog, she pulled several napkins from the dispenser and cleaned her tennis shoe as best she could.

Moments before Ashleigh finished adding mustard, Leigh and Drew went back to their seats to wait for her to return. When they looked up and saw her making her way to get back to her seat, her face beamed. In one hand she carried a soft drink and a wad of change and in the other, her hotdog and lots of napkins. Ashleigh's joy was contagious and Leigh and Drew smiled back at her.

"Here's the change, Dad," Ashleigh said as she reached her father.

"That's OK," Drew said, taking her drink so she could sit down. "You keep it. You earned it."

The game continued under a warm September sun and Leigh watched as Ashleigh enjoyed her hotdog. If Ashleigh had been affected by what had happened at the concession stand, she did not show it. Leigh knew that Ashleigh would deal with it in her own way, just as she had the day at the food court. Leigh's thoughts were interrupted by the sound of her daughter's voice. "Hey, mom, wanna bite?"

Leigh smiled and shook her head. "You enjoy it."

Forty-two

Erin Greene gripped the steering wheel tightly.

It was the only thing she could do to try to keep from crying. It didn't matter how firm her grip was, however. It did nothing to stop the tears from rolling down her cheeks. She bit her bottom lip, but it trembled anyway. Every time she thought of Ashleigh, more tears came.

Erin was driving from the group home near Congress Park to Ashleigh's new home on Speer Boulevard and bringing with her the last of the boxes that contained her personal belongings. As she drove, she thought of the little girl who had come to the group home thirteen years ago. Morningside was Erin's first job as a supervisor. In a sense, Erin and Ashleigh had grown up there together. Ashleigh was a lanky, perky child when they first met. Now she was a beautiful young woman.

Though Erin was losing a part of herself and of Ashleigh, tears that fell now weren't because she was sad. A new life for Ashleigh was about to begin in a red-brick building that housed generous, well-conceived apartments. Ashleigh had long outgrown the group home and Erin would be the first to encourage her to move on with her life. Another step toward independence.

It was nearly three o'clock when Tia, Jaime and Drew helped Erin and Ashleigh bring the last of the boxes upstairs and into the apartment. Erin pushed her glasses up on her nose and rested her hands on her hips. She looked around the living room. It was filled with boxes yet to be unpacked.

"Well," Erin said in a breathless voice. "I guess that's it, everyone. That's the last of the boxes and now it's up to you guys to empty them."

She turned and headed for the door. "And that's it for me. I'd better get back before someone starts to wonder where on Earth I've run off to."

"Thanks for all the help, Erin. We appreciate it," Jaime said.

Ashleigh joined Jaime and they walked Erin to the door. Erin had promised herself on the way to the apartment she would not cry when it came time to say good-bye. It was taking all the willpower she had, but she was keeping her word. At the door Jaime stepped away to let Ashleigh stand beside Erin. Erin put her hands on Ashleigh's shoulders and squeezed. She did not want to let go.

"Well, the time has come, young lady. Are you ready?"

Ashleigh nodded. "I'm ready."

"You're on your own now, but you know you can call if you ever need anything."

"I know and I will."

She pulled Ashleigh into her and hugged her tightly. "You'll do fine," Erin said her voice a moment from breaking. Her words were more for herself, than Ashleigh. There was not a doubt in her mind Ashleigh would blossom in her new home.

Jaime opened the door and Erin stepped into the hallway.

"Thanks again, Erin, I'll be in touch," Jaime said.

They waved to each other and with that Erin was gone.

They began to unpack boxes. Drew and Ashleigh worked in the bedroom while Jaime and Tia stayed in the living room and kitchen. Jaime and Tia looked at each other when a knock came at the apartment door.

"I'll get it," Jaime said and started toward the door. "It's probably Erin, she must've forgotten something."

Jaime's surprise was obvious. "Leigh? What are…?"

Quickly, Leigh put her index finger against her lips. "I was hoping you'd answer the door," she said in a voice hardly above a whisper.

Jaime studied Leigh briefly. It had been more than a month since Jaime last saw her. The bruises and lacerations on her face had healed. She looked healthy and well, as though most of her strength had returned. She looked thinner than Jaime remembered, but in her black jumpsuit, she seemed energized and ready to go.

Jaime stepped aside. "Did you want to come in? Ashleigh's in the bedroom."

Leigh shook her head. "Can we talk? I really came to see you. Let's walk."

Jaime looked at Leigh, a curious expression on her face.

"I'll meet you downstairs."

A few minutes later Jaime found Leigh waiting outside the building. Her arms were crossed over her chest and she was leaning against the building, her eyes cast toward the sky. It was a cool early autumn day. Clouds covered most of the sky, but the sun, for the moment, was shining.

A hint of a breeze brought the feel of an early winter. Jaime was dressed in Levi's and a hooded sport sweatshirt. She pulled the top against her neck. Leigh pointed toward Cherry Creek, and they crossed Speer Boulevard, walked to the river and headed west along its banks. Lush greenery and gently rolling water met their view as they walked. The wide cement path was empty of the usual cyclists and joggers who rode and ran along the creek. They walked for several blocks without speaking. Only the passing traffic above them broke their silence.

Jaime glanced at Leigh. "You look well and rested."

"Thanks. I'm going back to work next week." She held up her arm, still in a cast. "I'm getting this off next week too and I'm still going to physical therapy. I'm ready for this to be behind me."

"Ashleigh said Drew is leaving in a few days," Jaime said.

Leigh nodded.

"To Seattle?" Jaime asked.

"But not for good," Leigh added quickly. "He's coming back. Ashleigh and I are planning a trip, too. Our first since she was probably ten or eleven. We're going to bring him home."

"It'll be wonderful. Is Ashleigh excited?"

"Excited," Leigh said, with a lilt in her voice. "She hasn't stopped talking about it. She wants to know every day when we're leaving."

"When are you leaving?"

"In a few weeks. We'll all fly back to Denver when Drew has finished in Seattle, but the drive out will give Ashleigh and me the chance to spend some time together. We're looking forward to it."

Jaime smiled. "Sounds wonderful. I'm happy for both of you."

Leigh looked at Jaime levelly. "If it wasn't for Ashleigh and Drew, getting back on my feet after the accident would've been a lot more difficult. They really helped me get through it, Jaime."

A lone cyclist zoomed by them. "On your left!" he yelled as he passed.

"I'm glad you let them," Jaime said. "They only wanted you to get better. Ashleigh would come back to my place and tell me everything. She loved being home with you."

They walked the length of a block in silence.

"Jaime, I've been doing a lot of thinking…" Leigh hesitated, trying to find the right words. She didn't know how to begin, so she just blurted out what she had to say. "I can't go through with it."

Jaime frowned and Leigh saw the confusion on her face. "I'm withdrawing my petition from the court," she said. "I just can't go through with it. I can't put Ashleigh through that and I want her to be able to make up her own mind. It's her life and I realize that now. It's all about choice and it should be hers."

Jaime arched her right eyebrow slightly. She stared at Leigh directly, trying hard to conceal her excitement. They waited for a small group of runners to pass.

"What changed your mind?"

"When you're lying in a hospital bed, and then spending the next several weeks recovering, it gives you more than enough time to think. I began to see what I wanted wouldn't solve anything. The accident was the best thing that could have happened. I used to think it sounded silly whenever I heard other people say that ... Now that it has happened to me, it doesn't sound silly. Don't get me wrong, I'm still not crazy about the idea of Ashleigh's diabetes and the thought of her getting pregnant."

"You and me both," Jaime said, watching the runners, who now had moved well ahead of them.

Leigh smiled and remembered her conversation with Drew.

"So I've been told. But if it were to happen, Jaime, I know I wouldn't have to deal with it by myself. I'd have help this time."

Jaime nodded. "Drew."

"He's different now. Maybe it's age mostly. But he's not the same man who left years ago. Maybe after almost sixty years, he's grown up and is ready to settle down. He'll be here for Ashleigh now and me. I know that now."

"You want that?"

"I do. Very much. I'm glad he's come back..."

Leigh stopped to collect her thoughts. She watched as water passed under the bridge they were about to reach. When she spoke again her voice sounded distant. "You know, I often wondered what it would be like if Drew and I got back together. I didn't imagine it could be like this ... And, then, Ashleigh. I didn't realize it until we spent so much time together how much time we had been apart ... I visited her all the time at Morningside and she'd come to the house, but when I think about it now, we didn't do much, I mean nothing like we've done together in these last six weeks."

"Do you want to change that?"

Leigh looked at Jaime, shielding her eyes from the sun with her hand. "I do. For so long I thought I needed to be an outside influence for Ashleigh so that she would learn more on her own without me meddling. I thought she'd gain more experience and independence if I were less of a mother figure in her life."

Leigh stopped a moment, realizing the impact of what she was saying. She shrugged. "I don't know now if that was right or wrong. Seems like I've missed out on so much."

"I don't think there is a right or wrong way to do what you did. It wasn't easy," Jaime said quietly. "You did what you thought was right. You must have done something right rearing Ashleigh, she's turned out all right given her circumstances."

"You have to give Erin a lot of credit," Leigh said.

"Erin was wonderful for Ashleigh. But Ashleigh's earliest years were your responsibility. I didn't have to know you then to know it wasn't something you took lightly."

Leigh nodded. "Thank you. I needed to hear that."

"Erin took Ashleigh as far in life as she was supposed to. Now the road changes direction a bit," Jaime said. "Who knows what happens from here? New people will come into her life and help her. She'll learn from them and they'll learn from her."

"Will you be one of those people, Jaime?"

Jaime smiled at Leigh. "More than anything else I'd like to be."

They walked another block and turned around. The breeze that had been at their backs, now lightly touched their faces. As they walked, Leigh thought of the afternoon she and Ashleigh played Chopsticks on the piano. She remembered what Ashleigh had said to her.

"You know for the longest time I didn't think my daughter loved me."

"It's my guess for a long time you didn't give her reason to."

Leigh nodded. "Perhaps you're right. After the hearing, I was sure she never wanted to see me again. And then after the accident she didn't think twice about coming to help me to recover and gain my strength back. Ashleigh told me something one day at the house that I didn't think I'd ever hear again coming from her."

Jaime met Leigh's gaze and held it.

"She said she loved me. When I think about it and what I wanted for her, that's when I began to question what I was about to do. I couldn't go through with it because it wouldn't be fair to Ashleigh ... I was being selfish, Jaime, I only wanted what was right for me. There are more feelings and lives to consider here than my own."

"You're doing the right thing with Ashleigh," Jaime said.

"I know," Leigh returned, her voice quiet. "I know that now. What's it about for anyone, really, but choice."

Jaime put a hand on Leigh's shoulder. "Tia will love the news and so will Erin. What about Ashleigh and Drew? Have you told them?"

"I have a feeling Drew already knows. We've talked about it. He's just waiting for me to say something. I'm going to tell both of them tonight."

They walked a block in silence. Leigh kept her attention fixed on a distant traffic light changing from red to green, but her mind was on the first day of Ashleigh's hearing. Leigh had lost track of the countless hours she had spent thinking about it. The thoughts often made her physically sick when she replayed them. When she spoke her words were slow and deliberate, her voice almost throaty.

"They made my daughter out to be a fool in court. As though she didn't know anything. They thought they knew everything about her. They talked to her a few times and called themselves experts…"

Jaime glanced at Leigh briefly before she spoke. "They were only trying to give you what you wanted, Leigh."

Leigh nodded as she studied her palms, not letting Jaime see her eyes. She seemed almost embarrassed.

"And Winston ... He was my saving grace. He spared me the pain of questioning her hard. I was grateful for that. I think he knew I had already heard enough from the others. He knew it hurt me terribly to have to sit there and watch what was going on and he didn't want to add to it."

"I think, perhaps, it was equally as bad for you, Leigh. You thought that's what you wanted for Ashleigh," Jaime said quietly.

"Well, I was wrong."

They looked at each other. There were smiles on their faces.

"Remember the day at the food court?" Leigh asked.

"I remember."

"I didn't think I could ever feel that kind of pain again. Ever. But I did."

"When?"

"The day of Ashleigh's hearing. I walked in the courtroom and the pain just filled me and it got worse as the hearing went on. I didn't think I'd make it through. I must've asked myself a thousand times 'what am I doing here? What the hell am I doing to my daughter'?"

Jaime looked at Leigh earnestly and nodded. "You didn't say much during the hearing."

"It was all I could do just to sit there. I kept thinking we're here because of me, because of something I wanted. I wanted to have my daughter sterilized. I think I must've been insane. I ... I guess I didn't realize the impact of what I was trying to do, until everything started to happen ... Then it hit me all at once. There were several times I just wanted to bolt from the room. Do you understand what I'm trying to say?"

Leigh looked at Jaime, but she did not expect an answer and Jaime did not give her one.

"What about the day we were at the food court, Leigh? I thought for sure that incident had sealed your mind for good about your wishes for Ashleigh."

"It almost did. I went back a few days later and sat in the same place.

There weren't any kids there this time and I made sure Ashleigh saw me. She beamed from ear to ear when she saw me sitting there."

Jaime smiled with Leigh.

"When she went back to work, an older man came to the table and said he was her supervisor and asked how I knew her. When I told him, he told me about the incident you and I saw."

"Did you tell him you saw everything?"

Leigh shook her head slightly. "I didn't say anything. But what he said has stayed with me. He said Ashleigh handled herself very well. Better than what they expected. He said they expected to have problems like that and had planned to train the workers on what to do." Leigh gave Jaime a sideways glance. "You know the good thing? Ashleigh hadn't had any training yet. He said she just knew what to do. I can't tell you how happy that made me feel."

"Has Ashleigh ever said anything to you about that afternoon?" Jaime asked.

"Never. What about you?"

Jaime shook her head.

"Let's keep it that way," Leigh said. Her mind was occupied with thoughts of the incident at Coors Field, but she said nothing to Jaime.

Jaime nodded in agreement.

"I've decided I'm going to write about this," Leigh said.

"In a column?"

Leigh took her eyes from the path for a moment to look at Jaime. Leigh looked different in the late afternoon light. Her eyes had a luster in them that Jaime had not remembered seeing since they met. They seemed a deeper blue than she remembered. More like sapphire than the cool blue she saw the first day they met. She smiled slightly at Jaime before returning her attention to the path.

"Probably a series of them. Or maybe even a book. I was thinking more like a novel. Who knows? Maybe I'll say something that will help someone."

"You have that ability," Jaime said.

They reached Eighth Avenue and the entrance to the apartment building.

"Jaime, you fought so hard for Ashleigh, I think you should be the one to tell her everything is over," Leigh said.

Jaime considered Leigh's request. "I would love to tell her, Leigh, but it really should come from you and Drew. I'm OK with that and I appreciate that you wanted to tell me first. Ashleigh can fill me in when I see her again."

Jaime opened the door. "Are you coming in?"

Leigh shook her head. "I'm going home. I'll see Ashleigh tonight when Drew brings her home for dinner." There was a twinkle in her eye. "Besides, I need to get home. My new Cabrio is being delivered this afternoon."

Jaime laughed. "You bought another one?"

"I couldn't resist. It's just like the other one, black and everything. And I have to get home because I'm trying a new recipe. It's a celebration of sorts, for several things."

"Ashleigh's new living arrangements?"

Leigh nodded. "And Drew coming back and my decision. It's all cause for celebration. Last night Drew said he's finally finished the sculpture he's been working on. He's going to show me before dinner tonight. I'm dying to see it."

Jaime grinned widely. She would love to see the look on Leigh's face when Drew showed her A Mother's Love. "Sounds wonderful."

"I'm hopeful," Leigh said quietly.

Jaime fixed her attention on the buildings across the street. "I am, too."

Their eyes met briefly, then Leigh turned her attention for a moment to the street. Jaime watched as she took the keys to the rental car from her purse. Leigh opened the car door, but before she got inside, she turned to Jaime.

"We'll talk soon," she said and got into the car.

She waved as the car pulled away from the curb and Jaime watched until the car became one with the rest of the traffic.

By six o'clock most of the boxes had been unpacked and Tia had gone home. Jaime took one long look at Ashleigh's new home and then at Ashleigh and felt utterly happy for her. She tousled Ashleigh's hair. "It looks good, Ashleigh. It's the perfect place for you."

"Pretty soon, I'll go to work from here. Will you come see me at the food court tomorrow, Jaime?" Ashleigh asked.

She nodded. "I'll come after the noon rush and we can eat together."

Jaime looked at Drew then nodded that she was ready to go.

"Come on," he said. "I'll walk you down."

When they left the building it was Jaime who spoke.

"Leigh says you're showing her the sculpture tonight."

Drew laughed slightly as he nodded. "It's done and I'm very happy with it."

They walked in silence toward the curb. Jaime had wanted to apologize for the comment she had made to Drew the afternoon in the hospital cafeteria. She did not know when she would see him again, so the time was now. She hesitated briefly before she spoke.

"Drew, I want you to know that I'm sorry for saying you wouldn't do anything different if you had the chance to do everything with Leigh and Ashleigh all over again. I was wrong for saying that. It wasn't my place and I'm sorry."

"You were right, though."

He stopped to study the features on her face. She was a beautiful woman, with sensitive and caring eyes and a deep disposition to match. Shortly after that conversation, Drew had began to compare Jaime to jade, a precious stone with colors that ranged from white to dark green to amber. The jade was nearly as hard as a diamond. With its smooth, hard texture, the jade was a stone that required a sculptor's great patience when carving intricate works of art.

The end results made the sculptor's labor worthwhile.

When polished, a finished jade stone had a sheer, glassy luster. It had a beauty that made one want to reach out and touch. That was Jaime. Her beauty, easily seen on the surface, went deeper still.

"I'm glad you were honest and straightforward with me," Drew said. "It reminded me what Confucius said about the jade … there's truthfulness about the precious stone. The strains in it are not hidden and add to its beauty, like truthfulness. It's smooth and shining, like intelligence. You have the qualities of jade, Jaime. Remember that."

They were silent.

Drew went on, "Ashleigh really likes you. She talked nonstop about you the day we looked for rocks. She said you had a sister."

Jaime nodded and the thought of Sarah filled her completely. "She's been gone from me a while."

"Maybe someday you'll tell me about her."

"Maybe."

She looked at him. She had grown to care deeply about him in the short time she had known him. She felt close to him, as if he would understand anything she told him.

"So, you're leaving in a few days?"

He nodded.

They stopped at the curb. They hugged for a long moment and Drew didn't immediately let go when Jaime pulled away. She retrieved the car keys as she walked toward her RX7, her long hair flowing behind her in the late afternoon breeze. She unlocked the car door and was about to get inside when Drew called to her. She looked to him.

"Thanks for wanting to help Ashleigh. It means more than you know," he said.

She smiled and waved at Drew and got inside the Mazda and within moments she was gone. Drew watched until he could no longer make out her image inside the car. He called out to her, as though she still stood beside him.

"There's an easiness about you, Jaime, the way wheat bends into the wind. Most of us could only hope to be blessed with such a grace ... I'll remember your love for Ashleigh and your desire to help her succeed in a life that only pushes people like her away ... So long for now, Jaime. I'll see you again someday."

Leigh, Drew and Ashleigh sat down together to enjoy Leigh's recipe of stuffed chicken breasts and wild rice. Leigh had told Drew of her decision while Ashleigh was in the shower. They decided they would be together at the dinner table to tell their daughter.

"First," Drew said holding up his wine glass. "A toast! A toast to Ashleigh's new home."

Leigh raised her wine glass and Ashleigh her water glass. The room was filled with the sound of glasses coming together. When Ashleigh set her glass down, Drew called her name and she looked at him.

"Your mother and I have something we want to tell you."

Ashleigh looked from her father to her mother. Her eyes were wide with wonder.

"Sweetie," Leigh said over the lump that had formed in her throat, "I

… I have been doing a lot of thinking here these last few weeks with your father home and you being so good taking care of me. I … I have you both to thank for helping me recover … and I wanted to…"

It was proving harder than Leigh thought. Leigh's hand was resting on the tabletop and Drew covered it with his. She took a deep breath. "Sweetie what mommy is trying to say is that the case is … over. I could never, ever put you through something like that. I love you and I want your life to be yours. I want all your choices to be yours ... I…"

Before Leigh could say another word, Ashleigh sprang from her place at the table and fell into her mother's arms. Tears flowed freely between them.

Hours later, after Leigh cried long and deep at the sight of *A Mother's Love* and with Ashleigh asleep in the bedroom down the hall, Drew and Leigh walked quietly to theirs and closed the door.

From there, their clothes fell where they may. Drew laid her gently down on the bed and held her gaze. Their hands met and he folded his over hers. They began to caress each other's hands, stroking them, fitting them into shapes together. Then Drew stroked the length of her bare body with the back and tips of his fingers. Soft, so softly, that she could hardly feel his touch. He covered her with gentle, downy kisses. And they loved each other long into the night.

They lay entwined for a long time, with only the darkness between them. Then he spoke to her, thinking of the song.

"I never meant to be unkind."

She knew the words immediately and whispered, "I know."

Moments later, when he spoke again, his voice was husky and quiet.

"It was the last thing on my mind."

"I know," she said, softly.

"And I *will* love you better," he said.

"I know."

And in the darkness, there was no other sound except their breathing.

Forty-three

Jamie couldn't wait for the workday to be over. She was playing tennis with Ashleigh at Washington Park at 6 p.m. She had been so excited all day, she felt like she was going to jump out of her skin. She glanced at the time. Fifteen minutes until 5 p.m. Close enough.

She walked to her car. The weather was perfect. She couldn't have asked for a better day to walk onto a tennis court for the first time in years. Jaime was picking Ashleigh up at her new apartment and she had all her equipment in the car. It wasn't as bad as Jaime thought it was going to be when she got out her old Prince racquets. And Sarah's too. She could still see herself in the garage gripping the handle of Sarah's racquet. She placed her hand within the same indentations where her sister's hand had once gripped so tightly.

Jaime smacked the racquet hard several times against her palm. She smiled, somehow knowing that Sarah wouldn't mind if Ashleigh used her racquets. Jaime had purchased three cans of Wilson tennis balls, though she knew nine balls wouldn't be enough for her and Ashleigh. Of course they were going to spend more time chasing balls than hitting them, but three cans would serve their purpose.

By the time Jaime and Ashleigh arrived at Wash Park, the afternoon had turned pleasant and calm. Jaime was pleasantly surprised, grateful that she felt little uneasiness as they opened the gate and walked toward the center of the court. Perhaps it only took stepping on a tennis court again with Ashleigh to make her realize how much she had missed the game.

"You're going to let me use Sarah's racquet?" Ashleigh asked as Jaime handed it to her with a smile that covered her face.

"I can't think of anything that would make Sarah happier, Ashleigh," Jaime said as she popped open a can of tennis balls. She closed her eyes at the familiar hissing sound and smell of fresh, new tennis balls. Jaime took out her racquet and began to bounce a ball against the racquet in a rapid, even pace on the ground.

Ashleigh watched wide eyed. "Wow! You're good!"

Jaime laughed and quickly blinked away tears. She couldn't believe how good it felt to do such a simple motion with a tennis ball.

She pointed with her racquet and they walked onto the tennis court together. They spent the next hour hitting (or trying to hit) tennis balls. The balls went in every direction, including one that Ashleigh hit over the fence and into the water. And the first time Ashleigh had managed to hit a playable ball back in Jaime's direction, she returned it with such precision and pace that Ashleigh just watched it sail right by her.

"Wow! You're good! That ball came back really fast!" Ashleigh said as she looked over the net to Jaime, who was grinning so widely, her face could hardly contain her smile. Jaime knew Ashleigh wouldn't know that because she hadn't played in years most of her shots would be rusty and her timing would be off. But of course that didn't matter.

Before they knew it, an hour had passed and the sun had dipped behind the tall trees. When Ashleigh hit the last ball into the net, Jaime trotted toward it. Ashleigh watched as Jaime collected a ball between the side of her foot and her racquet, picking it up with ease. Ashleigh tried to pick up another ball the same way, but after much effort, she had to bend down to get the ball with her hand.

"Come on, Ashleigh," Jaime said. "Let's go get that ball that went in the water."

They collected their things and walked toward the gate. They reached the water's edge and saw the number 3 Wilson tennis ball bobbing in the water.

"That's ours," Ashleigh said and pointed.

Jaime used the tip of her racquet to get the ball out of the water. She carried it in her hand as they headed toward her car.

"Can we play again sometime, Jaime?"

Jaime nodded and put her arm over Ashleigh's shoulder. "Yes, yes, we can," she said quietly. "We can play every night of the week if you want."

By the time Jaime made it home, what heat there had been had cooled following a light rain. Puddles made small pools in the streets. The earth was wet and fresh with moisture and evening shadows were beginning to grow. A hint of breeze blew lightly through the trees and with it came the feel of fall. Autumn was already caught in some of the trees. The air was thick with the scent of wet, fresh-cut grass—a far better scent than the streets of Denver had to offer, which was in equal parts, diesel exhaust, bus and car fumes.

Jaime stood at the back of her garage, listening. She had become accustomed to the stillness of living in Washington Park, the same way the eyes become accustomed to seeing in the dark, as though she were the air now that was part of it. She took the racquets out of the car. Before she put them back on the shelf, she took out Sarah's racquet and placed her hands around the grip. Her smile was bittersweet.

Jaime wondered what would have become of Sarah had she lived. Maybe she would have overcome what had happened and gone on to play professional tennis. Maybe she would have used the money from her trust fund and gone to college. Maybe she would have become an attorney or a doctor. Maybe she would have married and settled down, had children and lived in a rambling house in the Colorado mountains she had always loved so much.

The possibilities made Jaime smile, though not for long.

Maybe she never would have gone beyond what had happened. Never played tennis again. Maybe Sarah would have become a woman adrift, in an endless search for direction. Maybe she would have lived a meandering life, with a series of false starts and unhappy endings. There would be no pinnacle of tennis. There would be no Wimbledon, no top seed ranking, no crowds to cheer her on.

But there would be. At least in Jaime's mind. And in her heart, where memories of Sarah remained. Where they would stay unforgotten through the passage of time.

Forty-four

The autumn wind blew crisp and cold.

At least it wasn't raining as it had been the first and only time Jaime had come to Boulder to visit Sarah's grave. It was hard for her to imagine that more than six years had passed since her sister's death and she had only come once. But she did not have the strength to return until now.

The windows were down in the RX7 and the wind moved easily through the car, tousling her hair as she headed west on U.S. 36. There were no songs on the radio, just the sound of the wheels moving along the highway. As she neared the cemetery, Jaime looked to make sure an old gym bag she brought on the back seat. Inside were fresh flowers and something else she planned to leave on her sister's grave.

Last night she had dreamed again she was running. So much time had passed since she had the running dream that she had almost forgotten it. Though it always seemed so real as she ran through the encompassing fire, Jaime began to notice each time she had the dream it bothered her less. She was certain the dream meant her own death was imminent and, eventually, she would be consumed by the inferno that surrounded her.

But that never happened. Everything that fell from her body burned to a cinder, but each time the shell of her came through unscathed. She began to notice after each dream she felt stronger, more confident. She began to allow herself to think the dream meant something good, nothing foreboding, as she had allowed herself to believe.

Everything she shed as she ran, her jacket, her clothes and her skin, was her former self, an erstwhile image, one that had kept her prisoner for years. Last night, the dream had not bothered her at all.

Along the way to Boulder, she realized what the dream meant. It consumed her as quickly as fire would a piece of paper. She squinted at the thoughts working within her. She realized for the first time that she was not running from anything, but toward something. A settling peace spread through her as though she stood in a quiet field watching the sunrise.

She knew now what it was.

A new life.

The running dream was, at that moment, an epiphany.

It was not the end, but the beginning. The dream was telling her she was free, liberated and released to start living life again.

Jaime looked up. Patches of thin, white clouds covered a turquoise sky. Wind pushed and scattered them in all directions. She reached the cemetery and stopped near Sarah's grave. She took the red, pink and white carnations wrapped in baby's breath from the bag. They were fresh and fragrant. From this distance, on this early autumn day, rich, green grass could be seen covering Sarah's plot. The sight made her happy as she walked toward the grave. At the end of her sister's section, Jaime noticed a cemetery employee tending to one of the graves.

When Jaime reached her sister's grave, she studied the headstone. Gray letters were engraved on a mauve stone that stood two feet above the ground. There were matching stones for her mother and father for when the time came. Jaime looked to her father's headstone and under his name was the word, Father. On Sarah's right was her mother's stone. The word Mother was engraved beneath her name. Three graves standing like mute sentinels. Her father was on one side, her mother on the other, as though they would protect her in death from what they could not in life. Jaime looked around. There wasn't a headstone for her or any room nearby for another one. She smiled sadly, somehow expecting this, to be separated, even in death.

Tattered pink and white silk carnations protruded from a holder attached to the headstone. Jaime wondered who had brought them. They were old, faded and dirty from whatever the wind had brought along to settle on them. They seemed slightly bent in a northerly direction, but had been firmly planted in wire so that even the strong winds so common along the Boulder foothills could not have shaken them free. She began to adjust the flowers, bending and shaping them to stand straight again. She was so busy and deep in thought she did not hear the cemetery worker approach.

"Afternoon," he said quietly.

The sudden sound made Jaime jump.

"Sorry," the man said and flashed a small smile. "Didn't mean to disturb you."

"It's OK," Jaime said and she continued to straighten the last of the flowers.

When she finished, she stepped away from the headstone to study them. "Do you know who brought those?" Jaime asked the worker, a tall, wiry man.

He came and stood next to Jaime and pushed his tattered cap up on his head. Jaime saw the deep creases in his neck and forehead. The short-sleeved green work shirt he wore revealed weathered, scrappy arms, indicative of years of hard work under the sun. The name on his work shirt, Paul, was written in script.

"I do," he said looking from her to the graves beyond Sarah's headstone. "I've been tending these grounds for almost thirty-five years and I know just about everyone who comes and goes from here."

He thought a moment while removing his gloves. "It was a couple. Nice looking. I'd say maybe late forties, early fifties."

Jaime described to him her parents.

"Yep," he said, readjusting the cap to the center of his forehead. "Sounds like them. They were here in May, I believe, though I'm not sure exactly, but sometime during the spring."

He was right. It would have been the anniversary of Sarah's death, May 24. Her parents had come and gone to Denver without contacting her, though that didn't surprise her. Nothing did anymore.

"This one here," he said pointing at Sarah's grave with the gloves he held in his hand, "is a quiet grave."

Jaime looked at him with narrowed eyes and shook her head. "Quiet?"

"Quiet," he repeated. "She doesn't get too many visitors. Look over there."

Jaime looked in the direction Paul was pointing.

"Those people are here all the time. Look at all the flowers."

Jaime saw the flowers, along with a windmill and chimes, which were silent now in the stillness of the afternoon.

"This is only the second time I've come since my sister died," Jaime told Paul.

"Your sister, huh," he said. "It's sad she died so young."

"I don't think my parents will ever get over Sarah's death," she told him. "Nor will they ever forgive me for what happened. As far as they're concerned, I was the one who took Sarah and everything she was supposed to be from them. They'll always blame me. Blame is the easiest thing to put off on someone else and knowing that, I've come to accept it, I guess, at least that's what I tell myself."

"Are they still in Boulder?" Paul asked.

Jaime shook her head.

"Do you know where they live?"

"Somewhere near Tampa, south of it, I think. My aunt told me."

Jaime was quiet a moment. She looked at Paul, wondering if he was bored by what she was telling him. But he had leaned forward and had tilted his head slightly to the right.

She shrugged and went on. "I have their phone number. My aunt gave it to me. Sometimes I dial it. It rings and rings, but no one has ever answered." Jaime was quiet a moment before she spoke again. "They live in a house with a pool in the backyard."

"Do they swim?"

"Never have. It's a token thing for Sarah, I guess. My sister was a really good tennis player. She was supposed to turn pro. After we'd play tennis and she had practiced all day, she used to love to swim to cool down."

Jaime stopped, feeling a stream of sadness in the center of her chest. Together they looked at Sarah's headstone.

SARAH RENEE MONROE.

Below Sarah's name read her epitaph:

Our Beloved Champion

Gone But Not Forgotten

Alive Forever In Our Hearts

Sadness kept her from saying anything. Jaime removed her gym bag from her shoulder and set it on the ground. Paul watched Jaime take out a GI Joe doll, one of the originals.

"Was that your sister's?" Paul asked. Jaime smiled and nodded as she smoothed GI Joe's army fatigues back into place.

"I had one, too," she said almost embarrassed. "We didn't play with Barbie dolls or toys like that when we were kids. We were both sort of tomboys ... You know, we did sports and played cowboys instead of house. I guess our mother must've known from an early age because I don't remember her ever getting us any girl stuff for Christmas."

They laughed and then Paul watched as Jaime moved closer to Sarah's grave. Jaime looked from the fully bearded GI Joe doll to the headstone and said to Paul, "When I stopped playing with toys, Sarah did, too. Everything I did, she did. I knew she looked up to me and I tried my best not to let her down. As I think any big sister should do."

Jaime looked over her shoulder to Paul. His arms were folded against his chest, the gloves limp in his hand. His expression was serious, almost sad.

"After what happened to Sarah," Jaime went on, "she stopped doing everything else, tennis and everything. She regressed deeply and stopped doing everything except playing with all our old toys.

"About a week before she started high school, she put everything away. I thought when Sarah went to high school things would get better, but it just went from bad to worse. I can still hear my mother talking to my dad about Sarah, saying how worried she was that Sarah simply refused to do anything except play with those dumb toys."

Emotion welled in Jaime's eyes and she cleared her throat before she spoke. "A few weeks before I started my freshman term at college, I was outside my parents' bedroom. They were talking and it was late. My mother said, 'I just don't know what else to say. This has got to stop. Sarah is starting high school soon and she's still playing with those damn dolls. I'm tempted to just go in there and take all those toys away from her and hide them. Burn them if I have to.'"

Jaime mocked the sound of her mother's voice.

"My father disagreed, though. But she countered it was the only thing she could do. She told him over and over that this was just no time for toys…"

Jaime's voice trailed off and she looked at GI Joe in her hand.

"Are you going to leave him here?" Paul asked with gentleness in his voice.

"I've thought about it," Jaime said, shrugging. "But, I'd better keep it."

He nodded. "Probably best. People leave sentimental things like that here all the time. They're here one day and gone the next. Then they get upset when they learn it's gone. Who knows why people do it? They do it for all kinds of reasons, I guess."

"I bet you've probably heard all kinds of stories working here."

He chuckled a bit, as he nodded. "All kinds," he said.

Paul stepped away from Sarah's grave. "I'd better get going. You stay as long as you want. And don't worry, I'll keep good watch over your sister's grave."

"Thanks," Jaime said and she held back her tears.

Paul winked at Jaime and she smiled and waved as he turned and walked away, putting on his gloves.

Jaime glanced at the headstones, lined in neat, quiet rows and returned GI Joe to her gym bag. She took one long last look at Sarah's grave. A blue northerly wind pierced her. And she heard the chimes rustle softly. She pulled her Boston University hooded sweatshirt close to her neck. She listened to the wind as it came off the Flatirons, as it whispered and moaned in and around the stones.

The sun had dropped low in the sky, casting long, slanted shadows behind the gravestones. A faint mist had settled over the horizon, and later there would be fog, but she would be gone by then. Back to the life she left behind, somehow different now.

Jaime rested her hand lightly on top of Sarah's grave, the cold spreading evenly through her fingertips. She left it there for a few moments.

Before she turned to leave, she slipped her hand inside the front pocket of her sweatshirt and pulled out a tennis ball. She turned it over. It was the number 3 ball that she and Ashleigh had used the first time they played tennis together. Jaime could see herself retrieving the ball from the water. She could feel Ashleigh's hand on her shoulder. She tossed it up and down several times, then she bent down and placed it on the ground, in front of Sarah's headstone. She left the cemetery in silence.

In the rearview mirror, she could see Paul tending to the grave with the windmill and chimes. She thought about how easy it is sometimes to talk to strangers. Or maybe it was just easier to talk to him because he was, after all, the keeper of her sister's grave.

During the drive back to Washington Park, Jaime watched dusk settle, turning the horizon a dusty pink. She pulled to the side of the road and stared at the sunless sky for what seemed a long time, then made the rest of the journey home. She loved twilight, the way it made her feel. She recalled a column Leigh wrote one Christmas about being grateful and for the hope that is part of tomorrow.

There is something about the hope of a new day that pushes people onward, in an Easter Sunday sort of way. Perhaps it was hope, after all, that kept Jaime going the years after Sarah had died. A small fire that burned.

She could see the landscape move outside her window as she began to drive. She thought of the countless times she had made this same drive with Sarah and her mother and father. They were just black and white memories now, the color and the images long since faded. She took the Boulder turnpike south to Interstate 25 that would take her to the Washington Street exit. She reached her home and turned off the engine. She listened for a moment as the car settled, studying her new home. She would welcome her first spring in her new home with a yard. It was good to have grass surrounding her home again instead of cement.

Jaime got out of the car and began to walk the length of her red-brick steps. She walked slowly, looking at the trees that lined her yard. Leaves protected the branches in the spring and summer, but in the winter they were on their own. Trees have to be strongest in the pall of winter to face the wind and snow and survive until spring. With autumn closing in, some of the leaves had begun to fall. She bent down to collect a few. As she walked, she let them fall from her hands like snow and she trembled in the dying light that now covered the length of the yard.

She thought about the running dream. In the end, like the trees, she too was left with only her nakedness. She felt weary from battle, but somehow refreshed. She knew she would survive. She thought about the familiar and tattered poster that had been hers since high school. It now hung by a thumbtack in her study. On it was a winter scene of sunlight splintered through naked trees half buried in snow. She thought of the quotation by Camus written in italics in the cold shade of the empty trees:

"In the midst of winter, I found there was,
within me, an invincible summer."

Jaime remembered being at a shopping mall with Sarah when the poster had captured their attention. She was drawn to it immediately and bought it. She was still reminded of that day every time she looked at the poster.

She never understood what the poster meant, until now. It was all of her and more. She thought how lonely and empty trees looked without leaves. Their emptiness would last the winter, until spring, when leaves would cover the trees again.

All things become new. All that remained of her now, too, was her nakedness. An empty shell.

She felt stripped and exposed. Open and uncovered.

It was the last that was left of her, the best.

She was ready for the dawn, a new sun rising.

THE END

PLEASE WRITE A SHORT REVIEW

Hello Dear Reader,

Thank you for reading An Invincible Summer. Now that you have finished reading my book, if you could find a few minutes to write a short, candid review on my Amazon Author page that would be greatly appreciated. I would like to thank you in advance.
http://www.amazon.com/dp/B015ZZFP4K

Copyright

Book Cover Design by Laura Stumbaugh

Stay connected with the author

Visit her author central page on Amazon:
https://www.amazon.com/author/bettaferrendelli

Follow her on Twitter: @BettaWriter

Sign up for Betta's newsletter on her website:
www.BettaFerrendelliBooks.com

Follow Betta on Facebook:
www.facebook.com/BettaFerrendelliAuthor

Or correspond by snail mail: P.O. Box 147105, Edgewater, CO 80214

Other books by Betta Ferrendelli

The award-winning Samantha Church Mystery Series:

The Friday Edition

Revenge is Sweet

Dead Wrong

Coming in 2016

Cold Case File No. 95-2159

Visit: https://www.amazon.com/author/bettaferrendelli